JACK MURPHY
TARGET DECK

Target Deck is a work of fiction. Names, places, and incidents either are products of the author's imagination or are used fictitiously.

© 2012 Jack Murphy

Printed in the United States of America

http://reflexivefire.com

First Edition

For the Glory Boys
1st Plt A/co 3/75

1

Deckard woke up underwater.

Bubbles escaped around the SCUBA regulator clenched in his mouth as he checked the glowing hands on his wrist watch. Time can cease to exist while submerged. Maintaining neutral buoyancy, he floated, his wet suit insulating him against the cold that threatened to creep in regardless of the warm water.

Pulling the rubber sleeve of the wetsuit back over his watch, he breathed evenly, if a little too fast, recognizing the first signs of pre-combat jitters. He was burning through oxygen faster than normal.

In the darkness, the mercenary could feel, rather than see, the presence of his team. They floated alongside him in silence, waiting.

Samantha Diaz struggled against the handcuffs, rubbing her wrists raw.

"How about we play a little game."

Jose Ortega stood in front of her, his arms folded across his chest. The ratty black mustache on his upper lip wiggled as he suppressed a laugh.

"Yeah, let's turn off the lights and play a game of who's in my mouth?"

Ortega's crew broke out laughing, anticipation in their eyes. They lounged around the master bedroom, wearing flamboyantly bright t-shirts with stenciled designs from designer labels. Their hair was identically slicked back with the same product, jeans with the same prefabricated tears and wear marks that came pre-worn from the store.

"Try not to cry like a little bitch," the cartel leader demanded. "We already suffered enough of that from your father."

Samantha lunged, the handcuffs digging deeper into her wrists.

Ortega bent down and grabbed her by the hair.

"You were stupid to come back," he said with rotten breath. "Now you pay the price."

Reaching into his pocket, he flicked open a switchblade. Running the blade under the inside of her shirt, he began slicing through the fabric to the cheers of his lieutenants.

"Everyone will know that the Diaz family produces nothing but whores."

Several of Ortega's men got to their feet, their hands moving towards pants zippers.

The explosion was deafening.

Two walls immediately collapsed followed by smoke and what sounded like thunder strikes that were sent skipping through the bedroom.

Gunfire erupted from the multiple breach points created through the cinder block walls, screams cut off by short controlled bursts of gunfire. New voices filled the room, speaking some strange language that Samantha was unfamiliar with.

When the smoke began to clear, she saw Ortega laying on his back with splotches of crimson staining his over-priced shirt. Attempting to speak, a strained gurgling sound was the best the cartel don could manage.

The heel of a combat boot came down on his throat.

Grinding his boot into Ortega's neck, a man snarled, his lips curled back, bearing teeth like fangs.

"Get security up," the man ordered in English. "Nikita, get those bolt cutters over here."

A brown skinned man with Asian eyes moved forward, slinging his rifle over one shoulder, gripping the cutters in his hands. As he maneuvered the chain links of her handcuffs between the shears, she noticed that he was wearing a wetsuit, dripping wet despite the fact that they were nowhere near the ocean.

Grunting as he closed the bolt cutters the commando severed the links with a loud snap, freeing her from the bed post she was chained to.

Muffled shouts sounded from outside. One of the soldiers cracked open the bedroom door, peering outside before pulling the pin from a fragmentation grenade. Rolling it outside, the grenade exploded, the voices suddenly going silent. Taking another glance outside, the grenadier turned to the large gringo with his foot still on Ortega's throat and said something in what sounded like Russian.

Looking up from Ortega's lifeless eyes, he replied in a similar rapid fire manner in the same language.

The man who had cut her free dropped the bolt cutters and took a knee next to one of the gaping holes created by the breaching charges, his rifle at the ready, waiting for targets to present themselves.

The gringo undid a waterproof bag that had been riding over his shoulder, producing a stack of papers before moving towards her.

"Ms. Diaz, I need you to-"

"Need me to what?" she asked pressing a .357 Magnum Colt Python revolver into Deckard's cheek.

"Uh," the mercenary paused. "Where did you get that?"

"Ortega kept it in his waistband under his shirt."

"I didn't see you reaching for it."

"You should be more careful, *puta.*"

"Ma'am, I just need you to sign the-"

"Don't tell me what to do jackass. I-"

Her words were interrupted by Nikita cutting loose with a staccato burst of gunfire, the wall he was taking cover behind was chipping away under enemy return fire.

"I don't think we have time for this."

"Don't have-"

The ground shook as an explosion rattled somewhere in the drug lord's compound.

"What the hell was that?"

"My boys blowing the front gate," Deckard informed her.

"Your boys?"

"You know, my mercenaries. Your father contracted us but with him being killed seventeen hours ago, I'm afraid we are now here illegally, which is why I need, I would like, for you to sign the-"

"Sign?"

"The contract, extending its duration until we can finish the job we were originally hired for."

Nikita lobbed a grenade through the breach and resumed firing.

"What job?" she yelled over the noise.

"To take care of your drug cartel problem."

Outside it sounded like the fourth of July back stateside where she had attended university in Texas.

"What the fuck is going on out there?"

"My platoons just drove their assault trucks into the compound. They are in the process of mopping up the rest of Ortega's men."

"I can't sign a contract with mercenaries, I'm a deputized police chief, not the provincial governor."

"Actually, he was killed twelve hours ago."

"The provincial judge?"

"He was with the governor," Deckard said looking out of the corner of his eye towards the door, with the massive revolver still stuck in his face. "The chief prosecutor too."

"Shit."

"Yeah, so if you could just sign here," he said handing her a ball point pen.

"And you work for me?"

"That's the idea."

"And we clean these motherfuckers out?"

"Precisely what I had in mind."

Samantha snatched the pen out of Deckard's hand and signed on the dotted line.

"Initial there."

Another explosion sounded.

"Okay," Deckard said flipping through the stack of papers. "Initial here."

Samantha grimaced, sketching her name all over the papers.

"Right, and one more time right here."

"Anything else."

"That should do it," Deckard said sliding the papers back into his bag. "But do you mind getting the cannon out of my face?"

Samantha looked at him long and hard before lowering her newly acquired pistol.

The mercenary posted next to the door leaned out, sending a barrage of gunfire down the hall.

"Pleasure doing business with you," Deckard said, taking her by the hand and helping the woman to her feet. "We've got work to do."

2

Outside, a dozen assault trucks were arrayed around the compound. The vehicles looked like porcupines with machines guns pointing outwards in every direction.

A final rattle of gunfire sounded, ending the fire fight and leaving the survivors in a sudden, awkward silence.

The compound itself was situated on top of a narrow plateau, built up by Ortega to act as the fortress from which he ran his cartel. Inside the stone walls were his personal villa, a barracks, a cafeteria, garages, and even an Olympic-sized swimming pool. With the kind of money the drug lord had, virtually no expense was spared. This was reflected by gaudy statues of horses and scantily clad women in the courtyard.

Nerves still frayed, Samantha stared wide eyed at the bodies of the drug lord's minions littered around the plaza.

"How did you get in here in the first place?" she asked Deckard as they walked down the steps from the villa. The compound had been heavily fortified with machine gun nests, guards on the high walls, and heavy gates at the entrance.

"They let us through the front gate," he answered flatly, nodding towards the tanker truck parked on the far side of the compound.

"Once I found out that Ortega still had contractors digging a well, we knew he had to be getting weekly water shipments given the amount of people he housed here."

"But how-"

"We rode inside the water tank itself," he said kicking at some bushes alongside the villa.

Bending down he picked up several sets of oxygen tanks normally used for recreational SCUBA diving.

"We borrowed these from a dive shop down on the coast. The driver never even knew that we were inside the water tank that he was transporting."

"Risky."

"I hope that isn't a complaint," Deckard said with a smirk.

"Not at all," she said forming fists with her hands, trying to control the shakes.

"As you can imagine, we didn't have a lot of time. We

weren't scheduled to hit this place for a couple more weeks, after we had gathered more intel and did some mission planning."

"You came for me? Why?"

"Give me a minute and then we'll head down to the police station."

Deckard walked between mercenaries scurrying across the compound in desert fatigues as they carried out their assigned tasks. He searched the back of several of the assault vehicles before finding what he was looking for and dragged out a green duffel bag.

Samantha turned around, unsure exactly why, as the American began to strip out of his wetsuit. While he dressed, a black Mercedes with tinted windows pulled into the court yard.

"Hey, Deck!" someone yelled from the car window.

"Yeah?"

"We found Ortega's vehicle. It's got level seven armor, in case you want to go outside the wire with a little less visibility."

"Sounds good," she heard him say. "Prep two of the trucks to run a few minutes behind us in case anything happens. They can circle in a lager route just outside the city."

"You got it."

When she turned around, the commando had exchanged his wetsuit for a pair of jeans and a black t-shirt. Sitting on the tailgate of the truck, he pulled on a dry pair of boots before shrugging into body armor adorned with various pouches for ammunition and grenades. Throwing the duffel bag back on the truck, he slung his Kalashnikov rifle over one shoulder.

Ortega's armored luxury vehicle purred as the driver sat on the hood, checking the load in his pistol before sliding it back into its holster.

"How far out are the logistics vehicles?" Deckard asked.

"Any minute now," the driver said.

"Take the wheel, let's get out of here."

The driver motioned for her to follow. Samantha slid into the backseat next to him as the driver snapped on his safety belt. Slamming the doors shut, the car weaved through the wreckage of what was left of the fortress' heavy metal gate. Accelerating down the dirt road on a decline, she could see a pair of headlights trailing them in the distance.

"I suppose you want some kind of explanation," the

American said breaking the silence.

"That would be nice."

"With the situation here in Oaxaca deteriorating, your father reached out to us. He hired us to come in and conduct an area assessment, figure out the topography of the local cartels, collect intelligence, with the possibility of going overt. As you know, he didn't have much faith in your government when it came to cleaning up the mess down here. I came in with an advance party of five men and we worked out of a safe house in town-"

"What was he paying you with?"

"Unreported confiscations of drug money."

"The confiscations that got him killed."

"It was Ortega's money so it makes sense."

"So what happened after he was killed?"

"To tell you the truth we were preparing to withdrawal. Our arrangement with your father wasn't all that legal to begin with. Then you came onto the scene."

Samantha stared out of the window. A couple ancient deuce and a half cargo trucks came up the hill, forcing the driver to scoot over the edge of the road.

"Those are our supply trucks, we brought everything with us."

"With you from where?"

"That isn't important right now. Once we decided to come after you, I had my two platoons fly in. The logistics vehicles left the airport staggered back from the assault element by about thirty minutes. The flight was logged as commercial air traffic. Once they got on the ground the police and airport officials were bribed or coerced, or both."

"Strong armed."

"So now I have a question for you, why did you come back to Mexico?"

Samantha resumed staring out at the passing hills.

"When I found out that my father was killed I came to take up his post as police chief. I knew no one else would take the job. He was the third chief to be kidnapped and killed in as many years."

"Gutsy move."

"But not enough apparently."

"Bullshit."

The woman clenched her teeth.

"Just a few hours after I was deputized, Ortega's crew picked me up, grabbed me right off the street."

"It's in the past. With Ortega out of the way, we can go after the big dogs."

Approaching the city, they drove under an overpass. A decapitated corpse had been strung up and hung off the side of the bridge. The message, scrawled in blood, was written on the sign nailed into the body's abdomen. *This is what happens to police, dog fuckers.*

"How far out are we Pat?"

"Ten minutes from the city."

"Where can we take you that you will be safe?"

"Nowhere is safe."

Turning, Deckard looked into large brown eyes. He had seen that look enough times to be scared of it. Ortega's .357 was stuffed down the front of her pants.

She was out for blood.

3

Deckard threw the door open as Pat brought the car to a halt outside the Oaxaca police station. Holding his Kalashnikov at the ready, he proceeded up the steps, striding over a body riddled with bullets as Samantha followed close behind.

A second corpse lay in the entrance, graciously holding the door ajar for them to pass through.

"Better call and cancel that guy's dinner plans."

The female police chief snorted.

"Cartel scum."

Behind them, the engine squealed as Pat peeled off to position himself behind the building, just in case everything went sideways on them.

"*Alto!*" someone shouted at them from down the hall.

Samantha spoke in rapid fire Spanish that was too fast for Deckard to follow.

Stepping from behind an over turned desk, with a snub nosed .38 revolver in one hand, a portly man in a police uniform crossed himself. Obviously, he hadn't expected to see his new boss again, not unless she was hanging under an overpass somewhere.

In the corner, a muted television showed a broadcast of a masked man brandishing a machete from behind a podium as he gave his speech. Deckard did not need to hear the audio to know the revolutionary was fixing to lop some *federale's* head off. Over the last few months Mexico had begun its final decent towards chaos, the federal government not controlling anything outside of Mexico City. Everyone with a gun was moving to fill the vacuum and the disarmed civilian population was forced to resort to the machete, the traditional weapon of peasant uprisings in the Latin world.

Continuing their conversation in their native language, the two police officers led Deckard into the offices. Peering into one of the adjacent jail cells, Deckard spotted the bales of narco-dollars wrapped in cellophane, safely locked behind bars.

"They didn't come for the money," he said curiously, referring to the cartels who would want their money back.

"No, *senor,* the police officer on duty said. Just a few opportunists thinking they might find some easy money. Word

14

must have leaked out on the streets."

"They had me," Samantha said. "They thought the money would be theirs to reclaim whenever it suited them."

"How many police officers do you have on call?"

Samantha looked at her subordinate, who in turned shrugged his shoulders.

"One, including me. The others left, ran away. They will be swallowed up by the Jimenez cartel," Samantha said referencing the largest and most powerful drug cartel in southern Mexico. "That or they will go to work with them."

"Along with whatever is left of Ortega's organization," Deckard added.

"We have to move on them fast."

"I agree, but first we need to move the money to our new headquarters. We can keep you safe there as well, along with-" Deckard looked at the sole beat cop in Oaxaca city.

"Officer Lopez," the policemen responded with a half assed salute.

"Right, let's get moving."

Lopez switched back to Spanish, asking his police chief something. Deckard only caught on to one word, *Inteligencia* .

"I'm not CIA."

"That's right, you're some kind of gun for hire, huh? Then what do we call you mystery man?" Samantha asked.

"Black will do for now."

"Well, Mr. Black, I don't know-" her words were cut short as an old rotary phone sitting on one of the desks began to ring.

"*Como?*" Lopez said, holding the phone to his ear.

"*Si,*" he paused before cupping his hand over receiver. "It's for the *gringo*."

"I guess that must be me," Deckard said taking the phone. "Yeah?"

Heavy breathing sounded over the phone before someone spoke, "We want the money."

"Who is this?"

"A friend of Mr. Jimenez."

"You want the money? Come get it."

"Leave this place now. You don't belong here."

"We'll see who's standing when the smoke clears."

"Take a walk and don't come back. That is the deal."

15

"Make your play."

Another pause.

"I already have."

The police station was suddenly plunged into darkness as someone cut off the electricity.

4

Deckard pulled Lopez out from behind the desk as a barrage of auto fire chopped through the thin Formica board. Tucking the stock of his Kalashnikov into his shoulder he punched the first cartel gunmen through the door with a double tap. The second shooter got off a burst with a MAC-10 submachine gun that exploded the television screen behind him before Deckard gunned him down.

"We need to extract!" he shouted into his radio as more *sicarios* pushed their way into the police station.

Samantha's .357 nearly took the head clean off the shoulders of one of the shooters. The gunfire was deafening indoors.

Pat's transmission came through garbled and unreadable.

Moving into rooms adjacent to the hallway, the gunmen took cover as the two police officers offered suppressive fire. One of the *sicarios* lobbed a fragmentation grenade down the hall, a gift from post-Cold War stockpiles left over from one of Central America's dirty little guerrilla conflicts that had been delivered to the cartels.

Deckard didn't hesitate. Reaching down, he palmed the grenade and overhanded it back down the hall before turning and driving both officers to the ground under his weight. Overpressure washed over them, filling the dark narrow confines of the police station with smoke.

Taking a knee, Deckard indexed one of the remaining shooters, his silhouette visible through the haze. Squeezing the trigger, the assassin spun around under the force of the 7.62 rounds that knocked him to the ground.

"Get the money," Deckard said taking charge. With an unknown number of gunmen attempting to make entry, he knew they wouldn't be able to sustain themselves in place for long.

Lopez was turning the key and opening the jail cell when more shooters exploded through the rear entrance, somehow getting passed Pat. Deckard didn't know how and didn't care to dwell on what that meant for his friend.

Throwing himself back down to the dirty linoleum floor, the AK-103 chattered off another burst, striking one of the black-clad gunmen in the chest and knocking him backwards into his companion behind him.   Deckard noted the black combat fatigues and paramilitary gear. Only the best for Jimenez' men.

His follow up shot drilled the remaining gunmen, sending him stumbling back out the rear door in a splash on crimson.

More gunfire raced up the hallway towards him, sending splinters flying in all directions. Deckard rolled to his side the enemy fire traced passed him and into the gunmen's comrades at the other end of the hall who committed the fatal and costly mistake of attempting to catch him in an envelope.

Getting to his feet, he keyed up his radio once more, speaking a single phrase into the headset he wore.

"Prairie fire!"

Lopez looked up at him over the giant bale of cash on his hands.

"We're trapped," he said choking on his own words, sweat running down his face.

Pushing the police officer aside, Deckard snatched up one of the office chairs and flung it through a window. It smashed through the glass and landed outside in the alley.

"Go," Deckard said, letting his rifle hang on its sling.

Samantha threw her bale of money through the broken window before grabbing Lopez' bale and hurling it out after the first wad of cash.

Deckard reached for the pouches on his combat rig and grabbed two of his own grenades. Carefully pulling the pin out of each while keeping the spoons held in place was tricky. Outside the offices, he could hear the enemy regrouping, someone shouting orders.

As the two police officers cleared the broken window sill, Deckard leaned out of the doorway. Tossing the grenades to either side, he ignored the panicked screams of the cartel assassins as he double backed towards the window. Running, he hurtled up and out, brushing against the jagged glass that jutted out of the sides of the frame.

Coming down on the hard concrete, he almost stuck the landing before slipping on a piece of trash and landing on his backside. Inside the building, twin blasts shattered most of the remaining windows, the walls nearly buckling under the pressure of the explosives.

"*Dios mio*," Lopez said helping him to his feet.

Flicking his wrists, Deckard shook the grenade pins from his fingers.

"Let's get out of here before they figure out what happened."

Letting the officers reclaim the bales of greenbacks, Deckard took the lead, stalking down the alley towards the back of the police headquarters.

"Prairie Fire, this is Sierra Six," he said into his radio.

"Go ahead Six."

"How far out are you?"

"Two minutes," the Russian accented voice sounded above the static.

He knew they needed to keep moving.

The Quick Reaction Force was not going to make it in time.

The alleyway wound by a rusting car hulk that was propped up on cinder blocks before terminating back out on the street. Glancing around the corner, Deckard saw two blacked out SUVs with all doors thrown open. Four cartel hit men were maintaining rear security with German made Heckler and Koch sub-machine guns pointed absently into the night sky.

"*Jose!*" one yelled as a bloodied figure came stumbling out of the rear exit of the police station. Streams of blood flowed from punctured ear drums. Blinded by the blast, he tripped and fell in a heap in front of the parked trucks.

Deckard sighted in, lining the red dot of his rifle's reflex sight on one of the cartel men as he bent over to pick up his comrade. Maybe sensing his impending doom, the gunmen looked up, spotting Deckard in the shadows just as he stroked the trigger. The Kalashnikov bucked into his shoulder, the Mexican assassin catching a face full of lead.

The three remaining members of the cartel hit squad spun towards him, weapons ready. Their firefight was interrupted, hi-beams flashing across the SUVs and temporarily whiting out their vision as their eyes struggled to readjust.

The black Mercedes slammed into the SUV that the gunmen had foolishly clustered themselves around. Weighing in at over two tons, the car broadsided the truck, crushing two gunmen as metal mixed with flesh. Both vehicles were nearly lifted off the ground by the force of the impact before gravity slapped them back down to the pavement.

The last gunmen had avoided the wreck by mere inches. Now he leveled his MP5 at the driver's side window. Holding the trigger down, 9mm parabellum rounds spider webbed the multi-layer laminated glass. As per industry standards, the bullet proof window maintained its integrity until Deckard stepped from the alleyway and expended the rest of his magazine into their antagonist.

The driver's side door on the Mercedes was flung open in a plume of smoke, Pat coughing as he emerged from the cloud.

"Nice shot," he said through teary eyes.

"What the fuck was that Pat?"

"Improvising."

"Now how the hell are we supposed to clear out of here?" Deckard asked, pointing with his muzzle toward the smoking wreck that up until a few moments ago had been their ride home.

"The suspension on it was fucked anyway," Pat shrugged. "Ortega should have had it switched out months ago with an armor package on it that is this heavy. Inconsiderate bastard."

Two more SUVs were now racing towards them from down the street. Samantha and Lopez were caught in the open as they jogged over to Deckard and Pat, taking cover behind the car wreck. Deckard dropped his empty magazine, exchanging it for another full thirty rounds. The fumes of leaking gasoline were now overtaking the stench of garbage that permeated throughout much of the city.

Machine gun fire rattled out in several long bursts from behind them. Throwing himself to the ground, Deckard saw two Samruk assault trucks approaching from the opposite end of the street. Gunners went cyclic, cutting a stream of fire that crisscrossed over the enemy SUVs. The Quick Reaction Force had arrived on target and not a moment too soon.

With the windshield caved in by twin streams of 7.62 PKM rounds, one the SUVs swerved sideways, tires bursting as it skidded over the curb and slammed into an empty mechanics shop. Fixating on their second target, the machine gunners riding in the turret of each truck drilled the driver before walking their tracer fire down into the engine block.

The black SUV decelerated abruptly, slowing to just a few miles per hour. The windows were shattered, the bodies inside torn open when the truck played bumper cars with what was left of the Mercedes and finally came to a halt.

"Exfil. Now," Deckard ordered.

Lopez rose on shaky feet, the veteran cop and *de facto* combat soldier of the streets of Mexico, was still in disbelief after their several near misses. Samantha spurred him on with a few curt words, dumping the money bales onto one of the assault trucks.

"Sorry about that, Deck," Pat apologized. "It got to hot out here when the cartel showed up. I had to circle around the block and try again."

"Everything turned out okay, so we're both off the hook this time."

Pat grunted as he climbed on the back of one of the Iveco assault trucks, his ribs still bruised from the beating he had taken several months ago, including a shot gun blast to the chest, barely stopped by the body armor he had been wearing.

Deckard still sported some bruising of his own where his nose had been broken during that engagement.

Compulsively checking to make sure a round was seated in the chamber of his Kalashnikov, he found himself a seat and the trucks peeled out, headed back for the dead drug lord's compound. Scanning the streets as they flashed by, he knew the night wasn't over yet.

"Over here," Manuel whispered to his comrades. "This is the place."

The police officers had received a frantic phone call from Ignacio, one of Jimenez' lieutenants. The assault on the police station had failed, something that had never happened to the *sicarios* before. Crazy stories had the lieutenant spooked, something about some gringo running around with enough guns to even have the heavily armed cartel nervous. Manuel didn't believe the rumor and didn't care. Jimenez wanted the money, and Manuel hadn't seen a paycheck in months.

"We set the ambush here," he said to the rogue police officers. "They should be heading down this road in a few moments."

The terrain consisted of rolling hills and light vegetation. Not much cover to speak of, but with the terrain advantage of the high ground and the concealment of night, they would have little difficulty in raining lead down on the two vehicle convoy that they had been told was approaching.

After receiving the initial phone call, Manuel had to act fast, assembling the ten police officers and arriving to interdict the convoy with minutes to spare.

The Mexican cops got down in the prone position with American made rifles and Russian manufactured light machine guns, eyeballing the road in wait.

That was when the first shot sounded.

Manuel turned, the gunfire coming not from their front but from behind. The gunman next to him suddenly lay still, slumped over his machine gun.

The ambush line panicked. Some fired down onto the kill zone, pointlessly expending ammunition on the barren road. Two others realized the shot had come from their rear, firing equally useless bursts into the night at a target they couldn't see. The two slightly smarter gunmen who had at least identified the cardinal direction from which the attack had come from where the next two to be killed, taken down by high caliber rifle rounds spaced just a second apart.

Confused, and fearing some kind of double cross, one of the police officers jumped to his feet. He fired his M16 on fully automatic, slaughtering the nearest policemen before he could even figure out what was happening. Flicking his selector switch to semi, Manuel fired a quick series of shots into the idiot's chest, who fell to the ground in a cloud of dust.

Another corrupt cop lay sprawled on the ground, the sniper's bullet smashing his skull, leaving the gunman unrecognizable.

Manuel saw the muzzle flash in the distance. The enemy sniper had positioned himself to the rear of the ambush line, cleverly concealing himself in the saddle between two hills.

The remaining police officers might not have seen their salaries in months, but they knew when they had seen enough. Dropping their weapons, they ran down the opposite side of the hill, headed for the road. Manuel screamed down at them, cursing their cowardice, just as a .300 Winchester Magnum bullet slapped him between his shoulder blades.

Deckard looked on, confused as the assault trucks raced down the road. A small handful of uniformed Mexican police officers ran across the road and disappeared into the night. They had seen the muzzle flashes as they neared the compound and were prepared for an ambush. Apparently, they had thought better of it.

Reaching over, he grabbed Pat by the shirt sleeve.

"What the hell was that about?"

6

Five minutes later, the Samruk International mercenaries guarding the gate moved aside, letting the two Iveco assault vehicles into the compound. The soldiers of fortune were hard at work unloading equipment, building defensive positions on the roof tops, pulling rotations on guard duty, and other preparations for their latest campaign.

Deckard jumped off the back of his truck and frowned, seeing a figure approaching from Ortega's villa on crutches, limping his way towards him.

"I thought I told you to stay in Astana, Frank."

"I know, but I stowed away on one of the supply trucks anyway. I'll be damned if I was going to spend another day locked up in that damned hangar."

After a labyrinthine journey from their previous mission in the Pacific Ocean back to their headquarters in the capital of Kazakhstan, the wounded Samruk International members had been evacuated to the hospital. The few who were still able to walk were immediately paid and put on indefinite leave. Frank was discharged from the hospital a week later, having been treated for several gunshot wounds. Others, like Charles Rochenoire were still laid up, recovering from more serious injuries.

He and Deckard had spent the next month recovering from their injuries in a hangar at the Astana airport where all of the PMC's equipment was being stored. Deckard had often half joked that considering the nature of their previous mission, he expected a JDAM to land in his lap at any day now. Amazingly, that day had not come.

Mostly they had sat around drinking beer and playing spades.

"I had a feeling you might say that."

"Playing solitaire in a empty hanger just isn't my thing."

"You should have seen what happened on the way here. The most half assed ambush I've ever seen. They fired before we were anywhere near the kill zone, then dropped their weapons and ran as we finally rolled up to them."

"Chicken shit motherfuckers," Frank laughed. "Hey, what's that?"

24

Deckard followed his gaze over to Samantha hefting a oversized bale of money out of the truck.

"What? Samantha or the money?"

"Both." But Deckard could almost see the dollar signs forming in his eyes.

Walking towards her, Frank whipped out his folding knife, ready to cut through the layers of cellophane wrapped around the stacks of greenbacks. Deckard caught his wrist, stopping the blade a few inches from the plastic wrapping.

"Watch yourself."

"What's the idea, dude? We just want our pay day, you know, on account of how hard you got us working."

"Bullshit," Deckard grunted. "The cartels put ammonia and bleach between the layers of wrapping so that when dumb asses like you try to cut through them, the two chemicals mix and create chlorine gas. Sends a message to any of their couriers who decided to skim a little off the top, same goes for enemies who might manage to acquire some cartel cash."

"Fuck me."

"Where are our protective masks?"

"I think they're still on the back of the deuce and half," Frank said referring to the two and half ton cargo trucks that he had arrived with.

Deckard had ordered literally tons of gear, a battalion's worth. Now that battalion had been decimated down to a little over two platoons, they were left with a surplus of gas masks among other military items.

"Get a couple guys to put those masks on and open these bales up on the roof. Since you are so enthusiastic, and crippled, you just became the unit treasurer and pay agent. Tomorrow, you can have the boys line up and collect their paycheck."

Frank looked hurt, but for once held back his unsolicited commentary.

Slipping out of his plate carrier, Deckard set the body armor down in the corner of Ortega's living room next to his AK-103 which was left propped up against the wall. He kept his pistol belt in place, knowing it was important to keep some critical items on his person at all times. The belt held his Kimber 1911 pistol and holster, as well as several grenades, escape and evasion gear, and a few other bare necessities.

The living room was in the process of being converted into Samruk's Operations Center or OPCEN. Hard cases had been flung open, wires tangled across the carpet, computers were already plugged in and humming quietly.

A young man moved across the room, fumbling with the computer equipment in short, jerking motions. Starting up an electronic projector, he connected it to one of the laptop computers, displaying a large image of their operational area against the wall.

"Hey, who are you again?" Deckard asked.

"MY NAME IS CODY," the kid responded in loud stunted words.

"Damn, try using your indoor voice, okay Cody?"

"IT'S NOT MY FAULT. I HAVE ASPERGERS."

"We have hamburgers here? I'm hungry enough as-"

"NOT HAMBURGERS, ASBERGERS."

"What the hell are those?"

"I'M NOT STUPID YOU DICKHEAD."

"Where the fuck did you come from-"

"Holy shit, Deck," Frank said, crutching his way into the chaos of the Operations Center. "I haven't had the chance to introduce you to Cody. He's the guy I was telling you about. Remember, the hacker I worked with in the past? He helped us with that job in China."

"Okay, got it," Deckard said turning towards him. "But what the hell is wrong with him? Did he get into Ortega's stash or something?"

"FUCK-"

"Hey, hold on, Cody," Frank said holding a hand in the air. "You can just go back to doing what you were doing. Don't worry about it."

Turning abruptly, the hacker went right back to work with his electronics as if nothing had happened.

"Cody's got Asperger syndrome," Frank explained.

"What's that?"

"It's like a low grade form of autism. He's socially awkward like you wouldn't believe but he knows this computer shit. He's a genius when it comes to math, code, programming, stuff like that. We communicated by e-mail in the past when he would do freelance jobs for me so I never really noticed it before."

"Are you sure this is right?" Deckard asked. "Or legal?"

"Since when has that ever gotten in your way? He's fine, just a little strange. I promise you, this guy will pay big dividends in the future."

"GODDAMN-"

"I got this Cody, chill out!"

"Does he have tourettes as well?"

"Hey," Pat said leaning through the doorway and poking his head into the operations center. "Nikita just came strutting back into the compound."

"What do you mean, *back in*?" Deckard snapped.

Nikita stood in the courtyard with his SIG Blaser sniper rifle slung diagonally across his back. He held a Mexican police officer prisoner, the captive's hands secured behind his back with plastic flex cuffs.

"What the fuck is he doing freelancing like this?" Deckard demanded. "Someone go get the Sergeant Major. What is this guy doing, trying to win the Tom Berenger award or something?"

Nikita shrugged his shoulders in response. His English

was about as bad as Deckard's Russian.

Apparently the sniper had sneaked out of the compound after Deckard's departure, running his own solo operation. Now he knew what the gunfire on the ridge had been about on their way in. Nikita had triggered the ambush before they drove into the kill zone. It wasn't that he wasn't grateful. The sniper had great initiative, if poor judgment.

Just then, Sergeant Major Korgan arrived, looking for Deckard. He must have already been told the news.

"Security is up," the Sergeant Major reported. "We've got the perimeter secured and will rotate the guards in accordance with our op-tempo."

One platoon would provide security and other base operations while the second platoon conducted combat operations.

"Take control of this prisoner," Deckard said. "Get him searched and secured then prepare him for interrogation."

Korgan nodded, taking the police officer by the collar, relieving Nikita of his prisoner.

"We'll deal with Wyatt Earp later," he said referring to his renegade sniper. "We've got work to do."

7

"Alright, take your seats and let's get started," Deckard said as he set down his cup of coffee. He was already running on fumes. He'd been running recon in Mexico for nearly a week when he made the decision to launch the hostage rescue on Ortega's compound. Calling back to Astana airfield in Kazakhstan, he mobilized the Private Military Company that he was now the *de facto* owner of to get the ball rolling. After the assault on the police station, he knew he needed to get some sleep but transitioning right into twenty-four hour operations was necessary. They wouldn't have long to complete and close out their contract with Samantha before the Mexican government made a power play.

As of now, the mercenaries were the new guns in town and heading for a showdown with Jimenez. The projection against the wall of their Operations Center displayed a map of Central America.

"Here we are in Central America," Deckard said glancing at Frank. "For those us you who are just joining us."

Cody worked at his laptop, zooming in on where Southern Mexico met with Guatemala and the Yucatan peninsula.

"Our new base of operations is centrally located in the state of Oaxaca courtesy of Ortega," Deckard stated, while Cody pinpointed their location the map with a red dot. "To the north is Veracruz, to the west is Guerrero, south is the Pacific Ocean, and to the south east is Chiapas. Continuing east from there is Guatemala.

All hands were on deck, sitting in chairs confiscated from Ortega's mansion or standing towards the back. Squad Leaders, Platoon Sergeants, and other key leadership were getting a full brief now that they were all in country.

"Central America for the most part is both mountainous and covered in jungle, which is why there has never been an invasion north-south or south-north throughout history aside from perhaps the Panama invasion in 1989 which was able to make use of US air power. The climate is generally temperate but varies from dry plateaus and deserts, to rain forests and mountains.

"The terrain here in Oaxaca varies from lightly vegetated rolling hills, like this," a slide showed a panorama of the country side that looked like the backdrop for a Sergio Leone movie. "To dense forest transitioning into jungle in *la sierra norte* located to our north east.

"While Central America is traditionally divided up into personal fiefdoms for dictators, the rich, and military officers, Mexico in this case suffered under nearly seventy years of single party rule from the Institutional Revolutionary Party or PRI. The PRI acted as an oligarchic type of institutional dictatorship. This power sharing structure among the elite was finally crushed in the year 2000 when the rival PAN party member was elected president. Today, the old politics of Mexico are somewhat irrelevant as the Mexican government controls little if anything outside Mexico City.

"While the Mexican military is fragmented and corrupt, their best infantry brigades remain under the command of the central government and have proven somewhat effective in combating the drug lords. The more effective units seem to be the Marines and the FES, Mexico's maritime commando unit.

"Those of you who served in Sankar and other Kazakh Special Forces units are already familiar with the mechanics of drug production and trafficking from dealing with this issue in your own country but here is a down and dirty on the local situation."

The majority of the mercenaries in Samruk International were veterans from Kazakhstan. As Russian speakers, Sergeant Major Korgan was translating for his men who didn't speak English.

Deckard continued his brief, giving the team a brief overview of the history of drug smuggling and drug trafficking organizations in Mexico before narrowing in on the recent activities of the Ortega and Jimenez cartel. With the Mexican military pushing hard on the Zetas and other cartels in the north, cartel activity was being pushed further to the south where they were currently located in Oaxaca. The province had been something of an oasis in the middle of the drug wars until the crack down in the north forced the cartels to adapt and find new centers to move drugs through.

The brief went on as Deckard laid out the information that he and his recon team had gathered over the last week.

30

Little did he know, the enemy was also beginning to conduct an intelligence estimate of Samruk International.

8

The moon hung high in the night sky, obnoxiously bright flood lights keeping the soccer field illuminated at all hours in case the boss wanted to play. Tonight he was kicking the ball back and forth with a member of his Praetorian Guard, the Personal Security Detachment that never left his side. They were his best, and more importantly, his most loyal.

Following a winding road that traced its way to the summit of a jungle mountain was an aging, decrepit church. The glass windows were shattered, green foliage sprouting from the sediment that collected on the roof tops. The holy site remained in a state of disrepair, cast aside for new ventures. As the Jimenez cartel grew they bought up large swath of land in Oaxaca, in other cases they just moved in and claimed it for themselves.

The church was just a relic from a bygone time, the rest of the compound was built upon and ancient fortress built by the Spaniards during the colonial years, all surrounded by high walls and gun towers. The location itself was unique, the steep cliffs and rough jungle terrain on all four sides of the compound made it nearly impenetrable.

Still, it was the sight of the church on the way in that had initiated the churning in Arturo Carranza's stomach. Reaching into the pocket of his slacks he produced a white handkerchief, making sure to blot the sweat from his hands before the cartel leader acknowledged his presence. Arturo did his work and did it well, but not of his own accord, not in Oaxaca, and not with permission.

"Arturo," Jimenez beamed from across the emerald green field. "You grace us with your presence."

Wiping down his palms, he shoved the handkerchief back in his pocket.

"At your request, sir."

Even at one in the morning.

The goalie batted the ball back to the cartel leader who caught it with the insole of his soccer cleat.

"And I have," he responded. "I take it you've heard about Ortega."

"It wasn't *federales*," Arturo croaked in his defense.

Arturo was young, ambitious, and highly educated in American and European universities. His skin was just as white as that of his former class mates in The London School of Economics. He was a member of one of Mexico's elite families. Jimenez of course, was not. He came to power by seizing it from others. Arturo was born into it. Young, ambitious, and scared shitless by the man that both rivals and allies called The Beast.

"Then who?"

Jimenez wound up, swatting the ball down the field. The security man guarding the goal made a halfhearted attempt, lunging for the ball and missing. He knew well enough to let his boss win.

"I've established contact with my agents," Arturo swallowed. "They will be reporting in shortly."

"I sent a couple squads of assaulters to intercept them at the police station when I found out that they had rolled into town. My town."

The goalie held the ball in both hands over his head, tossing it back to Jimenez. It made contact with the ground and bounced towards him.

"Gringos," the cartel leader said, his foot stomping down on the ball to stop it. "Some of our informants in the area saw gringos in military trucks."

Arturo was supposed to provide any and all early warnings to the cartel in the event of Mexican military incursions.

"Luckily, they were not like the Mexican military vehicles," he continued.

The Mexican intelligence agent breathed a sigh of relief. He was off the hook, if only for the moment.

"So it seems I know something you do not. Something that you of all people, whose business it is to know, should already know for yourself."

Jimenez circled around the soccer ball until he was facing his pet intelligence operative. It was the eyes that scared Arturo. Those crazy eyes. They were the eyes of a man who had butchered his way to the top. He would have made the Aztecs proud.

"*Mercenarios*. That is what I think," he said nodding to himself. "They cleaned out two squads just back from their training in Guatemala. Find out who they are Arturo. I want names. I want to know who they are and where their families sleep at night."

"Yes, sir."

Taking a step back, Jimenez launched the ball at Arturo. As it rocketed into his chest, he caught it with both hands.

"My men will make you comfortable in their quarters until those calls of yours begin to come in."

Suddenly, he was flanked by two cartel members each grabbing him by an arm. Looking down at the ball in his hands, his mind struggled to construct the pattern of the ball. Rather than black and white checkers, there was something else he recognized. Seeing the holes for eyes, nostrils, and a mouth, he dropped the ball. Recoiling in disgust, the two security man held on to him tightly. A human face had been sewn into the ball.

"Do not fail me Arturo," the cartel leader's words called after him.

9

"We have been working him for half an hour," Sergeant Major Korgan reported to Deckard. "Nothing so far. He is more scared of Jimenez than he is of us and keeps calling him The Beast."

"We'll see."

The two mercenary leaders weaved between the custom made Iveco assault vehicles. They had all been refueled and shotgun parked, nose facing towards the gate, and ready to move at a moment's notice. Deckard had the trucks constructed for Samruk International months prior. They featured an up-armored cab that sat a driver and passenger, who acted at the vehicle commander. In the back were eight seats that were bolted back to back, four on each side. The passengers in the back sat facing out, ready for enemy contact. A rotating gun turret topped it off with a PKM machine gun in the pintle mount.

Inside the garage, the prisoner that Nikita had captured was handcuffed to a pipe sticking out of the wall. Two Kazakh soldiers stood guard with the AK-103 rifles at the ready while Pat questioned the prisoner. Standing with his hands on his hips, the former Delta Force commander shook his head.

"Take over," he said looking up at Deckard. "I know you are fluent. I got sent to DLI to learn Thai, not Spanish," Pat complained about the Defense Language Institute.

"What do we have so far?"

"I've been asking him about who he knows in town that works for Jimenez. Apparently Jimenez is one bad dude. He has this guy scared out of his mind. He told us all of his own background information but won't divulge anything about the cartel."

"Nothing a little sleep deprivation and twenty four hours of questioning can't fix. He'll break."

"You know as well as I do that we don't have that kind of time. The clock started ticking the second we hit the ground. The Mexican military will be on its way once word gets back to them in the morning. How much time do you think we have?"

"A couple days at most."

The elite infantry brigades that were still loyal to the Mexican government were fighting a desperate, American sponsored, offensive against the Zeta cartel up North. It would take them time to divert resources and re-deploy. But it wouldn't be long.

"We need to escalate the level of violence," Pat said. A veteran of thousands of strike operations in Iraq and Afghanistan, he knew that this wouldn't be like previous campaigns. This was a blitz, and whichever side could react the fastest would be the one walking away from this battle.

"I've got an idea," a female voice approached from behind the two mercenaries.

Samantha pushed them aside and walked into the garage to face the prisoner. She began firing off Spanish at him in stunted machine gun bursts. The prisoner pleaded, his bushy eyebrows turned upward. He was trying the puppy dog routine.

In one smooth motion, Samantha drew her .357 Magnum and sent it crashing into the side of the prisoner's head, hard enough to draw blood.

"Where are the drugs?"

Bringing the heavy pistol barrel down on his forehead, the prisoner yelped, looking towards the two Americans for help.

"Where are the drugs?" Samantha was screaming in her native language.

The pistol whipping continued as she brought the gun down on his face repeatedly.

Deckard was about ready to stop the interrogation. She was getting out of control.

Then the prisoner started talking about the drugs.

Cody displayed Google Earth on the projector screen, zooming on the Pacific coast of Oaxaca. The section displayed was completely barren.

"So he was bullshitting us," Deckard said.

"NO, WAIT, HOLD ON."

"It sounds right," Pat said, his arms crossed in front of

him. They stood in the OPCEN, pouring over what little data they had, trying to substantiate the information that Samantha had pried out of their prisoner. "The Colombian military captured a couple narco-subs last year. They were built up-river, deep in the jungle-"

"I bought this new imagery from a private intelligence firm," Cody interrupted, a little more subdued. Deckard had to admit, the kid was in the zone around computers.

"Here is the latest satellite photography," Cody said bringing it up on the projector.

"Still nothing," Pat sighed.

"I will keep looking," Cody said.

"Hold on," Deckard stopped him. "Zoom in on the Southeastern part of the grid square."

Cody enhanced the image, showing a close up of an empty coast line.

"Now go back to the previous imagery."

Going back to the older image, Deckard walked in front of the projector, tracing the coastline with a finger.

"Now back to the new one again."

The image flickered over Deckard and he began tracing the coast again.

"Son of a bitch," Pat cursed.

"The coast is different," Cody exclaimed.

"It's this cove right here," Deckard announced. "You can see the cove just fine on the old imagery, but on the new pictures it has completely disappeared. Someone camouflaged the entire cove and now it is blending in with the surrounding terrain."

"The perfect covert submarine pen," Pat finished for him.

"Get First Platoon in here and we will do a quick brief. We have to capitalize on this intelligence before the opportunity is lost. I want to be rolling out of the gate within the hour."

10

"VDO, VDO," Deckard announced over the radio net. The convoy of assault vehicles slowed to a stop. The VDO or Vehicle Drop Off, was where the assault element would depart on foot and begin marching towards their objective.

That it had been a long night was an understatement. They had pushed off in the early morning hours, driving overland across bumpy terrain on dirt roads, going off road altogether at times to take short cuts, avoiding the main avenues as much as possible. It was a long drive that had threatened to rattle the fillings out of their teeth but they had made it to the VDO just before dawn.

As commander, Deckard had allowed his men to doze off in their seats as long as one troop stayed awake per vehicle. It was always possible, if unlikely, that another ambush was out there waiting for them somewhere. It was a tactical decision, he needed his men as fresh as possible when lead started to fly, even allowing himself to nod off for a few minutes until the rough terrain shook him awake.

While the PKM gunners in the turrets and drivers would remain with the vehicles, the rest of First Platoon jumped off the vehicles and gathered around Deckard. Unfolding a topographical map, Deckard illuminated it with a small, red lens flashlight.

"This is our current location," Deckard said using a twig to pinpoint their location for his men. The mercenaries were mostly of Kazakh extraction, members of a Private Military Company that he had inherited from his former employers. There were a number of American and European troops thrown into the mix, Special Operations soldiers he had brought on as instructors who had stayed around after the initial contract.

"We will move by foot from here on out to our objective here," he said, pointed out the cove. "We suspect that this area here is a camouflaged base for submarines that the Jimenez cartel is using to smuggle drugs from Colombia up the Pacific coast and eventually into the United States. We could be wrong, it could be a dry hole in which case we'll turn back around and high tail it back to the compound. Once we get into position we will search the area but it should be pretty clear, there is either a

38

hidden cove tucked inside the coast or there isn't. Search and destroy. Any questions?"

Deckard's Russian had improved to the point that he could struggle through a mission brief.

"Good. You've got five minutes for final Pre-Combat Inspections."

The mercenaries quickly applied gun oil to their AK-103 rifles, checked magazines, refilled hydration bladders from five gallon water cans on the trucks, and made ready to initiate movement to the objective.

"Cody, this is Six," Deckard spoke into his radio. "Radio check, over."

"I READ YOU LIMA-CHARLIE."

The kid was smart but it would take some time for him to get used to Cody's halting use of the English language.

A hint of daylight was just beginning to break on the horizon when Deckard put the men into a single file and they began marching towards the distant sounds of ocean waves breaking on the shore. The smell of sea salt clung to the breeze, a welcome relief from the stifling summer heat.

Leaving behind the low lying shrub land, the mercenaries had to break bush. Moving single file, Deckard eventually found a game trail to walk on and pushed through. Weaving through the jungle foliage and interspersed palm trees, they covered as much ground as they could, moving about a kilometer. Checking the Garmin GPS device that he wore on his wrist like a watch, Deckard could see that they were about halfway to the objective.

Sweat beaded on his forehead as he led the mercenaries through the jungle. He had thirty two assaulters total which should be enough for the kind of attack he had in mind. He hoped.

Driving on, they crept forward until the jungle opened up at an outcropping of smooth gray rock. Looking over his shoulder, he motioned the Kazakh assault element forward. In the jungle, it would be difficult, if not impossible, to maneuver if they came under fire and he was glad to be out of it.

Staying low, he leopard crawled over the rocks, eyes scanning in the early morning light. Blinking, his senses were not, in fact, deceiving him. The terrain in front of him was perfectly uniform other than a slight sagging in the middle.

"So that's how you make an ocean bay disappear," he said under his breath.

A massive tarp had been stretched from the rocky cliffs all the way across the cove. Large metal pickets had been hammered into the dirt or metal hard points drilled into the rock itself where the ends of the tarp were secured with thick metal rings. The fabric itself had a photo realistic printing etched across its length and width showing a beach front. The cartel obviously had it done professionally by one of the defense firms that printed up special camouflage sheets to hide military vehicles and facilities.

"Six this is Frank," his OPCEN leader crackled over the radio in complete disregard for the correct verbiage that was supposed to be used on the assault net. "What's your progress, over?"

"We just arrived at the target," Deckard whispered into the microphone attached to the headset he wore. "It looks like the bay we are looking for has been camouflaged over. I'm going to get in close to do a leader's recon before the assault."

"Roger, Frank out."

Turning around, Deckard crept back to his men waiting in a skirmish line right where the jungle receded from the rocky area. His Russian had improved in leaps and bounds since he first took command of Samruk International but it still left a lot to be desired. Repeating himself for clarification a few times, he got his point across. The assaulters would maintain their security position while he and Sergeant Fedorchenko did a leader's recon.

Whenever a maneuver element knew it was going to perform a raid on an enemy target it was important to be as deliberate as possible and plan out each phase of the operation. In this case they were dealing with an irregular target, it wasn't as simple as an enemy compound or camp. No one knew what they were really facing at this point.

They needed a close recce to confirm what their prisoner had told Samantha. The prisoner that Nikita had brought back had described a secret submarine base commanded by a cartel boss that they called Captain Nemo.

Fedorchenko was one of his best men which was why he had been promoted to Platoon Sergeant after Samruk hit a black site in the middle of the Pacific a while back. When the leadership in his platoon had been killed off during the hit, he had manned up, taken control of the other men, and defeated the enemy. They had pulled off the impossible, if at a heavy price.

Deckard gritted his teeth as he freed his Ka-Bar fighting knife from its sheath and began to cut through the heavy tarp that concealed the bay from overhead observation.

Here we go again.

Cutting a Y-shaped slit through the fabric, he put the blade away, and quietly swung through the hole feet first. Setting down on a slope, he let go of the tarp and half stepped, half slid down the embankment, making as little noise as he possibly could. Slowing himself, he put two gloved hands up in front of him to stop his forward movement before he slammed into a wooden crate at the bottom.

The tarp bounced overhead, making a slight whipping sound as the sea breeze rolled across it. Underneath the covering, half of the bay had been boarded over to create a dry dock. Wooden pylons jutted from the water, connecting a somewhat haphazard boardwalk of floating dock segments. Crates and pallets were scattered everywhere. A lone guard patrolled the pallet yard in the distance.

Ducking down behind cover, Fedorchenko was already at his side.

Keeping their Kalashnikov rifles at the ready, their trained eyes swept the enemy hardsite, identifying key targets. At the far side of the dock they could make out the mast of the narco-submarine that Nikita's prisoner had described. It was bigger than Deckard had expected, about the size of an old Japanese midget submarine straight out of the WWII.

On the south side of the dockyard were a couple dozen 55-gallon drums. Besides a place to off load contraband, the sub pen also served as a fuel depot where the midget subs would refuel before heading back to Colombia. Deckard sized up the operation in moment. There were no roads into or out of the remote hidden cartel base.

The Colombian farmers would grow the coca plants and sell them to the cartels, who would refine the product in drug labs deep in the jungle. From there the cocaine would be loaded onto the locally constructed submarines and clandestinely transported north to southern Mexico. The subs would bring the drugs, off load them in the sub pen, then head home. The drugs would then be loaded onto boats to be taken to yet another location in southern Mexico for distribution where they would then be taken overland across the US border for sale.

The sub pen was a site known as a "trampoline" by the cartels. The term normally referred to a way station between where the drugs originated, in Colombia and Bolivia, and the United States that was utilized by aircraft being flown by smugglers. Their small airplanes would need to stop somewhere to refuel on the way to Florida. The days of sky pirates were mostly over now, the Coast Guard having shut those corridors down years ago.

Now the cartels had evolved by using submarines instead. The voyage all the way to the United States would be too taxing for the small submarines so instead they would have to sell the drugs to the Mexican cartels and let them take responsibility for moving the product to market.

A clever set up, Deckard had to admit.

At the north end of the dock were several connex shipping containers that had been converted into living quarters for the staff that worked at the submarine base. With the sun now hanging in the early morning sky, he knew that the staff and the rest of the base's security would be waking soon. They had arrived just in time, the night guard would be exhausted and ready for a shift change. The Colombians were probably catching up on some sleep before making the voyage back home. Now the men of Samruk International just had to act fast enough to exploit the opportunity.

"I want that submarine," Deckard whispered to Fedorchenko. "We can use something like that."

"Deep sea fishing?"

"You are from a land locked country, what do you know about deep sea fishing?"

"I have dreams you know."

"Alright, let's get the boys down that embankment and have them start taking cover behind these crates. It looks like they are loaded full of cocaine. White powder sandbags should be able to stop a few bullets once the shooting kicks off."

"Da."

Deckard maintained eyes on the objective, monitoring the guard as he absentmindedly paced the docks until a shift change that would never come for him. Fedorchenko glided back up the embankment and through the hole in the camouflage canvas that hung over the sub pen. A minute later, the assaulters began filtering down into the pallet yard. One by one they took up positions behind the crates, training their weapons on the guard and the living quarters.

Positioned on the extreme right hand side of their assault line was a machine gunner with an Mk48. An assistant gunner moved with him, carrying additional belts of 7.62 ammunition. The Mk48 was the size of a light machine gun such as the M249 SAW but packed the 7.62 punch of a larger general purpose machine gun such as the M240B. The Belgium made weapon was a gift from another merc outfit that Samruk hand tangled with in the recent past. The Kazakh soldiers were finding the Mk48 to be plenty effective for immediate support by fire.

Deckard's only concern was that one of the cargo containers that served as living quarters was situated behind the other. In the restricted confines of the submarine pen, it was impossible to get any kind of flanking fire. The second container was outside of their cone of fire and there wasn't much they could do about it at the moment.

Nodding at Fedorchenko, he acquired the lone guard in the holographic reticule of his rifle sight. The Kazakh Sergeant was in charge of his platoon and would be the one to initiate the raid. Easing his safety from safe to semi-automatic carefully as not to compromise their position by the loud distinctive click that Kalashnikov selectors make, he gently squeezed the trigger.

The guard seemed to react a moment before the rifle barked a stream of fire.

Before he could turn around, the Mexican triggerman was thrown backwards as if tugged off balance by invisible puppet strings. Propelled backward, he slipped off the edge of the dock and fell into the water with a belly flop. Deckard sent two more shots just as Fedorchenko fired but they proved redundant, the shots passing just over the guard as he collapsed into the sea.

Thirty audible clicks sounded as one. The Kazakh mercenaries were ready to get some. Deckard made a quick mental note to teach them how to wrap the selector switch in electrical tape to prevent the clicking sound, something he'd picked up on another battlefield in one of his previous lives.

The Mk48 went cyclic, the gunner holding down the trigger for fully automatic fire.

The Samruk mercenaries turned their guns on the living quarters, giving the enemy the wakeup call of a lifetime. 7.62 bullets sparked as they punched through the flimsy metal walls of the connex containers, the Mk48 sweeping fire from one side to the other as the gunner traversed the gun on its bipod legs. Several bloodied cartel members stumbled out of the container in their boxer shorts. The mercenaries made short work of them, each sprawled on the ground in seconds.

Then someone threw a grenade, just to prove that no good plan survives first contact with the enemy.

The explosion ripped through the docks, sending splinters of wood into the air. Several of the 55-gallon drums in the fuel yard exploded, the burning heat singeing the hair on Deckard's arm where he sleeve had been rolled up. The gasoline flooded across the submarine pen, burning with an intensity that drove the mercenaries back. The fire was intense enough that it was threatening to overtake their position. The gasoline used to power the submarine had spilled into the water leaving the surface layer of the water on fire.

"Fire in the hole!" Fedorchenko yelled, depressing the transmit button on his radio. It was an operational code word that alerted the entire platoon to evacuate off the objective as fast as possible, only to be used during extreme emergencies.

As one, the platoon stood up from their positions and peeled off, filing back up the embankment. Through the flames, Deckard could see the black outlines of human beings. Their forms shimmered in the heat mirage coming up off of the fire. It was difficult to discern their movements through the haze but they were there.

The heat was growing in intensity, the crates that the mercenaries had taken cover behind were now on fire. If they didn't hurry, the enclosed submarine base would become their tomb. Freeing knives from their sheaths, the mercenaries began cutting more holes in the canvas to escape from rather than wait their turn filing through one opening. Like rats trapped in a cage, their actions took on a certain kind of urgency.

Deckard stumbled up the embankment. Reaching up, he grabbed the canvas and slashed it with his Ka-Bar fighting knife. The smoke burned his eyes, causing them to water. As if Mexico could get any hotter, they had found a way to trap themselves in hell itself.

Clenching both sides of the slit he had cut, Deckard lunged forward and back out into day light and fresh air. Gasping, he looked around at the other mercenaries. They were coughing from smoke inhalation and had the black soot of carbon under their noses and around their red eyes. Fedorchenko gave him a thumbs up. All of the men had made it out of the inferno.

Doubled over, Deckard spat a black tar ball on the ground before standing up straight. The fire had burned through a large portion of the camouflage tarp covering the bay. The submarine would be able to escape the flames and there was no way to flank around, the embankments around the sides of the bay were too steep and rocky to maneuver around.

Unless there was an alternate way to intercept the submarine before it escaped.

Before he knew it, Deckard had jumped onto the canvas and was running across it. The fire was melting through the fabric and holes were sprouting up all around him. The commando tripped, falling on his face as the fire popped another tether from the fabric, causing it to go slack. Struggling to his feet, Deckard ran. More holes continued to appear in the camouflage covering, the entire mess threatening to collapse at any moment and plunge him into the inferno below.

Going for his knife, Deckard lunged forward and slashed the blade across the canvas. Grabbing the edge with both hands, he somersaulted forward and through the opening he had cut. Hanging on, he could feel his gloved hands beginning to slip. It was only by some miracle that he had judged his position on the covering correctly.

He was dangling directly over the metal connex containers that the sub crew and security personnel lived in. Releasing his grip, Deckard fell the ten feet to the metal roof, his boots coming down hard, knees bent to help break his fall. The sub pen was now a haze of black smoke, the heat threatening to overwhelm him. Under his combat gear, even the veteran soldier felt as if he might pass out, a sure death sentence. If the fire didn't get him, the smoke inhalation would.

Moving to the lip of the connex, he hooked the inner part of his boot on the edge of the container and held on with one hand, lowering himself off the side in a spider hang. Kicking off with his foot, he dropped the rest of the way to the wooden dock.

Putting his Kalashnikov back into operation after having it slung across his back, Deckard ran in the only direction available, towards the sunlight that barely penetrated the smoke.

The entire dock rocked into the water, causing him to stumble once more. The fire was eating through the wooden pylons, making the entire platform unstable. Tears streamed from the corners of his eyes as the smoke began to sting. With his legs driving him forward, Deckard knew his body was red lining.

Suddenly, he burst out into daylight, the sun hanging in the morning sky above the ocean. Behind him, the canvas that had been concealing the bay collapsed into the fire with a whoosh of hot air and black smoke. By now, most of the flames had been smothered by the collapse or extinguished as the dock sank into the bay.

A bullet exploded at Deckard's feet, wooden splinters sent tearing into his pant leg. Rolling behind a forklift, he came to a knee as a cascade of auto fire clanged off the metal framework of the heavy lift vehicle.

"You okay down there Six?" Fedorchenko came up on the net.

"I'm not dead," Deckard replied into his radio.

Peering from behind his cover, he saw the trigger man who had been shooting at him disappear down into the mast of the midget sub. Metal on metal sounded as the port hole slammed shut. White water churned behind the sub as it began to pull away from the dock.

"We're trying to flank around but we have to hack through the jungle to get to you."

"See you soon," Deckard terminated the transmission and broke from cover in an all-out sprint.

Boots pounded across the sinking dock, the sub quickly picking up speed as Deckard chewed up the ground between himself and his target. Unfortunately, he was running out of dock. The pier was about to end as he vaulted into the air. Weighed down with nearly forty five pounds of weapons, ammunition, and body armor, he managed more of a leap than a jump, coming down hard on the metal fuselage of the submarine. Slipping, his feet splashed into the water as he found purchase, grabbing a hold of a periscope that snaked from the top of the sub.

Pulling himself up onto the submarine, he moved towards the mast sticking from the center of the giant metal cylinder. It was amazing that cartel engineers were able to put together a functioning midget sub in a dry dock somewhere deep in the Colombian rain forest. It looked like something straight out of a WWII movie. The porthole was tightly secured he discovered, grunting as he gave the handle a few tugs. Inside he could hear frantic voices arguing in Spanish.

Looking over his shoulder, Deckard could see his platoon of Samruk soldiers at the edge of the bay, looking out to sea as their commander grew distant, the submarine making haste for the open ocean.

"Six-" the Kazakh platoon leader's voice crackled over the radio.

"I've got an idea."

Deckard wasn't carrying any breaching charges or other explosives aside from a couple flashbangs and fragmentation grenades. He had one chance to improvise something before the sub filled its ballast tanks and plunged beneath the waves. Unzipping his med pouch, the American pushed through his tourniquets, bandages, and celox gauze before he tore free a plastic IV bag full of Hextend fluid. The IV was meant to be given to gunshot victims to help boost their blood pressure after massive blood loss.

Deckard had other ideas.

Tearing a flashbang from its pouch, he used a roll of white medical tape to secure it to the IV bag, wrapping several lengths around the two items to hold them together. Pulling on the hatch, the mercenary commander did his best to identify where the locking mechanism was located. Placing the IV-flashbang satchel over it, he taped it in place on the hatch with more medical tape.

He had created an improvised water impulse charge. Normally, C4 plastic explosives would be used in conjunction with a container of water. Water didn't compress under pressure so when an explosive charge was placed behind it, the force of the detonation pushed the water straight through anything in its way. Holding the satchel in place, Deckard yanked the pin from the flashbang and ducked behind the submarine's mast.

The flashbang went off with a shock wave that would have left him bleeding from the ears if he hadn't been wearing hearing protection. Looking over the lip of the mast, Deckard saw that his MacGyver antics had paid off. A ragged hole had been blasted through the hatch. Flinging it open with one hand, he kept his distance as gunfire shot up and out of the porthole.

Dropping another flashbang down into the darkness, Deckard waited for it to detonate before throwing his weight over the lip and down the ladder leading into the sub. The interior stank of the sulfur residue left behind by the flashbang in the enclosed space.

The inside of the sub was poorly lit, several yellow bulbs mounted on the ceiling and running the length of the sub barely illuminating anything at all, especially now that several had been shattered by the flashbang.

The shadow of a man stumbled towards Deckard. He was having a coughing fit. Holding the side of his head, he ran into the ladder. He had been completely disoriented by the blast inside the enclosed compartment. Deckard grabbed the cartel man by the collar and slammed in into a bulkhead, knocking him unconscious.

The air shifted, something moving behind him. Twisting at the hips, Deckard shot his foot out in a mule kick to his rear, catching an approaching gunman in his mid-section. Doubled over, he stripped the pistol from the would-be killer's hands and drove his knee upwards and into the man's face.

Two down.

But midget submarines sometimes have a crew-

Gunfire sparked off metal, bullets ricocheting down the sides of the metal submarine as the rounds found flat surfaces to ride along.

-of three.

Deckard didn't bother to transition to his rifle or snatch for the 1911 he carried in a holster at his hip. Using the black pistol he had relieved from the second submariner, he pointed the muzzle deeper into the sub where he had seen the muzzle flash of the enemy gunman.

Dropping to a knee, he felt the angry bite of hot metal chopping through the air just above his head.

Milking the trigger, he squeezed off a three round burst from the Glock pistol he held. The enemy yelped, dropping his weapon. Rushing forward, Deckard had to high step it across the metal catwalk that ran down the length of the sub. He caught the

Colombian in mid-reach as his bloody fingers stretched for the Ingram MAC-10 submachine gun that he had dropped.

Captain Nemo.

Deckard never gave him the chance. A final shot echoed inside the submarine and the cartel submarine captain sprawled out on the catwalk with a bullet hole in his forehead.

Dropping the Glock's magazine, Deckard racked the slide, ejecting the round in the chamber before casting the pistol aside.

Samruk International was expanding its capabilities with a fledgling brown water littoral Navy.

11

Black smoke spiraled into the blue morning sky as the mercenaries cleared the jungle and began making their way back to their assault trucks. Each of them was a little lighter than they had been on the way in to their objective, having drank water and expended ammunition before, during, and after they trashed the cartel's hidden submarine base.

It was a skill set that they had been trained on in Kazakhstan, honed on the battlefield in places like Afghanistan and Burma. Destruction was what they did, it was what they were good at. There were two kinds of violence in the world. There was the senseless killing perpetrated by terrorists, politicians, and cartels on one hand but on the other there also existed a type of creative destruction wielded by those who stood in their way. These days, it seemed that the former was far more common than the later.

The mercs walked in an extended wedge-shaped formation. This distribution gave them the most versatility in a firefight as each man could fire to his flank without risking injury to his teammates. The point man raised a fist into the air, halting the patrol.

"I've got contact up here," the point man whispered into his throat mic.

"Enemy?" Fedorchenko asked.

"Maybe," came the reply. "They're armed."

Deckard ran up to the front of the formation to get a better look. He felt the fatigue in his body. He needed to get some rest. The grind of back to back operations would take him down eventually.

Standing across the rocky terrain was a line consisting of a dozen gunmen. They stood stoically in their olive colored fatigues. Balaclavas concealed their faces while they held a variety of rifles at port arms, motionless in the morning heat. Even at a distance of a hundred meters, Deckard could tell that several of the smaller gunmen were actually women.

"Who are they?" Fedorchenko said as he moved up from behind him.

"Zapatista rebels. Usually they stay in their home turf, farther south in Chiapas."

"Why don't they open fire?"

"Because they are putting on a show," Deckard said sardonically. "Tell the boys to lower their weapons. These guys are here to deliver a message; not get into a dust up with us."

The Kazakh Sergeant began barking orders. The men quickly arranged themselves into a defensive perimeter, their weapons kept at the ready just in case things went hot.

"I'm going to go meet with them, Fedorchenko," Deckard told the Platoon Sergeant. "If I'm not back in ten minutes, or you hear gunfire, I'm probably dead. That would be your queue to bound your men up and assault right over these assholes."

"Are you sure?"

A faint trace of a smile crossed the commander's face.

"Sure," Deckard said with a shrug. "Why not."

As he began walking towards the Zapatista rebels the Kazakh Sergeant looked to his men, signaling for two of them to accompany their commander. Ravil and Nuro picked up and trailed behind Deckard acting as a small security detachment.

Squinting in the morning light, Deckard scrutinized the rebels. They wore military fatigues with well-worn black leather boots. Their non-military status was flaunted by the wearing a jewelry, most of them adorned with traditional Mayan necklaces and bracelets. The web gear they wore was positively ancient, probably leftovers from one of the dirty little wars that the United States fought in Central America during the 1980's. In their hands were mostly aging American made M-16 rifles with a few Kalashnikov's spread out between them.

None of the rebels moved a muscle as he approached.

"Let us pass," Deckard said, his mind struggling with the words as he transitioned from Russian to Spanish. "Our fight is not with you."

"We want to talk to the one who is in charge," the rebel directly to his front spoke, his mouth moving under the balaclava.

"That's me."

The two accompanying Kazakh mercenaries looked at each other in confusion, the conversation lost on them.

"Come with us."

"Come with you where? Who the hell are you?"

"*We are the forefront of the revolutionary movement!*"

the rebel burst out.

One of the female Zapatista's took him by the arm, speaking in rapid Spanish in an attempt to calm him.

"Please come with us," she asked Deckard. "It is only a short way. Our commander would like to meet you."

"Very well," Deckard said before clicking the transmit button for his headset and speaking in Russian again. "I'm going to be going a short way down the hill to meet with one of the rebel leaders. Same rules are in effect."

"Roger Six, stay in touch. I'm getting tired of you freelancing on us," the Platoon Sergeant responded.

The rebels moved on either side of the three Samruk mercenaries, leading them down a narrow foot path. The rocky terrain wasn't nearly as difficult to negotiate during hours of day light as it had been during the dark on the way in. Deckard kept his AK-103 at the low ready while stepping over the rocks until the group had descended down the hill. Rounding a rock formation that was jutting from the side of the hill, they came upon a hasty camp fire, a half dozen vehicles surrounding the camp in a semi-circle.

The Zapatista rebels stepped to the side to allow Deckard to enter the camp. Striding into the middle of the rebel camp confidently, the American's eyes swept the area for threats. A male rebel joked with a female rebel near the rusted out Toyota pickups. Four more fatigue wearing Zapatistas played a game of cards on the hood of another truck.

"Green hat go," a man said to Deckard.

He sat in the center of the camp, outfitted in the same uniform as his comrades. Pistol and shotgun cartridges were strung into his web gear like a *pistolero* from times gone by. Behind the balaclava, Deckard could see the crows feet at the corners of his dark brown eyes. A nickel plated revolver rode on his hip, his fatigue jacket left open where a blue neckerchief was tied around his neck.

"Do you know what that means?" the rebel spoke to Deckard in nearly perfect English.

"Supposedly it was a slogan used by Mexicans during the Mexican-American War of 1846. American soldiers wore green hats at the time. This is where the word gringo came from."

"A popular explanation," the Zapatista laughed. "But it

is more likely that the word referred to the Irish of the St. Patrick's Battalion. Even before that in the 1700's, the Spaniards used the term to describe people who couldn't speak Spanish very well, especially the Irish. Irish need not apply, that is from America, is it not?"

"From our past, yes."

"You know something of history," the Zapatista said. "That gives me a small measure of hope."

Deckard said nothing.

"Hope that we can reach an agreement," the rebel elaborated. "As you can imagine, we are concerned about a military unit of mercenaries led by gringos invading Southern Mexico. We are all a little on edge given the Mexican military's excessive measures in both Oaxaca and Chiapas."

The Mexican military had cracked down on the Zapatista rebels on a number of occasions, engaging in a wanton slaughter as the rebels fled into the jungles of the Yucatan. Then there was the suppression of peasant uprisings in Oaxaca, all with US tax payers footing the bill a number of years ago.

"These soldiers you bring with you, they are brown, but they sure as hell are not Mexicans."

"Outsourced," Deckard said hooking a thumb over his shoulder as the black smoke still rising over the submarine base behind him. "You communists don't get it. Globalization isn't all bad."

The rebel leader bawled, laughing out loud, still giggling as he attempted to light his pipe.

"Gringo, you've got a lot to learn," he lectured. "Our movement isn't just communists but you see, we are also anarchists, socialists and libertarians. Everyone who opposes the current oligarchic power structure imposed on us joins with the Zapatista movement. We are the only game in town as you say. Together, we are not the fiendish communists your press would make us out to be. We just want the right to farm our own land without the exploitation of government and corporations, the two of which are nearly impossible to tell apart since this great new deal was imposed on us, you know it, *free trade*. NAFTA."

"I took down Ortega, now I'm here to take down Jimenez," Deckard stated. "And anyone who gets in my way. I really hope that you won't be one of them."

The men playing cards looked up, the game interrupted

as hands suddenly got a little closer to firearms slung over backs or holstered on hips. The blue smoke from the rebel leader's pipe hung in the air for a long moment. Deckard swallowed. He'd flopped his dick on the table and hoped it wouldn't get pounded with a brick.

"You can call me Commadante Zero," the Mexican said, waving dismissively.

"Black," Deckard gave an alias for an alias.

The Zapatista rebels went back to their game of spades.

"Tell me gringo, do you work for the Yankee intelligence services?"

"No."

"Not anymore?"

"Not anymore."

"What happened?"

"I didn't feel the love."

Commadante Zero laughed.

"You and me both. So if you are not an agent of imperialism than what brings you south of the border?"

"A call for help."

"America has already *helped* us enough, but thank you just the same."

"It was a cop, one of the good ones. He would have gone to you if he thought your movement could mount an effective resistance against the cartels. The Zapatistas have been weak since you were chased back into the jungle by the Mexican military. You of all people know this. Your troops carry rusted, shot out weapons. When was the last time they did any hard military training?"

"As you can see, we don't exactly have the budget of your Defense Department, or your mercenaries in this case. We are a people's movement."

"What if you could be more?"

Cammadante Zero took another puff from his pipe.

"I'm listening."

"I can provide trainers, commandos who have seen war the world over. These men are experts in unconventional warfare. We can issue your men the modern weapons we capture from the cartels."

"But?"

"But this communism nonsense still bothers me.

Marxism died a long time ago and isn't coming back. I don't hold any illusions about what Southern Mexico will look like after we leave but I need your assurance that you will lead your people into something that resembles a democratic process. Replacing an oligarchy with an autocracy is unacceptable to me."

"I thought you were a gunslinger," the rebel leader said with a nod. "I had no idea that you were an idea man. I'm happy to hear that we think along the same lines."

"Don't play me on this."

Commandate Zero looked up at Deckard.

"Why don't you sit down for a moment."

"I've got work to do."

"It will take your men at least another half hour to finish hiding that submarine that you captured."

"You've got eyes and ears," Deckard inferred.

"Yes," Zero said. "We have them everywhere."

12

Deckard grounded his kit in their newly acquired gear room. After setting his rifle down, he ripped the Velcro cummerbund from his plate carrier and lifted it over his head. He was drenched in sweat and covered in black soot. While first platoon was out taking care of business, second platoon had been preparing the Ortega compound as their headquarters, getting everything ready for ongoing operations. One of the garages had been emptied, cleared out to make way for a load out room.

It was only by sheer chance that he was able to effect a marriage of convenience with the Zapatista rebels. He had proven his *bonifidis* to the rebels by taking down Ortega and striking out at Jimenez. The populist movement hated the cartels and the violence they brought to Mexico just as much as anyone else who wasn't entranced by the romanticism that surrounded the drug lords.

Drugs brought with them drug culture. Just as the addict made their entire family sick with their addiction, drugs could make an entire culture sick, their very identity seared into the drug mythology. In a country like Mexico where the government was hopelessly corrupt, the criminals were often seen as heroes. They were the underdogs.

In the third world there were few alternatives to the human-destroying authoritarian governments. Some gravitated to the cartels as a way to advance in life, at least until they no longer had a life to speak off, snuffed out by rivals or comrades for growing too powerful. Others allied themselves with the leftist rebel groups. If he had to pick between the two, Commandete Zero and his rebels were clearly the better choice. Say what you would about the Zapatistas, they were a homegrown rebellion seeking some kind of reformation. There wasn't really an equivalency between the rebels and the butchers in the cartels.

Keeping his war belt on, Deckard slung the AK-103 over a shoulder and headed out. He needed a cup of coffee. What he really needed was a few hours sleep but there was a war to fight and Samruk was working on a very limited time line.

Stepping out into the hall, Deckard's footsteps echoed down the empty halls. When he came to Ortega's arms room, he

56

stopped at the door to look inside. Nikita stood with his back to the door. He was running a cleaning rod down the barrel of a massive .50 caliber Barrett Anti-Material rifle. It was one of the many weapons that they had liberated from Ortega.

Sadly, the large bore rifle was nothing more than a show piece to the cartel. It was just an expression of machismo, they hadn't even bothered to attach a scope to it. Nikita would give the rifle a cleaning, get the rifle zeroed, and put it to use. Use the enemy's weapons against them, it was the perfect battlefield recovery.

Nikita slowly turned his head to look over his shoulder at Deckard. His eyes were cold, his face expressionless.

Deckard moved along. Now wasn't the time.

Several months ago they had stood together on the deck of the Crown of the Pacific. It had been a super-cruise liner that had sunk to the depths of the Pacific Ocean. By that point they were both barely on their feet, wounded by the fight of and for their lives. Samruk International had been put through the meat grinder, reduced from a full battalion to only a few platoons.

For reasons that confounded those who remained, they had survived the ordeal. Samruk had pulled off the impossible but it wasn't pretty. Their bodies had slowly healed, but Deckard knew that Nikita's mind had never really left that ship as it slipped beneath the waves towards the ocean floor.

Crossing the courtyard, Deckard looked over the security positions on his way. Pairs of Samruk mercenaries stood guard at intervals along the compound walls. They were still in the process of building up fighting positions with sandbags, bricks, and mortar. RPG launchers and PKM machine guns had been assigned to each position. So far, so good.

Entering Ortega's mansion, Deckard weaved through more of the mercenaries as they moved about. They would be switching out, some of them bedding down for the some sleep, others relieving the guard force so they could get some sleep before heading out on new missions once the intel was developed. Right now their battle rhythm was a little haphazard, but they'd get it figured out. Probably just in time for them to wrap things up and head out, or so Deckard suspected based on previous experience. Inside the OPCEN, he found Cody hard at work behind his computer. Projected on the wall was an organizational chart that attempted to break down the structure of the Jimenez cartel.

Deckard poured some coffee into a Styrofoam cup and took a seat. Scanning the link chart that Cody had made, Deckard knew he was sharper than he had given him credit for. Rather than a typical pyramid type hierarchy, Cody had accurately described the cartel as being largely horizontal.

The big problem with link charts was that Special Operations forces had a tendency to think that terrorist organizations had a strict chain of command and that they were all carefully organized into individual terror squads. This was the result of American military officers looking at terror networks through their own cultural lens. They thought that terrorist groups were organized along the same lines as the US Army.

In fact, terrorist groups functioned around loose associations. Only the most disciplined cells would be rigid or military like in their structure. They were dangerous, but quickly targeted and eliminated by strike teams. It was the disorganized chaos that proved to be a real threat. In Iraq for instance, terrorists from around the world flooded into the country to take part in the Jihad. They circled around linkmen, financiers or ringleaders. Many times they were divided up into task oriented cells. One cell would build an IED, another would set it in place, and yet another would detonate it.

There was no General in charge, not even a Captain, but maybe a lieutenant in some cases. Mexican drug cartels dispensed with the backward aspects of Arab culture, harnessing the power of the free market for their organizational structure. They franchised.

Individuals and small gangs would work on a contract basis, job to job, for the cartels. Often, they were in turn being sub-contracted from another larger player who was the actual link man to the cartel itself. It wasn't uncommon to have various franchised cells running operations who had absolutely no idea who they were working for. They ran drugs, conducted contract killings, and were so compartmentalized that they had no idea who or why they were killing.

As backwards as the Islamic terrorists might have been, they had an ideology. The nebulous cartel structure had none. Even the name *cartel* was more of an invention of the media than anything. No such organization actually existed.

The Mexican Drug War was the first 21st Century conflict. It was a post-political war waged by non-state actors who had no motivation aside from full-auto capitalism.

Deckard sipped his coffee as his team began to filter into the OPCEN and take seats. Samantha walked in and sat down with her arms crossed in front of her. Frank hobbled along on his crutches until he found an empty chair, his new war wounds competing with the old ones as he washed down some pain killers with coffee. Sergeant Major Korgan commanded the attention of the Kazakh Sergeants as he sat down next to Deckard, his presence filling the room. He was from the old school and in Kazakhstan the old school was the Soviet Union. Pat stood with Fedorchenko, waiting.

Finishing off his coffee, Deckard turned and tossed the cup in the trash. He found himself looking twice, his eyes just picking up something in the corner of the room. It was Nikita. He stood in the only shadow in the room, his back to the wall. The sniper's eyes were locked onto the organizational chart projected on the wall. He was memorizing the names.

"Let's get started," Deckard said as he got to his feet. "This is going to be a situational report to make sure everyone is on track, so we have several orders of business. First off, the attack on Jimenez' submarine base was a success although we encountered a few complications. The compound itself was very professional. Well hidden terrain wise, camouflaged with some top of the line vinyl, the base was constructed in an organized manner, and the submarine was very sophisticated especially considering that it is essentially a homemade deal. Their only mistake was in being overconfident in how well they were hidden. They only had one guard posted-"

"Thankfully, you didn't let that stop you from burning the place to the ground," Pat blurted out with a laugh. After Action Reviews took on a different flavor in the unit Pat was from. Delta Force played by their own rules. Deckard was glad he'd talked him into an early retirement and signed him to Samruk.

"Shit happens," Deckard said with a smile. "The good news is that we captured the submarine for use in future operations and have it cached somewhere safe. Also, we made contact with the local Zapatista rebels. They want the cartels out of their home as much as we do so I've come to an agreement with their leadership. We will be sending a cell of trainers and advisers to work with them. If our advisers feel confident in the intentions and motivations of the Zapatistas they will begin conducting operations with them."

Samantha frowned.

"You cut a deal with the Zapatistas? Through who?"

"Commandate Zero."

"Holy shit," she snorted. "You're something else."

"You disagree with my decision?"

"No, they have popular support and oppose corruption. As a perpetual outsider it seems that you are able to establish rapport with people who the American government and the cartels would never touch."

"We'll see how it works. These guys could be an asset to us and help act as a stabilizing force once Samruk pulls out of the region."

"We also took a prisoner," Fedorchenko reminded him about the man he had knocked out on the submarine.

"Have you gotten anything out of him yet?"

"He told us that the guy you shot in the face on the submarine was Captain Nemo himself. This clown that you brought back was his right hand man. He's Colombian of course and doesn't know the local players."

"That intel guy I told you about should be here soon," Frank interrupted.

"Who?"

"You don't remember me telling you about my boy Aghassi?"

"No, I'm afraid not Frank."

"He'll be here shortly," Frank said knowingly. "Aghassi could find a whore in a Wahhabi Mosque. Once he starts working the intel piece we will be able to build a real target deck."

"Our other prisoner did start naming some other local heavies," Pat added. "They are low hanging fruit but it's a place to start."

"I don't really care if it's a dry hole at this point. We need to keep up the momentum while we work on developing some better targets and start filling out this chart," Deckard said pointing to the cartel organization chart. There were a lot of blank slots. "Sergeant Major?"

"Second Platoon is conducting rehearsals and Pre-Combat Inspections as we speak," the Kazakh reported.

"This isn't a time sensitive target so roll when the men are ready."

"Understood."

"Sounds good, Sergeant Major. Make sure the men are getting at least five hours of sleep between guard and combat rotations."

"We are working out the schedule," he responded in his thick Russian accent. Korgan had been the first Samruk International member that Deckard had met when he arrived in Kazakhstan for the first time and had liked the man immediately. There had been a Serbian Executive Officer whom he had a different opinion about, but that problem had been resolved.

"There is one more thing," Cody said in a hushed tone.

"What's that?" Deckard said prompting him.

"The *nacrocorridos* about Jimenez."

"I told him that it is nothing to worry about," Samantha said shaking her head. "We already know that he's an asshole. We don't need to waste time worrying about his crappy folk music."

"These songs are unique," Cody insisted.

The *narcocorridos* were type of Mexican folk music that had become massively popular throughout the country and even into parts of the United States. The songs glorified the violence of the cartels and extolled the virtues of the quick thinking gangsters as they outwitted the authorities. They portrayed cartel leaders as Robin Hood type characters that the peasant class could relate too. They might have sounded silly to gringo ears but they were no laughing matter in Mexican culture. Gangsters even hired musicians to write songs about them, the most powerful cartel leaders paying hundreds of thousands of dollars for a hit tune composed from a romanticized version of their life story.

"The *nacrocorridos* that Jimenez had made about him are flat out creepy," Cody went on without pausing for breath. "They talk about him skinning people alive, raping dead bodies, weird shit man. Some of them are even about how he worships the devil. The songs refer to him as The Beast."

"He is trying to make people scared of him," Samantha stated.

"I don't think so. These folk songs are supposed to help the locals relate to cartel leader. They are to make him popular in the eye of the public."

"I don't think songs like this would make him very popular amongst a very Catholic Mexican public," Deckard said.

"I'm just sayin'," Cody continued. "Watch your back out there."

With the briefing adjourned, Deckard followed Frank out into the courtyard. Everyone was quiet for a moment and all of them were taking advantage of it to catch their breath. Samruk hadn't even been on the ground for a full twenty four hours and they'd already killed one cartel, pissed all over another, and formed an alliance that the US State Department would certainly frown upon.

The Kazakh mercenaries that stood at the sandbagged positions near the gate began getting restless. They aimed down the sights of their rifles at something approaching on the other side of the wall.

Frank's cell phone began to ring.

"Yeah," he said, taking the call. "Cool. Got it."

"It's okay," Frank yelled to the gate guards. "He's one of us. Open the gates!"

Deckard hurriedly translated into Russian before they had a shoot out on their hands.

The mercenaries nodded before one of them climbed down the ladder and swung open the gates. The gates were still a mess since they had blasted their way in earlier but an ad hoc repair job held them closed for the time being.

As the gates parted, Deckard could see a cloud of brown dust roll in along with a beat up 1990's model Saturn sedan. The muffler was being dragged in the dirt behind it. Once the rust bucket came to a halt in the court yard, the Kazakhs swung the gate closed and resumed their post.

"Goddam piece of shit," the driver coughed out as he slammed the door shut.

Deckard frowned as he and Frank walked over to the newcomer. The car had American license plates.

"Did you drive here?" Deckard asked.

"Sure did," the driver turned around to face him. He had to look up at Deckard to see him. The newcomer was short with a mop top of black hair and a gnarly looking mustache. "I hit the road an hour after Frank gave me a call about some hot action south of the border. Drove all the way from Oklahoma."

"You know I would have flown you in, right?"

"Can't do it brother. On the no-fly list."

"You're fucking kidding me."

"Well not me but some dude with my name is and those costumed clowns that pretend they are security guards give me a hell of a time whenever I try to fly."

"What's your name?"

"Ahmed Aghassi."

"I don't remember seeing him on the target deck."

"He was some Iranian fuck hiding up in the mountains of Afghanistan who was advising Al-Qaeda cells throughout the country."

"Tell him the fucked up part Ghassi," Frank interjected.

"I was on the mission that killed him," Aghassi said as his eyebrows bobbed over his eyes.

"So you waxed some Iranian with that same name as you out in Afghanistan?"

"Yeah."

"And his name is still on the no-fly list?"

"Takes a while to get the names of dead terrorists taken off the list," Aghassi muttered. "Years apparently."

"What the fuck?"

"You said it brother."

"Alright," Deckard said. "Frank vouches for you so let's get the job interview out of the way. Who the hell are you really?"

"Everyone calls me Ghassi. I grew up speaking Farsi at home-"

"Where is home?"

"I told you already. Oklahoma."

"Which is where you drove from."

63

"Yeah, so it's like this, my parents emigrated from Iran and I grew up in the States. I joined the Army as an interpreter and learned Arabic in DLI as a third language-"

"Frank told me you spoke Spanish."

"I do, I picked it up in High School. So some computer program picks my name out of a hat because of my background and language skills and the next thing I know I get approached by some shady dudes at work. That was how I got recruited to the Intelligence Support Activity."

Deckard nodded for Aghassi to continue. He had worked with ISA numerous times when he was in Army Special Operations units. They did intelligence and reconnaissance work, mostly for SEAL Team Six and Delta Force. Frank had also served in that unit after a stint in the Ranger Reconnaissance Detachment or RRD, although Deckard still suspected that Frank must have lied his way through the battery of psych evals he was required to take as part of the entrance exam.

"You know the deal. Afghanistan, Iraq, and a few other places. I probably worked the intel piece for a few of your missions," he said to Deckard. "I got out a couple years ago and did contract work."

"Where?"

"Back in Afghanistan. I lived as a *kuchi* with a native family."

"Bullshit." The *kuchis* were nomadic people who roamed the wastelands of Afghanistan.

"No really man. I spoke the language, I'm brown, and with a Bin Laden beard I look just like one of them. I had a female Afghani intelligence agent pose as my wife and we took in a couple orphan kids to travel with us in our caravan to complete the picture. We moved all over Southern Afghanistan collecting intelligence for our clients."

"Sounds pretty rough."

"You got no idea man, I feel like a stranger in my own country every time I return home."

"Okay," Deckard said making a decision. "You're hired. I'll give you a couple hours to come up with a list of what you need and then you can interface with Samantha, our local police liaison, and you can start working on building an intelligence network-"

"That's cool. I will coordinate with her and whatever

sources she has. For now just give me a new car and I'll roll."

"What?"

"Here you go hoss," Pat said walking up from behind as he tossed a set of car keys to Aghassi. "Take the white Toyota, it will blend in on the streets here."

"Thanks bud."

"You sure about that?" Deckard asked Pat.

Pat shrugged.

"Let's see what he can do."

13

A triple strand of det-chord formed a flex linear charge that was affixed diagonally across the front door of the single story building that served as living space and a headquarters for one of the many drug gangs that inhabited Oaxaca City. It exploded in a shower of debris that woke people from their beds several blocks away. Mothers hid with their children under beds. Mexico was a war zone and they knew what would come next. This was their reality.

Deckard stepped out of his Iveco assault truck as he watched four Samruk International assault teams storm the compound, swarming through the now empty door frame. In moments, it was all over. Not a shot had been fired.

"Six this is Zhen," the Platoon Sergeant's voice crackled over his MBITR radio. Zhenis had received a battlefield promotion to his rank like Fedorchenko. Now Zhen ran second platoon while Fed ran first.

"Go ahead."

"Objective secured. Five fighting age males, no civilians. Initiating our search."

"Roger that, Zhen."

"Zhen out."

Deckard changed channels and reported their status up to Cody back at the OPCEN. Samruk functioned very well on a system of merit based ranks in which those with greater responsibility drew higher pay. However, they didn't have any real Officers in the Private Military Company. It was a Sergeant's game and they liked it that way. Still, Deckard now found himself playing the role of Platoon Leader while Zhenis was busy leading his men.

Deckard had to be the one thinking several steps ahead. Where were they going next, how would they get there, and how would they respond to any roadblocks thrown up in their way? This was his responsibility.

Several assaulters popped up on the roof to pull security and watch for any enemy counter-attack.

Striding up to the doorway, Deckard watched the Kazakh mercenaries flexcuff and blindfold each prisoner one by one before patting them down and segregating them from each other.

Cell phones, a few pistols, and other assorted pocket litter was found between the five prisoners. When one of them began to complain as he was pushed down onto his knees against the wall, one of the Kazakhs jabbed him in the ribs with his rifle barrel and barked at him in Russian.

"Six, you might want to take a look at this," Zhen said over the assault net.

"What is it?"

"Found something in the back yard."

Deckard walked through the house as the mercenaries continued to pull it apart searching for weapons and potential intelligence information. Out back Deckard kicked through the dust towards Zhen. The backyard was really just a strip of dirt covered in feathers and rusty chicken wire. The dried skeleton of what had once been a tree was the only notable feature.

"What did you find?"

"Look up," he said pointing into the tree.

Deckard squinted in the darkness, the exterior lights of a nearby house was the only illumination. Raising his AK, Deckard triggered the tactical light attached to the rail system on his rifle and trained it on the bare branches.

Intermingled and concealed with the branches was a complicated antenna farm of UHF and VHF dipoles that were tacked onto the branches. Other equipment had been painted the same color as the tree and nailed into place to create a frequency division duplex. Whoever had set up the clandestine antenna station clearly knew what they were doing.

"What the hell," Deckard muttered.

Looking up at the roof he spotted two solar cells angled in the direction that the sun would be rising from at dawn. Looking back down at his feet, Deckard started brushing dirt aside, probing with his fingers. Finally he found the coaxial cable and followed it from the antenna system back to the house where it snaked through a small hole cut through the cinder block wall.

"Bring one of the prisoners in here," he said to Zhen. Deckard scanned the inside looking for a false wall. His men had taken to their task with enthusiasm, a couch was flipped over, a mirror broken, and shattered glass spread across the floor, but they had not turned up anything notable.

Zhen pushed one of the prisoners into the room.

He looked to be in his mid-twenties and fighting a losing battle with acne. The American drew his 1911 pistol and quickly snapped off two shots, one on either side of the cartel man.

"Where is the receiver for the repeater system outside?" he asked, leaving no room for compromise and no doubt as to the consequences of anything less than a truthful answer.

"There," he said pointing to the corner of the room. "Behind the panel."

Deckard took a closer look and sure enough, there was a false wall. The seam was almost impossible to detect at a glance and he had to use his Ka-Bar to wedge it in the crack and pry the plaster panel away from the wall. Inside was a rack of black radio receivers bearing the name of a well-known European telecom company.

Changing channels on his own radio he flipped over the command net to talk to their headquarters at the Ortega compound.

"Standby for video," he said.

"Got it," Cody replied.

Turning on his helmet camera, the image panned wherever he happened to be looking. Using a GoPro WiFi attachment was an improvised measure to beam the signal back to the satellite communications set up on their assault trucks and then back to their headquarters. Cody had called it a ghetto rig, but whatever he did to it seemed to work.

"What am I looking at?" Deckard spoke into the headset microphone.

"Looks like a TRG 6030 transceiver and some more low-grade receivers for microwave."

"Hold on, I'll walk outside and show you the antenna farm."

Hurrying back outside, Deckard look up into the tree and shined his tac-light again for Cody's benefit.

"Professional job," Cody said in his clipped manner. "Decent concealment."

"What kind of range do you think this thing has?"

"About five to ten kilometers on its own but this is a repeating station. If you look at the setup it is clear that this is just one sub-station in a much larger network. With the repeater turned on you can push out to fifty kilometers and then on to infinity depending on how many repeaters are in the network."

"What kind of commo could a station like this push?"

"Whatever you want," Cody answered. "No need for a land line, wireless, or the internet as far as this network stretches."

"So it is basically a pirate net."

"With encryption available on the civilian market they will have set up a dark net that can't be traced or tapped into by the authorities since it's completely off the grid."

"And they can use it to coordinate drug shipments, assassinations, and other cartel business," Deckard thought out loud.

"It looks like they also have some equipment to help hide their frequencies from the authorities."

"No wonder why they are running circles around both the US and Mexican governments."

"Take it apart and bring it back here. Don't break it. I will take it apart myself and tell you how it works."

"Roger Cody, Six out."

Deckard switched back onto the assault net and gave the order to begin dismantling the antenna array. He wasn't ready to call it their big break against the Jimenez cartel but it was another chip in their armor. If Samruk International could penetrate the enemy's communications system they could get inside the cartel's decision making process and destroy them from the inside out.

In the meantime, Deckard knew that Jimenez himself was out there somewhere in the night. Deep down he knew that the drug lord was sitting down with his top men at that very moment and plotting his counter attack against Deckard and Samruk International.

14

Aghassi sat at the end of the bar nursing a beer.

A rooster clucked and flapped its wings up into a storm of loose feathers that drifted through the bar. Locals filtered in and out, some stopping for a drink. Others to loiter or smoke a cigarette. At the other end of the bar a couple twelve year old girls took turns slamming tequila shots. The intelligence specialist shrugged and went back to his beer as the rooster made a beeline for the door.

He had been at this game for so long that he felt more at home here than he did back in the town he grew up in. He had left Oklahoma as a kid and joined the Army. Getting picked up for various intelligence projects that wanted to capitalize on his linguistic abilities had seen him spending long periods in third world countries, often under deep cover. Whoever the kid from Oklahoma had been got lost in the fold somewhere along the way.

The door swung open just long enough for the rooster to make his escape. The flash of sunlight from outside made Aghassi squint his eyes. The guy passed out and drooling on the bar next to him was unresponsive to it all. The newcomer that walked in was different from the other locals. He wore expensive Diesel jeans and a black t-shirt featuring pictures of flying skulls. His haircut was one of the latest Mexican trends with pointy sideburns and lots of hair gel.

Taking a seat, the trendy dude had to wait to ask for a beer. The girls were ordering another round.

"You're not from here," Aghassi said to him in Spanish. "I just got into town myself."

"Yes," he nodded. "I'm here on business. How about you?"

"The same. I'm a truck driver."

The newcomer laughed.

"Got it."

It was widely known that once the drugs came in from the south that the drug cartels loaded them into tractor trailers that had been up-armored with metal sheets to look like something out of Mad Max. They were then loaded down with the narcotics and escorted by modified pickup trucks which were also armored and had machine gun mounts in the back. Some of the convoys could stretch out into as many as a hundred vehicles.

"Dangerous work," he commented.

The convoys would race up the drug corridors in the middle of the night hoping to avoid being ambushed by rival cartels. These days Mexico was more dangerous than Iraq or Afghanistan.

"It isn't as bad as they say," Aghassi said trying to sound cool about it. "And it pays well."

"That is the important thing," the Mexican laughed as the bar man finally brought him his beer.

"What do you do?"

"I'm a manager for a corrido band," he answered referring to the traditional type of Mexican folk music that had now been taken over by the narcocorrido or drug ballads that glorified cartel life. "My brother is the singer."

"I'm surprised you had to come from out of town to find work."

"My brother is a big name up in Sonora. We go wherever the highest paying clients are."

Aghassi tried to hide his surprise at the turn of luck by sipping on his beer. Jimenez controlled all of Oaxaca with Ortega out of the picture so there was no doubt as to who the client was.

"That's interesting."

"Hey, Deckard."

"What is it?"

"Turn off that WiFi for your helmet cam. It's turning you into a moving hotspot and broadcasting your location to the world."

"Thanks Cody," he said reaching up and flicking off the WiFi and his helmet camera. The antenna array had been taken apart and loaded into their assault trucks. They were just now rolling off the objective with their five prisoners.

"This isn't Cody," the voice crackled over the internet.

Deckard's thoughts froze for a moment as the Iveco truck rounded a corner and set out for the Ortega compound. Someone had penetrated their comms system and broke through their crypto. Granted it was just an off the shelf system which wasn't very sophisticated but his heart skipped a beat on realizing that unknown parties were tracking and listening in on the Samruk mercenaries. Now they were announcing themselves.

"Is Jimenez in the room?" he asked finally.

"Nice guess but this is your former employer."

Even worse.

The voice gave him an address in Oaxaca City.

"We want to talk."

"You guys still bitter about the Colombia job?"

No one replied.

"Who was that," Cody suddenly burst over the net. "I couldn't hear them but I could hear your responses."

Deckard began looking at the Falcon View navigator program running on the tough book computer mounted in his truck.

"Christians In Action," he answered. "They broke into our net."

"I WARNED YOU-"

"We'll take care of that later," Deckard cut the computer technician off. "Hit Internacional Road and then turn right on Eduardo Vasconcelos," he then told the driver. "We're taking a detour."

The streets were dead. Not a soul dared to show their face after dark. Up until recently Oaxaca City had been spared the extreme violence that had plagued much of Mexico. It was only as the Mexican military truly began cracking down on the cartels to the north, under the aegis of an American foreign aid and military program, that the drug barons began getting displaced to the south. Squeezed up against one another, cartel bosses like Ortega and Jimenez arrived in Oaxaca and began warring with each other. Just a few months prior the entire province had been considered an oasis for tourists. Even the US President's daughter vacationed there.

The aging colonial buildings and churches clashed with the pastel colored homes and commercial warehouses as the

Samruk convoy sped through the night. Deckard sat back in his seat, watching the vehicle icons move across the map on the computer screen as they were updated by the GPS hockey puck stuck to the side of the truck with a magnet.

His dance card was filling up fast. The fact that the CIA wanted to talk made him more nervous than if they had been trying to kill him. What did they want?

Turning onto the main throughway, Deckard told the driver to continue straight as they headed into the outskirts of the city.

Turning onto another road they went up hill and the houses began to spread out until they found a lone bungalow style home sitting by itself on the incline. The lights were on inside and two sedans were parked out front. It looked a lot like a trap.

The mercenaries silently glided off their vehicles and surrounded the house in an L-shaped formation. They were prepared to open fire if they were being baited into an ambush. Two of the assault trucks trained their PKM machine guns on the house while the others faced outward, scanning to exterior threats in the surrounding hills. Cicadas could be heard humming above the sound of idling truck engines.

Deckard walked right up to the front steps and looked through the screen door.

"Come on in," a voice said from inside. "It's just us."

Deckard pulled open the door and stepped into the living room.

"No bullshit, olive branch and all? I never thought I'd see the day," the mercenary quipped.

The living conditions in the house were austere. A few pieces of furniture, an ancient television set, some empty beer cans sitting on the coffee table. Just enough to make the CIA safe house look as if it were lived in.

"You're the one with the strike team outside," said the older guy sitting on the couch. "We're pretty passive here in Oaxaca. We might have a guy or two working out of the consulate for protection but we save the contractors for Somalia and Yemen. Until now at least."

"We should be so lucky. Based on my observations you might want to increase your security around here."

"No need," said the second CIA case officer. He was a

73

younger agent of Hispanic origins. "We are flying out tonight. We're done here."

"But that hasn't stopped you from shadowing my moves."

"Relax Deckard, it's our job," he replied. "Remember?"

"I didn't feel the love."

"I'm Grant," the older CIA veteran said smoothing out his collared shirt with one hand and motioning to an empty chair with the other. "My associate is Felix. Why don't you take a seat."

Deckard's eyes flicked across the room one last time before he sat down, laying his AK-103 across his lap.

"You embarrassed us by rolling into Oaxaca like this. We had no forewarning that some merc outfit was going to just fly in and start a shooting war."

"You'll have to offer my apologies to the Director."

"Well, we started tracking your movements electronically and once we realized it was you we pinged Langley and requested permission to have a sit down. To our surprise they immediately approved this meeting."

"I suppose they've got a lot questions that they would like to ask me."

"That they do but this isn't an ultimatum. Not anymore. Listen, Deckard, I realize that we didn't know each other when you were with the Agency but all those knuckle draggers down in Ground Branch had good things to say about you even if you pissed off the mafia working on the 7th floor. We know that we got caught asleep at the wheel."

"Again."

"Yeah," Grant said breaking eye contract. "Yeah."

"You would think that the Agency owes me one."

"Listen, things have changed. We're still trying to piece together how it all happened. The investigation is unofficial of course but we watched the entire national security apparatus stand up and get pushed to the brink without any discernible reason. We know it was an attempted coup on US soil. A couple people were forced into retirement, some others moved around, you know the deal."

"That accountability that the CIA is oh-so-famous for," Deckard replied, growing bored with the conversation. "What do you want from me?"

"The real question is what you want," Felix piped in. "You brought down Ortega and are gunning for Jimenez. We want to know what your next play is, we want to know what your intent in this region is. Everyone in the Pentagon and at Langley is nervous as fuck about you stomping around in combat boots in our own back yard."

"I'll be damned if I'm going to show you my playbook."

"It's a poor choice of words," Grant said looking at his partner. "Besides, we know already know how you do things. Fire and maneuver. You're a soldier not a spy, I get that. We have no allegiance to Ortega or Jimenez and your goals might coincide with ours on this issue. But we need assurances."

"We want to disable to the cartel and weaken them enough that there is an opportunity for law and order to prevail in Oaxaca. I put a bullet in Jimenez's dome and I'm out of here."

"That's all we needed to hear."

"But?"

"But the Mexican Marines and other Infantry battalions are already receiving re-deployment orders. Jimenez has some kind of in with the Mexican intelligence services, we don't know the details but they have an arrangement."

"Kickbacks."

"No doubt about it but Jimenez is putting pressure on those contacts to help him solve his mercenary problem and those intelligence contacts are pressuring the administration in Mexico City. They've got the Mexican President by the balls on something. The Army and Marines are beating up the cartels pretty hard up north. We're happy with the progress they are making but now the President is ordering two battalions worth of troops to mobilize and redeploy to Oaxaca to take you out."

"Good luck."

"Look Deckard, what do you have here? A hundred guys? You won't last long. To tell you the truth we don't want these troops pulled off the target deck that our office has them working up north. Several of the meanest cartels in Mexico are at their end game thanks to our efforts and we don't want to see this opportunity squandered at the very last moment. As it stands, those Mexican troops should arrive by ground transport in Oaxaca within 48 hours."

"You've got some pull with the administration yourself. Cancel the orders. Give me some breathing room down here and

75

I'll be out of the picture. Give me five days, maybe a week."

"The Agency is prepared to do just that but right now we don't have the ammunition we need against the Mexican President. He's getting uppity with Washington. It's election season down here and he's busy demonizing the United States to shore up voters. He has to blame the corruption and failure of governmental services on someone. Certainly it isn't a homegrown issue, so it's gotta be the gringos."

"That's quite a dilemma."

"We need the leverage ourselves and so do you if you don't want the military coming down here and pushing your shit in," Felix explained. "So this puts you in a position to help yourself and the Agency at the same time."

"I'm all aflutter," Deckard wisecracked. "Do tell."

Grant flopped a stack of stapled papers on the table.

"We're cleaning out Mexico of the most troublesome cartels. Like you, State's unofficial policy is to reduce the cartels' power down to a manageable level. Manage them like we managed the Italian mafia back home. A level of corruption that we can all live with, we know they are not going away anytime soon. The problem is this fucking Lebanese faction running the financial side of things for the cartels out of Cancun."

Deckard picked up the dossier and began scanning the photos. "I'm listening."

"Bashir Safadi is the primary money washer for drug cartels throughout the southern cone. Not just in Mexico either. He's Lebanese by descent, hit Mexico in the 1980's and dug in as a financier. His money laundering organization controls Cancun where they are constantly building hotels that sit there empty so that narco-dollars can be reported as profits from tourism. Bashir also controls the airfield at Cancun which pilots from Venezuela and Colombia use as a trampoline. They stop at the halfway point between their home countries and the US to refuel at Cancun."

"What does this have to do with me?"

"Like I said, the Agency is doing some house cleaning down here in Mexico. We're hoping for a less unruly drug trade and a more business oriented government. This Bashir guy has got to go. He's making our job very difficult by acting as the cartel's banker and hiding their slush funds."

"You want me to take him out?"

"Not just take him out, we also want you to capture his secret stash of video recordings that he keeps in his penthouse there on the main strip of Cancun."

"Blackmail."

"Right, that's how we'll keep the Mexican military off your ass and how we'll keep the Mexican government looking towards the United States for foreign trade rather than those fuckers over in China."

"How long do I have? I can probably fly a team in within the next day and get eyes on the target."

"We have a private jet waiting for you at the airport here in Oaxaca City right now. If you need additional personnel we can ferry them to Cancun as well."

Grant reached into a gym bag next to his chair.

"We've got an identification package done up for you. Give us the word and we'll set up a meeting with Bashir to get your foot in the door. You'll be an investment banker flying in from New York."

"I don't know anything about investment banking."

Felix laughed.

"Neither do they."

Deckard stood and walked towards the door.

"One more thing Deckard," Grant stopped him. "I need to know."

"Know what?"

"What really happened out there on that ship in the Pacific? I need to know the real story."

"Some other time," Deckard said and let the door slam shut on his way out.

Aghassi downed his fifth beer and slammed it down on the bar.

"That is interesting."

"We're a lot alike," the music manager said, "We go where the money is."

"I hear that," the American signaled the bartender for another round.

"My brother's band is up at the compound every day working on their narcocorrido for Jimenez. He is offering six figures to some of the top names in the industry to write a song about him. He wants it to go viral on the internet."

"So what's your role in all of it?"

"I just handle the business aspect of it for my brother. My brother was mom's favorite," he laughed. "He was the talented one."

"I've got a brother myself," Aghassi said, keeping his target engaged. "So you've actually been up in Jimenez's compound a few times?"

"Oh, yeah," the manager said as the bartender brought their beers. Taking a swig, he offered Aghassi a cigarette before lighting up himself. "That place is pimp. He's living the high life for sure."

"How big is it?"

"Man, it takes up an entire mountaintop. Soccer field, indoor pool, bowling alley, he's got everything up there. It's like a little city," he paused. "Except clean!"

"How much of the compound have you seen?"

"I don't know," the manager puffed on his cancer stick. "Most of it I guess. They took us for a tour when we got there but we still haven't met Jimenez. Supposedly he will come and hear the song played when we finish so he can give final approval."

"Do you think you could draw up the floor plan?"

"What the hell are you talking about?"

"If you're in it for the money, I can offer money."

"You must be out of your mind. You know who Jimenez is and what he does?"

"You're almost done with your song for him, you said it yourself. It's easy money."

"No way."

"You'll be back in Sonora with a hefty bonus in your pocket and your boss will be none the wiser."

"You must be crazy."

"Ten thousand dollars. American."

The corrido manager took a sip of beer, rolling the idea over in his mind. One thing he loved was money.

"Ten thousand cash," Aghassi emphasized.

"Deal."

15

Several pressing issues were exploding in Deckard's face all at the same time.

Their COMSEC obviously needed work since the CIA had broken into their net. Aghassi just called in that he was developing a Recon and Surveillance mission to penetrate Jimenez' compound for purposes of intelligence gathering and wanted a sniper on standby to support his operation. Deckard was himself en route to the airfield to catch a CIA black flight out of the country and then back into Cancun to meet with the cartel's money man. Then Cody told him that their new contractors and gear just arrived at Oaxaca airport.

The convoy was heading back to the airport to meet up with the new Samruk International employees and to drop Deckard off for his Cancun excursion.

By now they were familiar with the airport. Deckard and his recon team had scoped it out before the main element arrived. It was a flat strip just outside the city, long enough for large international aircraft. The airport was surrounded by a chain link fence topped off with barbwire. Swinging around towards the main concourse, Deckard could see a gray colored Gulfstream V jet idling on the tarmac. It sported tail number N44982 but no other markings.

The mercenary grunted to himself. When the airplane wasn't flying assassins like him to do dirty deals for the CIA it was probably flying rendition flights from Yemen and Afghanistan to Poland and Estonia.

Deckard had already paid off the security guards so the front gate hung wide open, allowing the convoy to drive right onto the airfield. A dozen contractors stood milling around two pallets, waiting for their ride. The cargo plane from the States had dropped them off and quickly departed. None of them were armed and he had not dispatched a reception committee to meet them on time to issue out weapons. It was an oversight on his part and another indication that he needed some sleep and some time to gather his thoughts.

The driver of the lead vehicle slowed to a stop and Deckard pushed open the armored passenger door before stepping out into the oppressive night heat.

The silhouette of a powerfully built man walked from the pallets and shook Deckard's hand.

"Never a boring moment with you," the contractor taunted him with the slightest hint of a German accent in his voice.

"You complaining?"

"Never!" the German laughed.

Kurt Jager was a former German GSG-9 Counter-Terrorist operator that Deckard had sub-contracted from another Private Military Company called GUARD. It wasn't his first collaboration with Samruk international. A skilled linguist, Kurt's grasp of the Russian language had been a huge help in interfacing with the Russian-speaking Kazakh mercenaries that made up the bulk of their troops.

"My boys will help you break down these pallets and pack the gear on the trucks. We're already carrying some dismantled communications equipment we pulled off an objective tonight so we'll radio for a deuce and a half to drive down here from our compound to help carry everything back."

"Sounds good."

"Did all the kit I ordered get put on those pallets?"

"Almost, some of the ammunition missed the flight but everything else is there. We also had one guy miss the flight. Some former SEAL named Webb."

"Typical," Deckard said shaking his head. "I'm assigning you and several other personnel to our FID cell."

"We have a FID cell?"

FID, or Foreign Internal Defense, was a usually a mission where an Army Special Forces team would train indigenous guerrillas and lead them in combat operations. Now the mercenaries would perform the same mission working alongside the Zapatista rebels.

"We will make sure you have constant comms with our OPCEN but you'll be working for Commandente Zero."

"You're kidding," Kurt blurted. "You know I've have dealings them those guys in the past?"

"Well, let's hope they don't recognize you," Deckard smirked. "I've got a plane to catch."

16

Deckard came awake with a start.

"We are on final approach," the co-pilot said.

"Already?"

"We can do DC to Kabul in twelve hours, baby. You slept right through landing and takeoff at Nassau. We picked up a package from the Agency for you," the middle aged CIA pilot pointed to the closet built into the fuselage of the aircraft. "Might want to change into something else. You will scare the squares out in this tourist shit hole in that Soldier of Fortune getup."

"Thanks," the mercenary replied as he stood and stretched his back. It felt like a dozen joints popped all at the same time. His knees and lower back creaked, he was sore all over, and his quadriceps threatened to seize up due to dehydration. The two mercenaries he had brought along with him remained sleeping in their chairs. The Gulfstream was outfitted to transport fifteen passengers so there was plenty of room for them on the aircraft. Their body armor and weapons lay in a pile on the floor.

The co-pilot disappeared back into the cockpit and Deckard got to work. When you are completely exhausted and going into the drone zone a few hours of sleep feels like you just woke up after hibernating for the winter. Although his body was still recovering from the abuse, his mind was moving a mile a minute.

In the Gulfstream's small bathroom he threw water on his face and then used the squirt bottle of liquid soap to wash his hands, arms, and face. Wetting down his hair he used the same soap to wash the dirt and debris out. Silently, he cursed the CIA agents in Oaxaca. They gave him an out but they sure as hell gave it to him on short notice.

The digital camouflage uniform he wore was stained with streaks of white. It was salt deposited in the fabric from sweating through the uniform several times a day. Stripping out of it he discarded the pants, blouse, and t-shirt the corner of the bathroom and continued wiping himself down as best he could. Somehow, he had to look like an investment banker when he met Bashir.

Ignoring his nudity, Deckard stepped out of the bathroom and went to the closet. Inside a garment bag was a gray Hicky-Freeman suit that had clearly been tailored to his measurements. He knew that the CIA kept an extensive file on him but this much information was ridiculous. Bracing himself against the wall, he felt weightless for a moment as the jet began dumping altitude.

Quickly, he pulled on the pants, threw on the white button down shirt, and shrugged into the suit jacket. He left the fruity colored tie in the bag, leaving the shirt collar open. Sitting back down he began tying the shoes that came with the suit.

In the side pocket of the garment bag was the identity package he had been promised. There was a smart phone with touch screen, a wallet packed full of credit cards and cash, and a US passport with his picture that bore the name Granger Black. The package was professionally done. The phone was pre-loaded with an address book full of phone numbers leading to various CIA front organizations. There were previous phone calls programmed into the call log and bullshit text messages stored in the memory all to make it look like it was used if anyone looked it over. The wallet included various business cards, including Granger Black's. The passport was stamped up from London to Rome to Zurich.

He'd scanned the documents that Grant had given him in Oaxaca and then read them more carefully prior to take off. Bashir traveled with a Personal Security Detachment, or PSD, wherever he went. They were former Lebanese Strike Force members from Beirut, trained by US Special Forces Soldiers. There was no time to plan the logistics of a large scale Direct Action strike with a platoon of Samruk mercenaries. In days, if not hours, the Mexican Marines would be raiding Samruk's compound and hunting them down like dogs if he didn't do something in the meantime.

In order to get close to Bashir he would have to go in undercover. The two mercenaries he brought along were backup and would probably have to wait for him in the Gulfstream. If everything went pear shaped he would be on his own for the foreseeable future. His weapons and equipment would have to be left on the aircraft. Once again he was flying by the seat of his pants and cursed the CIA for it. A bunch of Mormon accountants and Jesuit Lawyers from Harvard, Princeton, and

Yale, it was no wonder that a Special Operations soldier like Deckard never got on with them very well.

When the wheels touched down on the tarmac the two mercs shook awake, looking around for a moment before collecting themselves and reaching for Kalashnikovs.

As the Gulfstream taxied onto the parking apron on the airfield, Deckard checked himself over in the mirror one last time. Running a hand through his hair he found it coarse and thick despite the impromptu washing. His face was drawn, he had lost some water weight over the last few days. His eyes were sharp even if his body wasn't back to full capacity. Grabbing a bottle of water from the on board refrigerator, he downed half of it in one gulp.

When the plane halted the co-pilot came forward and dropped the folding stairs down to the ground.

"Good luck bud. We've done of a few of these that turned out to be one way trips for our passenger."

"Just keep the engines running," Deckard said dryly. "This shouldn't take long."

Frank winced as pain shot up his bum leg. He swallowed a few painkillers before tapping out a pinch of Copenhagen snuff that he packed into his lower lip. War is hell.

In front of him was the communications array that Sergeant Zhen's platoon had dismantled and taken off an objective with them. It had taken him a while to piece it together. The VHS receiver, microwave relay, and duplex were laid out on the floor the way it would have been when it was operational. It was a strange combination of communications gear to say the least.

After running recon patrols with the Ranger Reconnaissance Detachment, or RRD, for a number of years he had been recruited to the Intelligence Support Activity. ISA was perhaps the most secret, most compartmentalized asset within the Special Operations community. They conducted deep penetration missions behind enemy lines to gather intelligence for SEAL Team Six and Delta Force missions. Frank would go out with a partner, sometimes he'd go out alone, spending long stretches by himself in the mountains of Afghanistan.

His primary specialty within ISA was as a HUMINT, or Human Intelligence collector; however he had to cross-train with the knob turners as well. They taught him how to use bleeding edge signals intelligence equipment, how to break into communications networks, intercept enemy transmissions, and conduct traffic analysis. Although a knuckle dragger by trade, he had enough background to put together and understand what he was looking at presently.

The enemy they had faced in Afghanistan and Iraq had been tenacious to say the least. It was a case of military Darwinism. With SEALs, Rangers, and Delta grinding away at the terrorists, the dumb ones didn't last long. The smart ones were the mullahs and cell leaders who cynically used their followers for terrorist attacks. Those guys, the foot soldiers, were dangerous in that they often had no interest in actually surviving their attacks. ISA helped US Special Operations units in knowing where the bad guys were and sometimes helped them in the killing.

As the war stretched out over a decade the enemy adapted, countering American tactics, and forcing them to innovate on a daily basis. Frank had seen the enemy make some impressive moves but the Mexican cartels were in a category all their own. Their funding, equipment, weapons, and tactics, as well as their technical sophistication blew the Taliban and Al Qaeda out of the water.

The cartels had established a pirate net that piggy-backed on the pre-existing telecommunications infrastructure in Mexico. The cartel had clearly done a cost to benefit ratio analysis and realized that they could save on costs by hopping across the civilian cell phone towers but then convert to VHF to make it harder to trace their calls and maintain their COMSEC.

The way it would work was that a cartel member would place a call with his cell phone to another member. The call would bounce across the commercial microwave relay towers used by civilian cell phone traffic. In addition, the cartels would raise their own microwave relays on communication masts in order to fill dead zones or help confuse anyone trying to track them. The signal would bounce across the network until it reached a specific repeater which would then use multiplexers and converters to convert the signal from CDMA to VHF.

CDMA, or Code Division Multiple Access, was the backbone channel access method used by civilian cell phone carriers while VHF, or Very High Frequency, was typical of ham radio operators. VHF was considered obsolete with the military having transitioned over the High Frequency and Ultra High Frequency so the mechanisms used to track VHF were being phased out. Because of this, American forces were unable to trace VHF signals. Al Qaeda knew this and adapted accordingly forcing Frank's unit and others to scramble for a solution.

That solution was found but now the cartels were using the same technique with a much more elaborate system. Factor encryption and frequency hopping into the mix and the cartels had a black cell phone network that would be damn difficult to penetrate. It shouldn't have come as a surprise. How else were the Colombians coordinating with dozens of cartels to smuggle drugs without having their communications intercepted by the DEA?

Frank spit some dip into an empty Gatorade bottle, going over it all in his mind.

The prisoners they had pulled off the same objective as the communications equipment were spilling their guts to Samruk interrogators. It was fortunate that the mercenaries had caught the cartel members off guard and by surprise. They had just arrived back in Mexico from a cartel training camp in Guatemala. Apparently Jimenez ran a training center off-site in the Central American country away from the prying eyes of other cartels and gringo spies. They sent their shooters down there for military training, including heavy machine guns, mortars, long range marksmanship, room clearing techniques, and explosives.

It only got more ominous from there. Jimenez had one hundred men in the new training complex he had built down there currently undergoing training. They were due to graduate, with certificates of achievement and everything in another week. With Samruk's assault on the cartel, Jimenez would be pushing to abridge the training or yank them out of it altogether in order to get some warm bodies into the fight.

If that happened it would be a disaster for Samruk and

the people of Oaxaca. They had to intercept the cartel para-
military soldiers before they could arrive back in Mexico. Their
OPSEC was tight, the cartel men had been blindfolded and
bussed down to the training center. None of them could locate it
on a map.

But they did know that the hidden base had a VHF relay
system to talk to the rest of the cartel in Mexico. In fact they had
been adamant that the pirate net extended from Colombia all the
way north, maybe even into the United States.

Now it was just a matter of figuring out how to back
trace the signal and pinpoint the location of the training center.
Then they had to get Samruk shooters to the camp.

Frank had a few ideas on both counts.

It was time to make some phone calls.

Kurt Jager supervised the packing of a deuce and a half
truck full of weapons and ammunition. Samruk had inherited a
sizable weapons cache from the Ortega compound and taken
some more guns from Jimenez' boys. Now the mercenaries
would be transferring them over to the Zapatista rebels they were
to train. They could mothball their shot out rifles, but the
guerrillas were going to need some more serious firepower for
their so-called revolution.

The German was uneasy with Deckard's alliance with the
communist fighters. On one hand, the locals saw communism as
the only viable alternative to the cartels, the corrupt Mexican
government, and western trans-national corporations invading
their land. He didn't blame the people of Oaxaca and Chaipas
for turning towards the Zapatisas but he was skeptical of their
long term ambitions. Communism didn't have many success
stories to brag about.

War was full of unsettling compromises. German,
American, and other coalition forces had also trained and armed
ambiguous groups in Iraq and Afghanistan. It seemed that this
would be no different. Deckard was also hedging his bets.

Only train them to do the specific tasks that we need them to execute in order to defeat the cartel, had been his parting advice to Kurt. He was to get them to a point where they could square off with the cartel but not duplicate the capabilities of Special Operations units. Not that they had time for that anyway. The former GSG-9 commando had a hasty program of instruction sketched out in his notebook. Some marksmanship drills and tactical training would probably be all they would have time for.

In the meantime he had selected three other contractors to accompany him. Thankfully they were former 7th Special Forces Group members. They spoke Spanish and had previous experience training soldiers in South and Central America. It was a good thing, too. They would need every edge they could find if they were going to be successful.

"Load up," he ordered.

The four man FID cell jumped onto the deuce and a half and bolted the ramp shut. As the truck rumbled out the gate two assault trucks pulled up to escort them. They would be taken to a rendezvous point where the rebels would then take the four men and the weapons to their base somewhere in the jungle.

"Wait, wait," Frank bust out as he stumbled alongside the truck.

The brakes squealed as the truck came to a halt.

"What is it?" Kurt asked.

"When you get out there and link up with the rebels I need you to pick a few and have one of your guys to be on standby for a mission."

"What mission?"

"A recon down south!"

17

It was eight in the morning when Deckard walked across the tarmac in Cancun towards the half dozen heavies that were waiting for him. The sun was already beating down on his head and shoulders, the rising humidity hinting at the crippling heat that would come later in the day.

"No bags?" one of the Lebanese men asked as he approached.

"Nah," Deckard said. "I figure I'll be shooting out on a flight later tonight anyhow."

A thick necked gangster stepped forward with a metal detection wand in his hand. He wore a blue tracksuit and had a ghost of a beard that was supposed to be a substitute for his non-existent jaw line.

Deckard went along with the routine. He got wanded and then patted down. They quickly looked over his wallet and cell phone before handing them back. The passport was given slightly more scrutiny as the guy in the tracksuit flipped through the pages before returning it. They walked him into the terminal and straight through customs without having to submit any paperwork or have his passport stamped. The Lebanese men moved in a circle around Deckard as they escorted him through the automatic doors and out into the arrivals lane outside.

A black Ferrari waited for him.

"Over here," the driver waved to him.

Deckard looked left to see the six man security detachment climb into a white panel van behind the sports car. He would be on his own with Bashir for at least a few minutes.

"Pleasure to meet you," Deckard said as he opened the passenger side door. He was glad that it was a convertible with the roof off because it was difficult as it was to squeeze his frame into a car that rode so close the ground.

Bashir looked him dead in the eye as they shook hands.

"And you," he smiled.

Shifting, the Lebanese money man stomped on the gas and they peeled out, accelerating down and out to the main strip of hotels at Cancun. The emerald green waters shot by on their left hand side while empty hotels flew past on the right. Deckard noted that they looked almost bombed out like some scene he had seen in the Middle East. They were half constructed in most cases, sitting empty. They only existed to launder drug money through.

"Staying long?" Bashir said taking his eyes off the road as they continued to accelerate to look at him.

"I'm afraid not," Deckard said casually. "They want me back in Manhattan but I'm happy to stay as long as needed for us to come to an agreement that we are both comfortable with," he forced a smile.

"I would love to do some business with your firm," Bashir looked back on the road in time to swerve around a tour bus. "I've heard good things about McLaughlin and McLaughlin."

"We have extensive experience in Central America," Deckard confirmed.

It wasn't just a predisposition due to the information the Agency had given him. There was definitely something way off about Bashir. His mannerisms were overly confident, he looked at Deckard like a starving man would look at a bloody steak.

The Lebanese gangster's eyelashes batted every time he blinked. They were so dark that it almost looked as if he were wearing eye liner. There was something elegant about his face, like he was someone who took care of himself. There was a gentleness to it that was countered by the look in his eyes.

They were pushing a hundred and twenty miles an hour as Bashir held onto the wheel with both hands. He wore a black shirt that was left unbuttoned to leave much of his chest exposed. Since it was tucked into his slacks, Deckard could see that he wasn't carrying a firearm. He did some quick calculus in his head.

He could incapacitate Bashir, take control of the car, kill him, and make a run for it. It sounded great but it would never work. They were on a narrow strip of beach and highway. The white van was just a minute behind them filled with Bashir's hired guns. Deckard could try to lose them inside one of the hotel complexes but it was a zero sum game. He needed access to Bashir's private DVD collection if he, and the CIA, would have the leverage they needed over the Mexican government. He'd have to keep playing the game and ride this thing out.

"So what is your specialty with the firm?" Bashir asked. "Double Dutch?"

Deckard caught on that now he was talking shop, specific money laundering techniques.

"Not so much," he replied. "We're a progressive group that looks east these days. We wash the money through Turks and Caicos, Montserrat Island, and a few other places in the Caribbean before packaging it into financial derivatives that we invest in China and elsewhere in South East Asia."

"I've been having issues with our accounts up north as of late."

"We understand. Your money is safer in Asia. Even anonymous Swiss bank accounts are not as anonymous as they used to be. My firm understands the need for privacy and security that our customers look for in an investment bank."

"I look forward to talking about it with you," Bashir said as he pulled into the drive way of one of his five-star hotels.

No sooner had they stepped out of the Ferrari and a valet was slipping in and pulling the sports car away to be parked.

"This is where you live?"

"Year round," Bashir laughed, causing the wrinkles in the corners of his eyes to become pronounced. Deckard knew from the dossier that the cartel money launder was 53 years old but he looked like someone in their mid to late thirties.

Another attendant held the door as they walked into the marble floor lobby.

"You should think about staying a few days, make yourself comfortable," Bashir insisted. "I'll tell you something about the women down here," he hinted.

"Oh?" Deckard said, feigning interest.

"In Mexico you can go to the strip club and the girls will let you put your finger all the way up her pussy to the last knuckle."

"Sounds like a gas."

"Americans think it is nothing but wetbacks down here but I've carved out a paradise for myself."

The words were chilling when taken into account with the dossier files Deckard had read. He knew exactly what kind of paradise Bashir had in mind. Looking over his shoulder and through the glass door he saw that the white panel van was nowhere to be seen. The bodyguards must have pulled around back assuming that their principle was safe inside his own establishment surrounded by his own people.

There were guests wandering around the lobby, as Bashir's flagship hotel was actually staffed and operated as an actual business. Mostly young honeymooners enjoying the beach life and the night life of Cancun. Bashir led him deeper into the hotel passed several fountains to an elevator that was roped off and guarded by two strong men.

"This goes straight to the penthouse," Bashir said.

One of the guards inserted a key into the control panel and the elevator doors parted. Stepping inside, the guard punched the single button for the top floor for his boss before letting the doors slam shut.

"Very nice," Deckard complimented. "So what is the next big project out here?"

"I've got architects drafting the plans for a water park, a casino, and a few more hotels. I think they will go forward but the gears of government need some lubrication as I'm sure you can understand."

"Perfectly."

"Nineteen stories," Bashir boasted as the doors swung open at the top floor.

The office was indicative of a man who had more money than taste. The walls and ceiling were painted in pastels, modern art hung on the walls, and some movie memorabilia was scattered about including a life size mannequin bearing the costume armor of a Spartan warrior. Deckard fought to control his facial expression in front of his host.

"Impressive."

"Several magazines want to feature the penthouse but you know how it is," Bashir said non-nonchalantly. "I value my privacy."

The Lebanese man sat down behind his desk as he motioned for Deckard to take a seat as well. As he sat down in one of the leather seats beside the desk his eyes absorbed everything in a single snapshot. He was in one of two leather chairs. An armed guard that he wasn't supposed to notice stood behind him at his seven o' clock. On the desk were closed MacBook, an ash tray, a cellular phone, a remote control, a pencil, and lamp.

"Can I offer you a drink?"

"Johnny Walker Black. On the rocks."

Bashir picked up the remote control and pressed a

button. One of the adjoining doors swung open and a woman done up like an escort walked in. She stood at about five foot two and ninety pounds and wore a very revealing hostess outfit. Bashir gave her Deckard's order and asked for a gin and tonic for himself before sending her on her way.

Once she had departed he offered Deckard a cigarette which he declined. A plan was formulating in his mind. He had a narrow window of opportunity and had to make it count. Lighting up a smoke with his Zippo lighter Bashir smoked his cigarette underhanded with his thumb and middle finger.

"If I can convince you to enjoy Cancun for a few days I promise you won't regret it. While you are here we can conclude our business and begin transferring several sizable accounts once our lawyers get the paperwork done up."

"I thought I was supposed to be pitching you," Deckard smiled. "But please continue."

"As I was saying, you can have any girl you want here. Any taste, any size."

"Really?"

"I prefer them small," Bashir shrugged as he took another puff on his cigarette. Reaching out, delicately tapped the ash into the ash tray. "It is okay to indulge yourself here. No one will say anything."

"What do you mean?"

"As they say, the United States is a nation of prudes. When a girl reaches sexual maturity she has become ripe. For whatever reason, your laws do not account for this. It is a very easy thing," Bashir continued. "I invite them over to swim in one of my pools. Sometimes I promise them nice things, a designer handbag, nice clothes, whatever they like."

Deckard couldn't believe how brazen Bashir was. He didn't even try to hide it but rather offered his own pseudo-intellectual justifications for why it was okay for him to rape girls who had barely reached puberty.

"I've never had them turn me down because they know that I love them. It is perfectly natural of course and helps their self-esteem as they grow older to know that they are desired by older men. Most of the time I let them play movie star and we make some movies as well."

There was a knock and the hostess came back into the office with their drinks.

"Is that something I can convince you to stick around for?" Bashir asked.

Deckard palmed his glass of scotch off the hostess' tray. "I'll pass."

Without missing a beat he hurled the contents of his glass at Bashir, causing him to recoil backwards in shock more than in pain. Springing to his feet, Deckard hooked an ankle under the Mexican hostess' feet and swept her to the ground. By now the lone body guard in the room was closing the distance towards him.

Deckard didn't want the body guard drawing his pistol and going for lethal force which was why he had taken a restrained approach. Reaching out, his fingers tightened around the pencil laying on the desk even as Bashir thrashed about and knocked his ashtray and computer to the floor with the crash.

Pivoting on the balls of his feet, Deckard bent at the knees and prepared to receive the bodyguard's attack. The mercenary held the pencil in his right hand, the eraser at the end pressed into the palm of his hand, his middle and index finger resting on either side of it while the point stuck out. As the bodyguard reached out, Deckard deflected his hand and struck out with his right. The tip of the pencil was guided into the bodyguard's neck where it stuck in place. Deckard immediately moved his two fingers out of the way and pushed the pencil the rest of the way into his neck by palming it forward until he slapped skin.

Bashir had by now wiped his face down with his shirt and was fumbling for the remote on his desk, no doubt for the panic button. Deckard slapped it out of his hand before the bodyguard collapsed to the floor where he began convulsing. Grabbing the money launderer by his greasy hair, Deckard slammed him face first into the desk. His head bounced off the surface before he slid off to the side and fell to the ground.

"You," Deckard pointed to the hostess and began speaking in Spanish. "Go in there," he pointed to the coat closet. "Go inside, turn the light off, hide in the corner, and don't come out."

The woman nodded his understanding.

"Now!"

She got to her feet on shaky legs. That didn't stop her from stepping over the still twitching body on the floor on her way to the closet.

Reaching inside the bodyguard's waistband, Deckard confiscated a Glock 19 pistol.

Bashir was moaning on the ground.

Pushing the point of one of his shoes under him, Deckard flipped Bashir over onto his back. Blood flowed freely from his broken nose.

"I'm not going to give you the opportunity to lie to me. You've got me interested alright, but not in the way you were hoping. Where do you keep the movies you made?"

"W-w-who are you?" he stammered.

Deckard reached down and twisted his nose eliciting a sharp scream. They were alone up in the penthouse aside from the one guard he had taken down already.

"Where do you keep the movies?"

"In the basement," he groaned.

"How do I get there?"

"It's the sub-basement. That private elevator is the only way down."

"You have the key?"

"In the desk drawer."

"Let's go for a walk."

Deckard dragged Bashir up to his feet and pushed him back to the desk. Inside he found the key and then pushed the pedophile towards the elevator. He held Bashir by the neck with the Glock 19 pressed into the small of his back.

Calling up the elevator, the door opened.

"I don't need to tell you what will happen if you try anything stupid. You can still make it out of this alive if you play your cards right," Deckard told him a bold face lie.

As it was, it would be a miracle if either of them survived another hour.

Deckard grabbed the key and turned it into the slot. The elevator snapped shut and they began descending down into what he suspected was Bashir's private house of horrors. He played it off like it was all fun and games, but people like Bashir were hardcore psychopaths. They dropped below the lobby and the basement. The digital counter above the doors was blanked out when they reached the bottom.

"Move," Deckard ordered as the doors opened. He pocketed the elevator key before following the cartel financier out.

They were underground where the air was moist and cool. The chambers had to be specially engineered well ahead of time as they were now below the waterline. The main hotels, bars, and clubs in Cancun were all situated on a narrow patch of land sandwiched between the ocean and an inter-coastal waterway. The entire commercial ribbon was essentially a long island with a highway, a beach, and a bunch of buildings crammed in between.

They came to a heavy metal door with a numerical punch code pad.

"You know what to do."

Bashir entered the code and the door unlocked. Deckard pushed Bashir into the door. It swung open as the automatic lights kicked in and Bashir collapsed to the floor.

"What. The. Fuck."

It was a film studio wired for video, sound, and special effects. A large bed had been set up in the center of the room. Digital video cameras were arrayed around the bed on tripods and professional Hollywood quality lighting was hung on rails from the ceiling. Children's stuffed animals and dolls were stacked in one corner of the room.

Against one of the walls were restraints bolted into the concrete. Other handcuffs, gags, and restraining devices were sized extra small for the young "actresses" in Bashir's movies.

"Come here," Deckard grabbed Bashir by the throat and yanked him up.

The rapist struggled, his feet stumbling over each other as Deckard dragged him and slammed him into the wall. Wrapping one of the leather restraints in place around Bashir's neck, Deckard did up the buckle. He began fighting back so Deckard punched him in the gut, which would have doubled him over except that he was now choking on the leather collar. Next he used similar leather restraints to secure his hands. Bashir was now tied to the wall, as helpless as his victims had been.

"Tell me where the recordings are and I will let you go."

"You can't do this to me!"

"I'm just here for the recordings. You are not the job, I have no interest in you."

"It's all on discs. Over there," Bashir motioned to a side room.

Deckard looked inside. It was packed with cameras, portable lighting equipment, boom microphones, and other production equipment. Inside he found rows and rows of jewel cases on a book shelf.

He ignored Bashir's howls of terror. Deckard wanted to leave the torture chamber as soon as possible. Looking over the jewel cases he saw that Bashir's obsessiveness bled over to cataloging. Deckard clearly wasn't the first of his guests that Bashir had tried to coax into his predilections. Most of the names on the discs were unknown to him but a few jumped out as belonging to Mexican politicians. Not all of the names were Mexican either. Maybe ten percent were American. As his eyes quickly swept over them, he recognized a few as sitting US congressmen.

Looking around he found a camera case with a sling attachment. Discarding the pull out padded inserts on the floor, he packed the bag full. There were so many discs that he began tossing the jewel cases as well to make room for the discs. Outside, Bashir was sobbing and whimpering to himself.

Slinging the camera bag over his shoulder, Deckard walked back out into the studio and looked at the pathetic worm that he had strung up to the wall as he had done to so many of his young victims.

"You have to let me go now," Bashir pleaded. "I did what you wanted. You have to let me go!"

Tears streaked down his cheeks.

Deckard walked over and fished around into the money man's pockets until he found the Zippo lighter that he had seen him with earlier. Opening up the fuel cell, he dumped the lighter fuel on the bed in the center of the studio.

"What are you doing?" Bashir whined.

Deckard flicked the Zippo next to the lighter fluid.

"Hey, what are you doing man?"

Another flick and the sparks ignited the sheets, starting a fire.

"What are you doing, you said you would let me go!"

"I know."

"So let me go. The job wasn't me, you said that yourself!"

The flames were spreading behind Deckard. Soon they would engulf the bed, the carpeting, the drywall, and everything else in the film studio.

Bashir's eyes were pure panic. He was used to causing pain and eliciting terror in others but of course he had no tolerance for pain himself. His pain was the only kind that he could feel. He was a maniac.

Deckard was more of a sociopath. He could never fit in with the rest of society, he could never conform to what society wanted in a person. But the similarities between him and Bashir ended there.

"You said you would let me go!" Bashir's eyes were wild with panic.

"I lied to you."

The flames were growing hot at Deckard's back.

"What?!"

Deckard's eyes were ice. They looked right through Bashir.

"You are going to burn."

"Wait, wait, wait!"

Deckard walked towards the elevator. Before he left he found the climate control panel and made sure the vents were wide open. Down in the sub-basement it was especially important to make sure the flames were fed with plenty of oxygen.

"You can't do this to me! You can't just leave me here!"

Deckard stepped onto the elevator and turned the key. The doors shut, leaving Bashir to his fate.

18

The closet door suddenly shot open and the hostess hugged her knees a little closer to her chest. Bashir's visitor, the man who turned out to be an assassin, stood in the doorway.

"You are going to hear the fire alarm go off in a few minutes. When that happens you need to leave. Don't come back."

She nodded.

"Is there an emergency exit?"

"Through the other room, there is a door leading to a staircase that goes to the next level down."

"Okay, take that once you hear the alarm."

Deckard shut the hostess back in the closet and readjusted the camera bag strap on his shoulder. He was forced to ride the elevator back up to the penthouse. There was no other escape from the dungeon and popping out in the lobby would very likely place him at ground zero for a triple cross fire with no cover or decent plan of egress. He had the Glock and one magazine from the bodyguard forcing him to think on his feet and come up with other options.

He had propped up a chair to hold open the elevator door to prevent the shooters standing by down in the lobby from calling the elevator down and coming up after him. Deckard could already see black smoke wafting up through the shaft from below and into the elevator.

Following the hostess' instructions he walked through a parlor room that contained the late Bashir's salt water fish tank. Finding the stair case he tried one door and found that it led to a bathroom. The second door took him to the spiraling stairs that went to the ground floor.

The mercenary began hurrying down the stairs when he heard shouts, the voices reverberating up the confines of the emergency stairwell. Looking over the railing, he could see the forms of Bashir's shooters rushing up to meet him. They were fast. The PSD had seen the smoke coming from the elevator shaft, tried to take the elevator to the penthouse only to find it blocked, and were now coming up the stairs to find out what was going on. Deckard estimated that it had only been three or four minutes since he left Bashir to his fate.

They would meet somewhere around the tenth or eleventh floor, a meeting Deckard didn't care to have if he could avoid it. There were more cartel shooters flooding up the stairs behind the bodyguards and he didn't have enough bullets for them all, assuming he even got the chance to shoot. On the seventeenth floor landing he exited through the emergency door and quietly shut it behind him. With a little luck, he would be able to slip past them entirely.

Moving down the hallway he could see that the entire floor was being refurbished. Drywall and stacks of wood lined the hallway. The walls were covered in plaster and waiting for a coat of paint. A couple workers carrying buckets of plaster moved across the hall from one room to the other, paying Deckard no mind as they talked to each other in Spanish.

Ducking into one of the rooms that was being renovated the mercenary walked out onto the balcony. It was going to be a little dicey but these things always are, he told himself. Below, hotel guests were coming out of their hangovers and scuttling along like little ants to the beach with their umbrellas and coolers. Squinting in the sunlight, Deckard could see the flashing red and blue of police lights several miles down the strip.

That was fast. The local Mexicans would never get such a reaction from the police if they got into trouble. That kind of hustle was reserved for Cancun's franchise owner.

After placing his wallet and cell phone into his pants pockets, Deckard discarded the suit jacket and undid the buttons on his sleeves. Securing the camera bag tightly across his back, Deckard started towards the balcony when he had a last minute thought. Turning back, he grabbed a fist full of screws from a box laying on the floor and pocketed them as well.

Back out on the balcony he held onto the railing and swung his legs over the side. Down on the ground, the tourists continued about their business none the wiser to any of the insanity that was going on in their hotel. Taking a deep breath, he knew he had to act fast. The cartel gunmen would figure out his ruse sooner or later and block the exits. Here he was, hanging over the edge of the balcony on the seventeenth story of a hotel in Mexico with a camera bag full of highly questionable material.

Not one of my finer moments, Deckard thought to

himself with some resignation.

Reaching down to the bottom rail he kicked his feet out and let himself hang under the balcony. Gravity attempted to have its way with him, his sweaty hands struggling to maintain a firm grip. Slowly, he began to swing his legs back and forth. Sweat ran down his face and dripped down his shirt. Swinging harder and faster, he built up momentum before angling his legs towards the balcony below and releasing his hands.

Air whistled in his ears as he landed with a crash. Stumbling backwards he almost tipped over the railing of the lower balcony, threatening to go end over end to his death. Both hands instinctively snapped onto the railing to prevent him from falling.

Looking at the sliding door, Deckard realized that he might have screwed himself but breathed a sigh of relief when he found it unlocked. There was a double bed inside and someone was in the bathroom with the shower turned on. He moved across the carpet as silently as he could, slowly turned open the dead bolt and eased the door open. Once in the hall he reached into the side pocket of the camera bag where he stashed the Glock and moved back to the stairwell.

With an ear pressed against the door, he listened for a few moments before continuing. The cartel gunmen had indeed continued up to the top levels of the hotel. Rushing, Deckard took the stairs four at a time, falling forward and turning at the last moment to prevent a face plant into the wall before going down the next flight. The camera bag bounced on his back as he raced to the ground floor.

Out of breath, he hit the landing on the third floor when the police officers he had seen from the balcony finally arrived and began making their way up to the penthouse.

"Fuck," Deckard said under his breath. He took the door again, searching for a way out. Halfway down the hall he found a thirty-something blonde exiting her room with a beach bag.

"Excuse me," he said, pushing her out of the way and walking into her hotel room.

"Hey," she said curling her nose at him. "Who the hell are you?"

"Shore patrol."

"What?"

Deckard flung open the sliding door and was back out on

another balcony. This time the fall wouldn't be enough to kill him, just enough to hurt really, really bad. There was a swimming pool below but of course it was just a little too far for him to jump to. Immediately underneath him were some plastic pool chairs.

The woman chased after him, letting the door slam shut behind her.

"Hey dude," she squeaked. "Get the fuck out of my room!"

"I'm working on it," Deckard responded, climbing over the railing.

"What are you doing? Are you on drugs?"

Examining the side of the building, the walls were smooth with no way to climb down, no drain pipes to slide on, not even another balcony to drop down on. He was on the third floor leaving about a thirty foot drop down to the poolside.

"Holy shit," someone cried out from below. "Look at this action hero!"

Swimmers in the pools stopped and looked up at Deckard hanging off the outside of the balcony. Tourists lounging about set down their cocktails and stared at him in bewilderment.

"That dude is crazy!" someone wearing a Hawaiian shirt yelled. "He's gonna jump!"

Just then a banging came at the hotel room door behind him followed by muffled screams.

"Oh, no," the blonde exclaimed.

"It's the police," Deckard explained. "They are after me, not you."

"It's not the police, that's my fiancé," she said listening to the screams coming from the other side of the door. "He must know there is another man in the room with me!"

Now everyone at the pool was looking up at Deckard.

"Do it!" someone said. Then in unison they began to chant, "Jump-jump-jump!"

"Should I let him in?" the girl asked.

Looking over his shoulder Deckard could see the door bulge with each thud as her fiancé began trying to kick the door in.

"Who is your fiancé?"

"He's a linebacker for the Miami Dolphins."

Deckard turned and jumped from the balcony.

It was far from a graceful landing. As a former para-trooper Deckard knew how to execute a Parachute Landing Fall which was meant to help cushion your impact with the ground and prevent injury. Keeping his feet and knees together, he brought his fists up in front of his face for protection. Making contact with the concrete, he stayed loose and rolled to the side, flopping over some pool furniture.

For a moment he saw red and was vaguely aware of the crowd cheering his epic wipe out.

Struggling onto his hands and knees, he was scraped up and bruised pretty good. His entire body felt jarred like he had just been in a car crash.

"That was gnarly man!" one of the partiers said helping him to his feet.

"Thanks kid," Deckard grunted. "Now get the fuck out of my face."

The kid took a step back, seeing that Deckard was bleeding from several cuts he'd received during the fall.

"I'LL KILL YOU MOTHERFUCKER!"

Looking up at the balcony he had just jumped from he could see that the Miami Dolphins linebacker had made short work of that door, expecting to find a stranger having an amorous encounter with his fiancé.

"Go Jets!" Deckard yelled back.

The NFL player began climbing over the railing himself as the blonde woman jumped on his back, wrapping her arms around what little neck he had to try to stop him.

The pool party was in stunned, awed silence by the spectacle.

Exit stage left.

Deckard readjusted the strap of the camera bag again and began skirting around the side of the hotel. Behind him he could hear the football player still threatening his life. He could also hear the muffled siren of the hotel's fire alarm coming from inside. Moving into the pump room for the pool, he scanned for police or cartel men, finding that the coast was clear. They were still occupied searching the top floors for both him and Bashir, who was no doubt a crispy critter by now.

Moving around to the front of the hotel Deckard found a dozen police cars parked in the roundabout next to the main entrance. The doors on many had been left ajar as the corrupt cops had stampeded into the hotel. Reaching into his pocket he found some of the screws that he had taken from the work site inside and began placing them under the rear tires of each police car except for one that he reserved for himself. The task was completed in a little over a minute and he hopped into the police cruiser he had left untouched.

The cops had been in such a hurry that they even left the keys in the ignition for him.

Pulling out of the hotel parking lot, he executed a hasty three point turn and was off on the main highway just as the fire department was pulling in. Above the hotel, a column of black smoke rose into the beautiful blue sky.

Driving along the highway, he was suddenly feeling good. Real good.

Another dead asshole and he was slipping away none the worse for wear.

Coming up to a police checkpoint, Deckard flipped on the cruisers lights and sirens, blowing right through it as the policemen on duty waved him on.

Fishing around for his CIA issued cell phone, he reminded himself that the mission wasn't over yet.

"You fly plane?"

"How the fuck did you think you got here," the CIA pilot answered the mercenary's question.

The two Kazakh trigger pullers that Deckard had left in the Gulfstream as a security detachment had been playing twenty questions with the two pilots since he had departed.

"You spend lot of time in airplane?"

"It is what I love," the pilot responded proudly. "I did my twenty in the Air Force. I couldn't stop flying if I wanted to."

"You fly plane," the second mercenary interrupted. "Meanwhile, your wife at home playing like promiscuous Uzbek whore!"

The two mercenaries burst out laughing.

"Laugh it up you little brown fuckers!" the pilot fumed. "It's only a matter of time before we invade whatever country you two are from!"

Hearing his smart phone ring, the pilot answered while the Kazakhs continued to have some fun as his expense.

"It's him," he shouted to shut the two of them up. "He's coming in."

The mercenaries flipped a switch and they were all business, throwing on their plate carriers and readying weapons.

"Shit," the pilot cursed. "Start it up!" he yelled to the co-pilot sitting up in the cockpit. "He's coming in hot!"

A smooth extraction had been too much to hope for.

Stepping on the gas, the police cruiser raced across the bridge, passing over transparent turquoise waters as Deckard left Cancun and shot down the road that led through the mangrove swamps. Looking in the rear view mirror he could see several black military type vehicles belonging to the *federales* chasing after him.

His subterfuge slowed down the police but they had figured it out fast enough to call in the big guns. At least the Army hadn't shown up yet.

Clearing the hump in the middle of the bridge, Deckard decelerated slightly as he felt the rear wheels sliding out from under him. Bringing the police car back under control he gunned it down the highway. He held the steering wheel with his hands placed at the nine and two o' clock positions to help make the hair pin turns at high speed that he would need to negotiate.

When he came to the first turn, he held the wheel tight, slowly spinning it until his forearms crossed over each other. The cruiser protested the harsh treatment but Deckard pushed the vehicle to its limits until coming out of the turn when he quickly brought the wheel back to the 12 o'clock position.

Passing another one of Bashir's abandoned hotel projects, Deckard took the car squealing around another turn towards the airport. Looking in the mirror again, it seemed that he had bought himself some breathing room.

Reaching for the smart phone, he redialed the pilots.

"Hey, we kicked the engines," the pilot picked up. "Where are you?"

"A couple minutes out. Head away from the commercial terminals and stop on the taxiway. I'm going to have to ditch the vehicle and meet you there. They are right on my ass."

"We haven't been granted clearance by the tower yet."

"Fuck clearance if you don't want to spend thirty years in a Mexican prison!"

Deckard threw the phone in the passenger seat next to the camera bag as the car threatened to careen off the side of the road. He had noticed on his way out of the airport that they had gone under an overpass. The highway actually passed under the taxiway that connected to the two landing strips at Cancun's airport.

Now he was flooring it down the straightaway, the needle on the speedometer creeping up over a hundred miles an hour. The aging police cruiser wasn't a Ferrari but it was getting his ass out of Dodge and that was all that mattered at the moment.

Up ahead was some kind of modern art type monument in between the two lanes of traffic where he saw the police were quickly establishing another checkpoint. They were probably shutting down the airport itself at that very moment but hadn't caught on to which plane he had come in with yet.

Deckard slowed and cut the wheel again, crossing the median and blasting into the opposing lane of traffic. Tactical driving was a piece of cake once you overcame your aversion to breaking every traffic law known to man. The police looked dumbfounded at Deckard as he shot by. The oncoming lane only had a few cars on it and it was easy for the drivers to avoid each other even as they honked their horns at the renegade cop car.

He slowed slightly to avoid traffic when passing through a four way intersection. By now the *federales* were back in sight in his rear view mirror, giving chase as he closed on the airport. He had hoped for a little more stand off when he made his move, but it was what it was.

When he came up to the overpass, he pulled the car off the side of the road while grabbing for the phone and the camera bag. Once the car came to a halt, the mercenary dove out of the door and scrambled up alongside the over pass. Climbing up the embankment to the taxiway, he pushed and clawed his way through the thick bushes.

The black *federale* vehicles screamed to a stop down below, the pop of gunshots searching him out. Coming to the crest of the hill, Deckard hit the ground as a bullet cracked over his head. Crawling forwards, he could hear the federal cops breaking brush behind him. They couldn't move the way Deckard could, but they were closing the distance.

Careful not the silhouette himself, he reached the top of the embankment just in time to see the Gulfstream V turn onto the taxiway in front of him. Rolling over, Deckard palmed the Glock 19 pistol and began firing downwards into the bushes to give some suppressive fire. Normally he wouldn't fire on law enforcement officials but these were the goons who had lent Bashir top cover while he ran his child porn operation. They did more crime protection than law enforcement.

The twin engines on the Gulfstream whined as it grew closer. The *federales* were hugging dirt, unable to react to persistent contact the way infantry troops would. Once the Gulfstream pulled around the folding stairs dropped down. Both the Samruk mercenaries piled out and ran to Deckard. Aiming their AK-103 rifles they sent a barrage of semi-automatic gunfire down the embankment and into the idling *federale* vehicles.

It was just in the nick of time Deckard realized as he noted that his Glock was in slide lock as he had fired his last round.

"Cease fire," Deckard ordered. "That's enough, we're getting the hell out of here."

Deckard grabbing the Kazakhs by the sleeves, the three turned and ran for the Gulfstream, climbing back inside.

The pilot was through playing games and disengaged the air brakes. The private jet jerked forward nearly throwing Deckard back out of the door as he was retracting the folding stairs. He barely got the door shut and locked into place before they swung onto the runway. Blowing off the warning from the control tower, the CIA pilot hauled ass the down the runway throwing the three mercenaries in the cabin to the floor as he sped for takeoff.

The Gulfstream was only halfway down the runway when it lifted off the ground and soared into the sky.

19

"We're not out of the briar patch yet," the pilot growled.

"What is it," Deckard asked as he braced himself in the door to the cockpit. They were still gaining altitude rapidly.

"From the radio traffic I'm hearing it sounds like they scrambled fighters from Merida the second they realized that you were making a run for the airport."

"Fighter jets?"

"F-5's."

"Weapons?"

"Raphael Defense air-to-air missiles."

"Shit."

"Yeah. Thank god for our Military Assistance Program in Mexico."

"I take it Havana is out of the question as an escape route?"

"We are heading for Grand Cayman but we will never make it. We will be intercepted in less than ten minutes. They got a head start on us and will clear the Yucatan in a few minutes."

Now the co-pilot turned around.

"What the hell happened down there?"

"Classified."

"I should have known. Whatever happened, you stirred up a real shit storm."

"Couldn't be helped."

The pilot leveled out the aircraft as they reached 30,000 feet. With the co-pilot looking out the opposite side of the window, they both scanned the sky.

"Three o' clock," the co-pilot announced. "Nice size formation."

The pilot nosed their aircraft towards the lone cloud formation off in the distance, the shadows shifting in the cabin behind Deckard as the jet changed its heading. The co-pilot was listening to something in his headset.

"Two F-5's. They are reporting to the control tower that they are eight minutes to intercept."

"We'll make it," the pilot announced but Deckard saw the sweat beading on his forehead.

The dark clouds in front of them were quickly moving to fill up the cockpit's windshield. Once inside they would gain visual concealment but Deckard knew that modern aviators often flew by instrument alone.

"I appreciate what you guys are doing," Deckard said nervously. "But getting into those clouds isn't going to hide us from their radar."

The pilot's eyes remained fixed on his instruments.

"We know what we are doing," the pilot lectured him. "This happened to us in Switzerland last year. The Swiss Air Force tried to ground us as we flew through their airspace. Some jerk off in their parliament didn't like us flying captured terrorists from Kabul to Morocco so they tried to intercept us with a couple fighters."

"What happened?"

"We disappeared."

"How?"

"Classified," the pilot shot back.

Finally, the cockpit went dark as they blasted into the cloud formation. The co-pilot leaned over what looked like a navigation panel and starting flicking switches. It was then that it dawned on Deckard that beneath what looked like a normal console was actually something entirely different.

"I had wondered how Red Squadron had infiltrated into Pakistan while evading the military's radar systems," Deckard said referring to the SEAL Team Six raid that had killed Osama Bin Laden. "They got flown in on some of those nifty stealth helicopters from 160th Special Operations Aviation, but you can only do such much to conceal the radar profile on a rotary wing aircraft."

The pilot and co-pilot looked at each other.

"They tested those stealth packages at Area 51 out in Nevada so they must have known what their limitations are. Yeah, you can reduce the radar signature by using composite skin and radar absorbent paints," Deckard thought out loud. "But those rotor blades would create a huge blip on Pakistani radar none the less. So there had to be something else involved. Maybe special electromagnetic interference?"

"Don't know what you're talking about," the co-pilot asserted.

The pilot began circling the jet around inside the clouds,

keeping them concealed from the F-5 fighters searching for the CIA black flight somewhere in the sky below, all while transmitting electronic counter-measures.

"The Mexican pilots are getting into an argument with the control tower. They don't see anything and neither do the radar operators," the co-pilot announced.

"We'll keep circling until they run low on fuel and have to return to Merida. They burned a lot of gas scrambling out here so it shouldn't be long. Once they head back we'll shoot over to Grand Cayman as fast as we can," the pilot said.

Deckard walked back into the cabin where his two mercenaries were clutching their seats nervously. Grabbing another bottle of water, he took a seat.

He had to admit, the pilots had pulled off a pretty slick maneuver by using cloud cover to visually camouflage their presence while going hot on some classified microwave weapons system to conceal their radar signature. Microwaves have the unique ability to slip through the seams of enemy radar installations and insinuate themselves into the circuitry. They sneak in through the back door and spoof the radar system or cause it to malfunction.

More than likely, this had been the secret sauce that had allowed the SEAL Team Six operators to covertly slip into Pakistani airspace aboard 160th Stealth Black Hawk helicopters. The helicopters themselves had stealth characteristics like the F-117 Stealth Fighter, but these had to be combined with microwave spoofing techniques to completely hide radar signature created by the beating rotor blades.

In this case, those same microwave weapons were perfect for concealing CIA black flights. The airplane could look perfectly normal on the exterior as not to arouse suspicion when it arrived in airports but could "go dark" to evade detection during covert operations. Deckard took a sip of his water.

Clearly, the CIA wasn't hurting for funding.

The Iridium satellite phone was picked up on the first ring.

"*Nam?*" the man answered in his native language. For a moment he was confused as to where he was and who he was talking to.

"It is a Gulfstream V. The paint job is gray but there are no commercial labels or official seals. The tail number is N44982," the caller told him.

"Good work Arturo," the Arab thanked him while committing the information to memory.

The Mexican intelligence official had become his go between with the Jimenez cartel and himself. It was now clear that the CIA would be of no use to them. They were perfectly happy to see the Jimenez cartel liquidated. The Arab worked for vested interests who were determined to ensure that this never happened. If Jimenez went down, there was no telling how many of the drug corridors would collapse if the American set off some kind of domino effect. They had to nip this problem in the bud.

The Arab smiled. He was good at troubleshooting these types of problems.

"You are sure he is on this flight?"

"Yes," Arturo said. "My contact in the *federales* personally saw him board this plane just before the pilots made an illegal take off in Cancun. I would have left the problem in your hands but before I could intervene our air force sent up a couple fighters."

"Did you have them stand down?"

Fear clenched the Arab's gut. On one hand if the Mexican Air Force shot down the jet it would save him the trouble, the job would be complete. On the other hand, he would be stuck with seven mad men that he would need to find a way to get rid of.

"No, I was too late but somehow they managed to avoid the fighters. The Air Force is still trying to figure it out. It may have been some type of radar cloaking."

"But you are sure they are returning to Grand Cayman?"

"Almost certain. My sources indicate that the island was their stop off point on their way to Cancun and they were heading back in that direction when they dropped off the radar."

"I will call you when it is finished."

"I would appreciate that my friend," the intelligence agent sounded uneasy. "Jimenez grows...impatient."

"This ends today. You will hear from me soon."

The Arab terminated the call and set the phone down.

In the muffled interior of the garage he could hear his seven charges initiating their prayers. The chants to Allah reverberated off the walls, filling the garage with their religious incantations. The Arab winced, his fingers tracing the thick scar tissue on his forearm. In the Caribbean heat it felt like the scars were tightening up on him. Soon it would be time for more plastic surgery to relieve the pain, his constant reminder of who he had been in a past life.

The Arab packed away his satellite phone and edged around the side of the Toyota van towards the prostrated Muslims.

"It's time."

20

Deckard rubbed his eyes.

They had just touched down in Grand Cayman. It was only noon and it had already been a damn long day.

"We're refueling and taking back off for the States," the pilot announced. "This plane is hot as fuck right now and we need to disappear it, slap on some new paint, and re-register it before using it operationally."

"And us?"

"There is a Learjet coming in from Miami that will pick you up and then fly you back to Oaxaca. They are about ten minutes out. In the meantime you need to find something for your two pals to wear when they transfer aircraft."

"Got it," Deckard said, popping the final DVD out of the laptop computer he had been using. They had played cat and mouse with the Mexican Air Force for another forty five minutes before the fighter jets ran low on fuel and returned to base. Once the CIA pilots had turned off their jammers, Deckard had used the plane's laptop and satellite connection to get onto the internet and connect to one of Cody's remote servers. He had blasted out the contents of the DVDs filling the camera case, uploading the contents of something like seventy discs before they landed on Grand Cayman.

"I'm also being told on our net that there will be an agent on the Lear who will take control of whatever you were supposed to collect in Cancun."

"Sounds good."

Transitioning to Russian, he told the two Kazakhs to stay put while he exited the airplane with the camera bag over his shoulder. The pilots remained in the cockpit while the ground crew for Owen Roberts International Airport refueled the plane.

He smiled at a few of the other private pilots as he walked to the hangar. They were in between flying rich tourists in and out of the Cayman Islands and waiting for their passengers, or on some aircraft maintenance. One of the pilots held open the door for him as he walked into the hangar. Inside, he quickly found a locker room where the airplane mechanics stored their equipment and stole a pair of coveralls and a work bag. Next, he headed into the small break room and opened the camera bag.

Popping open the microwave, he dumped the pile of DVDs inside. Before closing it, he reached into his pocket and threw the CIA issue smart phone in as well. Slapping the door shut he set the timer for ten minutes and punched the start button.

This wasn't his first rodeo.

If he simply turned the blackmail material that he had collected over to the CIA then he would lose all control over it and the Agency might very well claim that they had never heard of it or their deal with Deckard. By turning it over, he would lose any leverage over the Mexican authorities as well as the CIA. No, he would instead dole out the filthy material in bits and pieces, holding it over the Agency's head as well. They probably didn't realize that American politicians would appear on the recordings which gave him even more pull when the time came for a power play. Once he got back to Oaxaca in one piece he would have Cody e-mail approximately a quarter of the recordings to Grant so that he had something to work with when they approached the Mexican government with the information.

Looking through the microwave's window, he watched as the discs begin to melt. With the task complete, he stuffed the coveralls into the bag and walked back outside to the Gulfstream.

"Hey," he said to the two mercs as he climbed aboard and tossed them the bag. "Put these over your uniforms and then pack all of our gear into that big work bag. We're going to switch planes in a minute."

Inside, he grabbed another bottle of water from the refrigerator. It was hot as hell out on the tarmac.

"This is your ride," the pilot said, pointing to a white Learjet taxing towards them.

"Good deal," Deckard said spotting the plane as he looked through the cockpit glass. "Thanks for the ride. I'll take you two as drivers any day."

"Never a dull moment, huh?" the pilot laughed as they shook hands.

"I've been hearing a lot of that lately," Deckard said turning to shake the co-pilots hand.

They had worked well together. Two professionals, they had known exactly what they were doing every step of the way and had pulled his ass out of the fire when he needed it most.

"Until next time," he told them.

"Fuck next time, get the hell off our jet!"

By now the two Samruk mercenaries had donned the coveralls and gotten their gear packed up. The bag was heavy with three plate carriers and three rifles so one of the men hefted it over his shoulder for extra support as they climbed down the stairs.

"This one here," Deckard pointed out the approaching Learjet to his men. The three of them walked across the tarmac to meet it as the plane continued to taxi down the runway towards them. They stopped at the edge of the parking area for private aircraft and waited.

Behind him Deckard heard a crash and turned around in time to see a red Toyota van that had just smashed through the chain link fence surrounding the airfield. The van barreled down the pavement towards the private jet lot at full speed.

"Get those guns out," Deckard ordered the Kazakhs. "Get them out!"

The brakes smoked as the van slowed and rocked on its suspension system. The side door slid open and six men clothed in white from head to toe leapt from inside the van to the tarmac. Without waiting to close the door, the driver gunned it towards the CIA Gulfstream V.

One of the Kazakhs reached into the bag and tossed Deckard his AK-103 rifle. Deckard racked the charging handle, stripping the first bullet from the magazine and chambering it. Bringing the rifle to his shoulder, he aimed down his sights at the red van just as it slammed into the Gulfstream and detonated.

The mercenaries were instantly knocked to the ground as the shock wave washed over them. Having just finished refueling, the wings were full of jet fuel and the airplane went up in a giant fireball that rose and curled into the air before swirling into a cloud of black smoke. The fire on the ground spread across the pavement, pieces of hot metal thrown in every direction. Deckard pushed up to a knee as debris were still falling. The blast had struck him like an invisible sledge hammer to the chest.

Shaking off the over pressure from the explosion, it was the heat of the fire that caused the three men to cover their faces with their hands and backpedal away.

116

Through the wavering blur of the heat mirage coming from the fire and off the tarmac, Deckard spotted one of the men dressed in white running towards him. He could see the tears streaming down the man's eyes, his mouth was open, screaming something that he was unable to hear above the ringing in his ears. The clothing was Islamic and he had something clutched in his right hand. That was enough for Deckard.

Bringing his AK to the ready he shot the man twice through the chest. His target collapsed to the ground and detonated himself. An arm was torn from the body by the blast and sent end over end into the air. A leg went in the opposite direction. Scraps of flesh went everywhere.

Five more suicide bombers rushed across the flight line towards the three mercenaries. They were running at a dead sprint. Now he could make out their words.

"Allah Akbar!" they screamed in unison.

The two Kazakhs finally pulled their rifles out and put them into operation. With three AK's in the fight they began working the opposition from side to side, putting two shots center mass. At this point they were unconcerned with whether or not their bullets detonated the explosives in their suicide vest or not.

One by one they flopped to the ground, two more self-destructing. As hot shrapnel shot over Deckard's head, the Samruk mercenary to his side collapsed to the ground. He had to leave his comrade for a moment while they still had targets rushing their position.

The Kazakh who was still on his feet fired a burst into the final suicide bomber. The 7.62 rounds impacted his shoulder and spun the terrorist to the ground. Sobbing, the terrorist threw his detonator to the ground and put his hands in the air, the arm on the injured side hanging lower than the other. Blood soaked his white tunic as tears continued to poor down his face.

Struggling to his knees the bomber kept his hands as high as he could, attempting to surrender.

"Don't shoot," Deckard ordered. "We can take him-"

Before he could finish his sentence, the surrendering bomber exploded. His head separated from his body as the explosive vest went off and spun through the air. Hitting the tarmac, the head bounced across the pavement like a soccer ball before rolling off into the grass.

Deckard blinked. The threat was no longer a concern so he turned to their casualty. Rolling the Samruk mercenary onto his back, he saw that a piece of shrapnel had penetrated his team mate's skull. Suicide bombers often embedded nails or ball bearings into the explosives they used for increased carnage. The Kazakh's eyes stared up at him, empty. There was nothing he could do for him.

The Learjet was already turning around and preparing to take off. They were not sticking around after what had just happened.

"Go stop them," Deckard told the remaining Kazakh. "Take our bag with you and I'll be right behind you."

Deckard managed to fling the body over his shoulders in a fireman's carry. Holding onto an arm and leg with one hand, he carried his AK in the other, chasing after their only chance at a ride out of the hell zone they had been trapped him.

The Kazakh managed to wave down the pilots as they turned the Learjet around. They opened the door and helped Deckard load the corpse on board. Once inside they got the door closed and prepared for takeoff. The fire was still burning fiercely behind them. They had lost two CIA pilots and one mercenary in the surprise attack.

Deckard's mind raced. None of it made sense.

An agent in khakis and polo shirt came forward while Deckard was still catching his breath.

"Where is the package?"

The Learjet lurched forward, causing everyone to hold on to something while they blasted down the runway and lifted off.

"Where is the intel you collected," the agent repeated once they got airborne.

"Destroyed," Deckard answered.

"What do you mean it was destroyed?" the agent asked as he went red in the face.

Deckard pointed out one of the windows to the fire raging back at the airport.

"Destroyed in the explosion."

21

The sun was dropping below the horizon as Deckard and his partner carried their fallen team mate to the waiting deuce and a half truck. The Learjet immediately took off and left them behind, the agent on board furious with Deckard and half suspecting that he was playing a game of his own.

He was still turning the events over his hid mind, replaying them again and again. The presence of Jihadi suicide bombers was bizarre to say the least and the timing of the attack was incredible. Once they got the body loaded, Deckard stood there thinking about it some more. They had Oaxaca airport more or less under their control for the time being.

The bombers had been the hardcore Islamic extremists that you find in Afghanistan, Iraq, or Palestine. The kind of crazies you expect from the Wahhabi sect originating in Saudi Arabia. He had come across those types before, but on a resort island like Grand Cayman? Somebody transported them there and managed the logistics. More importantly, someone had steered the kamikaze attack directly to the CIA black flight at exactly the right time. The enemy knew precisely where and when to strike. How could their Operational Security have been breached so thoroughly?

Then there was the final nail in the figurative coffin. The last bomber had tried to surrender only to have his suicide vest go off after he discarded the detonator. The terrorist cell leader had to have been in an overwatch position somewhere nearby. The s-vests must have been dual primed, a second detonator rigged with a remote control as an insurance policy against any of the bombers falling into the hands of law enforcement. Someone watching the airfield saw the bomber try to give himself up and detonated the explosive vest remotely.

"Hey, you okay?"

Deckard looked up and saw one of the Samruk men hanging out the driver's side window.

"We've got two missions about to kick off simultaneously. They need you back in the OPCEN."

Deckard turned and climbed aboard the truck. With a puff of black smoke from the exhaust pipe they left the airport. It was a quick drive to the Samruk compound. Jumping out of the back of the truck, he walked into the OPCEN where Cody and Frank sat quietly, monitoring several ongoing operations.

The projector was in standby, a blue rectangle was the only image being projected on the wall.

"The Agency just cut our ISR feed," Frank said without looking up from his computer. "You did something to piss them off."

"Cody?"

"Yeah?"

"When I uploaded those videos to your server I also dumped the contents of the smart phone. You'll find the e-mail for a Case Officer named Grant. I want you to mail him about twenty five percent of the videos I uploaded."

Cody's hands flew across the keyboard.

"It is sending now," Cody said as they watched the green bar on the computer screen move as it uploaded the MPEG files. "Ok, it has been sent."

"What is going on here?"

"A lot since you've been gone," Frank answered. "We got word through interrogations of how Jimenez has nearly a hundred men down in Guatemala conducting para-military training. He has recalled them and they will be leaving tomorrow morning."

"We have to ambush them before they get here," Deckard said. "If they arrive in Oaxaca they will go underground and fight an unconventional war."

"That's what we've been working on. I've been in touch with the Agency since you took off on whatever errand they had you run. The Guatemalans have had enough with the cartels so their military was more than happy to provide an aircraft. The real trouble was locating the camp."

"They should be about five minutes out," Cody announced.

"We can't know for certain until this fucking ISR feed gets unscrambled," Frank said irritably.

"So the Guatemalan military provided an aircraft for us to use and gave up the location of the camp?"

"No, it is somewhere in the highlands not far across the border. That area is facing its own cartel insurgency and the government forces don't have much of presence there. I looked over the antenna array you brought back from that objective before you left and figured out how it worked. Cody and I were able to back trace their signals part way into Guatemala as it skipped across cell phone towers. At some point it hit a repeater station and the frequency was converted into VHF which we were unable to trace."

"And not even the CIA or NSA has the assets in place to track something as antiquated as VHF. Who uses a walkie-talkie these days?" Cody interjected.

"Well, thanks to Al Qaeda playing these games with us in the Middle East we have developed the assets. Now with the war winding down, many of those assets are being shifted to Central and South America, lucky for us."

"How did it go down?"

"As I understand it they flew an F-16 from a carrier to Galeta Island and then on to the target area that I determined. The fighter was outfitted with a Liberty Blue SIGINT collection package that allowed us to determine where the VHF signals were terminating. I would compliment you Deck, you really forged an alliance with Uncle Sugar instead of burning bridges like you usually do. They came through for us, but then," Frank pointed to the blank projection on the wall, "you went ahead and fucked it all up."

"OP-1 just called in the airfield as being clear," Cody announced. "I'm going to radio the Dakota and give them the green light."

"Wait until they get a load of who is on some of those videos with underage kids," Deckard frowned. "I think that ISR feed will be coming back up any second now."

"At least we got a location for the camp. It is up in the mountains of Quiche, about fifty klicks south of the Mexican border. We got our boys loaded up in a Guatemalan Air Force Dakota and off the ground just before you got back. They are almost on target. Oh, I almost forgot to tell you. We also borrowed some static line parachutes from the Guatemalan Army."

"The Kazakhs aren't airborne qualified," Deckard choked.

"They will be in about three minutes when Pat kicks them out of the door at five hundred feet," Frank said before spitting brown Copenhagen juice into an empty Styrofoam cup.

Just then the ISR feed kicked back in, some stooge in

Langley having shit his pants when he spotted the House Minority Leader on one of Bashir's videos with a fourteen year old girl and made a desperate phone call to the US Air Force who was flying the drone circling over Guatemala. Deckard had documented evidence against some very powerful people, and that in turn made him a very powerful person.

Deckard's jaw dropped as he watched tiny black forms falling out both doors of the Dakota airplane. Their parachutes were inflating just moments before they collided with the jungle airstrip below them.

Kurt Jager was impressed.

The Zapatistas had been living in the jungle long enough that they knew the terrain and knew how to move in it. The entire mission had been a rush to interdict the cartel para-military soldiers before they could depart the camp and cross back into Mexico. More than once it looked like they had faced obstacles that they would not be able to overcome only to have everything work out at the last moment. Having a certain three letter agency greasing the wheels certainly didn't hurt.

He had not even met Commandente Zero but one of his sub-commanders when he requested two Zaptista rebels to take along with him and Pascal, one of the former 7th Special Forces Group Sergeants that Deckard had contracted. They had a half assed comms system but it worked. Kurt had just crept into their Observation Post and got eyes on the objective area. He got on his MBITR radio and called the all clear to the Mission Support Site. The airstrip was empty and quiet. The MSS consisted of Pascal and the other Zapatista who used a SATCOM radio to communicate with their compound back in Oaxaca.

The mission had been green lit.

UAVs could do a lot of reconnaissance work, but nothing beat having actual recce operators getting eyes on the objective.

Kurt Jager and Gomez, his Zapatista partner lay on their

bellies in the thick growth next to the airfield trying to ignore the mosquitoes buzzing in their ears.

They didn't have to wait long. In minutes the Dakota was roaring overhead, coming in low and a slow on a heading parallel with the muddy jungle airstrip.

Pat stepped out into the darkness, the scorching hot exhaust from the airplane and smell of burning fuel stinging his eyes for a nano-second before gravity whipped him down and away. His T-10Charlie parachute was snapped into a static line running the length of the inside of the Dakota aircraft so that when the line was extended, it caught and yanked his parachute out as he fell.

As the round parachute deployed, the straps dug tight into his thighs and shoulders. Rocking from side to side by the suspension lines, he reached down and released his assault pack, lowering it on a nylon line below him. The former Delta Force operator couldn't see the ground through the darkness but he wasn't taking any chances, he had a bad experience jumping from an airplane not all that long ago.

Everything was quiet for one single moment as he drifted down through the night. Hearing his assault pack make contact with the ground, he prepared to land by pulling an overhand slip and tugging down on the main lift webbing of the parachute. Keeping his feet and knees together, Pat rolled to the side as his boots hit the ground.

Laying in the dirt, he breathed a sigh of relief as the parachute deflated around him.

As jumpmaster, had been the last out of the aircraft and was now able to see that they had successfully landed on the jungle airstrip. The surrounding terrain was rough mountain highlands and would have been a death warrant had they drifted off the drop zone.

Moving with urgency, he quickly shrugged out of the

parachute harness. He had to establish a Control Point with Sergeant Major Korgan while the assault elements had to move out to their objectives. They were only a platoon strong and needed as much of an element of surprise as they could get. Cartel guards were probably already waking up the rest of the camp.

Pat reached into his M-1950 canvas gun case and secured his Kalashnikov and then grabbed his assault pack. He wore his chest rig with additional magazines for the rifle under his parachute rigging for the jump so he would have it close by when he needed it. The Kazakhs were coming off the runway, some of the them limping, a couple were being carried by their buddies.

Their first parachute insertion had taken place after only a few hours of instruction and then they were jumping out of a plane at only five hundred feet and at night. They knew that they would take a few casualties on the drop but it was a calculated risk. They could treat a few broken ankles and use the injured for static security when they got back to the compound. It all had to be weighed against the casualties that they would take if the 100-man para-military force engaged them in direct combat, on their terms, and with the home field advantage in Mexico.

Better to sort these fuckers out here and now, Pat thought to himself.

Gunfire was already breaking out, the odd green colored tracer round soaring through the night sky when Pat got his long whip antenna up and broke squelch.

"OP-One this is Alpha-One," he said into the hand mic.

"This is OP-One," Kurt Jager's voice came over the command net.

"Our boys are hitting their RV and will be moving out shortly. Are there any complications we should know about?"

"Just one," Kurt said from his Observation Point somewhere nearby. "We have spotted the ingress route to the camp. It isn't wide enough to get vehicles up but looks like a footpath."

Pat was the Ground Force Commander and ultimately in charge of the entire mission with Deckard out of the picture.

"We are already light on personnel after the jump," Pat told him. "Can your element break down the OP and lay in an ambush along the trail?"

"Give us a couple minutes. We'll link up with our MSS and get it done."

"Good copy. Alpha-One out."

Reaching down, he turned a knob on the radio in his assault pack to change to the channel over to the assault net.

"Zulu-One this is Alpha-One."

A burst of static came over the net.

"Alpha-One, this is Zulu-One."

It was Sergeant Fedorchenko, the platoon Sergeant who would actually be leading the assault on the nearby training camp."

"Are you a Min-Force with men, weapons, and equipment?"

Minimum Force was the minimum number of personnel that they had determined in planning would be needed to destroy the camp. Pat suspected they had already lost a few to injuries during the jump.

"Yes, we are up," Fedorchenko said. He spoke in heavily accented English, but his voice had plenty of enthusiasm in it.

"You are cleared hot to take the primary objective."

"Roger, out."

Technically, Pat was the one that should be saying *out* since he initiated the conversation but he had better things to worry about. Just then, Sergeant Major Korgan shuffled up to his position with a Samruk trooper slung over his shoulder.

"Three men with foot and leg injuries," Korgan reported. "None of them are able to walk."

Pat checked three men off in his head.

"Let's get the other two pulled over here and they can pull security."

Corporal Abykeyev led his element forward. He guided the squad through the camp's one hundred meter flat range and then passed their obstacle course where various high beams and monkey bars had been arranged for physical training. The Kazakh mercenary had committed the layout of the camp to memory after studying the overhead photography he had been given during their hasty planning session.

The Corporal was a veteran of The Lions, called Arystan in his native language, they were Kazakhstan's elite commando force. When Samruk International opened for business in Astana he was among the initial recruits. Since that time he had seen action with the Private Military Company working as a mercenary in Afghanistan, Burma, Mexico, and now Guatemala. He could also add a combat jump to his list of professional accomplishments. In just a few months he had seen more action than he had during nearly a decade of service in the military. The Corporal was unmarried and had no family to speak of. Soldiering was what he did, it was what he was good at and he had no interest in any other profession.

He was now the senior Squad Leader in Fedorchenko's platoon, in charge of Weapons Squad. In addition to the four countries they had fought in, there was another mission that none of them talked about. They were the survivors and had no desire to relive the operation that had nearly killed them to a man. Samruk had been a battalion sized unit. Now they were just a couple platoons. However, the unit had absorbed many different weapons, recovered from dead enemies during that mission such as the three Mk48 machine guns he had in Weapons Squad.

There was a large berm line at the edge of the shooting range that was supposed to stop bullets during training. It was the last covered and concealed position before they spotted the actual living area and planning bays that the para-militaries used for class rooms.

Using hand and arm signals, he got his squad on line with each other, the three machine gunners distributed evenly down the line. To the left of each gunner were the assistant gunner and an ammunition bearer.

Signaling forward, the squad moved as one over the berm to establish a Support By Fire line.

Sergeant Fedorchenko had his three rifle squads moving in their own assault line as they crept towards the camp from a different angle than the Weapons Squad with their machine guns. They had heard a few pop shots since the Dakota blasted over the runway to drop them off. Those shots were just warnings from guards posted somewhere else in the area to alert the camp.

The first effective fire they took came as the assaulters rose over a hill and came into view of the large tents and cadre huts. There were five large military tents in a semi-circle that could fit about twenty men in each. Three large huts made out of plywood served as hootches for the instructors and probably supply sheds for additional weapons and training ammunition.

Flashes lit up the camp ahead of them like miniature firecrackers, popping off left and right. The mercenaries hit the ground as the enemy gunfire kicked up dirt to their front, other shots cracking over their heads. With a skirmish line of twenty four riflemen, they immediately returned fire.

Suddenly, the entire camp lit up with muzzle flashes, gunfire searching through the night.

Fedorchenko was about to order his men to bound forward when the Support By Fire line opened up. Three 7.62 Mk48 machine guns went cyclic, chewing through four hundred round metal link belts of ammunition in seconds. The machine gunners directed their fire into the camp and traversed from side to side to rake the enemy positions.

"First Squad!" the Platoon Sergeant yelled. "Bound!"

While second and third squad continued to fire at suspected enemy positions, First Squad picked up and each man rushed forward for several seconds before dropping back down to prone.

"Second Squad, bound!"

Second Squad replicated the maneuver, moving up alongside First Squad. Meanwhile, Weapons Squad was drenching the cartel base camp with hot lead, pouring into the tents and huts. Without warning, one of the huts exploded in a brilliant flash. Several cartel men jumped up from their firing position with their backs lit on fire. They flailed around in a panic like giant human torches for a few seconds before the Samruk mercenaries made short work of them.

From the much smaller secondary explosions, Fedorchenko had his suspicions confirmed. They were storing ammunition inside.

"Third Squad, bound!"

The Platoon Sergeant moved with Third Squad, hanging to the rear where he could best see and direct his platoon.

Fedorchenko continued to bound his men up squad by squad. Cordite hung heavy in the air, the disgusting sweet smell of gun powder seeping into their sinuses while sweat streaked down their faces. They were almost ready to clear over the camp itself when all hell broke loose.

The flash from each shot was bright enough that it lit up the trees around the camp around the machine gun nest. The .50 caliber M2HB hammered into the assault line as Second Squad was bounding up to the camp. Fedorchenko watched helplessly as one of his men had his head taken clean off by the heavy machine gun.

The sneaky bastard had kept the gun quiet, waiting until the mercenaries were right on top of them before firing where it would be like shooting fish in a barrel. The .50 caliber rounds chewed up the assault line. All three Mk48s back at the Support By Fire line fixated on the enemy machine gunner, their triple stream of fire sweeping across the wall of sandbags around the gun.

One of the mercenaries hurled a fragmentation grenade. It landed on the wall of sandbags and exploded, shredding the fortification but the .50 cal kept shooting. Finally, the Mk48 gunners walked their automatic gunfire over the enemy position one final time and the heavy caliber gun went silent.

"Get on line!" the Platoon Sergeant ordered.

Some of the men needed a quick boot in the ass to get

them back up and moving again after the onslaught. Squad Leaders enthusiastically provided one. They needed to secure the objective fast, before the enemy could mount a counter-attack to repel the mercenaries. Reaching into a pouch in his plate carrier, Fedorchenko palmed a pen flare gun and thumbed down the spring loaded trigger before firing a single red flare into the sky. It was the signal to the Support By Fire line to shift off the objective to prevent friendly fire.

The assault line got to their feet in one single element and all three squads crossed through the camp with their rifles pointed forward. What they discovered there was a massacre of death and mayhem. Bodies were strewn across the ground in whichever undignified position they had fallen. There were dozens of them, some with neat and tidy holes in their chest, but most had been machine gunned into ground beef.

Sergeant Fedorchenko halted the assault line so that smaller, four man elements could clear each tent and the two remaining huts. A single shot sounded in the night. The teams reported back that they had found one of the para-military trainees attempting to hide under a bed. They'd shot and killed him when they saw a pistol in his hand. The other structures in the camp were declared clear of any living enemy presence.

Barking at his men, the Squad Leaders pushed the assault line forward until their Platoon Sergeant declared that they had reached the Limit Of Advance, an imaginary line just past the objective and out of hand grenade range. From there the Squad Leaders began to inspect their men and Fedorchenko began calling forward men who had been prearranged into special teams. The Aid and Litter team came forward to treat friendly casualties.

They had to backtrack to where the .50 cal had opened up on them. As the Platoon Sergeant had suspected, all three were KIA. Each .50 caliber bullet was about the size of a human finger, if you got hit with one of those you probably were not going to survive. The bodies were collected in one place to be taken off the objective when the platoon moved out.

Next, the search teams were called forward. The Kazakhs worked in two man teams to search the enemy dead. One would provide security while the other carefully lifted the body to check and make sure that they had not pulled the pin on a hand grenade and left it under their body with the spoon depressed. It was a grisly business. The mercenaries had to hold their noses in many cases. If the cartel member had a jumper in the door when he was killed, he would shit his pants as his muscles relaxed. With this task completed they would search through pockets and pouches. It went fast since many were only half dressed, Samruk's unexpected airborne jump having woken them from their sleep.

The tents and huts were also searched over, although no one could even get close to the ammo dump which was still crackling with pops as ammunition cooked off in the fire. The scorched human bodies created by the explosion were left in place.

Maxim, one of the Squad Leaders approached Fedorchenko.

"We have three killed but are otherwise up on men, weapons, and equipment," he reported. "But we can hear some of the enemy who tried to escape. They are hidden in the brush and we can hear some of them groaning and struggling to breathe."

"Very well," the Platoon Sergeant replied. "I will stay here and prep the demolition. Take the assault line forward of the LOA and secure prisoners if possible."

Fedorchenko went into his assault pack, pawing through the C4 explosives he had brought along for the task, his mind already thinking about the best way to destroy what was left of the training camp when gunfire broke out behind him.

"That can't be good," Deckard said looking at the Predator UAV feed projected in their Operations Center.

The circling UAV captured the scene below in gray and black thermal vision. They had watched the assault on the camp nearly stall for a moment before Fedorchenko pulled the men together and got them moving again.

On the opposite side of the flat range, they could see ten

heat signatures running along a path through the bush and up to the range itself. From there the cartel gunmen would be behind the actual assault element. Who knew how many friendlies they would be able to take out before the platoon could re-orient itself, displace the Mk48 machine guns to a new firing position, and assault through the new enemy force.

Deckard had no doubt that they could and would do it, but taken by surprise like that, he might have a single squad coming home rather than a platoon.

The cartel men must have been stationed down below the hills as look outs along one of the major roads so they could warn the base camp of any Guatemalan military presence. They had not expected a combat jump on their compound and now the gunmen were rushing back to reinforce a camp that they didn't realize was already wiped out. If they did, they probably would have beat feet all the way back to Mexico and called it a day.

Suddenly, the reinforcements stopped in their tracks. Through the thermal camera on the UAV, Deckard could see specs of black flying off the human forms. It was a black hot camera, which meant everything in black was something hot. It picked up on the infrared light given off by human body heat. What this meant in practical terms was that Deckard was watching small bits of flesh being stripped off one gunmen's body as they were ambushed.

"Looks like Kurt has it under control," Frank said, spitting another wad of dip into his cup.

The Zapatista's didn't lack anything in courage, but Kurt knew from previous experience that their marksmanship left much to be desired. This was why he watched in shock as one of the cartel gunmen spun around in a macabre dance of death as Gomez launched a fully automatic stream of gunfire from his AK-47 into their adversary.

Kurt Jager zeroed in, taking single precise shots that dropped the cartel men one by one. Bullets sliced through the foliage above his head as one gunman attempted to return fire.

Thinking quickly, Kurt had his four man element occupy an ambush site once he had found an elbow in the trail leading to the airfield. He and Gomez lay in the prone looking down the long axis of the trail while Pascal and his Mexican counterpart occupied the short end. The result was a deadly L-shaped ambush. The two Zapatistas were instructed to fire on full auto in order to keep the enemy's heads down more than to effectively engage. This would be done by the two former Special Operations soldiers who would shoot with their rifles on semi-automatic.

The tree that the German had taken cover behind provided more concealment than cover as it was so thin, but it was all that was available and even that was being shredded. It was a frantic several seconds of both parties yanking on triggers and searching for targets. The Mexicans were shooting at muzzle flashes in the night, if they even had the chance to fire at all. The joint mercenary and Zapatista force fired on one gunman after the next until nobody was left standing.

Kurt breathed a sigh of relief.

They had gotten lucky.

Very lucky.

"Contact rear," Fedorchenko said keying up his radio.

"That's a friendly Blocking Position," Pat announced over the net. "Wait one."

The Kazakh listened to the onslaught behind him, wondering what was going on until their commander got back on the assault net.

"You're clear Zulu-One. The threat has been eliminated. Continue with the mission and give me a one minute warning before you initiate any demo."

"Roger Alpha-One."

Documents, laptop computers, cellular phones, and

anything else that could yield any kind of intelligence value had been rounded up by the Samruk mercenaries and put into several kitbags to be transported back to Oaxaca.

As would the prisoner they had captured.

The assault squads had finished their sweep out behind the objective where perhaps another dozen bodies had been found. They had been attempting to escape the camp when the bullets of the Mk48 gunners chased them through the trees, creating a wall of lead that they ran right into. One of those that had survived was expectant, he would not live much longer with bullet wounds through both legs and his stomach. He was dully relieved of his misery with a single mercy shot.

Another had very serious extremity wounds through his lower leg, and a second that had nearly amputated his forearm. Using tourniquets, the Kazakhs got the bleeding under control and the platoon medic administered some pain killers. He was their trophy and they weren't going to let him die on them now.

Several blood trails had been discovered leading away from the kill zone, a few lucky ones who had escaped the camp but the amount of blood they had left behind cast serious doubt on how much longer they had to live. They would probably try to hide in the bush until dawn, quietly bleeding out until they succumbed to their wounds. At any rate, the mercenaries didn't have the time to follow up with a tracker team and were not interested. Whomever made it out of the camp would not be returning to Mexico to give them a hard time, that much was certain.

"Alpha-One this is Zulu-One."

"Go ahead Zulu."

"One minute."

The mercenaries carried their dead, kit bags full of confiscated material and their prisoner off the objective with Corporal Maxim leading them back to the airfield. Corporal Abykeyev would remain in place with his weapons squad until Fedorchenko left as the last man off the objective.

Twisting the pin on his fuse igniter, he initiated the time fuse before putting his nose down and smelling it. In the dark it was sometimes hard to see if it was actually burning or not.

"Burning," he announced into the radio.

All weapons and equipment found on the objective had been shoved into one of the cadre huts where they had strung out of ring main of detonation chord with five bricks of C4 plastic explosives tied into it.

Turning, Fedorchenko ran to catch up with his platoon.

Corporal Abykeyev watched with a smile as the gunner's faces were revealed for a second by the explosion that tore apart a second cadre hut.

They had burned through almost their entire supply of machine gun ammunition and each gun team had jumped with five hundred rounds distributed between them. With about one hundred rounds left per gun that meant that they had riddled the kill zone with 1,200 rounds of 7.62 ammunition.

With their task completed, he pulled one gun at a time off the Support By Fire line in case of the unlikely event that any more bad guys decided to show up. Once he pulled everyone back they got back into a squad wedge formation and went to meet up with the rest of their platoon at their rendezvous point back on the airfield.

Pat was kneeling, listening to his hand mic, when the platoon came humping back to meet up at their rendezvous which was conveniently co-located with his Control Point.

Their dead were laid down next to the CP, their weapons and equipment secured for transport back to Mexico. The former Delta operator looked down at the three men, one of whom was headless. They did not have any body bags and the frank reality of war simply would not disappear. The bodies were mangled, twisted forms of what had been living men just moments ago. There was no hidden message or soul shaking epiphany to be found in the corpses of the dead as found in Hollywood films. There was only an unshakable finality to be found that, as unsettling as it was, could not be undone.

"Fedorchenko?"

"Right here," said a Russian accented voice from behind Pat.

"Detach two men to Sergeant Major Korgan to go and link up with our recce element then have the rest of your men start balling up and clearing parachutes off the runway. The Dakota has refueled and is already back in the air."

"I understand."

"Fedorchenko?"

"Yes?"

"Make sure your men knew they did good work out here tonight."

"I will."

As the Ground Force Commander, Pat had to be thinking several steps ahead. For instance, he had to set the conditions for Samruk to make a successful exfiltration from their area of operations. Sergeant Major Korgan would conduct his link up with Kurt Jager's recce element and then escort them to the Control Point to avoid any blue on blue incidents. If a couple Zapatistas carrying guns walked up on the airfield, there was a very high probability that one of the Kazakhs would shoot them dead, mistaking them for enemy combatants.

The rest of the Kazakhs slung their weapons and began recovering parachutes off the runway. They would have to be secured and bagged up in a black garbage bags that each troop had been handed before the jump. If even one parachute was unaccounted for, it could get sucked up into the Dakota's turbine upon landing, cripple the airplane, and leave them stranded in Guatemala. Once Fedorchenko gave him an up on getting the parachutes secured, Pat bumped up to the air net to talk to the pilot and instructed him that he was clear to land.

With the whine of the Dakota's engines buzzing through the night air somewhere off in the distance, Sergeant Major Korgan returned with the four-man reconnaissance element. Their lack of translators or any bilingual Spanish to English capability prevented them from interrogating the single prisoner that the Samruk mercenaries had captured. With Kurt and Pascal joined up, they could now engage in some tactical questioning

135

while they waited for the Dakota to land.

"Kurt," Pat said to the former GSG-9 operative. "See what you can get out of our prisoner."

Kurt and Pascal knelt down next to the prisoner. He was hanging his head, partially in shame, partially in shock from his injuries. Even on painkillers, he was pretty tore up.

"What's that?" Kurt asked.

There was a white plastic stick between his lips.

"Fentanyl lollipop," Pascal answered. "The medic hooked him up with some good shit."

"You must be kidding," the German said frowning.

"Not at all. We used them in Special Forces when one of ours or civilians would get injured. It helps keep the casualty calm and relaxed."

"It's going to be hard to talk to this guy when he's high on opiates."

"Wake up," Pascal barked at the prisoner in Spanish.

The prisoner's head shot up, his eyes wide and blood shot.

"We need to talk," Kurt told him as the Dakota came sweeping in over the rugged highlands.

"He says he was with the Kaibiles, Guatemalan Special Forces. He told us that he defected from the military last year when the Jimenez cartel established their training camp and offered significantly higher pay. He trained the cartel men in small unit tactics, urban warfare, and light and heavy weapons."

Deckard crossed him arms in front of him while he listened to Pat send up his Situation Report. There were numerous news reports of the Kaibiles soldiers running rogue and working for the cartels so none of it surprised him much until Pat got to the end of his report.

"The prisoner is also telling us that they were waiting for an explosives expert to arrive tomorrow so that they can begin learning how to construct IED's. The cartel is very interested roadside bombs apparently."

Leaning forward, he and Frank listened closely. This was what they had been afraid of.

"This guy doesn't know the trainer's name, only that he is a specialist being brought on for the job. They called him, The Arab."

Everything was quiet in the OPCEN. Deckard has suspected for a long time that insurgents, terrorists, and criminals across the world were sharing information and working together on a much more profound level than most people suspected. Part of it was a side effect of the inevitable spread of communication technology but he had a wakeup call many years ago in Iraq.

It had been early on in the insurgency but the Special Operations community was noticing that the Iraqi insurgent's IEDs were getting increasingly sophisticated. They were learning and evolving in leaps and bounds. The improvised bombs would be concealed in the road and painted over. Some would be detonated by cell phones so the coalition forces started using frequency jammers. It wasn't long before the insurgents were making bombs that detonated when a constant transmission had its frequency jammed as an American convoy came down the road.

Deckard and his team were given the task of hunting down and eliminating the IED training cell responsible for developing the technology and techniques involved. To their surprise, the men they were hunting down turned out to be former Irish Republic Army bombers who had gone freelance. Before Iraq, they had worked with FARC in Colombia and Hezbollah in Lebanon.

All the villains in Gotham city were ganging up on Team America.

For Deckard, it was no longer a question of whether or not these links between so-called non-state actors existed, he had seen it for himself. The real question was whether or not they were facing a global insurgency. Rather than isolated regional conflicts in Mexico, Iraq, Nigeria, the Philippines, Burma, Afghanistan, and elsewhere, perhaps they were all the same conflict. Was it possible that all of these rebel movements were responding to the same economic and social inputs? The notion of the state was becoming increasingly obsolete with people losing faith in their own governmental institutions.

From Mexican drug cartels to Islamic groups like Hezbollah, their goals were not to take over and stage a revolution, rather they wanted to carve out their own version of economic free zones where they could pursue their own criminal activities. In some cases, groups like Hezbollah or even the Japanese Yakuza crime gangs often provided better social services than the government.

But Mexico was something different. It was a post-political conflict, a violent non-religious jihad for the sake of commercial business interests where the players were often contractors who didn't even know who their boss was much less have some kind of unified ideology. Unlike the Islamic extremists, the Mexican cartel wars lacked even a misguided cause to fight for, there was not much else but cold hard cash.

"Six, I have to break down the TOC. Our ride just touched down."

"Roger that Alpha-One," Deckard said into the microphone on Cody's desk.

"Six out."

22

Cody's computer pinged as a new e-mail landed in his inbox. The computer technician's hands breezed across the keyboard, pulling up the message. It was from Grant, the CIA's Oaxaca man. He only offered a phone number and the words, *call me*.

Deckard was watching the UAV feed as the mercenaries packed onto the airplane, taking their dead and wounded with them. Of course the prisoner was being given free airfare as was Kurt Jager's recon element.

"HEY, THAT GRANT FUCKER WANTS YOU TO CALL."

Deckard almost jumped out of his seat. Sometimes Cody could be smooth like sandpaper. He would have shitcanned the computer expert but his work was wired so tight that they would have to put up with the abrasiveness. He took the mobile phone that Cody handed him and started punching in the number displayed on the computer screen. Deckard wasn't exactly a pussycat himself so maybe he didn't have much ground to stand on with Cody to begin with.

"Oh, shit. What does Emperor Palpatine want," Frank said sarcastically.

Deckard hit send and held the phone to his ear.

On the projector screen, he watched the Dakota lift off and turn north. The Predator UAV tracked the aircraft for another few seconds and then peeled off, heading back to whatever covert drone base the CIA flew it out of in Central America.

Grant picked up on the third ring.

"What happened to the smart phone I gave you?" he asked immediately.

"Had a bit of an accident along with your DVD's."

"Did it?"

"Lucky I had them backed up while we were still in the air just in case those Mexican F-5s shot us down. Even without me, the mission could then continue, thank god."

"Stop being a smart ass. We lost two pilots in the last twenty four hours, those guys were legends back here at Langley."

"You are not the only one that has lost people."

"No shit. Well, then you understand why this is personal for us now. That attack in the Caymans has everyone shitting bricks back here. That came out of nowhere and now everyone is running around trying to plug leaks that may or may not exist. No one is blaming you, not yet."

"You better keep it that way Grant. We were clearly the targets. Your pilots were collateral damage, it isn't something I'm proud of. I'm responsible for this, but not in that way."

"We know that Deckard. Just understand that everyone is on a razors edge right now and it doesn't help that it looks like Mexico is finally going to implode sometime in the next couple of weeks. We've got low-vis JSOC and DEA elements guiding the war way up north of you against the cartels but we just had another Mexican Infantry unit defect to the other side."

"We can discuss my rates after I mop up this mess in Oaxaca."

"I heard what your man was saying over the radio net."

"Using the Pred to listen in on us, huh?"

"Don't act surprised. We have a jihadist suicide attack in Grand Cayman and then hours later we find out about an Arab bomb maker coming to train cartel gunmen in Guatemala. I don't believe in coincidences."

"I was thinking along the same lines."

"We want that prisoner, especially if he can get us to The Arab."

"How about that thing you were supposed to do for me after I sorted out Bashir," Deckard interjected. "How is that coming along?"

"It is already done. We showed those videos to select members of the PRI and PND political parties in Mexico City. You've got six or seven days. After that the political pressure on both sides of the border will overwhelm those assets altogether and you will be on your own. They will divert military forces down to Oaxaca at that point. Obviously, it would behoove you to be gone before that happens."

"You can have the prisoner. We don't have any use for him, he leads us nowhere in our fight against the Jimenez cartel."

"I'll be in touch."

Deckard hung up.

140

23

Arturo huffed up the stairs, far more winded than a man his age should have been. To many nights meeting with contacts in smoke filled bars and strip clubs had resulted in his health declining over the last several years. He had been in peak physical condition when he had first joined Mexico's Center for Research and National Security, or CISEN.

Arriving at the top floor of the warehouse he punched in his pass code and passed through the door and into his offices.

Inside was his staff of three additional CISEN employees. They were shuffling around the office preparing reports and analysis to be forwarded up to Mexico City. The covert CISEN office included two full time analysts and one intelligence officer in addition to Arturo. They were responsible for keeping tabs on Oaxaca and acting as the federal government's eyes and ears. The bosses were not so interested in cartel activity but wanted a heads up if the Zapatistas movement ever started acting up again.

In the meantime, they could collect information on the Zapatistas to be ready for the moment when the government had the political will to send the Army back in and crush them once and for all.

The intelligence agent sat behind his desk and wiped his sweaty palms on his pants. It was a job, or at least it had been. It didn't pay that well but the fringe benefits were outstanding. It was an open secret at CISEN that the field agents were well compensated for staying out of the way of the cartels.

Since showing up in Oaxaca, he had developed a cordial relationship with Jimenez and Ortega. A few times he even acted as a source for back channel communications between the two cartels when it looked like they might have gone to war with each other. Arturo had helped keep the peace, and the tourist dollars continued to pour into Oaxaca.

Until now.

He resisted the temptation to reach for the bottle of whiskey he kept in his desk. He'd been buzzed for days and was now taking uppers just to be able to continue to function.

Both chiefs up at CISEN and the Jimenez cartel were locking his balls in a vise. They wanted to know what the hell was going on and they wanted to know yesterday.

Swallowing, he reached for his cell phone and dialed one of his American contacts.

"Are you in your office?" the voice on the other end of the line asked.

"Yes."

"I found some of the information you wanted about your mercenary problem."

"Who are they?" Arturo asked, completely exasperated.

Jimenez was going to kill him if he didn't start getting results. He listening intently as the voice began to talk about the gringo mercenary force that had arrived in Oaxaca.

"Deckard?" Arturo spat. "What is his first name?"

The voice continued.

"I see. How did they manage to pull that off?"

The sweat was beading on his forehead again.

"And in Kazakhstan? That doesn't make sense. Who are these guys really?"

The voice elaborated again. At one point Arturo looked up at the clock on the wall. He could hear the second hand ticking between heartbeats. His guts clenched in knots. Finally, he flung open his desk draw and grabbed for the whiskey. Popping the cap, he took a long swig to calm his stomach.

"NSC is tracking this?"

The voice had to be exaggerating.

"Yes," the American answered.

"Now what?"

"Now what? You know what. Take care of it."

"You're fucking kidding me!"

But Arturo was talking into a dead line. The voice was gone.

The CISEN agent looked down at the bottle of whiskey as the phone slipped from his fingers and bounced off the floor. He felt numb. But not numb enough. He reached for the bottle.

"Gentlemen," he called across the office. "Bring it in, I need to talk to you."

The three intelligence men got up from behind their computers and walked over. Arturo had them working day and night. Everyone had been pulled off their regular assignments monitoring the communist movement, narco-groups, and their own entrepreneurial activities. The mercenary situation had their

142

undivided attention for the last several days. Each of the Mexican CISEN employees looked exhausted.

"I want to thank you for the hard work you've been putting into this matter over the last several days," Arturo said while looking each of them in the eye one by one. He was actually starting to feel a little relieved now that the pressure was off him. They finally had a resolution and would no longer be between the proverbial rock and a hard place.

"This office is being liquidated," he continued. "Unfortunately, the situation between local drug traffickers, our government, and these mercenaries will be not resolved, at least not in the immediate future. For reasons unknown to me our government will not be deploying soldiers to Oaxaca to bring this Private Military Company under control. I can only speculate that someone, somewhere is holding something over the heads of CISEN and maybe the federal government. At any rate, it no longer matters. Our mission in Oaxaca has concluded."

The three veteran intelligence men looked at their boss and then at each other. This was not what they had expected.

"Close out your workstations and return home gentlemen. I will initiate the containment plan when I leave and will contact you with further instructions over the next few days."

His subordinates looked shell shocked.

The entire state of Oaxaca had just been written off by their own government.

"Listen," Arturo lectured. "Don't just stand there looking at me like I've got a dick growing out of my forehead. Close out whatever you were doing and walk."

The intel agents snapped to and returned to log out of their computers and pack up whatever personal belongings they might have laying around. Arturo was feeling good, feeling in charge for the first time in a long time. Taking another shot of whiskey, he lit up a cigarette. One by one his men filed out the door with gym bags or cardboard boxes filled with their things. None of them muttered a single word under their breath as they went out the door.

Arturo stubbed out his cancer stick. He wished them luck, he really did. They would need it too. Each of them was about to become a hunted man.

Getting to his feet, he retrieved the five gallon gas can they kept sealed up in the closet. Unscrewing the lid, he began pouring it around the office, on the desks, on the floor, finally turning it upside down and spilling what was left in the center of the office. He then began opening filing cabinets and dumping their contents in the center of the room. The files would be destroyed anyway, but he needed some kindling for the fire.

When he had finished, Arturo flicked his lighter under a few sheets of paper to begin burning the pile of paperwork. He then returned to his desk and pounded down another few mouthfuls of whiskey. Once again, he was in charge of his own destiny.

The fire was beginning to really take off, burning up the paperwork and crawling up the walls, following the gasoline through the office. Arturo smiled.

Eat it or Jimenez eats you.

Reaching under his jacket, he palmed the Beretta pistol he carried in a shoulder holster, yanked it free, pressed the barrel against the side of his head, and squeezed the trigger.

The gun went bang, the office burned, and Arturo felt nothing.

24

Deckard watched the flatlands roll by, the green fields shooting past while the distant hills seemed slow to keep pace. It was the kind of wide open and rugged terrain that the men from Kazakhstan could relate to. The countryside was beautiful and had been a popular getaway for tourists from all over the world until recently. It was a shame, but with the Mexican military cracking down on the cartels in the northern parts of the country, some of the more violent groups had been pushed south.

Oaxaca had always been a pit stop between Colombia and the United States for drug runners, but now this particular drug corridor was being fought over here rather than in the drug plazas up north were it was increasingly difficult for them to operate under the constant pressure of Mexican troops and American military advisers. The turf battles like the one that Jimenez and Ortega had been fighting was referred to as *heating up the plaza*. Now that battle had shifted with Ortega taken out of the picture. It was a Jimenez cartel versus Deckard Private Military Company brawl.

While Deckard saw it in the context of military science, he knew that in the machismo culture of the cartels that Jimenez would see it as two men squaring off to see who had the bigger balls. Deckard had set the pre-conditions he needed just to get his foot in the door. The battlespace had been prepared first with reconnaissance, then by capturing a foothold with Ortega's compound that they could operate from. Next he had found a way to keep the Mexican government from interfering as a spoiler force and prevented cross border interlopers from jumping into the fray from Guatemala. Jimenez was isolated, but far from finished.

Now the real war would begin. It would be man to man and man for man once they started shooting again.

The three assault trucks reached the coordinates they had selected for a Landing Zone out in the Oaxaca countryside. Fedorchenko's platoon was recovering from their mission the previous night while the other platoon ran the drop off mission. The trucks formed up into a hasty triangle-shaped security perimeter while they waited for the rendezvous time.

Pat pulled the prisoner they had captured during the

airfield seizure off one of the trucks and sat him down on the ground. The prisoner wasn't doing so hot, but they would let the CIA goons worry about that. They just needed him to survive long enough for the hand off. They had pumped him full of IV fluids to get his blood pressure back up so that Samantha could put him through a few hours of interrogation before they departed the base. Since then he had been kept on a steady dose of painkillers.

The former Guatemalan Special Forces soldier hadn't been able to tell them much more about the so-called Arab than he had told them during the tactical interrogation on the airfield. The information was compartmentalized and he only knew that their explosives expert was supposedly en route. With more time and resources, the Samruk men might have been able to stage an ambush for this Arab but those were two things they were in serious lack of when they pulled off the target.

Deckard hoped that the CIA would be able to take what information the prisoner did have, correlate it with other sources of intelligence, and splatter the bomb maker's brains but deep down he wasn't very optimistic. He had a sick feeling that he hadn't heard that last of The Arab.

While they sat and pulled security on the surrounding countryside as they waited, the Kazakhs lit up some cigarettes and shot the shit, breaking each other's balls like soldiers the world over.

Pat should have been recovering with the rest of the Samruk men who had just come off the mission. Being in a leadership position was often even more exhausting than the combat positions. The responsibility and decision making could take a lot out of even a seasoned Special Operations soldier and it showed on his face. He had pulled off the impossible in under twenty four hours by throwing that mission together with Frank and Fedorchenko. However, he had still insisted on accompanying Deckard out to the LZ. He wanted a word.

Deckard could see that on his face as well.

"I need to talk to you."

"What is it Pat?"

"I need you to start acting like you are in charge around here."

"I thought I was."

"So did I until you took off for a vacation to Cancun."

146

"You know the deal. I had to get work done or we would have Mexican Marines all over Oaxaca, Special Forces Brigades surrounding our compound, and GAFE blowing down the front door."

"Bullshit. I got left out there throwing together an airborne operation at the very last moment before those guys were to cross over the border and we came back with three injured and three dead. This organization needs its actual leadership in place for this operation."

"I couldn't send a platoon in to Cancun, it wasn't that kind of deal."

"So what? You needed someone who can conduct low visibility operations? Work clandestinely in denied areas? What the hell was I doing in Afghanistan and Iraq for eight years? You could have sent me to do that job."

"I didn't think of it that way, I felt that it was my responsibility."

"You are not working singleton operations anymore Deck, this is the big league, totally different than a five man Delta assault team or anything else we are used to working with."

"I know."

"So why are you out running around like some Corporal in Ranger Battalion? I heard about that stunt that you pulled when you hit the submarine base. What the hell were you thinking running out there by yourself like that?"

"Someone had to stop the submarine from getting away."

"Who cares about one submarine? What if you got killed, then what would happen to this operation? You need to start thinking about the big picture and stop acting like somebody with a death wish."

"I don't have a death wish, I just want to win."

"Bullshit, everyone here wants to win but we haven't been doing the same stupid shit you have. Frank told me you haven't been the same since that shit went down in the Pacific. We lost a lot of guys out there, I get that but we're going to lose a lot more out here if we are not smart about how we handle this."

"Yeah, I get it."

"We've got our ducks in a row. Now is the time to make sure everything we do is wired tight."

"With a little luck we can close this deal out in a few

days. Wear Jimenez down and corner him."

"Aghassi is working it. Cody has narrowed down the location of a few more repeater systems and the prisoners have given up some information that helps flesh out our target deck."

"Good," Pat said, finishing his sermon. "And thanks."

"For what?"

"For hiring me to do this job."

The sound of rotor blades beating the air thumped, growing closer each second.

"America should thank me," Deckard said. "I'm running a jobs for vets program out here. Although, I'm surprised that I managed to lure you away from Delta."

"Things are changing. Lots of guys getting fired or quitting the unit these days. Delta isn't really the place to be anymore, it's turning into a stepping stone to various commercial interests."

"Like Samruk?"

"We'll see," Pat laughed as the helicopter neared.

The two mercenaries lifted their prisoner to his feet as they spotted the inbound gray colored Eurocopter.

"Most of the Delta dudes I knew are going to work for these guys," Pat pointed to the helicopter. "Big money in CIA contracts but that isn't for me. There are some good dudes doing those contracts but also lot of tools that just want to sit on the base or some cushy safe house end up there too."

"Doesn't sound like that is the life for you."

"Nah," Pat yelled as the helicopter set down fifty meters in front of them. "There are some real dildos shooting designer steroids and banging horrendously ugly Kurdish prostitutes. I like to be at the forefront which is where Delta was, but now the war is winding down and everyone is looking for an exit strategy."

As the Eurocopter touched down it blew out of wave of dust around it that washed over the Samruk mercenaries before the rotors brushed the loose dirt away. The door opened and a muscle bound contractor jumped out wearing a plate carrier and a short barrel M-4 slung over his shoulder. His sleeves were rolled up to display numerous tribal tattoos which almost overshadowed the five hundred dollar Oakley sunglasses he wore.

"Big money, huh?" Deckard egged Pat on but the former

Delta operator just shook his head.

Deckard looked back at the Kazakhs manning the perimeter. With the wars in Afghanistan and Iraq coming to a close many American Special Operations soldiers would end up taking high dollar security contractor jobs. But what about those like Pat, those .0001%'ers who could care less about the money and wanted to go back into combat.

Where were they going to end up after the smoke cleared?

Nikita eased the selector switch on his new Heckler and Koch 417 rifle from safe to fire.

"My contact is right around the corner," Aghassi's voice sounded in the earbud that the sniper wore. "I'm sending him out now."

The sniper settled into position, getting as close to the ground as he could and remaining still. He could hear voices around him, probably just some kids playing. When he was sent out to meet up with Aghassi on short notice, the intelligence handler made it clear that their mission had to be conducted at a certain time and place. Unfortunately, it had to be during daylight and there weren't any better sniper hide positions available so he was left hanging out in the open, watching a string of haciendas from a distance of eight hundred and fifty seven meters according to his laser range finder.

He had been trained by the best, a former South African Recce commando named Piet who Deckard had hired to train all of Samruk International's snipers. Nikita knew how to construct an appropriate hide site by digging in if he had had some time to insert early and construct the hide during periods of darkness. As it was, he'd just have to rely on a few new toys to keep him concealed while the children kicked a soccer ball around right next to him.

One of those news toys had arrived on the pallets that

Deckard had flown in from the United States, a sniper variant of the HK 416 rifle carried by Delta Force, MARSOC, and OGA operators. The 417 was the same design but larger than the 5.56 model as it was chambered for the well tested and seasoned 7.62x51 that snipers utilized on battlefields all over the world. With an accurized 20-inch barrel and twenty round magazine, Nikita would be able to quickly and effectively place semi-automatic fire out to one thousand meters, depending on various mitigating circumstances including but not limited to wind speed, what the target was doing, and even whether or not he had gotten a good nights sleep.

He eyed the target building through the Schmidt & Bender scope mounted on the top rail of the rifle. It was a single story building with a small storage type room built on the roof with cinder blocks atop which sat a basin that collected rainwater. There was one barred window and a single door. A lonely string of barbwire lined the front lip of the roof.

Someone was down the street burning their trash in the middle of the road.

The children continued to bat their soccer ball around right next to Nikita. They were unaware of his presence, at least for the moment.

"It creeps me out how similar the villages and cities in this part of the world look like the kind you find in Iraq," Aghassi said over the radio.

Nikita depressed the small transmit button that was wrapped around his non-firing hand with Velcro to reply.

"I don't know," he said in broken English.

Prior to working for Samruk International, Nikita had like many other of the Kazakhs, been a member of his country's elite commando unit known as Arystan. As a member of Arystan he had conducted operations across the steppes and mountains, and sometimes in the cities of his country fighting Islamic extremists. Most of them were foreign fighters from Uzbekistan, Afghanistan, and elsewhere. Some of them were linked to Al Qaeda. It wasn't until he signed on with the Private Military Company that he began being deployed abroad.

The ranks of Arystan had been composed of some of the bravest men that Nikita had ever known, but in retrospect he had to admit that they were severely lacking in many technical matters. The way Samruk International did things was much

150

more deliberate and much more surgical.

"Heads up, here he comes," the intel man informed Nikita.

"Blue hat?"

"That's him."

Aghassi had been quickly establishing a network of informants in Oaxaca City and the surrounding area. Usually the art of spycraft required years to develop a ring of assets but Aghassi was throwing caution to the wind. They were working in a semi-permissive environment and there was no shortage of people who would talk to him because they had grievances with the cartels. Many of them had lost sons and daughters to the senseless narco-wars they fought. The intelligence man was ignoring normal protocols and making compromises with his personal security in order to quickly move amongst the civilian population and collect information. Having access to Samantha's long time informants did not hurt either.

He had hit a road block with one particular family. The nephew worked in the Jimenez compound up in the mountains as a general contractor. He knew specific details about the inside of the drug lord's fortress that Samruk would find useful. However, no one in the family would get involved with Aghassi out of fear. They had lost several family members to the cartels and didn't want to lose another. There was already a group of Sicarios right down the street from the family that pressured the entire neighborhood.

Aghassi had to cut a deal. He would have the sicarios put out of business in exchange for the information he wanted. They agreed. The nephew would lure the sicarios out of their safe house and then run. Nikita would provide the talent needed to complete the task.

The kid in the blue ball cap strolled right up to the front door and started banging on it. The cartel hitmen were known to be taking their siesta at home this time of day after a long night out on the town. Now the kid was screaming. Aghassi had told him to get the hit men real riled up and tell them that some left over Ortega cartel men were stealing their cars parked outside. Finally, the distraction worked. When the boy saw the Sicarios opening the door, he bolted down the street.

Nikita exhaled, his finger tightening around the trigger.

He waited an additional second for all four men to make

it outside.

The range was already dialed into his scope which would allow him to fire and compensate for the bullet drop caused by gravity. With a four mile crosswind, the sniper knew he would have to hold a half mil into the wind to compensate.

The crosshairs in the Schmidt & Bender scope lined up on the first shirtless gunmen who had exited the house. Shifting his point of aim for his wind hold, he held his sights on his target let the first round fly. The bullet carved a path through the heat mirage rising off the desert sand, leaving a trail of ripples in its wake.

Crimson blossomed on the sicario's chest a moment before he collapsed in the middle of the street. One of his comrades looked over upon hearing him fall and was similarly dropped dead in his tracks by Nikita's follow up shot as he quickly transitioned between targets. The third man dropped to the ground, thinking that someone was firing at them from down the street, not understanding that a sniper had them in his sights. The Kazakh sniper frowned, having to adjust the position of the rifle by aiming down at the pavement in front of the cartel shooter. Going into the prone had been a smart move on the gunman's part as he now presented a smaller target but knowing which direction the gunfire was directed from would have been more useful.

Nikita squeezed the trigger twice firing one shot in succession of the other. The 7.26 Long Range bullets skimmed down into the street and ricocheted off the pavement before penetrating the top of his target's skull.

The last man fired off the pistol in his hand at absolutely nothing in a panic before Nikita drilled him in the chest.

"Targets are down," Nikita announced over the net.

"I got the kid back in the car with me. We are peeling out now."

"I will be at the rendezvous in five."

Throwing his hood off, he sipped on the camelbak straw clipped to his sleeve, gulping water down. As he got to his feet the four children playing soccer stared right through him in amazement. They had frozen the moment they heard the shooting, not fully grasping what was happening. Now they were looking right through a man who had appeared from nowhere. He looked like a disembodied head floating in the air with a large black rifle suspended beneath him.

As one, the children took off running back to their parents.

Nikita kicked the abandoned soccer ball after them but it was ignored. They would come back for it later on once they worked up the courage. Most of them would tell their parents that they just had a close encounter with Dorian Gray.

As a sniper, he was convinced. Both the HK 417 and the new uniform that had come in on the pallet had worked flawlessly. As he knelt back down to police up his expended brass shell casings, a background sensor embedded in the collar of the uniform detected slight changes in light conditions and immediate surroundings. Slowly, the uniform began to shift colors and intensities to blend as closely as possible to current environmental conditions.

The Canadian company that manufactured the technology called it ChromaCamo after the Chromatophore in Chameleons that allow them to change their skin pigment. The uniform was still being looked at by the lazy and bloated US Army acquisition process, but Deckard knew the company's CEO and managed to secure a specially made recce cut of the ChromaCamo for his sniper before the entire project would get bought up and classified by the Special Operations community.

Placing the spent brass in his pocket, Nikita held the 417 at the ready just in case of chance contact and began heading out to the cross roads where he would be picked up by Aghassi.

As he walked, the ChromaCamo uniform continued to alter its color, changing from sand and foliage colors to that of rock and slate as he moved from his firing position and slid down hill towards the road. Back at their compound he had sat down on one of Ortega's imported Italian couches while watching television and a fellow Samruk employee nearly jumped out of his skin when he noticed that Nikita had turned blood red, the uniform matching even unnatural environmental colors.

Reaching the base of the hill, the sniper walked to the side of the road as Aghassi pulled up in his car. The spy almost drove right past him, the camouflage doing its job so well that he almost went unnoticed while standing in the open. Pumping the breaks, the car came to a halt.

Nikita smiled.

They were just getting started.

25

Aghassi was on lead as they climbed up to the high walls that surrounded the Jimenez fortress.

It was actually an old Spanish Colonial fort as he had discovered while milking information about the site from his sources. According to local legend, it was built on top of older Mayan ruins on orders from an insane Spanish General who had been suffering from syphilis. Jimenez as it turned out was just the latest in a long line of blood thirsty maniacs who had occupied the top of the mountain. It seemed to be a tradition.

The climb was up a sheer rock wall while challenging it was not particularly technical in nature. He had been a rock monkey in a past life and made quick work freeclimbing up a crevice in the rock. As he moved up the wall he reached back to the rappelling harness he wore and pulled off pieces of equipment to secure into the cracks in the rock.

They had begun climbing just before midnight and were already several hundred meters up the cliff. Nikita was slowly climbing hand over hand below him. They had approached through the jungle after nightfall, walking as far uphill as possible before beginning their ascent upwards to the fortress. The only way into the compound was by driving up a single lane road carved out into the side of the mountain that was heavily guarded and monitored. At least that was what Jimenez was banking on.

Aghassi was ready to try the back door.

Retracting a spring loaded camming device, the half moon metal discs retracted which allowed him to jam it into the crack in the rock. Once he let go, the discs extended again and held tight to act as an anchor point. Their climbing rope was then secured to the anchor and each climber tied into it just in case they fell. While Nikita had some experience operating in the mountains, this was his first technical climb and he was struggling to grunt his way up the cliff.

While he lacked the finesse of an experienced rock climber, he was making up for it with the raw strength and endurance that one would expect from a professional soldier from Central Asia. The extra kit they carried on their backs probably was not helping matters either but the tools of the trade were necessary.

The cliff face transitioned seamlessly into the stone bricks where the fortress walls began. This was where things began to get tricky. A strain sensitive cable had been strung across the wall half way to the top that, if triggered, would set off an alarm and bring Jimenez' personal guard down on them. All it would take was one guard looking down over the edge of the wall to see the two mercenaries dangling below and it would be like shooting fish in a barrel.

Identifying a route to the top, Aghassi utilized hand holds and foot holds he found in the gaps between the stones that were about as wide as his pinky finger. Those might be considered to be huge by the standards of a professional rock climber but even he was struggling at this point. Sheets of sweat were pouring down his face as he finally got to the cable. Sticking a camming device between two stones he made another anchor point and tied into it to give himself a rest.

He shook his forearms out in an attempt to release some of the lactic acid that had built up in the muscle tissue. While his legs were not strained, his entire upper body was aching. He had a couple minutes before Nikita could muscle his way up into position so he began to prepare some equipment.

Jimenez was a real piece of work. As he had questioned contacts and sources who had been in different parts of the compound, Aghassi was able to put together the basic layout of what it looked like inside and develop an entry corridor for him to utilize. By aggregating all of the information he had collected he was able to discern which security devices had been employed and where they were located. His entry analysis then factored in the defeats for each mechanism and determined the kit he would carry into the objective.

Literally overflowing with narco-dollars, Jimenez had been able to hire some of the finest security specialists in America to fly down and install his alarm systems and help him develop a physical security plan. As it turned out, he also kept several IT technicians on hand to monitor the various systems he had installed in the compound. If Aghassi was able to figure out specifically which American security firm had been hired for the job he would be sure to drop dime on them to the FBI when he got back to the States. As it was, this was going to be the most dicey, surreptitious entry he had ever conducted.

When he did his risk analysis he figured that it would be worth it, even if success was a long shot. Penetrating the cartel's electronic network, his clandestine telephone system, and whatever else they could find would make it much easier to take down the cartel piece by piece as Samruk International broke into its full stride in Oaxaca. If the mission was compromised, he and Nikita would certainly be killed but it would not force a change in the overall operation parameters. Jimenez already knew that people were trying to kill him.

Aghassi wore a Kifaru Koala pouch that rested over his stomach and was held in place by a harness that was strapped across his back. Inside was a silenced Glock pistol in a quick draw configuration, the rest of the space taken up by his breaking and entering equipment.

Suddenly he was torn away from the wall, the nylon loop he had secured himself to the anchor with strained as the dynamic climbing rope stretched beneath him. Looking down he saw Nikita at the base of the wall. Exhausted and in desperation, he had grabbed onto a sapling tree growing out from between the rocks. When it came free in his hand he fell free from the cliff and would have fallen to his death if he wasn't snapped into the rope.

Now the mercenary was swinging by the rope, the sling on his HK 417 rifle nearly choking him out.

"Son of a bitch," Aghassi cursed under his breath.

When Nikita finally stopped oscillating back and forth he was able to grab on to a handhold to stop his movement and begin climbing again. Completely out of breath, the sniper came up underneath him and off to one side. Nodding his head to his partner, Nikita unslung the rifle to pull security as best he could while Aghassi worked.

The cliff had been their first major obstacle, the strain sensitive cable would be the first system that he would have to defeat to continue onward. Although no serious thought was given to the idea of someone scaling the side of the mountain, whoever had installed the security systems had at least considered it.

This type of cable was usually woven through chain link fences and the like to detect people climbing over but served the same purpose on the stone wall of the cartel compound. The strain sensitive cable was of the coaxial variety that emitted an electrical charge down its length from the control panel to the termination unit located somewhere inside the compound itself.

Inside the cable would be an electrical conductor which was insulated and then encased inside a braided metal sheath. When human or animal movement created any kind of vibration by moving along the cable it would trigger an alarm. Given more time, Aghassi could find a way to stack alarms and give the enemy the perception that the cable was malfunctioning, that way they would disregard the actual intrusion. As it was, he had to desensitize the cable as best he could and then they would carefully climb over it. The security contractors could have installed a more thorough system but again, they had relied on the geography itself to keep unwanted visitors from approaching any way but by road.

Carefully cradling the cable in one hand, he slowly sliced through the plastic sheath that surrounded the cable. With that task completed, he closed his folding knife, stashed it in the Koala pouch and pulled out a collapsible plastic canteen. He then attached a modified screw top that he had glued a small tube to that ran from the canteen. Just as a medic would advance a catheter into a patients arm for an IV drop, he pushed the tube into the cable.

Nikita lowered his rifle for a moment, wiping sweat from his brow.

Aghassi then squeezed the plastic canteen, pushing the water down the tube and into the strain sensitive cable. When all the water had been pushed into the cable, he withdrew the tube and zipped everything back in place inside the Koala pouch. Filling the cable with liquid would prevent the sensors inside from bouncing, desensitizing it to the vibrations as they climbed over and around it.

Before moving on, he made sure the anchor was still secure and rigged it for an abseiling movement on the way back. They would quietly repel down once they completed their mission. Assuming they survived.

One at a time, they slowly and cautiously climbed over the cable, still careful not to disturb it. The cable was desensitized, not deactivated. At least the cracks between the massive blocks that made up the fortress wall facilitated their advance by giving them something to hold on to. They would free climb the remaining ten meters to the top of the wall.

At the lip of the ancient stone wall Aghassi was finding that the jungle growth made it even trickier to negotiate his way to the top. Peering over the edge, he did his best not to turkey neck it, but in the end it was too difficult to cling to a slick stone wall with plants growing out of it several hundred meters up with nothing to break your fall so he just took a quick glance. He didn't see or hear anyone so Aghassi grabbed the edge of the wall and pulled himself up for a better look.

There was no one on the walkway of the fortress wall in front of them, but with the area lighting turned on in the adjacent courtyard, he could see someone patrolling the wall on the other side of the compound with a sub-machine gun in their hands. From his angle, he couldn't see if there was anyone in the courtyard below, but that also meant that they couldn't see him.

"We're clear," he whispered to Nikita before slithering over the wall.

Drawing his suppressed Glock 19 pistol, the mercenary kept watch while Nikita gasped and made his way up to the top. Stone buttresses lined both sides of the thick exterior walls. Inside the compound were two courtyards, one with a soccer field where the outer walls merged with an old abandoned church, and the second courtyard was what they were looking into now. Across the courtyard was a single story modern building that had been erected amid the crumbling colonial architecture that housed the elite of the cartel, their bodyguards, and servants. Next to this was a larger two story red brick building that looked to have been built decades prior and refurbished only recently. There was a decent sized antenna farm on the roof for transmitting by satellite, VHF, and by microwave. This was Jimenez' private residence.

"Over there," Aghassi pointed to a tall circular tower that rose into the night sky. The old watch tower was similarly abandoned and left to waste. Situated on the outer wall, the tower had been built right between the two courtyards and was a part of the interior wall that separated them. Before Aghassi could make his move, they needed to get Nikita into position to cover him if something went wrong.

Staying low, they crept along the wall to the tower. The intelligence that they had been provided indicated that there was currently no way up to the top. The wooden ladders and stairs inside had long since rotted away; however, the roof remained intact. Over time it had become overgrown with vegetation sprouting up from the top. Climbing into a perch like that was usually a death wish for a sniper, but Aghassi would need Nikita's added situational awareness and the sniper's chance of discovery elsewhere in the compound was very high with constant roving patrols.

Digging through his assault pack, Nikita palmed a telescoping pole, a rolled up caving ladder, and an evil hooking metal device called an Afghan hook. The hook consisted of two metal bars with dozens of two to three inch spikes sticking out that made it look like a very nasty weapon but it was actually made to help Navy SEALs scale the high compound walls that were often found in Afghanistan.

Securing the base of the Afghan hook to the caving ladder, Nikita unwound it. The caving ladder was nothing more than two metal cables with horizontal metal rungs stretching between them. Next, he extended the pole to its full fifteen meters and locked it into place. Aghassi watched the roving patrol on the other side of the courtyard stop for a smoke break.

Next, the pole was clamped to the hook and ladder assembly via a small magnet at the end. Aghassi waited until the patrolling guard turned around, taking a puff off his cigarette.

"Do it."

Nikita swung the pole up on the back side of the tower until the hook disappeared over the top. Pulling the pole back, the caving ladder now hung from the side of the tower that faced out, concealed from those inside the compound. Collapsing the pole, Nikita placed it back in his assault pack. Before he began his ascent, he gave a hard tug on the ladder. When the ladder was pulled it released a second swing arm on the Afghan hook that came down and secured on the opposite side of the lip of the roof, locking it in place.

The Kazakh cursed to himself as he swung onto the ladder with both the assault pack and his rifle slung across his back.

Aghassi watched as the guard flung his cigarette down and rubbed it out under his shoe. He held his breath as the Mexican gunman turned around and began walking towards his position. Just when it looked like he would be forced into a confrontation, the guard turned and walked down the wide stone steps into the courtyard.

By now Nikita was almost to the top. He was using the overhand technique to scale the ladder to balance himself. With a flimsy cable ladder hanging in the air without support, it could be hellacious trying climb it because the climber's lower body would push the ladder out while the upper body pulled it in. The solution is for the climber to bring his arms behind the ladder and grip the rungs while climbing with his feet normally to distribute the weight evenly.

Once at the top he reeled the ladder in behind him and spoke into his radio headset.

"Spooky-One?" Nikita's voice came over the ear bud that Aghassi wore.

"I got you."

"Give me one minute and then move out."

Nikita crawled cautiously across the top of the tower. He had the best vantage point of anywhere on the entire mountain but if the aging structure caved in he was finished. It appeared that there were some lead shingles underneath the overgrowth that spilled over the edge of the tower, rather than decaying wooden beams.

Digging into his sniper tool kit he pulled free a set of garden sheers. Clipping short pieces of vegetation, he secured them to his 417 rifle with rubber bands. The Chromacamo uniform had already shifted color slightly to match the surroundings, the overall shading remained dark as it had been nighttime to begin with. He then made sure his suppressor was still fixed on the barrel properly. For this mission he had loaded a magazine of sub-sonic rounds. With the suppressor in place, each shot would be so quiet that the only audible sound would be the hammer inside the gun striking the firing pin. The bullets were great for low visibility work but only had an effective range of fifty meters or so before they lost enough velocity that they began to tumble through the air.

Extending the Harris bipod legs attached under the rifle, he set down into a position where he could cover Aghassi from.

"Ready," he whispered into his headset.

"I'm moving."

Aghassi began moving from the tower down the wall that partitioned the two courtyards. Down below, the roving patrolman was looking at the ground absently.

"You're clear."

They only had time to conduct a couple rock drills before the mission, no scale model, no rehearsals, they were flying by the seat of their pants. Aghassi wasn't even sure if he had all the right equipment he would need to penetrate the drug lord's server room.

Nikita came off glass. At close range there was no need for even the three power magnification that he had dialed the scope down to. The infiltrator below moved through the shadows towards Jimenez' villa. The guard had turned around and was heading back towards the stairs.

"Stop," Nikita whispered over the radio. "He's moving."

Aghassi crouched, holding his pistol at the ready.

Nikita looked through his scope, the crosshairs moving on the lead edge of his target as he walked. Someone called out in Spanish from across the courtyard. Looking over, Nikita saw that someone had walked out from the one story structure that Aghassi was heading to. He carried on a conversation for a few moments and then the guard turned to walk inside. Both Samruk operatives breathed a sigh of relief when he closed the door behind him.

"They are inside," Nikita informed him.

"Keep an eye out."

"I will."

The sniper watched as Aghassi hurried along the walkway on top of the wall to the opposite end of the courtyard. Once he reached the one story building he hung himself over the lip of the wall and lowered himself down. Gently, one foot at a time, he stepped onto the rooftop. Rather than enter on the ground floor where there would be the most security measures, he had opted to try the second story window into the villa which could be accessed from the adjacent rooftop as the two structures had been placed side by side.

The firm that installed the alarm and detection systems utilized layered security features but as he had found out, there were some gaps in them. The windows and doors on the bottom floor were wired into an alarm with contact strips; however, the second story windows were simply locked with a metal film embedded in the glass in case someone shattered it. Once the glass broke, it would break the circuit running through the metal film and trip the alarm.

Aghassi wouldn't be resorting to anything so crude. As their inside sources had reported, Jimenez attended religious services in the crumbling church at the front end of the compound this time of night. The lights inside his villa were turned off.

He slid a screwdriver under the widow and pressed up on the handle to make a small gap. Next, he reached into his bag of tricks and slipped a thin rubber airbag into the crack. Removing the screw driver, he connected a small hand pump to the airbag and began inflating it.

"God damned penis pump," he cursed. It was taking too damn long.

"We got all night," Nikita said sarcastically, having heard him on the net.

Below them, they could hear voices again.

"Maybe not."

"What is it?"

"They changed out the guards. Hurry up."

Reaching into the open Koala pouch, he palmed one of the metal bypass rods he carried and slipped it under the crack in the window created by the open airbag. The rod was L-shaped to come around and manually unlock door and window latches. It took a few tries but he finally managed to unlock the window and slide it open.

"He's coming up the stairs," Nikita hissed.

Aghassi grabbed the window by the frame and threw

himself inside and into the dark.

Nikita watched his partner disappear into the open window. A second later it was shut and the guard began his patrol unaware of the intrusion.

"Are we clear?"

"The guard didn't see anything," the sniper transmitted.

"Okay. Let me know if you see any activity around the villa."

"Roger."

Nikita was a silent sentinel at the top of the tower, gazing down on the entire fortress. In the second courtyard a dozen cartel men played a game of soccer. Stadium lighting allowed them to play all night if they wanted. One by one, Nikita stared at their faces through his sniper scope but came up empty. Jimenez was supposed to be taking his holy communion or some such at this time of night but he wanted to make sure.

When they had briefed Deckard on their mission plan just prior to heading out they had asked about the commander's intent behind the mission. Specifically the mission was to gather intelligence on the cartel but the overall intent of the operation was to destroy the cartel itself. If they had the chance to assassinate the drug lord himself as a target of opportunity, should they take the shot?

If I have to answer that then you don't need to work here, had been Deckard's reply.

"What in the good name of fuck is all of this," Aghassi

164

mumbled to himself.

He felt like he had just wandered onto a movie set. There were tables filled with weeping, half burned wax candles everywhere. Out of hundreds, only one or two were actually lit, making the room flicker with shadows. The air was thick with smoke and something unidentified. As Aghassi's eyes adjusted to the darkness he saw that he was in a bedroom.

Two women were passed out on the king sized bed, the sheets pulled astray. At least he hoped they were passed out. Tip toeing forward, he could see the naked back of one of the girls moving up and down as she breathed. The other lay on her back, her large breasts partially sinking into her armpits as her arms were flung over her head. Her massive chest was also moving. Bloody syringes and tie offs had been discarded over the side of the bed alongside the brown splotches of dried blood.

Mounted on the wall were various cured animal skulls, crosses, and other religious paraphernalia. A few books were laying around the bedroom by authors such as Aleister Crowley. On the dresser was a massive Smith and Wesson revolver. It looked like Jimenez was into some kind of Santeria type voodoo or something. He filed it away in the back of his head, even this type of intelligence could prove useful later on but having been raised a Baptist, he wanted to get the hell out of the bedroom as fast as he could.

Easing open the door, he slipped out and into the hall. The corridor was cold and dark, the air conditioning blasting up from the vents in the floor. Standing with the Glock in his hand, he listened for sounds of any enemy presence. Time seemed to stand still. The infiltrator had to fight off the feeling that he was being watched, that someone was right behind him. As he had been told by his sources, the second floor had no security cameras. After a full minute had passed he pressed the transmit button on his radio.

"Shooter-One."

"I got you Spooky-One."

"Can you see anyone moving around through the first floor windows?"

"It's dark, I can't see shit."

The next step was to get into the strong room on the second level, disable the cameras and motion sensors, then locate the server room. One thing at time.

The third door down on the left hand side would lead to the central monitoring room that controlled most of the security systems, at least those connected to it. Once inside, he would not be able to remotely open locked doors, but any alarm systems, cameras, and probably any other passive sensors could be shut down. It was a heavy metal door, set inside a metal frame, with a beveled bottom to prevent someone like him from slipping shims or rods through any cracks. The locking mechanism was controlled by a smart card reader.

Holstering the Glock, Aghassi went back into his bag of tricks. He had his own smart card modified with metal leads attached to the actual smart chip that ran in down the length of the card. To those leads he attached a logic analyzer with alligator clips. The other end of the cables terminated in a USB port. Reaching into the Koala pouch he removed his notebook computer, plugged in the analyzer and booted it up.

Starting up an analytical program, it quickly broke down in what sequence the card reader functioned, figured out what prompts it asked for, and what replies were expected. Once the digital recon work had been done, Aghassi packed up the card and sequence analyzer. He then plugged in a smart card reader to the notebook and stuck a blank smart card into it. Programming the card, he put it in the monitoring station's smart card reader, which picked up the false authentications and allowed him to open the door.

Dumping his kit into the open Koala pouch, he hurriedly stepped inside and shut the door behind him. He had thirty seconds to attack the alarm console inside a hard case on the wall before the alarms went off. The normal security monitor would just type in the pass code but he didn't have the code or the time to finesse that type of bypass.

Turning a key, he opened the alarm box and started pawing around through the guts of the alarm system. Using his screw driver he began disconnecting the leads, all of them just to make sure. No alarms sounded. The key had been provided to him by the kid that he and Nikita had saved from the sicarios that had threatened his family. He had been able to steal it while working on the compound the day prior to the night raid. It was one of the spares and the security monitor had left the key box unsecured for half an hour while making his rounds.

Next, he turned his attention to the monitor bank. With

the alarms switched off, Aghassi simply disconnected the power cable running to the console. The motion detectors would now be shut down and the cameras would not be recording anything that could be found later on after he left. There would simply be a blank area on the tapes if someone went looking.

He took a deep breath and let it out.

He was making progress.

Back out in the hall he headed for the stairs. It was so dark that he had to go into his kit and pull on a set of PVS-15 night vision goggles. There wasn't even any ambient light for the goggles to intensify so he had to use the infra-red illuminator to create some non-visible light. With his depth perception altered by the night vision goggles, he proceeded slowly and carefully.

The IR illuminator acted like a flashlight that was invisible to the naked eye but would at least allow you to see with night vision goggles when there was no ambient light.

Once at the bottom of the stairs, he panned back and forth, examining his new surroundings. There were dozens of guns hanging on the walls. Most of them looked like show pieces as near as he could tell through the green tinted night vision. The room was arranged as an entertainment area with overstuffed leather couches and chairs arranged around multiple flat screen televisions. The tables and bar area looked like they had been recently cleaned, the help having tidied up before going home for the night.

Aghassi began to think it though, trying to get inside Jimenez' head. His sources had told him that when the cartel's tech guru showed up every week or so, that Jimenez would clear the bottom floor of his villa. The technician would disappear inside for a few hours and then be escorted back off the compound. It was suspected that he was a professional flown in to maintain whatever system it was that the cartel was running for information management.

It was clear to Aghassi that the server room for the cartel's network was hidden behind a false wall or inside a concealed sub-basement somewhere. But where was the entrance? Where would someone like Jimenez hide it? The drug lord was known for his ruthlessness and brutal tactics. With what he had just seen in the bedroom, the Samruk mercenary could now add superstitious to the cartel leader's personality traits.

"Shooter-One?"

"I'm here," Nikita answered.

"How are we doing?"

"The roving patrol moved over to the second courtyard to watch his friends playing soccer. You are clear for now."

The former ISA operator began looking for seams in the carpet, maybe a trap door. Under night vision, his task was made about ten times more difficult. He bent over several times to run his hand along suspect areas. Unfortunately, it wasn't like the Scooby Doo cartoons where you just turn a candle holder sideways and a door pops open.

Or was it?

Looking over Jimenez's firearms collection, he came to a display case. The sign above the case read: *Goat's Horn* in bloody red letters. It was the nick name that cartels gave to the AK-47 rifle, referencing the distinct curved shaped magazine known by terrorists and soldiers alike the world over. Inside the case itself were gold plated Kalashnikov rifles, some embedded with jewels and other decorations. Aghassi could see large printed words behind the glass but could not read them with his night vision goggles so he flipped them up.

Activating a small red colored LED flashlight, he read the words written at the center of the displayed rifles.

The Beast.

What the hell is the beast?

At this point he had more than a hunch. Pushing on the display case he found that it didn't budge it, but when pulled, it smoothly eased open on ball bearing rollers.

Gotcha.

Jimenez hunched over the pool of holy water and began scrubbing the blood off his hands and arms.

The church had been built over a hundred years ago and

nature was slowly reclaiming it as her own. Everything, even the silent stone erected by the ancestors would eventually die, perish, and crumble back into what was before.

Strong pillars at each side of the church were encased in a tangle of twisting vines and overgrowth that reached up to the vaulted ceiling. There the creeping vegetation slowly gave way to the faded images of angels that stared at those below. The golden Catholic alter had long since been picked apart by looters, now there was just stone and shattered glass. Holes in the roof allowed a steady drip of water to create a pattering that echoed through the open space.

In place of the altar was an effigy of Santa Muerta. She was what this was all for.

The black robed skeleton wore a crown upon her head, the empty eye sockets hanging down at the sacrifice laid out before her. Jimenez looked away and back at his hands, the holy water now turning pink as he scrubbed away at the coagulated blood staining his skin. Wherever he went, she was close by. Her images were tattooed across his back, the hooded skeleton figure keeping watch. Drying his hands, the drug lord slipped back into his shirt.

Santa Muerta had not been pleased with him as of late. His blood offerings had not been sufficient. The rival drug cartel members he had decapitated, the police officers he had hung off of overpasses, the countless assassinations that kept blood flowing in the streets day and night. They were not good enough and she had blighted him for it. When would it be enough, did he have to bleed all of Mexico dry before she took pity on him?

He shed no tears when the dog Ortega met his end at the hands of the gringos but instead of going back from where they came, they instead turned on Jimenez, attempting to eat his organization alive. They had killed many of his gunmen in the city, raided their training camp across the border, and now his pet intelligence agent, Arturo had gone dark when he was supposed to be helping him defeat the gringos. The mercenaries were closing the net around him. It could only be a Yankee plot. They were defeating his rivals to the north and they sent hired guns to take care of the smaller cartels in the south.

The ten-year old boy had been purchased from a local village. The locals were also followers of her, of Santa Muerte. Not the false idols, but the one true Saint of Death. She asked

169

and you did not dare to disagree. The boy had screamed despite his instructions. They slashed open his veins and bled him dry around the alter. Soon, his eyes had grown distant and Jimenez knew that Santa Muerte had traveled inside the boy and taken him. Her empty eyes had met his. The small body now lay sprawled in front of the altar, the offering left for her to do with what she would.

Once again, the rulers of Mexico worshiped at the blood drenched altars of murder and human sacrifice.

She would now be satisfied.

Now she would grant him control over The Beast.

Nikita eased the safety switch on his sniper rifle to the fire position.

It was Jimenez.

The scope's reticle bounced across the drug lord's face. He had just stepped out of the church, his face an expressionless mask. His eyes were somewhere else, certainly not on this planet. This was the top of their target deck. Nikita had High Value Target number one in his sights and every reason to put a bullet in him, except one. Aghassi.

The soccer game ceased immediately and the body guards picked up their weapons before flanking Jimenez as they began walking across the field. From the tower, he was an invisible watcher of the entire scene below him. A voyeur that now felt helpless despite the precision killing instrument in his hands.

"Spooky-One, we have problem."

"What is it," Aghassi hissed.

"HVT number one is on the move with his guards."

"Shit!"

The sniper watched as the entourage passed through the gateway between the two courtyards.

"He is moving towards the villa."

"I'm almost in the server room," the spy said, clearly exasperated.

"I can distract them long enough for you to try to escape," Nikita offered. They both knew it was a death sentence.

"No, sit tight. Let the situation develop some more. I have an idea."

A completely stupid idea, Aghassi thought as he squeezed inside and swung the hidden door closed behind him. Now he was pinned between the display case the actual security door that would lead into the hidden room.

Through the cracks in the display case his coffin was suddenly lit up as someone flicked the lights on out in the living room. He heard muffled voices and doors slamming as they were opened and closed. One of the television sets was turned on.

Aghassi swallowed. He had been in some tight spots in the past but this was really bad. The Koala pouch was squeezed into his stomach making it difficult to breath. Sweat ran down his face and stung his eyes.

The only good news was that the alarms were disengaged so he didn't have to worry about any contact strips on the door tripping anything when they were disconnected. Now he just needed to pick the lock. It took a minute just to reach his picks in the confined space. The sounds coming from the television at least helped conceal any sounds he made while moving around.

Inserting a tension wrench into the lock, he applied light pressure while using a rake tool to knock the lock's pins into place by flicking the rake back and forth. A small commotion went up outside before he heard a beer bottle pop open. It was beer-thirty at the Jimenez villa.

Setting the distraction aside, Aghassi worked the rake around until the last pin fell into place and the lock cylinder rotated. Turning the knob, the pushed the door open as a whoosh of cold air blew across his face. It was literally a wave of relief after sucking it up in an upright coffin for nearly ten minutes.

Flipping down his night vision goggles on the swing arm they were attached to, he looked down the tunnel for several moments before stepping forward and silently easing the door shut behind him. As he had suspected, there were two sets of magnetic alarm strips that would have gone off if he had not intervened at the monitoring station upstairs. Reaching into his kit, he thumbed the switch on a white lens flash light to help guide the way.

"Shooter?" he clicked his radio on.

Static blasted into his ear.

"*KSHHHH*y-one."

"I'm going down into a tunnel system underground," he responded not sure how much Nikita would hear. "You won't be able to get comms with me."

"*KSHHH*er, Spooky. W*KSHHH*ere when you *KSHH*ack."

"Spooky out."

A stone stair case spiraled its way down to a lower level. The stones were smooth from decades of use, mineral deposits gathered on the walls from ground water seeping in. When he got to the bottom he noticed that the tunnel had an arched ceiling and appeared very old. It had to be a part of the original construction of the villa, built into the foundation and dug into the mountain. No way was it dug during the refurbishing when Jimenez chose the site for his headquarters.

Running along the side of the wall were a variety of cables. Taking a knee, Aghassi noted that some of them carried electricity, others were fiber optic communication lines. He was definitely on the right track. Shining the light down the stone corridor caused him recoil in fear as the beam was reflected back by a set of unblinking eyes. The rat scurried off without further comment.

He was aware of his nerves becoming slightly frayed at this point.

Walking through the tunnel he soon came to another door. He had no prior intelligence on how the sever room was secured or what it looked like inside. Without sniper overwatch, from here on out he really was on his own.

172

26

It took a good twenty minutes to pick the locks on the door. It would have taken longer if he had to bridge the wires on the alarm system but thankfully that was already taken care of. Aghassi was startled by the automatic lights as they suddenly kicked in. The bright fluorescent bulbs lit up racks and racks of computer hardware. Stepping inside, he closed the door behind him.

Banks of Cisco routers and switches blinked as they hummed along next to Juniper mobile and telephone devices, hardware for packet transport and time synchronization, firewalls and other network security devices. Up above, metal trays snaked across the ceiling where various network cables ran from one device to another.

Aghassi's attention shot to a server cabinet in the back of the room. Walking past the racks towards the servers, he also noticed several electromagnets stationed around the room. In an emergency, they could be used to sanitize hard drive platters, instantly wiping out sensitive data.

Reaching into the Koala pouch, the mercenary reached for his picks and raked open the lock on the cabinet. Inside he found several high-end IBM servers. He knew from previous experience that they would be running AIX and Oracle as a backbone for data management. Sun Sparcs were running Solaris to provide the file server services for Linux, Apace, and MySQL providing internet web services.

He had actually expected somewhat stronger security on the sever room, but the security plan designer must have felt that it was pretty secure as it was inside a hidden underground tunnel that could only be accessed from inside a very secure fortress. More than likely, the security measures had been put in place to ward off nosy employees and unauthorized cartel personnel. They didn't seriously think that a covert entry team could get this far.

Opening his notebook computer, Aghassi connected to the server with an ethernet cable. Once he was connected he duplicated a portion of the server's software that allowed him to surf the network as a digital drone and continue his stealth reconnaissance in the digital world. Installing a backdoor into the system took some time. There were several software safeguards in place that he had to bypass as quickly as possible. The clock was ticking, and every minute that passed increased the odds that he or Nikita would be discovered. If they weren't over the wall by dawn, they'd be stuck there all day.

With the code inserted into the servers, Cody would be able to access the entire network from the OPCEN back at Samruk's compound. From there, Jimenez' telecommunications infrastructure would belong to them.

It was a good thing too because the alternative would be to leave a wireless device connected to the router. The security manager or IT technician was due back to do his sweeps in a few days and once he discovered an intrusive signal being beamed out, they would be toast.

Finally, he copied a worm virus onto the network that would infect any laptop that connected to it. The nasty little bug would secretly be recording audio and video through the webcam and microphone on the connected laptop computers and then transmit the data back to Cody once the computer was connected to the internet. This was why breaking into the server room was so important, why it was more important than placing a bomb in the compound, or even assassinating the drug lord himself. Modern covert and counter-terrorism operations were about data. They were about networks and how to dismantle them. Whoever had access to the right type of data, whoever could aggregate it and analyze it, would be the one who took the enemy's network a part piece by piece.

With his work completed, Aghassi unplugged his notebook and put it away before locking up the server cabinet. He was extra cautious about making sure he left everything exactly the way that he found it. On the way out he closed the door and made sure it was locked before he walked back the way he came, his flashlight beam bouncing across the tunnel in front of him.

Aghassi wiped the sweat from his forehead for what seemed like the hundredth time that night.

Now came the hard part. Escaping with his life intact.

"Bitches," Jimenez huffed as he entered his bedroom. "Out!"

The two women moved in slow motion, lethargic as they oozed out of bed. They were still high.

"Now!"

The junkies staggered out, not even bothering to get dressed. His men would take care of them, one way or the other. He cleared off an area of his desk and laid his laptop computer down next to the weeping candle sticks. Santa Muerta had been appeased. Now she would grant him favor with The Beast that lived beneath his fortress. Night and day, it heard and saw everything.

Opening up the computer, he sat down wearing only his blood splattered pants.

With Arturo gone life had grown more difficult for the drug lord, but what had been lost with his pet intelligence agent had more than been made up for by The Beast.

With a few clicks, Jimenez opened up a program called Analyst Notebook which displayed a giant link chart showing how people were associated with one another. One by one he looked at the picture of each and every Judas Goat in his organization.

Using his cellular phone, he placed a call to his right hand man. Ignacio ran the nuts and bolts of franchising out tasks to various freelance agents from his base in Oaxaca City while Jimenez remained in his fortress up in the mountains. He would be waiting for the phone call.

Ignacio picked up on the first ring.

"Yes, sir?"

"It is time."

Aghassi peeked out from behind the display case before carefully swinging it open.

A dozen of Jimenez' men sat around the television screens watching European soccer. Engrossed in the sport, they cheered on, oblivious to the Samruk mercenary as he slipped behind them and up the stairs. He was almost to the top when the two naked, large breasted women he had spotted earlier in the bedroom stumbled on by. They disappeared into the corner room of the villa, slamming the door shut behind them.

Back in the security monitoring room, Aghassi clenched his teeth. It was a near miss. He was more than a little creeped out by what he had seen in the compound, his nerves shot, and was in a hurry to get the hell off of the objective. He had to take care not to get sloppy.

"Shooter-One?"

There was a slight pause.

"Are you clear?"

"For now, I'm back in the security monitoring room."

"The lights are on in the room you entered into on the second floor. Someone is there."

It had to be Jimenez. Nikita saw him entering the villa and he must have been the one who kicked the girls out of his bedroom. It would be a simple affair to walk into the bedroom and shoot him dead with the suppressed pistol.

Aghassi hurried to restore the security room to its original condition before setting the timers on all of the alarms on a sixty minute delay. The security manager would find everything in place the next day when the alarms came back online after he and Nikita had escaped.

"Shooter-One, this is Spooky-One," he said into his radio.

"Yes?"

"I'm going down the hall. We can finish this now."

"He's isolated?"

"I think so. It is now or never."

"Roger."

Aghassi had his pistol drawn and the door halfway open when he heard footsteps pounding up the stairs. Closing the door, he held the pistol at the ready. The footsteps continued down the hall. Easing his way out into the hall once the coast was clear, he could see that the bedroom door was open. Jimenez was having a pow-wow with his men.

Shooting across the hall, he cracked open the door that the two junkies had gone through. Neither could be seen so he stepped inside. Voices came from the adjoining bathroom. The giggles and girl talk made it sound like they were taking turns doing lines of blow.

"I missed my chance," he whispered into the radio. "I need an out."

"The sentry is on the blue side of the villa, the green side is clear." The sniper was using code words for the east and west sides of the building.

"Roger."

Looking over his shoulder, he waited for another explosion of laughter, using the noise to muffle the sound as he pushed open a window. One leg after the other, he slipped outside and onto a narrow ledge, shutting the window behind him. Taking a deep breath, he stepped off and fell down to the ground. With his feet and knees together, his legs acted like a giant piston to help break his fall. It didn't prevent him from gasping in pain as he scuffed up his knees and elbows though.

Readjusting his earpiece, he tried making contact with his sniper overwatch once more.

"I'm on the ground. Talk to me."

"The sentry is half asleep over on the far side of the building. From up here I can see a drainage ditch running towards the target wall we came up over."

"I think I see it."

Moving at a crouch, Aghassi walked through the grass until he found the shallow muddy depression. Getting down into it, he leopard crawled forward, arm over arm, happy to put as much distance as possible between him and the villa.

177

"We've faced some trying times. Times that have tried our faith," Jimenez looked up at the goat skull mounted on his wall. "But tonight we strike back. Tonight we strike back at the gringos and their colonial masters."

Jimenez spoke to his Lieutenants who he had called and gathered around him.

"The gringos come from the north and bring with them their military technology, their technology of oppression. But this technology can also be used against them. They forget that this is Mexico. The tax man, the pharmacist, the milk man, they all belong to us."

The cartel soldiers chuckled.

"And the telephone company, they especially belong to us. Both the real cell phone towers and the ones we build, they are all ours. Now let me explain," he took his time laying it out, assuring his men that he was still in control. "This computer program here compiles information. It takes the records of all cellular phone traffic in Oaxaca and shows us who is talking to who. We can look at it telephone to telephone like this," Jimenez pointed to the computer screen.

Displayed on the screen was an icon for a single cellular phone. Branches reached out representing each call made with the phone to other cell phones and land line phones showed incoming, outgoing, and missed phone calls.

"This is what normal cellular phone traffic looks like," the Jefe explained. With a few more clicks he brought up a new link chart showing one cell phone connecting to another single cell phone by incoming and outgoing calls.

"This," he said pointing to the screen. "Is what the phone calls of a snitch look like. No one uses their phone to call only one number, except those who have been given a drop phone for one specific purpose, to rat on their brothers."

The Lieutenants looked at each other for a long moment.

A few more clicks on the laptop brought up a new link chart showing side by side comparisons for two different phones.

"Now you see here, these two phones belong to the same person. One phone shows normal phone calls going out to his friends, family, and his brothers here in our family. However, the second phone is kept for one specialized purpose, to compartmentalize the calls to this single phone number from all the others. The Beast has sniffed out this information for us and there are many more like him but this cell phone belongs to someone in this very room."

Jimenez reached over his computer and grabbed the Smith and Wesson Governor revolver. Spinning in his chair, he bounced the hand cannon in his fist. The pistol was capable of firing .45 ACP rounds but more importantly it was designed around the .410 shotgun shell. The massive revolver was essentially a scaled down shotgun.

"Jose," Jimenez stated coldly. "This is your cell phone."

The cartel lieutenant took a step backwards, his hands coming up in front of him defensively. Whatever words he was about to say died in his throat.

"What do you want me to do about this Jose? This is a dead ringer as they say. One phone that only calls one phone, always in the middle of the night? You are a source and you have been talking to that whore, the former Police Chief's daughter. She works with the gringos now, you know that!"

Jimenez aimed down the tritium night sights, lining up the front sight post square on Jose's face.

"At least in death, you will serve Santa Muerta."

The drug lord squeezed the trigger and the revolver jumped in his hand with a flash, the recoil pushing the barrel up towards the ceiling. Jose's face disappeared in a splash of gore and shattered bone. He was dead before his body hit the floor.

Jimenez tossed the pistol back on the table where it landed with a heavy clunk.

"Next order of business-"

"SHIT!"

Cody looked away from the computer monitor and turned towards Frank. He had watched the entire exchange as it was recorded by the webcam imbedded in Jimenez' laptop. Aghassi's worm virus had infected the server, installed itself on the drug lord's computer, and started uploading through the cartel's own satellite uplink where it landed on Cody's computer.

"What is it?" Frank asked, setting down his spit bottle.

"Our entire human intelligence network is about to get rolled up."

"What the hell do you mean *rolled up?*"

"Jimenez correlated the calls made by the drop phones being distributed by both Aghassi and Samantha. It is right there on his computer, it looks like he used analysts notebook to compile the data."

Frank looked up at the projection on the wall showing Samruk International's target deck for the Oaxaca operation. There was Jimenez at the top, with his lieutenants under him, and then dozens and dozens of smaller cells that were franchised out on a contract basis for smuggling, killing, and other more technical tasks such as telecommunications and network security. What none of them had realized was that all the while, Jimenez had been building a target deck on Samruk and their network as well.

"Where is Deckard?"

Deckard walked across the freshly expended hot brass that rolled across the street.

"It is for you," the radio man sitting in his assault truck

said as he gave him the hand mic.

With Fedorchenko's platoon on stand down to recover from their airborne operation and Aghassi and Nikita running recon, Deckard was out on a parallel operation with Sergeant Zhenis and Second Platoon. They were back in Oaxaca City, mowing grass and churning through their target deck. After a brief firefight, they had taken down another ring of contract killers.

"This is Six," Deckard said over the command net.

"We have a problem."

It was Frank.

"What?"

"Our entire ring of informants is about to be liquidated. Spooky-One's mission was a success and they are on exfil right now. The virus allowed us to tap into the cartel's network but not in time to stop him. Jimenez had someone conduct a link analysis on all cellular traffic in Oaxaca."

Deckard's guts twisted in a knot.

"How bad is it?"

"We're trying to establish that now while we reach out to as many of our sources as possible."

Gun fire popped off somewhere deeper in the city. It was just a few shots, which soon turned into a spray. Seconds later, the heavy bolt of a machine gun thumped on full auto coming from a different direction, each blast echoing across the city.

"Start giving me names and locations," Deckard told him. "We'll see how many we can pull out."

As he listened to the gunfire, Deckard knew it was already too late.

Nikita pushed off the rock wall one final time and brought his hand behind him to slow his descent. The rappel rope was pulled through the figure eight snapped into his climbing harness as he lowered down to the slope. When his boots made contact, he braced himself against a tree. Aghassi came down right behind them.

Slipping on the muddy slope, Aghassi fell to his knees before struggling back up. They both looked at each other, shaking their heads. One too many close calls for one night. They needed a beer or ten.

Pulling the rappel ropes free, they pulled one end of the doubled up rope until it slid through the single carabiner they had left concealed on an anchor point up above. The one piece of equipment lodged deep inside a crack in the rock would be the only evidence left behind that they had even been there. The ropes and other gear went into a rucksack they had stashed at the bottom and the two mercenaries began making their way down the slope.

They had no idea as to what a shit storm they had just uncovered.

27

Deckard braced himself against the dashboard as the assault truck jerked to a stop.

"Samantha, call your source right now," Deckard spoke into the radio hand mic. "Tell him that we are right outside his house and are taking him with us."

The assault vehicles that the Samruk mercenaries drove were outfitted with eight seats in the flatbed in the back, four on each side sitting back to back. The moment the trucks stopped, they popped the quick release on their seat belts and slipped right off the edge and down to the ground. The turret gunner remained, maintaining security with their PKM machine guns. The assault teams formed together en route as they ran towards the target house.

"I'm calling now," Samantha replied.

"Tell him if he doesn't come with us that he won't be safe. We'll bring his family if need be but if he stays the cartel assassins are going to clean him out tonight."

"I'm dialing his cell, it's ringing."

The lead assaulter kicked the door, not to kick it in but to knock with his foot and get the home owner's attention. He didn't want to lean in front of the door and knock with his fist in case the residents decided to answer with a 12-gauge buck shot.

No one was answering, shotgun blast or not.

Looking down at his Falcon View navigation program displayed on a Tough Book computer, he saw that they were in the right place.

"I just talked him," Samantha reported from the Operations Center. "He's coming to the door now. I told him to make sure he is unarmed."

Suddenly, the door opened a crack. The assault team kicked it the rest of the way in and stormed the building. There was gunfire popping off all over town. Jimenez was having his right hand man, Ignacio, take out their entire network of informants. The Kazakh mercenaries and their Western advisers were not taking any chances. They secured the source and whoever else was home, bringing them back to the trucks for extraction.

Seconds later, the assaulters were already pouring out of

the house with the source and his wife, both flex cuffed and blindfolded for everyone's protection. Once Samantha confirmed their identities back at the compound they would have their restraints removed.

With his night vision goggles flipped up, Deckard could see all the way down the street with the occasional lights illuminating the area. His eyes went wide as tires squealed and smoked down at the intersection. A tractor trailer skidded to a halt, blocking off the road. Behind them, a second trailer pulled across the intersection, cutting off any chance of escape.

"Shit," Deckard cursed. "Light them up," he said flipping over to the assault net. "We're about to get hit."

Just then an RPG-7 gunner let off an RPG-7 rocket that streaked down the street. Passing between two assault trucks, it bounced off the road and detonated against a stone wall, crumbling it in a cloud of smoke. A second RPG followed hot on the heels of the missed shot, blasting into the armored front cab of the lead assault truck.

Gunfire rained down on the street from roof tops on both sides, the bullets plinking off the thick bullet proof windshield. A Samruk commando went down under a fusillade of gunfire right before Deckard's eyes.

Deckard clicked the hand mic in his hand.

"Blue building, right side of the road, fifty meters to our front. Do it."

PKM gunners churned through 250 round belts of ammunition as they sprayed the rooftops. Muzzle flashes traversed from side to side as they homed in on enemy gunmen. The drivers gunned it, one driver moving out before the men were fully loaded. One assaulter was flung off the back of the vehicle while his truck took off without him.

"Stop! Stop!"

As Deckard's truck jerked forward and then buckled as the driver braked, he flung open his door and reached out for the Samruk mercenary while firing his AK-103. With the butt stock wedged under his arm pit, it wasn't aimed fire, but intended to suppress the enemy along with the PKM gunners. Grabbing the fallen mercenary, he pulled him inside the vehicle, still firing with the door hanging open.

"Go!"

The convoy shot forward a second time. The first truck

had already smashed right through the garage door. Deckard's Kazakh driver expertly turned the wheel hand over hand, sharply turning while slowing just as they passed into the now open garage door.

The driver had to spin the wheel again to avoid the first truck. It was smoking as it had crashed into a large industrial metal rack loaded up with metal poles. The blue building Deckard had chosen to escape the kill zone turned out to be an aluminum shop. Aluminum scrap was stacked everywhere alongside the various hardware and tools of the trade. One by one, each vehicle squeezed into the metal shop until all five were out of the line of fire.

Somehow, the truck that absorbed the RPG round had limped in as well but once it stopped it was clear that it wouldn't be moving again anytime soon. The PKM gunner on the last vehicle rotated to cover his six o' clock and fired occasional bursts across the street.

Sergeant Zhenis jumped off the back of his truck and began barking orders in Russian. The platoon medic began treating a casualty who had been shot through the leg. It was too late for another mercenary, he had taken a round in the neck and had already expired. A pool of blood spread underneath him as his comrades lowered his body to the ground.

With Zhenis pushing his men where they needed to go, several took a knee next to the garage door. Others began climbing the metal racks all the way up to the roof. They moved up one at a time with their rifles slung over their backs. At the top, one found a hole in the roof that had been covered over with a piece of rippled sheet metal. Pushing it aside, he cleared the way and pulled himself up through the opening.

Deckard turned as the radio in his truck crackled.

"Six," Cody said on the command net. "We are inside the enemy's network. It is exploding with chatter. You've got every gunman in the city converging on your position."

"What am I up against Cody?"

"Everyone. Once Jimenez and Ignacio determined which source you were going to pick up they must have arranged the ambush. They let you drive into their trap. Sorry we couldn't catch it sooner but I'm still penetrating the network-"

"It is what it is," Deckard cut him off. "How many enemy are we looking at."

"Hundreds. Jimenez also put out a contract on our heads on his Facebook and Twitter feeds."

"He has a Facebook and Twitter account?"

"I'm afraid so, and most of Mexico is listening. Iganacio's soldiers along with every freelancer and wannabe sicario is descending on your position. I'm going to work on shutting down the part of the communications network that you are in and monitor the rest of it for early warning but it's going to take time. It would be faster if you took it out manually."

"Where is it?"

One of the windows suddenly shattered from the overpressure created by a nearby RPG blast. The stench of sulfur wafted through the humid night air.

"It is another concealed commo mast on the other end of the block."

Deckard thought it over, they needed to break out and he wasn't going to split his platoon in half to take out one communications repeater. It would weaken his own forces without much of a gain in his opinion.

"Get Fedorchenko's men rolling. We're going to try to shoot our way out. Have them bump to our freq when they get close and we will join forces."

"I'm on it," Frank announced over the net.

The PKM and both riflemen at the entrance fired controlled bursts, the gunfire shaking dust from the ceiling. Another RPG slammed into the exterior wall, rattling the building to its foundation. Deckard was amazed that the concrete wall was still standing. He looked around at the chaos and at the bodies.

"Let's go," he snapped. "Get that guy's leg bandaged, put a tourniquet above the wound and stop the bleeding then get that son of a bitch on the firing line to pull security!"

"You, you, and you," he pointed to three of the PKM gunners still on their trucks. Their weapons were useless indoors. "Get up on the roof and prepare to move. You," he pointed to the fourth gunner. "Dismount and orient that gun facing out that window." The final gunner was left in place to watch the entrance.

"Zhenis," he said keying his radio as he walked across the dusty floor. "Talk to me."

"We are taking fire from all directions," he said from up

on the roof.

"Roger that, which way will get us out of here the fastest?"

"Back the way we came, but first we need to get that trailer out of the way"

Enemy gunfire continued to rain down on the aluminum shop while the mercenaries on the ground returned fire. Outside, Deckard could see the lifeless forms of several cartel gunmen laying in the street.

"Prepare the men for movement," Deckard ordered the Platoon Sergeant. "I'm coming up."

Cody stared at his computer screen, trying to work through the problem. Frank had taken off to go wake up Fedorchenko and send his platoon out as a Quick Reaction Force. That was when the OPCEN door burst open. Pat stood there holding the door by the frame.

"What's going on?"

"Deckard and Zhenis are pinned down inside the city. Our entire informant network has been compromised."

"We need to get the other platoon rolling."

"Frank is on it."

Muffled gunfire could be heard outside, staccato bursts blazing away with a seconds pause between them. It was the perimeter guards up on the compound walls.

"We're getting hit," Pat announced calmly. "They are hitting the walls."

"FUCK."

"Tell Deckard to do what he can, but we're going to have to fight off this attack before we can go in and get him out. I'm sure the enemy coordinated it this way, but there is nothing we can do about it now."

Pat turned and ran outside as the gunfire continued unabated outside.

Cody turned back to his screen. Two and two came together and he figured out a work around for Deckard's problem. It was better than nothing.

Flipping through the various channels on Samruk communication's net, he began talking into his headset.

Aghassi pumped the car's brakes, tossing Nikita forward and waking him with a start as he slammed into the back of the passenger seat. He'd been dosing in the backseat since they pulled off target.

"Wake up fucker. We're not out of the briar patch yet."

"What you want?"

"Fedorchenko's platoon is pinned down inside the city," Aghassi informed him. "Just got the call out over the radio from Headquarters. We are being diverted to support them."

Aghassi sped up, his headlights leading the way as he snaked around the wide turns on one of the main avenues of approach through Oaxaca City. The brightly colored single story homes meshed with old Colonial buildings and churches that stood silently in the night. Aghassi circled around the hilltop that ran into the middle of the city until they came to a large open air amphitheater. Running along the side, and up behind the theater was a paved road leading to the cell phone towers at the top of the hill.

The Samruk mercenary stopped the vehicle as the headlights stopped on a chain link fence gate that was closed across the road.

"The cartel is bringing in every shooter they can muster down on our boys," Aghassi told Nikita as they climbed out of the car. "Cody wants us to disable that tower up there to help prevent the enemy from talking to each other and coordinating their actions."

"So much for beer," Nikita complained.

"No rest for the wicked," Aghassi said as he popped the

trunk and pulled out some tow straps. They had packed the car with recovery equipment ahead of their surveillance operation at Jimenez' compound. Running the straps up under the car and attaching them to the frame, the other ends were snap linked to the fence that was blocking their way. The locking gates of the snap links were facing up so that if they broke, the tow straps would snap down rather than up and smash the car's windshield.

Slowly backing up the car, Aghassi steadily increased the pressure on the gas pedal until the gate gave way and snapped open. Nikita quickly detached the straps and swung the gate the rest of the way open. The road wrapped around the hill as they drove up to the top and found the cell tower they were looking for. Aghassi shotgun parked before flipping off the lights and shutting the car down. Both carried their full equipment from the previous mission, but Aghassi added an AK-103 he had stashed in the car.

With their weapons held at the ready, the two mercenaries stood and looked out over Oaxaca City. From their vantage point they could see the entire panorama, lit up at night with golden pin pricks of artificial light. The night itself was hot and oppressive. Clouds of black smoke rose throughout the city obscuring their view. Gunfire rattled away, echoing from so many places that it was impossible to tell what direction the sound was coming from.

"Jesus," Aghassi muttered as he rubbed a hand across the stubble on his chin. "I had heard about this Deckard guy before but he really knows how to find the prettiest parts of hell, doesn't he?"

"You get used to it," Nikita said turning away.

Aghassi followed him to the tower where they both looked up at the various satellite dishes and microwave relay systems. It would take a lot of demo and a decent amount of time to rig it all in order to collapse the tower. They didn't have either.

"I can shoot them out like I did in Burma," Nikita offered.

"In Burma?"

"Yeah, it did the job."

"How about I just flip the power switch," Aghassi said hooking a thumb towards the generator shed.

"Okay," Nikita agreed.

Walking towards the tower, the Kazakh reached up and grabbed one of the metal cross members. Pulling himself up, he hooked a booted foot over the support structure and began climbing his way up.

"What the hell are you doing?" Aghassi shouted. Nikita was struggling to climb with his assault pack and HK 417 slung over his back. It made the intelligence operative nauseous to watch him as his uniform changed color and intensity as the Kazakh moved. It was like he was looking right through him sometimes.

"Those muzzle flashes to the East have to be Fedorchenko's platoon. You can hear the PKM fire. Get on the radio and make sure that Deckard has them turn on their IR strobes so I can mark their location. Once I get to the top I can offer fire support."

"That is a hell of a long shot," Aghassi said looking over his shoulder. "Are you sure?"

"Better than nothing. Shut down the power or my balls will get microwaved while I am in tower."

"Yes, sir," Aghassi said sarcastically.

As Nikita ascended the tower, he eventually found the ladder that had been retracted off the ground and locked in place. At least he could use it the rest of the way up. Aghassi went to work on the lock on the generator room. The massive fuel cell was outside sitting on a concrete foundation but the generator itself was under lock and key. It only took a few minutes with his lock picks before the cylinder turned and he was able to open the door. He picked a second padlock on the door to the console and opened it. Inside were a series of switches and one lever that controlled the master power distribution. Pushing it down resulted in the interior lights blinking out as well as shutting down the entire communications tower.

Back at the car, he dug into his assault pack where his tactical radio was located. A wire ran from the radio to a cable that ran up into the frame of the car through the glove compartment. Hidden in the roof of the vehicle was the satellite antenna itself. The low-visibility antenna was another piece of kit that Deckard had thoughtfully purchased with company funds and had flown in with the last shipment of supplies.

He turned the knob until he came to the channel for Fedorchenko's platoon assault net.

"This is Spooky-One," he said into the handmic.

Someone answered in Russian, causing Aghassi to frown.

"Spooky, this is Six," Deckard cut in. He could hear the rattle of gunfire across the net.

"We are in overwatch. Enemy comms are disabled. Break. Shooter-One is moving into position and requests that you turn on IR strobes prior to him going hot, over."

"Roger that," Deckard's voice sounded like sandpaper. "Glad to have you along for the ride."

28

"Turn on your shoot-me lights!" Deckard ordered.

Outfitted for urban combat, each Samruk mercenary wore a plate carrier and a low-profile ballistic helmet that their PVS-14 night vision goggles were attached to. They also had infrared light strips made by S&S Precision attached to their helmets. The V-lite was made out of a flexible strip that increased the visible area of the light that was Velcro'ed to the side of each team member's helmet. Squad leaders wore Manta strobe lights which flashed on and off and were even brighter. The infrared light was only visible under night vision goggles, a piece of kit that the enemy may have as well which was why they were usually turned off.

"Shooter-One, you see us?"

"Roger Six, let me get in position," Nikita reported from somewhere off in the night.

PKM gunners were now up on the roof of the aluminum shop with the assaulters. They extended the bipod legs from the bottom of the Russian machine guns and one was posted at each corner of the building for maximum fields of fire.

The Samruk men were taking some heavy fire, the machine gunners flinching and ducking down behind the lip of the wall every so often as the enemy walked in some tracer fire. Every time they saw a head and shoulders pop up on the rooftops the mercenaries would take aim and fire but it was like the cartel shooters were playing a deadly game of hide and seek.

The rooftops were haphazard and showed little sense of organization, mostly low one story affairs with additional structures built onto the side of the building or on the roof, much of it cobbled together with whatever materials were readily available. Deckard knew that his men had enough fire power up on the roof at this point that the enemy could no longer dominate the high ground uncontested. Now, the gunmen were pushing at their defenses here and there, looking for gaps. They would be finding their way closer and closer as they found ways to navigate around and through the buildings at ground level.

Walking alongside Zhenis, Deckard looked for a way for them to skirt over the roofs all the way down the block to the tractor trailer that was blocking them in.

"I see a way," the Kazakh said in Russian.

"Nikita is almost in place. Once he is set, we can take two squads forward."

Splitting the platoon in half would be a tactical disaster but both elements would be close enough that they would be able to support each other. At this point they had to make something happen or the enemy would nickel and dime them until they ran out of ammunition. Machine gunners had already been instructed to conserve ammo and two mercenaries had already climbed back down inside the building to pull additional belts of 7.62 off the trucks.

Another RPG rocket soared through the air, screaming over their heads before shooting out over the city and airbursting.

Zhenis looked at his commander.

"I'm going to have them bring up the Carl Gustav."

Nikita struggled to get into a stable firing position. One hundred and fifty feet up in the air on a giant communications tower was not exactly the best sniper hide. His Samruk sniper instructor had been a South African named Piet who taught him never to climb up into trees, water towers, or other such nonsense. When someone pulled the pin on a chaos frag you would be stuck up there. Nikita was obliged to agree but these were extenuating circumstances.

Digging around inside his assault pack he retrieved the climbing rope and carabiners that he had used at the Jimenez compound. Slinging the rifle, it was more than awkward to maneuver with one hand on the ladder. Running the rope back on itself and around the metal cross members of the tower, he used the carabiners to create a kind of improvised hammock that he could sit on. Carefully, he lowered himself onto the ropes and let himself sit down with his feet braced on the side of the tower. Finally, he got his HK 417 resting against the cross beam in front of him and popped open the scope caps.

Lowering his night vision goggles he could see the IR strobe lights flashing that marked the friendly platoon's position. Deckard was calling him over the radio so he responded, acknowledging that he spotted them. The tower provided Nikita with an amazing vantage point but it would be long distance, high angle shots that he would have to make to help thin out the opposition for his Samruk comrades.

Muzzle flashes lit up the night, a form of visible strobe lights that marked friendly and enemy positions alike.

The sniper took a deep breath and exhaled forcefully. Leaning forward, he powered up the Universal Night Sight, the night vision optics that complimented his long range scope for low visibility work.

Using a pocket sized laser range finder he ranged the distance to the warehouse his men were on at nine hundred and thirty two meters, a difficult shot to make on a good day and in a solid firing position. The external ballistics got more complicated however when Nikita began factoring in the high angle aspect of the shots he would have to make.

When judging range at a high angle up or down from the target, the distance to the target that the shooter would arrive at would be much longer than the actual flat range distance from his position to the enemy position. If the high angle distance to target, in this case nine hundred and thirty meters was dialed into his rifle scope, his bullets would impact much higher than the point of aim.

High angle, low angle, or no angle, bullet drop would be the same because the earth's gravity is constant, however the discrepancy between flat line distance and angled distance had to be compensated for.

A small level mounted to the side of his scope told him that with his rifle oriented down to the target building, gave him a reading that his gun was pointed down at 55 degrees. The cosine of a 55 degree angle was .57 according to a cheat sheet taped inside the scope cap. Next he applied the high angle formula to get his flat line distance. 930 meters multiplied by . 57 equaled a flat line distance of 530 meters.

Nikita used his thumb and index finger to slowly rotate the top dial on his Schmidt and Bender scope, counting off the clicks on the Bullet Drop Compensator until he arrived at the right offset, raising his cross hairs so that his bullets would strike center mass by compensating for the bullet drop caused by gravity at a range of five hundred and thirty meters.

Bringing his breathing under control, he exhaled in short evenly spaced breaths. A few rooftops over from the aluminum warehouse he saw a human form creeping along looking for a firing position of his own, a place where he could shoot at the mercenaries from a concealed position. Shifting in his improvised rope seat, Nikita let his sights land square on the gunman's back and keyed up his radio.

"Six," he whispered. "This is Shooter-One. I'm set, over."

A fresh round of gunfire exploded down below in the city.

"Send it!"

Nikita squeezed the trigger. He watched the gunman jerk, his muscles going tense. Through the green glow of the night vision enhanced scope, the would-be killer fell and died.

Deckard couldn't discern Nikita's individual shots above all the automatic gunfire and sporadic rifle, pistol, and occasional RPG shots but one by one, he noticed enemy muzzle flashes blinking out. Suddenly, the amount of effective fire they were receiving seemed to drop by half. It gave them some much need breathing room. Cordite from the PKM and AK fire their men were laying down hung in the air with the humidity, the sickly sweet smell invading his nostrils.

"We are prepared to move," Zhenis said as they crouched behind cover. "Two squads have been outfitted with extra ammunition and two PKM's will cover our movement for immediate fire support."

"How about our street sweeper?"

"Bringing up the rear."

"Let's do it."

The mercenaries slipped over the edge of the roof one by one and down to the adjacent rooftop. Machine gunners suppressed known and suspected enemy positions while Nikita was somewhere in the night providing precision fire. Once both squads and two PKM gunners were down they moved across the roof, staying low to avoid the continued onslaught of bullets that whizzed through the air. With the amount of lead kicking back and forth it was only a matter of time before someone caught a round in the face.

There was a small gap between the house they were on top of and the next building over. Hearing someone arguing in Spanish, Deckard looked down to see several shadows scurrying through the alleyway as they attempted to find a concealed route to the aluminum shop where the remaining two squads and their trucks were holed up. Yanking a pin on a fragmentation grenade, Deckard dropped it through the gap and stepped away.

"Fire in the hole!"

In the confined space of the alley, the effects of the grenade were absolutely devastating. Both the shrapnel produced by the grenade and the overpressure created by a blast had nowhere to go but straight out at the cartel gunmen who were using the alley as an avenue of approach. The building buckled under the mercenaries' feet as the blast shook the neighborhood.

Adjusting his night vision goggles by turning the focus knob, Deckard looked back down into the alley and saw body parts spread around with debris and the various other trash and refuse to be found in third world cities.

"We're clear."

Hopping the gap, the Samruk men continued across the rooftops. Gunfire from other rooftops came sporadically and was inaccurate until a single shot cracked out above the others. Orders and cries for help sounded in Russian, the Kazakhs throwing themselves down flat. Deckard followed suit, scrambling to a prone position. Another gunshot rang out as cement dust blew into Deckard's face.

Several Kazakh's pulled a downed team member behind a water basin, hoping for some cover from the gunfire but they had no idea where it was coming from.

"He is alive," one of the mercenaries told Zhenis as he asked what the status was. They had patted down the casualty and found no traces of blood.

"The bullet hit his ballistic plate. It knocked the wind out of him but he is okay."

Another shot punched through the water basin, a single stream of water spurting out and splashing next to Deckard.

"Shooter-One?" he called over the radio.

"I'm looking!"

Nikita used his night sights to peer into the shadows and crevices of the city, but a single enemy sniper could be hiding nearly anywhere, including inside a building and obscured from view.

Sweeping across the city, he finally found what he was looking for on top of the Hotel Fortin. The Hotel was down the street from Deckard's position but in the opposite direction from which they were heading. On the roof he could see a cartel gunman with a scoped rifle taking carefully aimed shots.

Nikita had to act fast before they suffered more casualties. He estimated the range to be about 700 meters, looked at his angle indicator and noted 70 degrees for a cosine of .34. 700 x .34 = 238 meters. The sniper adjusted his scope and settled behind the gun, his cheek pressed up against the stock in the exact same place every time he took a shot.

The enemy sniper fired from the top of the eight story hotel and racked the bolt on his rifle to load a fresh round.

Nikita had a difficult oblique shot, but it was the shot he had, not the one he wanted. Squeezing the trigger, he had no idea where his bullet went but he clearly missed. The target spun around as he heard something impact nearby. When he turned, he exposed his entire front side and chest to Nikita.

Even through the grainy green night vision, Nikita could make out some of his facial features. He could see he broad face, deep set eyes, and thick lips. As a sniper, you got to know your targets better than most other soldiers. That was what

Nikita liked about his job.

He sent a second shot. The HK 417 bucked into his shoulder.

The enemy sniper dropped his rifle before pitching forward onto his face.

"Got him," Deckard heard over the net.

"Pick it up! We're moving!"

The PKMs back on the roof of the aluminum shop were still roaring on advancing enemy but at least the enemy sniper had been put down. Moving one squad at a time, the mercenaries bounded forward from one roof to another with one squad in a static security position to cover the one that was advancing. The mercenaries were moving across the rooftops at a fast pace down to the end of the block where a large mechanics shop sat on the corner.

Looking through a window, Deckard saw that the shop was packed full of broken down cars in various states of repair. The front of the shop was locked up with barbwire fences. He could see gunmen running across the street, not to mention the front end of the tractor trailer that they needed to move.

Sergeant Zhenis brought up the rear as the second squad bounded up.

"It's going to get nasty once we get down onto the streets," Deckard said. "I want to get our two PKM gunners and the Goose gunner up on the roof of this shop for an added overwatch."

Zhenis looked up at the roof, it was about two man lengths higher than the roof they stood on. Giving some orders to his men, two of them formed stirrups with their hands with their backs braced against the wall. A third, with a long green metal tube slung over his back came forward and put his foot into their hands. The two soldiers boosted him up so that he could grab the edge of the roof and swing up.

198

Once on the roof, he removed the sling from the metal tube and connected the ends to create a big loop. The rest of the squad tossed up to him two packs containing four recoilless rifle rounds and several gunner's bags filled with linked PKM ammunition. Next, the mercenaries boosted the two PKM gunners up to the roof. The recoilless rifle gunner tossed them his sling so they could grab on to it and he pulled them the rest of the way to the top.

The recoilless rifle that the first mercenary carried was the 84mm Carl Gustav, a shoulder fired Anti-Tank weapon that fired a variety of shells ranging from High Explosive Anti-Tank, High Explosive Dual Purpose, flare, and smoke rounds. Popping open a locking lever, he swung the venturi at the end of the "Goose" out of the way and loaded a black round that looked like it had the top of it cut off with its flat nose. This specific round was an anti-personnel Flechette round.

Moving to the edge of the roof, the Goose gunner looked down to see the cartel shooters who had surrounded the tractor trailer and were building improvised fighting positions at the end of the road. They were laying in wait for the Samruk mercenaries to attempt a breakout. If they did, they would be shot to ribbons. First they needed to clear the way of excess enemy.

Shouldering the Gustav, the gunner used his thumb to prime the spring loaded cocking mechanism, aimed the weapon down into the street at the mass of enemy, and flipped the selector from safe to fire.

The entire street corner was turned from night into day for a fraction of a second as the flechette round fired. The Area Defense Munition blasted over a thousand metal flechettes at the enemy, causing nearly all of them to drop the ground immediately. Screams of agony ripped through the night as those still living howled in pain. The two PKM gunners raked the dead and dying with automatic fire to finish off the job.

By now the two squads of mercenaries had scrambled down to the street and ran to the tractor trailer. One of them jumped up in the cab and found the key missing from the ignition so he put the truck into neutral. The squads surrounded the cab, each man finding a hand hold wherever they could. With each of them throwing their weight into it and grunting in exertion, the semi-truck finally budged and began rolling.

Sergeant Zhen saw the truck lurch forward, unblocking access to the road.

"Get off the roof," he ordered the remaining two squads and two machine gunners still on top of the aluminum shop by calling over his radio. "Grab up the security element inside, mount the vehicles, and roll out. You are making a hard left on the way out and coming straight down the road towards us."

With the truck rolling down a slight incline, it smashed into several parked cars and came to a stop. Deckard wiped sweat from his face, turning around just in time to catch a vehicle screaming around the corner. It was a technical, a pickup truck with a .50 caliber M2 machine gun mounted on a pivot in the back. The gunner standing in the bed of the truck racked the charging handle.

"Technical!" he yelled.

The machine gunner let loose a fusillade of auto fire that cut through the night, red tracers pointing the way. The mercenaries ducked out of the street and took refuge behind parked cars as the hot metal screamed towards them.

The Goose gunner up on the roof lit up the night one more time, the blast nearly deafening the assaulters below. An HEDP round slammed into the pickup truck, the detonation lifting it clear off the pavement for half a second before it slammed back down and continued forward, now consumed by flames. The pickup shot past Deckard. As he turned to look he could see someone thrashing in the passenger seat, being burned alive.

"Get the fuck down here," he screamed up to their overwatch element. "Nice shooting!"

A muzzle flashed somewhere down the street. Fifteen AK-103's converged on it and that was the last they heard from him.

Four Iveco assault vehicles turned out of the aluminum shop, the PKM gunners in the front and rear turrets firing in multiple directions. Speeding up, they rounded around the corner to finally escape the kill zone and stopped to pick up the mercenaries. The fifth vehicle had been effectively killed. The mercenaries had tossed a thermite grenade into the cab before peeling out. Down the street, Deckard could already see smoke pouring out of the open garage door.

The three-man element that had been up on the roof of

the mechanics shop loaded up. The rest of the mercenaries found their seats, everyone trying to avoid the body bag loaded in the back of one of the trucks.

Deckard jumped onto the back of the last assault truck and sat down in one of the bullet proof ceramic seats that faced outward.

"Shooter-One this is Six."

"Six this is Shooter-One."

"Thanks for the help, we are clear of the kill zone and heading home. So should you."

"Roger."

"Six out."

Tapping on the cab's rear window, the passenger slid the bullet proof glass out of the way.

"Give me the hand mic."

The mercenary handed it to Deckard. He needed to get on the satellite radio to establish comms with the OPCEN.

"This is Six, we are clear of the killzone. How long until the QRF gets out here?" he asked Cody.

Nothing came over the airwaves but static.

29

Pat surged up the steps with a wooden crate over each shoulder. On the high walls, the Kazakhs from Fedorchenko's platoon were waging a pitched battle. Behind him, a 60mm mortar round slammed through the roof of what had been Ortega's garage and blasted the sheet metal sky high.

The Samruk men had been fortifying their compound for the last several days when they were not out on missions, and the sandbags and concertina wire helped keep the enemy at bay, but couldn't stop the barrage of gunfire and indirect mortar fire that had been slamming them for the better part of an hour. It seemed that Jimenez had called in about one hundred shooters to assault the mercenary base. They had approached from a defilade, in the low ground of an arroyo where they could not be observed until they were within range of small arms fire.

The former Delta Force operator suspected that Jimenez had the plan in place to assault Ortega's base at some point and when the mercenaries had disposed of him, the drug lord simply recycled the plan for his new enemy.

Sucking in as much oxygen as he could, Pat reached the top of the stairs and dumped the two crates of 7.62x39 ammunition. Using a multi-tool he cracked them open and pulled out two tins of ammo from each crate. Meanwhile, he could hear Sergeant Major Korgan policing the lines. He was up top with the men coordinating their fires. Below, Sergeant Fedorchenko was also carrying up more ammunition and had stopped to put a boot in the ass of their own 60mm mortar crew.

They only had one tube in the compound, the others had been given to Kurt Jager to use as commando mortars with the Zapatistas since they would be conducting more rural operations. That did not seem like such a good idea at the moment.

One of the mercenaries looked over his shoulder and yelled in Russian. He was clearing his back blast area before triggering an RPG rocket that exploded somewhere near the enemy position. PKM gunners braced their weapons against the edge of the wall and walked their tracers across the front lines each time the enemy tried to advance.

Using his multi-tool, Pat cut through the tops of the tins and began walking down the line, handing out boxes of ammunition to each soldier. Most of them had blown through five or six magazines a piece. One of the PKMs chewed through a belt and the gunner popped the feed tray cover, slapped another belt of ammo in place, and slammed it shut.

The enemy was coming right at them, like some crazed lunatic wave of suicide commandos. It didn't strike Pat as being consistent with the hit and run tactics that the sicarios used. Where was Jimenez finding these people? The Mexicans didn't have anything like a martyr culture as could be found in the Middle East.

Pat rushed down the lines, shoving the boxes of bullets in the cargo pockets of the men who were too busy firing to grab the re-supply.

The Central Asian mercenaries were grim, men of hard stock who grew up in the steppes of Kazakhstan. They hardly stopped to acknowledge Pat.

Then, as he proceeded down the line he found a kid wearing jeans and a t-shirt, firing an AK on fully automatic down at the general area where the enemy was.

"Cody?"

"FUCK!"

"What the hell are you doing up here," Pat said grabbing him by the shoulder.

"I'M IN THE SHIT!"

"Who the fuck is down in the OPCEN monitoring the comms gear?"

"I put Aghassi and the sniper on Deckard's position to help, then I came up here."

"So who is pulling radio guard."

"IF I DON'T GET TO KILL A MOTHERFUCKER THEN THIS WHOLE TRIP IS A WASTE FOR ME!"

Pat exploded. Grabbing Cody by the ear he yanked him off the line and towards the stairs.

"Are you fucking kidding me?"

"OW, MY EAR!"

"Get the fuck back down there and do your job!"

Headlights bounced across the hillside, closing in on the communication towers.

"Shooter-One," Aghassi radioed. "I need you down here fast. Looks like the jig is up. They are sending a goon squad after us."

A rope snapped as it uncoiled, just barely scraping the dirt at the bottom of the cell phone tower. Nikita came zipping down the line in his rappelling harness, slowing his decent at the last moment before he made contact with the ground.

"Was that fast enough?" he called over to Aghassi.

"Fast enough for Hollywood."

The sniper pulled the remaining rope through his figure eight attachment and joined his teammate. It looked like a lone van approaching from across the crest of the hilltop, opposite the direction they had taken from the amphitheater.

Nikita dropped an empty magazine and replaced it with a full one from his Mayflower low profile chest rig. Extending the bipod legs, he rested the sniper rifle on the hood of their car and waited for the van to close to an acceptable range. After sweating it out on top of the tower at Jimenez' compound, biting his nails all night, it almost seemed like he wouldn't get to do his job this time out.

Now he had blown through two magazines and killed somewhere around thirty targets, accounting for some fliers. The high angle shots he had made had been the most challenging of his sniper career thus far.

Nikita let the van get within three hundred meters before he took his first shot. He aimed low, towards the base of the windshield as bullets had a tendency to ride upwards with the curvature of the glass. Sure enough, the rounds were deflected slightly upwards as the glass spider webbed.

The sliding door was thrown open and one man managed to jump clear and tumble into the bushes as the van careened off the road and flopped over, rolling several times before really picking up momentum and flying off a cliff where it crashed somewhere down below.

The lone survivor stood up and dusted himself off, probably not comprehending what had just happened, maybe disoriented from his fall.

Nikita zapped him with one round through his neck.

Aghassi walked around the vehicle, got in, and turned over the engine. Nikita loaded up in the back again. Reaching for his radio he hailed the OPCEN.

"This is Spooky-One, we are RTB," he said, announcing that they were Returning To Base.

There was nothing but static on the other end.

"I say again, this is Spooky-One, we are RTB."

Finally, a voice crackled over the net.

"ROGER."

The pre-dawn light made everything look hazy.

Sergeant Zhenis had directed the convoy from the lead vehicle and gotten them out of Oaxaca City. They had made several more contacts and had to re-route around a half dozen hasty road blocks that Jimenez' men had raised at seemingly random places around the city, but they finally cleared the area and were well on their way back to the compound. Deckard had gotten off the radio with Pat and Cody after receiving an update. They had fought off the attack, but had been hammered by mortar fire. The enemy got so close that the Samruk International mercenaries had finally sorted the enemy out with hand grenades.

The four vehicle convoy turned onto Federal Road 175. While they usually drove completely blacked out with both headlights and tail lights taped up and the drivers using night vision goggles, it was now light enough that they flipped up their PVS-14s. The houses and buildings had thinned out as they headed back to their base up in the mountains just north of Oaxaca.

Deckard looked at the men sitting beside him in the outward facing seats. Their Asiatic features might have stood out in Mexico, but they fit right in wherever there was combat. They were tired, exhausted really, but would be ready to execute the next mission when the time came.

Leaning forward, he checked up on the rest of the convoy. The roads were well paved with a center median dividing the two lanes of traffic. Each vehicle maintained an even interval to minimize damage in case of an ambush.

Squinting in the early dawn light, Deckard saw something laying along the side of the road. His heart jumped a beat as they got closer and he saw that it was a bloated donkey carcass laying at the edge of the street.

The animal corpse and the lead vehicle in the convoy disappeared in cloud of smoke and fire. The assault truck spun around with its rear two wheels going airborne, the Improvised Explosive Device having struck the rear end of the vehicle. One of the doors was blown open. Body parts and scraps of flesh were tossed into the air.

The driver in the second vehicle had a moment of panic and slammed on the brakes. The third and fourth vehicles quickly established a security perimeter around the disabled truck.

Deckard jumped down to the pavement and stumbled forward.

Looking back, he saw that he had slipped on a dismembered foot.

It was still wearing a charred combat boot.

30

The sun was creeping above the horizon, the sound of chirping birds interrupted by the sound of car doors slamming shut. Two Sport Utility Vehicles unloaded nine men, each wearing black masks over their faces, each carrying a Sub-Machine Gun ranging from Uzis to the Swedish K. One of the masked men moved up the dusty driveway and to the front gate. Slipping a knife in the cracks between the two swinging gateways was enough to pop the latch open and allow the killers access.

The front of the white building had a large cross above the door. The men stood around, unconcerned for their safety while two other masked men came forward with sledge hammers. One of the men lit a cigarette while they waited. They had all the time in the world.

The men with the sledge hammers began pounding on the front door, one standing on each side and taking turns like lumberjacks hacking away at a tree. Maintaining a low grip on the handle they alternated swings, one after the other. Slowly, the metal door began to bend. The frame buckled under the force of the sledges at the top and bottom while the lock in the middle of the door held in place.

Inside the Christian mission, bedroom lights were flipping on.

Finally, the locking mechanism on the door twisted and snapped. The door swung open and the gunmen swarmed inside. The only one left in the courtyard was the masked man who was finishing his cigarette. Inside he could hear shouting in Spanish. Two of his men were indigenous personnel contracted for the job who could speak the language. The others were members of his regular crew.

Dropping what was left of the cigarette, the leader of the group left the cherry burning in the dirt and walked around to the back of the Christian hospital. According to the information he had received, the local holy man took in the invalids, taking them off their parent's hands and housing them in his hospital. Them and the addicts of course. Taking a seat on top of an old chicken coop, he reached into the breast pocket on his shirt and pulled free another smoke.

The back door burst open and the Padre somersaulted out with one of the masked gunman kicking him from behind. The Padre spoke a mile a minute in rapid fire Spanish as he clawed his way to his knees, pleading with the gunmen. The masked man swung a boot into his face that sent the Catholic priest back down to the ground in a heap. The gunman didn't understand a word he had been saying anyway.

As the sick, the recovering drug addicts, and the mentally retarded were paraded out of the hospital, the man sitting on the chicken coop flicked his lighter and puffed on his second cigarette of the morning. Deep horizontal scars climbed up his exposed forearms like the rungs of a ladder.

One of the invalids was laughing uncontrollably, his thick eye brows arched upwards as he looked at the ground and giggled about something. Another gunman came forward and slammed the butt stock of his Uzi into the young man's stomach, doubling him over.

Several of the patients were hugging themselves, some pleading with tears in their eyes. Some of the permanent patients, the ones with cognitive problems clearly had no idea what was happening. One of them began to clap her hands. The gunmen herded them all up against the brick wall.

The last person pushed out of the door was a female nurse. She was still in her pajamas, white panties and a t-shirt. Two of the gunmen began to tear her shirt off. She lashed out, trying to sink her nails into her attackers and received a fist in one of her eyes for her efforts. Slammed against the wall, they tore her shirt off, exposing her breasts. The panties were pulled down around her ankles.

"*Kiff*," the leader said, waving his hand with the cigarette between his fingers.

They had a job to do.

The gunman who had punched the nurse grabbed her by the hair and slammed her head into the wall. She sunk down onto her backside, trailing blood down the side of the wall. The Padre was yanked to his feet and stood up next to her.

As the dawn light peaked above the brick wall and cast golden rays on the side of the Christian hospital, some of the patients looked at the gunmen lined up in front of them. No one said a thing.

The leader exhaled a cloud of smoke. Finally, the Arab

208

ran his thumb across his neck.

"Kill them," he told the gunmen in Arabic.

Eight men racked the actions on their Sub-Machine Guns and fired.

31

"This is what failure looks like," Deckard said to himself.

Pat stood behind him as they both looked up at the metal frame road overpass for foot traffic. Counting from side to side, Deckard got a total of thirteen bodies hung underneath the overpass by their hands or feet. The corpses were bloated, their eyes lifeless. Wire and ropes were used to hang the bodies, where it now tugged tightly into the dead flesh of necks, wrists, and ankles.

Many showed obvious signs of torture. Some were disemboweled and others were missing fingers.

This was the fate of cartel snitches. By tapping into the telecom system in Oaxaca, Jimenez had been able to analyze the cellular phone traffic throughout the entire province. It was normal for intelligence operatives to give their sources cellular phones so that they could keep their clandestine activities separate from their personal life. Cell phones that only called one number, in this case a number belonging to Samantha or Aghassi, stood out like a sore thumb. It was a completely unnatural way to make phone calls. From there, the drug lord just had to match the suspect phone calls to the person in his organization who was making them.

This had probably been done through a combination of Direction Finding equipment purchased by the cartel through European defense companies and good old fashion human intelligence. Since Jimenez controlled large portions of the telecom network it was easy for him to listen in on phone calls. Once a suspect phone number was dialed they could listen in and find out where the source would meet his or her handler and a surveillance man could be detailed to stake out the site. From there the snitch could be identified and targeted for death.

Samruk had thrown the entire Oaxaca operation together on the fly, there was never any time for a high level of planning, rehearsals, or setting up of contingencies. Samantha had been doing the best she could with what contacts she had inherited from her father. Aghassi had taken over those contacts and cultivated a few of his own in just a few days. It was all done on an ad hoc basis and now they were paying the price. They had gotten sloppy and now people had died for their errors.

Only the one source that Deckard had gotten a hold of the previous night had come out intact or his family would be laying dead in an arroyo somewhere and he'd be hanging under the overpass as well. Currently, the family was secured inside the Samruk compound.

Also back at the compound were black bodybags waiting to be flown back to Kazakhstan. The bodies inside belonged to those who died defending the compound and those killed during the recovery operation, including the seven men killed by the IED strike. Deckard had picked up pieces of Sergeant Zhenis to fill one of the body bags.

"Boss," Sergeant Major Korgan called out to Deckard.

The Sergeant Major sat in the passenger seat of one of the four assault trucks guarding the approaches to the overpass.

"What is it?" Deckard asked.

Korgan paused.

"Aghassi found something."

Thirty minutes later the Samruk patrol rolled up to a white building with a cross hanging over the door.

Aghassi and Nikita stood outside the front gate. Aghassi held a handkerchief over his mouth and nose. The Kazakh sniper looked up at the sky absently. Carrion eaters were circling overheard, riding the warm thermals and orbiting around the Christian mission.

Deckard jumped down from his vehicle and walked towards his two reconnaissance specialists. Aghassi had sounded breathless over the radio. He told Deckard where he was and said that there was something he needed to see for himself.

"What's up?" Deckard asked.

"Around back," Aghassi replied, dropping the handkerchief for a moment. "One of the locals told me this is a hospital for recovering addicts and the mentally disabled."

The front gate looked undamaged but the front door had clearly been caved it with a battering ram or something similar. Turning around the corner of the building, he spotted an old chicken coop. His nose crinkled at an old familiar smell. It was the stench of death.

He was already numb by the time be turned the corner to the rear side of the building, he knew what to expect. He heard the steady buzz of the flies before he ever saw the corpses.

Bodies lay on top of bodies, maybe twenty of them murdered in cold blood.

At his feet was the body of a young woman, her face turned black with a layer of flies. She had been stripped naked, both arms hacked off at the elbows with a machete.

On top of the splatter of gore created by the execution were words written in blood on the concrete wall with the woman's severed arms.

Go home, Gringo.

Half an hour later the convoy rolled into the Samruk compound. It was a mess, several of the roofs were caved in, rubble was strewn everywhere. Plastic film and white wrapping from medical bandages and gauze blew across the courtyard.

The assault trucks turned around and shotgun parked, preparing for the next mission. The drivers got out and attached the hand pump to a 55 gallon drum of gasoline and began cranking it to refuel the vehicles. It was still early morning and the heat of the day had not yet arrived. Deckard felt sore in his joints as he walked towards the OPCEN.

Inside, he grounded his gear and weapon before taking a seat.

"You okay?"

Deckard blinked as he looked up at Pat. He hadn't realized that he had been staring into space.

"Yeah, I'm just weighing our options."

"You did the right thing."

"What do you mean?"

"I could see that old familiar look in your eyes when we left the Christian mission. I thought for sure that you would order us back into the city to start hitting whatever targets we could scrounge up, the kind of scorched earth policy that you usually opt for."

"It wasn't because I didn't want to. If we get baited into a second ambush we won't have enough soldiers to fight with and win against Jimenez. One more night like the last one and Samruk International will no longer be combat effective. We're running out of bodies."

"Jimenez must have ordered the execution of those hospital patients. The message was clearly directed towards us. He wanted to provoke a response. He wanted to bait you into another ambush that would finish us off. But we are also running out of time," Pat remarked. "Before long, the Mexican Army will reorient their forces to Oaxaca. Not every General and politician is involved in your sex, lies, and videotape scandal."

"If we go charging back into that city we'll get put through the meat grinder again. This isn't like Iraq, we don't have AC-130 gunships providing air support."

"And Jimenez is dug into his compound up in the mountains. It would take over a month to flush them out of there."

"Aghassi and Nikita could try to get in the same way as before, maybe they'd even get to take a shot at Jimenez but it wouldn't change anything. Another lesson from Iraq. We kill HVT number one and HVT number two takes over. The organization survives. If we kill Jimenez then Ignacio takes over the cartel. If we kill Ignacio then number three takes over and so on."

"We need to dismantle the entire network, the cartel has to be systematically taken apart."

"But we need strong intelligence information to do that," Deckard said while rubbing his eyes. "And all of our sources except one are dead and even he is out of circulation for his own protection."

"We are inside his communication network," Cody said,

interrupting for the first time, having been mesmerized by his computer screen. "But we don't have the resources to do a comprehensive traffic analysis and connect every phone number belonging to a bad guy and then figure out where he is. There are too many."

"Yeah," Pat said. "Jimenez had it easy, our sources were not hard to track because the way they used their phones was so unique."

"So what are our options?" Deckard asked.

"We have almost twenty prisoners chained up in the other building that we can squeeze for additional information. Who knows if it will be actionable or not," Pat added as an afterthought. "We also took a prisoner last night, one of the guys who attacked the compound. He's a babbling mess though."

"What do you mean?"

"I don't know if he is in shock or just schizophrenic. He keeps mumbling to himself about the beast or something like that."

"Okay, line up interrogations with each of the prisoners. I'm going to sit down with the source we brought in last night and have a talk with him."

"This is the deal," Deckard told the source that they had rescued the previous night. His name was Cezar. They sat on one of Ortega's imported leather couches in what had been his bedroom. The large man-sized holes in the walls marked the entry points that Deckard and his crew had blasted just days ago.

"I have a contact back State-side. We will keep you and your family safe for the duration of our stay in Oaxaca but that isn't much longer. We need to get you set up with something more permanent, even if we take Jimenez out."

"I will never be safe in Mexico," Cezar agreed. "I appreciate everything you've done for us."

"I want to get you set up with the witness protection

program in America. It means starting over from scratch but it will be in the United States and it keeps you and your family alive. I think I know someone who can arrange this, they work for the CIA. In exchange, he is going to want to debrief you on everything you've been involved with for the cartel."

"Whatever they want, I will tell them."

"Good."

The source was one of the truck drivers that traveled in armored convoys loaded full of drugs, transporting them north along the drug corridors where they would then be turned over to other cartels for transport, or they would pay a tax in exchange for safe passage up to the border. From there, the drugs were smuggled into the United States by underground tunnels, concealed in vehicles, or even carried on the backs of drug mules who huffed it through the desert. He had traded information to Samantha's father for a quick buck here and there, then when the police chief had been killed, Samantha became his handler.

"Right now I need whatever additional information you might have about the cartel. The cell leaders involved, shipment routes, whatever you might have been holding in your back pocket. Now is the time to cash it in."

The prisoner sat in the corner of the concrete cell hugging his knees while rocking back and forth. His lips moved silently, his eyes darting around the room yet oblivious to his two visitors.

"He's been like this since we captured him," Pat told Deckard. "We bring him food and water but he hardly touches it."

"You think he is traumatized or in shock?"

"Probably both but it makes you wonder."

"What do you mean?"

"You should have seen it last night," Pat explained. "When the base got hit those fuckers charged us in waves. They

215

got right up to the walls a few times. Our boys had to drop hand grenades over the side of the outer walls to repel the attack."

"Sounds like the NVA overrunning Lang Vei in 1968. My dad told me about it once when I was a kid."

"He was there?"

"So the story goes."

The prisoner's head shot up as he looked around frantically.

"Thebeastthebeastthebeastthebeast."

"What the hell is he saying?" Deckard asked.

"Something about The Beast. Apparently that is the local legend about Jimenez, that he has some kind of pact with the devil or something. Useful for keeping people in fear."

"And keeping them in line," Deckard added.

"Talk to Aghassi about it. He saw all kinds of weird religious shit inside Jimenez' villa. It freaked the hell out of him. He told me that Jimenez is all into that satanic type shit."

The prisoner continued to mumble incoherently.

"Looks like he made a believer out of those guys that assaulted our compound last night," Pat said with a shrug.

"We'll see."

Samantha reached down and picked up a monkey wrench she had found earlier in one of the garages. She held it in one hand and slapped the end of it against her palm, testing the weight of it.

Perfect.

Turning, she began heading back to the improvised jail cells where all of the cartel prisoners that the mercenaries had captured thus far were being held. Deckard had ordered that they be re-interrogated with a special emphasis on identifying key nodes in the enemy's organizational structure.

Two Kalashnikov totting Kazakhs were stone faced next to the door, standing guard. As the former policewoman's hand moved to unlock the door she heard footsteps coming up behind her.

"Hold on a second Samantha," Deckard said. "Where are you going with that wrench."

"I'm going to get answers."

"I have an idea. Maybe something a little less invasive."

Aghassi was with him, wearing shorts, a t-shirt, and flip flops he looked just like one of the locals.

"Which one of the prisoners is the hardest?" Aghassi asked. "I'll break him."

"That has got to be Ricky. He's been cursing and spitting at me and the guards since you guys brought him in. A real son of a bitch."

"Bring Ricky out here," Deckard instructed the guards, switching back to Russian.

Aghassi brought out two folding chairs and set them up facing each other in the garage. He sat down in one of the chairs and stared down at the ground. In the other room Samantha and Deckard could hear a scuffle and curses getting thrown around in both Russian and Spanish. Finally, the Kazakh mercenaries dragged Ricky out with his feet trailing behind him on the concrete floor.

"Sit him down."

The Kazakhs dully complied and slammed him down in the chair, opposite Aghassi. Restrained with handcuffs, the guards each placed a hand on the prisoner's shoulders to keep him in place.

"Ricky, you probably don't know who I am," Deckard explained while mentally switching back over to Spanish. "I'm in charge here. I run this compound."

"Fuck you," Ricky spat, glaring at him.

"Yes, fuck me. Now, listen. This guy sitting across from you came to me with some grievances. He walked all the way up here from the town and told me that I was holding someone prisoner who he wanted to speak to. That prisoner was named Ricky and he was responsible for killing his family."

"What?"

"Yeah, I don't know exactly which of your actions affected this man. Was it a random bullet you fired that punched through a wall and blasted his son's brains out? Was it one of your deliberate contract killings? Was one of the women you

217

raped his wife?"

"Hold on, hold on!"

"I don't know, I didn't ask, but his family is dead by your hand."

"Who is this man, I've never seen him before?"

Ricky was getting frantic. Just where Deckard wanted him. Walking over to Samantha he relieved her of the monkey wrench she had wanted to use on Ricky and handed it over to Aghassi. The Samruk intelligence agent's face was a blank screen. He looked like a ghost as he stared straight ahead at Ricky.

Deckard extended the monkey wrench to Aghassi and he slowly reached over to take it from him.

"I have some questions to ask you Ricky. Questions that you've been giving us a hard time with. Now we are going to try something different."

"What do you mean? You can't do this!"

"I'm going to ask you some questions. The first time you lie to me, the first time you break my balls, I leave the room. My guards leave the room. You remain in handcuffs and this man in front of you gets to keep the wrench."

Ricky swallowed.

"Now Ricky, tell me, who knows the most about cartel operations after Jimenez and Ignacio?"

Taking a deep breath, Ricky began to sing.

32

"Get me Kurt Jager on the Iridium phone," Deckard said storming into the Operations Center. "Get in touch with our Agency contact Grant as well and tell him we need to talk. Bring up our target deck on screen, it's time to start filling in the blank spots."

Cody's fingers danced across the keyboard.

"Frank, go get me the source we brought in last night. The truck driver. I need to have a word with him so have him wait outside."

Frank got up and walked out. Leaving the crutches behind, he still had a slight limp.

"Pat, go wake up Fedorchenko and tell him that I want the men on standby and ready to go on a moment's notice."

"You got it," Pat said as he followed Frank out the door.

"Kurt is on the line for you," Cody announced.

"Put him on speaker."

"Kurt?"

"I'm here Six, what can we do for you?"

"I need you to mobilize the Zapatista militia. We are getting to the end game and it's time to put the pressure on Jimenez. Is Commandante Zero ready to go?"

"Are you kidding me?" Kurt laughed. "We've been trying to hold him back since you gave him all these new weapons."

"Good. Samruk will handle urban targets inside Oaxaca City. I want the Zapatista soldiers to action targets in the rural areas that they are more familiar with."

"That's my opinion as well and it is shared with Commandante Zero. We've been prepping that mini-submarine you captured and have identified a landing zone on the western shore where the drugs are coming in."

"Get that mission rolling as soon as you can. Any other targets that Zero is looking at?"

"These people have lived here their whole life. They know where the cartel is out here in the hills and what they are up to. Their intel is pretty solid."

"Grant is holding for you," Cody interrupted.

"Okay, Kurt. You know the deal. Make it happen."

"Will do," the German said, signing off.

"Grant?"

"I'm here Deckard," the CIA officer's voice came over the speaker phone.

"I have an informant who's been outed. I need safe passage for him. He's willing to do a debrief."

"Who is he?"

"A drug courier. It's him, his wife, and his kid."

"What are you asking me for?"

"Witness protection."

"Give me his information, if he is who you say he is I will make it happen."

"Any progress on tracking down the Arab?"

"I was about to ask you the same thing. This guy is a ghost. Nobody knows who he is or where he is. I've got people working this around the clock, people are starting to get freaked out about it. There is nothing on this guy but myths and rumors. People have heard of him, are scared of him, but he's like some kind of boogeyman that no one can actually pin down."

"I'll keep an eye and an ear open for him."

"Pass on whatever you have and I will let you know if we locate him. Our databases are empty on this guy. If we find him and then you do what you do once I give you his whereabouts, I'll put as many people into witness protection as you want."

"Good to know. I will have something for you soon."

"I hope so Deckard. I will uphold my end of the bargain but we can't keep the heat off you forever. You are starting a war in America's backyard after all."

"We're not starting one Grant, we're finishing one."

Deckard walked over and hung up the phone.

"Let's take a look inside this communications network Cody."

The computer expert brought up a window on the projection screen showing thousands of telephones connecting to each other as well as showing the links between them. The infographic looked like a giant spider web.

"Once we identify who the leaders are in the cartel network, we can begin taking them apart faster than the cartel can react. When we get inside their decision making process then we've got them by the balls."

"But we have no way of knowing who is who," Cody explained. "This is just raw data. It means nothing by itself."

"Until now. We had a little talk with our prisoner, Ricky, and hit the jack pot. There is a paymaster for the Jimenez cartel. He's got so much money that it is just stacking up in safe houses and in the villa, he literally doesn't know what to do with it. When he has to pay his men, pay off officials, or hire freelancers he sends the paymaster to deliver the cash. This guy knows everyone and is the closest thing to the drug lord's secretary. He probably knows more about the interconnections between the cartel and Mexican society than even Jimenez does."

"Do we have his phone number?"

"No."

"Then how am I supposed to find him in all this mess," Cody said waving at the projection that displayed thousands upon thousands of numbers.

Someone knocked on the door to the OPCEN, interrupting the conversation.

Deckard opened the door and saw Samantha standing there with the source. Frank was lumbering down the hall behind them.

"We've arranged for safe passage for you and your family," Deckard told the truck driver.

Cezar suddenly had tears in his eyes.

"Don't thank me just yet, I need a name."

"What name?"

"Do you know who the paymaster was who paid you and the other drivers?"

"Kenny Rodriguez."

"Do you know where he lives?"

"No."

"Thanks," Deckard nodded. "Samantha, come inside. You too Frank."

Once inside the OPCEN, Deckard led her around to where Cody had his computers set up.

"I need to check your cell phone."

"What for?"

"I want the numbers of each one of the policemen you had under your command before they went rogue."

"Um, okay. If you think it will help."

Going through the address book on her phone, she began

221

reading off numbers to Cody.

"Frank?"

"What's up?"

"I want you to go round up Aghassi and tell him to hand pick three guys he wants to take with him for a low-visibility snatch and grab operation. I will fill him in on the details once he gets here."

"You like your coffee with cream and sugar?"

"Just be glad you still have a job here with that gimp ass leg."

"Funny," he grumbled as he headed back out.

Looking over at Cody, he had taken the phone from Samantha and entered the numbers into the computer within seconds. The man was an absolute savant with numbers.

"Cody, find me any phone numbers that Samantha's corrupt cops called."

Cody blew through the analytical program he used and brought up a phone number once he correlated one between each of the policemen.

"Here is one."

"That was my father's number," Samantha commented bitterly.

"What else do we have?"

Pounding out some more commands on the keyboard, Cody used the mouse and brought up a second number.

"This is the only other one that they have in common with each other."

"Now take that number and see who else that person has been calling."

"It's all over the map. Definitely Jimenez and Ignacio but also people spread all over Oaxaca City. Some of these numbers he dialed belong to the prisoners we are holding, particularly the leaders of their groups."

"That's got to be him," Deckard said. "That's Kenny Rodriguez."

Kenny Rodriguez was leaned up against the front tire of one of the assault trucks, sitting on the ground with his hands still in restraints. Deckard got down on one knee, grabbed him by the front of his t-shirt and pulled him in. Aghassi had just linked up with the two Samruk patrols where they were pre-positioned in formation and ready to roll into action. Aghassi's teamed had snatched him off the streets just minutes ago.

"This is how it works Kenny," Deckard growled. "You tell us everything. We want everyone in the city who is in charge of anything. Who runs the networks of spotters and linkmen that call information up to the cartel, who runs the kidnaps rings, who runs the assassination rings, who coordinates drug shipments, who runs the shifts of men who guard cartel assets, who is in charge of keeping the cartel's telecommunication masts up and running, we want them all."

Kenny's eyes were wide, his pupils dilated.

"Once we have what we want you catch a ride north and get a new name and new career selling used cars in Denver or Cleveland with the witness protection program. If you lie to me or refuse to talk, we still get what we want out of you but you lose your fingernails to a pair of needle nose pliers and then I dump you in the sketchiest part of town and make sure that whatever cartel buddies of yours are left see that you have been working with us."

"I will tell you whatever you want to know," Kenny squawked, his voice suddenly going high pitched.

"Load him in my vehicle," Deckard ordered the three Kazakhs with Aghassi. "Flex cuff him to the vehicle and leave his face uncovered. I want the entire city to see him as we pass by, that way he knows there is no way turning back. The only way forward is my way."

"Roger," the Kazakhs confirmed, dragging the cartel paymaster up by his arms and pushing him towards the lead vehicle.

Deckard walked along the convoy, looking up at the men as they squirted lubricating oil into the PKM machine guns in the turrets and assaulters re-checked their breaching equipment. They were all business and all knew that today was game day. They had to go big or go home.

They were pre-positioned just outside of the city. Now that everything was ready to go, he reached into his vehicle and retrieved his Iridium phone. Extending the antenna, Deckard dialed the number for his training cell working with the Zapatistas out in the hinterlands of Oaxaca and into Chiapas.

"Hello?" Kurt said answering the phone on his end.

"Green light any and all operations," Deckard told him. "Hit the high priority targets and move on down the list."

"We already have maneuver elements standing by and in position."

"Good luck."

"You too."

Deckard terminated the call and climbed into his truck. Kenny was crammed in the middle of the cab with his hands tethered through a metal roll bar that ran across the roof. Reaching for the radio Deckard keyed the handmic.

"Initiate movement," he said on the assault net. "We're heading down the main MSR through the city. Standby for targets."

The driver started down the road, picking up speed as the city lay sprawled out in front of them. Deckard turned in his seat and looked back at Kenny.

"This is what is going to happen Kenny. We are going to start driving around town and you are going to be our oracle and point out the house of every mid-level and above cartel member. Got it?"

Kenny looked away and nodded his head in a state of dejected defeat.

34

The Stewmaker followed a specific recipe.

In his line of work, he found that it helped to develop a consistent schedule, almost turning it into a professional ritual. Some of his fellow cartel members worshiped Santa Muerta, the Black Madonna, Chupacabras and all manner of nonsense. He was raised a strict Catholic without all the added window dressing that the working poor had ingratiated into their religion but these days the Stewmaker didn't have much of anything to believe in other than the six hundred dollars a week that the cartel paid him.

The money was good, but the work was somewhat time consuming, depending on how busy the cartel was. Last summer Jimenez had decided to heat up the plaza and wipe out some rivals. The Stewmaker had to dispose of so many bodies that his family had hardly seen him over the span of a couple months.

With a sigh, he dropped down to his hands and knees and poked the wood fire under the giant metal vat that he had started an hour ago. The recipe called for two hundred liters of water, brought to a slow boil, followed by two entire sacks of sodium hydroxide. Setting the metal poker aside, he swatted at some of the flies buzzing around, giant black fuckers that went straight for his eyes and ears.

It was the corpses that attracted the flies. Two of them lay besides the vat, their skin having gone gray, eyes sunken. Sometimes the bodies came in with obvious signs of torture and mutilation. Sometimes they came in with one clean gunshot wound through the head, sometimes they were riddled with bullets from head to toe. These two had severe cuts across their arms, signs of putting up a defense before they died from deep stab wounds in the abdomen. It looked like they had gotten into a sword fight but it wasn't the Stewmaker's place to ask questions. He worked disposal while someone else worked termination.

Lighting a cigarette, he watched the stew slowly come to a boil. He moved to put on some protective gear before dumping the bodies into the cauldron. First there was an apron, followed by heavy plastic gloves, and finally a face mask and goggles. Safety first.

Rubbing out his cigarette, the Stewmaker lifted the mask in place and hefted the first corpse over his shoulder. Handling dead weight was much more difficult than carrying someone who was still alive. Slowly, he eased the corpse into the bubbling stew. He dreaded what came next. The other corpse was the fat one. Grunting and straining, he managed to slide the second body into the vat.

The stew would cook for eight hours before he would extinguish the fire. He would stir the contents periodically and experience told him that all that would be left by the end was fingernails, toenails, and teeth. The stew would then be poured into 55 gallon drums, hauled out by pickup truck, and the contents burned at some remote location.

The fat one bobbed to the surface.

The Stewmaker used his fire poker to try to sink the body back into the mixture, but to no avail. He should have known better. Before dumping the body, he should have used a butcher's cleaver to slice open the stomach cavity and let the air out. No way would he be thrashing the corpse with a machete while it floated in caustic soda.

Discarding the gloves, mask, and goggles, the Stewmaker looked over at the two dozen drums stacked in the corner of his yard. It had been a busy month. He lived up in the hill country towards the border of Oaxaca and Chiapas where his activities could fly under the radar. The cartel would drop fresh corpses at his front door in the middle of the night and he'd get to work when he discovered them in the morning. Once a month, an envelope packed full of cash was slipped under his door. It was a nice arrangement.

The Stewmaker grew frustrated as he watched the fat body float across the surface of the vat. He knew better and should have taken precautions. Eventually, the lye would eat through the body and deflate it, but it was still irritating.

Just then, the front gate was kicked in and gunmen wearing black masks stormed his body disposal factory. Before the cigarette could drop from his mouth he was surrounded by ten gunmen. The Stewmaker put his hands in his pockets. That day had finally come. A rival cartel had come for him or the families of the victims hired some freelancers to do him in.

He did a double take as another masked man entered through the gate. He was smoking a pipe through a hole in his balaclava.

"Commandente Zero?"

The Strewmaker asked the question in a state of shock.

"The one and only!"

"I thought you were dead."

The Zapatista leader drew his hand gun and pointed it at the Stewmaker.

"Throw him in the vat with his friends," he ordered his underlings. "Let's see how he likes an caustic bath."

The Zapatistas slung their rifles and seized the Stewmaker by the arms, two others lifting him by the legs. He kicked and resisted but it was no use.

"Wait, wait, stop!"

The Stewmaker protested as they carried him over to his bubbling body stew. He continued to curse and scream all the way up until the point where the Zapatistas dumped him in head first, the guerrilla fighters shrinking away as the lye splashed.

"Go, go, go!" Kurt Jager pushed his Zapatista comrade up the ladder. Rushing up to the top of the ladder the two men climbed out of the midget submarine. The dorsal surface of the hull was just barely above the waterline, the mast sticking out a few feet further. In the dark of night, the submarine was invisible to their target.

Kurt looked at the Zapatista rebel and nodded his head. They both leaped into the ocean. The dark waters surrounded the former GSG-9 commando. As an experienced diver, Kurt remained calm and kicked his way to the surface. A second later, the Zapatista came up next to them.

The submarine had already disappeared from view as its screw turned and propelled it towards the landing area on the beach. The two soldiers were like baseball players who had just wound up and swung as hard as they could. They hit the ball just right and drove it right down the center, heading for the bleachers. They should have been swimming for the shore much like the baseball player should have been running for first base instead of watching to see if he hit a home run.

Instead they floated in the ocean, their eyes fixated on the horizon.

With the submarine pen destroyed by Deckard and his Samruk mercenaries, Jimenez had to revert back to the old system of ferrying the cocaine from Colombia on cigarette boats. The high speed sport boats would zip in and out at a certain time of night just south of Acapulco.

A ball of orange flame lit up the night, reflecting tiny red triangles across the ripples of the sea. The shock wave rocked over the submariners as they broke out with smiles. The submarine made contact with the docking station where the cigarette boats were offloading the drugs and had detonated. The trigger mechanism was stupid simple, two metal pie pans with a piece of Styrofoam between them separated the two electric leads going to the detonator. When the sub smashed into the boats or the dock, the Styrofoam trigger mounted to the nose was crushed, connecting the leads and detonating the TNT explosives that they had packed the sub with.

Fiberglass flew through the air as at least two of the sport boats were torn apart, the gas tanks going up in secondary explosions.

The only way they would get to Jimenez was death by a thousand cuts, and now they had once again cut off his revenue stream at its source.

As the fire began to die down, the two swimmers headed towards the shore.

35

"This peach colored house here on the left with the blue door," Kenny said pointing it out to Deckard. "That's where Jose lives. He runs a team of assassins."

"Truck Two," Deckard said over the radio. "This is Six."

"Six this is two, over."

"Peach colored house on the left. Blue door."

"Roger."

Truck number two broke off from the rest of the convoy and made a beeline for the house. Speeding up, the driver barreled through the front gate, blasting it open. The assaulters jumped off the truck and swarmed the house, quickly making entry.

"On the right, the two story blue building with a balcony over the front door," Kenny sighed. "That is where Julio lives, he kidnaps people for the cartel, it is his specialty."

"Truck Three," Deckard radioed. "Blue two story on the right. You are looking for Julio."

"Roger," the radio hissed.

Truck three left the convoy and stopped in front of the target building. Looking over his shoulder, he saw the mercenaries applying a flex linear charge across the front door. Seconds later, they blew it, rattling windows all over the neighborhood.

"Make a left hand turn at this intersection," Kenny advised.

"Hard left," Deckard informed the rest of the convoy as his driver brought them around the corner.

"Okay, this white building over here."

"With the green trim around the windows."

"Yes, that is where Alejandro lives. He runs an extortion enterprise for Jimenez, taking a cut from the local businesses."

"Truck Four, white house...on the right...green trim," Deckard said with a few stutters in between. He was quickly transitioning from Spanish to Russian, neither of which was his native language. "You want Alejandro."

"Roger boss."

Truck Four stopped short and the assaulters ran to the door. Identifying where the hinges were, the mercenaries shoved a Hooligan tool in the crack between the door and the frame. Another mercenary pounded on the flat end of the Hooligan tool with sledgehammer. When it had advanced far enough into the door jamb, the mercenary on the hoolie tool pressed it forward and the door splintered open. The assault team stacked on the door and moved in to clear the first room.

"The white three story building on the corner with the orange windows," Kenny said.

"Who lives there?"

"Ignacio's brother owns the building. He lives on the second floor and is a part of the cartel's inner circle."

"Truck Five, white three story on the corner. Floor two is where HVT number six lives."

"Roger," Truck Five's Squad Leader answered as they pulled up in front of the building.

Their target deck was now getting wiped clean almost as fast as they could fill it out with names.

"Six, this is Truck Two, over."

"Send it Truck Two."

"We are back in the convoy, over."

Deckard's vehicle kept at a slow roll as they coasted through the streets of nighttime Oaxaca City. As each assault element wrapped things up they would fall back into the convoy formation. They were not screwing around on the objective. They would force their way onto the target, kill any fighting age males that looked at them the wrong way and move on. Others would be flexcuffed and left behind for relatives to recover.

"Make a right hand turn here," Kenny informed Deckard.

"Hard right, hard right," Deckard said holding the handmic in front of his mouth.

"This pink building next to the church with the white shutters. They guy living there tortures people in the basement for Jimenez."

"Truck Six, pink building next to the church. Look for civilians being held prisoner in the basement."

"Roger."

Truck Six pulled up and the mercenaries jumped the ground and began placing their charge on the door.

"Six this is Truck Three, we are rejoining the convoy."

"Roger, Truck Three."

"So this yellow house next to the auto parts store is where-"

It went on all night as the oracle continued to spill his guts. The priority targets were cell leaders and those high up on the cartel food chain but targets of opportunity were nearly anyone associated with the drug traffickers. Kenny grew up in town and knew the topography of the city like the back of his hand, recommending short cuts and helping them as much as he could. He realized there was no turning back for him. He identified every target he could think of, some Deckard passed on as insignificant, others he prioritized.

The Samruk patrol moved so fast through the city and churned the enemy through the meat grinder so fast that they had interrupted the enemy's decision making process. Cody monitored the situation from the OPCEN and sent updates but the enemy was unable to react quickly enough to organize an effective resistance.

The cartel gunmen initiated one haphazard ambush which was easily repelled but after that they simply began to fire their guns into the air as a warning when the assault trucks were spotted rolling into their neighborhood. Even with warning shots, the convoy continued to snake through the city, staying one step ahead of the cartel's ability to self-organize.

By three in the morning, Samruk International had expended all of their demolitions and had to meet with a deuce and a half supply truck that the skeleton crew left at their compound dispatched to meet them. They had hit over fifty targets and had added dozens of enemy KIA to the kill list including several High Value Targets.

Getting back on schedule with magazines topped off and the mercenaries constructing new door charges as they drove, more targets were identified and struck one by one.

At four thirty in the morning, Deckard stood in the street watching his assaulters mechanically breach a door with a battering ram before flooding the structure with shooters. There were a few cracks of gunfire throughout the city, but under the dull golden glow of the street lights, everything was strangely quiet. A strange, disconcerting feeling crept over him. It wasn't some kind of sixth sense warning him of danger, it was something else, something different.

Finally, as the assaulters exfiltrated off the objective and loaded back onto their truck, he realized what that feeling was. Something had changed.

"You okay over there," Pat said as he opened the passenger door on the assault truck as it stopped next to him.

"I just realized something," Deckard said. He looked confused.

"What's that?"

"We won."

Pat nodded.

"I know."

"Now we need to finish this."

"I'll consolidate the men and vehicles," Pat said as he slammed the door shut.

The mercenaries stood in the courtyard of the Jimenez compound. It was strangely anti-climactic. They had expected a pitched battle all the way up the side of the mountain and right through Jimenez' front door. Instead they strutted right in without any opposition.

The villa was in flames. The fortress had been torched and left to history for yet another party to reclaim sometime in the future.

"The sever room is down," Cody informed Deckard over the radio.

"I'm not surprised," Deckard muttered, watching the building on top of it burn to the ground. They had probably used electromagnets on the hard drives and then set the place on fire. Once the antenna farm on the roof burned up then nothing was being transmitted in or out anyway.

"Not what I was expecting," Sergeant Major Korgan said from behind Deckard.

"I know," he replied as he turned out. "It's kind of a letdown."

"So whatchu gonna do PL?" Pat asked walking up to

him. It was a joke, in part anyway. Instructors in Ranger School were known for asking that question to confused students who had been made patrol leader.

"Good question, this place is a dry hole and speaking of dry holes, I think we've just about exhausted Kenny."

"Sorry boss," Aghassi said walking up to join them. "They blew out of here just as we arrived."

He and Nikita had been out running route and target reconnaissance for them all night, pulling double duty as sniper overwatch.

"We grabbed a few people we saw milling around on the way in and found out that Jimenez took his motorcade and headed into the city. Like I said, we just missed them."

Deckard reached into his vehicle and snatched the handmic again.

"Cody, is the cartel comms network completely down?"

"It is still useable as long as the repeaters are functioning but we don't have the ability to track it now that the sever room is cooked. I did see a spike in chatter just before it went down though. We do know that many of the phone numbers popping up at that time belong to Ignacio's crew."

They had put off striking Ignacio's compound. When the cartels fully conquered Oaxaca, Ignacio had taken over the city's cultural museum which was actually a converted convent. With its high walls and added fortifications, Deckard didn't feel that taking down Jimenez' number two man was worth the losses they would surely incur. Now it seemed that Jimenez had split from his mountain fortress and combined his forces with Ignacio.

"Gather the men," Deckard ordered Sergeant Major Korgan. "I know where they are."

With a few shouts, the assaulters gathered around their commander, waiting for his orders.

"I'm not good with Braveheart speeches," Deckard started. "But what the fuck else is new."

The mercenaries laughed at the movie reference.

"I will keep this short. What we do means more than what we say. Jimenez and Ignacio are holed up at their base back inside Oaxaca City. Today we finish this. Load the trucks."

The mercenaries broke ranks and ran to their vehicles, each engine turning over one right after the other. Rolling out of

233

the courtyard, Deckard's vehicle took the lead as they headed back into the city and whatever Jimenez had waiting for them.

36

Ignacio and Jimenez stood atop the tower at the center of what had been the Oaxaca Cultural Museum. Today it was another Jimenez fortress, this one serving as an Oaxaca base of operations that his number two, Ignacio normally ran for him. Based on the previous night's events, they had decided to combine their forces and make their final stand together rather than as two separately weaker elements. They were both running short on men, but together they had scraped together a few hundred fighters. The old cloisters, towers, and high walls of the former convent would be their Alamo.

"I understand," Ignacio said before hanging up and pocketing his cell phone.

"What is it?" Jimenez demanded.

"One of my *halcones* calling in," Ignacio said referring to one of the many lookouts posted around the city. Most of them were just kids with a cartel-supplied phone who called in reports for pocket change. "The mercenaries are on their way."

"Let's see this paper airplane fly," the drug lord said to the men standing beside them.

Down below, in the cloistered courtyard, cartel gunmen scurried along like ants as they stockpiled ammunition in key locations around the aging convent. Fortifications were being built up and preparations were made. With a little luck, the mercenaries would be in pieces by the time they stumbled up to the fortress walls.

One of the men ran across the edge of the tower with what looked like a giant model airplane in his hand. Reeling back like a baseball pitcher, he winged the miniature drone into the air where it quickly managed to gain some lift and buzz up into the sky. The Casper 250 had been purchased from an Israeli company through a cut-out operation and pressed into service by the cartel, although they hadn't had much use for it until now.

With an onboard camera and thermal vision sight, the pilot would fly the drone from the control and data uplink unit and report real time intelligence information to the strike force that was readying to intercept the foreign mercenaries.

Jimenez used his smart phone to place a call to the strike team leader as he walked behind the pilot and looked at the computer screen that allowed them to see what the drone was seeing. As the phone rang, the drone quickly gained altitude in the morning sky and reached the outskirts of the city.

Sure enough, an eight vehicle convoy had reached the city limits and was heading toward their location.

"Yes, sir?" the strike commander answered.

"Are you're men in position?"

"Yes, sir."

"They are coming in on Internacional Road. Eight gun trucks."

"We will move to intercept them now."

"I will hold," the drug lord said impatiently.

Jimenez watched as the mercenary convoy rolled down the main highway that cut through the city. On the live feed from the Casper drone, the assault vehicles looked like little toy trucks rolling down the street. The cartel strike team had ten vehicles of their own moving towards the road the foreigners traveled on. While the mercenaries favored light tactical vehicles for mobility, the cartel trucks were heavily armored.

With his latest drug shipment destroyed in Acapulco, Jimenez had ordered the armed escort vehicles immediately back to Oaxaca City. Normally, the cartel gun trucks would provide security for similarly armored tractor trailer trucks as the drugs were shipped up the corridor heading north on Mexico 95 where taxes would be paid to the Zetas to transport the drugs to the US border. Now that the shipment had been blown sky high, the drug lord intended to use the escort trucks as a strike team against the mercenaries.

On the screen, Jimenez watched the cartel truck parallel Internacional Road where the mercenaries were speeding towards the old convent.

"Veer left on this upcoming street," Jimenez said into the phone to the strike commander.

"That will put them right on Internacional when the two roads merge. They will be right on top of each other!" Ignacio blurted.

"Exactly."

The rattle of machine gun fire was the only warning before the Samruk mercenary sitting next to Pat was torn apart by machine gun fire. His body jerked and spasmed in the seat with each impact. Across from them, the former Delta Force operator watched as a convoy of enemy gun trucks merged onto the highway.

Machine gunners opened fire at a distance of just meters apart from each other. While the Samruk turret gunners manning PKM machine guns were relatively exposed, the cartel pickup trucks had been armored by improvising metal plating around the gun mount that had been built into the top of the cab of each truck. Even the belts of Armor Piercing Incendiary ammo that the mercenaries cycled through their PKMs was sparking off the armor plating.

Pat and the other mercenaries facing outward on the back of the assault trucks fired their own individual weapons opting for rapid fire or automatic with their AK-103s. They were suddenly right on top of the enemy and tactics flew out the window as it became a competition to see who could throw down the most lead.

The closest cartel gun truck ran a stream of auto-fire across Pat's vehicle that tagged their own machine gunner. Collapsing in the turret, Pat unbuckled himself and held tightly to the roll bar that ran down the center of the assault truck as the driver swerved across the road. As they screamed into Oaxaca City, houses blasted by in a blur of movement.

The two convoys were now like enemy ships of the line in the 1700's which had both come broadside with each other to unleash a volley of cannon fire and blasted each other to smithereens.

Clawing his way up into the turret, Pat took control of the PKM. Holding down the trigger, the Russian machine gun chewed through the rest of the belt of 7.62 ammunition, spitting bullets that rattled off the pickup truck's armor. The enemy gunner in the enclosed turret was protected from Pat's counter-fire except for an opening where his own M240B machine gun barrel pointed out but at least Pat was able to keep the gunner's head down and prevent him from firing.

The bed of the pickup alongside them was also armored with metal plates sticking up on both sides to protect the gunmen in the back. Pat looked around his working space and found a metal coffee can that bad been bolted to the side of the turret. Inside were some of the party favors he had been looking for.

Palming a fragmentation grenade, he yanked the pin and threw the grenade just forward of the pickup. With both vehicles moving at high speed, he had to compensate. The bomb landed in the bed of the pickup and detonated, tossing bodies into the air like rag dolls. The vehicle itself didn't explode like in a movie, but it did careen off the road with the driver slumped over the wheel and that was good enough for Pat.

Reaching for a fresh belt of ammunition, he struggled to get the machine gun loaded as the driver down below drove evasively. Slamming the feed tray cover closed, he pulled the charging handle and began firing as a second cartel gun truck moved up alongside them.

Deckard's head bounced off the side of the cab causing him to see stars. Kenny, who was still flexcuffed in the vehicle, screamed as the truck began listing off the road to one side. The windshield was splattered with blood. Blinking sweat out of his eyes, Deckard saw the driver hanging limply in his seat belt. The driver's side window was shattered. Somehow the armored cab of the vehicle had been penetrated. Momentarily disoriented, Deckard didn't know if they had hit another IED or what was going on but he had to conduct a dead driver drill if they were going to survive.

Reaching over, he elbowed the driver out of the way and grabbed the wheel with one hand. With his foot he kicked down and swept the driver's legs out of the way. Using the weight of his body and the kit that he wore, he leaned against the Kazakh to press him out of the way and give him some more room to work.

Driving while looking through a blood splattered windshield with one foot on the gas and one hand on the wheel wasn't easy. Then the turret gunner began shooting.

Through the spider webbed driver's side window, Deckard turned and saw an up-armored cartel pickup truck pull up next to them. The gunner in the armored turret rotated towards them and cut loose with a fusillade of gunfire that stitched across the hood of Deckard's Iveco assault truck.

Easing off the gas pedal, Deckard let the cartel vehicle overtake them slightly. His own turret gunner fired his PKM, the bullets bouncing off the armor welded around the enemy machine gunner.

Placing his hand on the twelve o'clock position on the wheel, Deckard knew it would be the only way to remember which position kept the vehicle driving forward. With his ears ringing, his eyes stinging, and visibility limited by blood splatter on the glass and the shattered windows, he felt claustrophobic and confused. He was trapped inside a metal kill box and the shit had most definitely hit the fan.

With the enemy pickup's rear quarter panel sliding parallel with the left corner of Deckard's assault truck, Deckard suddenly rotated his hand all the way to the left, bringing his hand on the wheel from the twelve to the six o' clock position.

At high speed, the vehicles made contact. As Deckard executed a PIT maneuver, the rear wheels on the cartel gun truck lost traction and began to spin out while the vehicle itself turned sideways as Deckard sped up, t-boning the vehicle for a second. A second was long enough for the PKM gunner in the turret to lower the barrel of his machine gun and let off a devastating burst into the bed of the pickup where the cartel gunmen were hunkered down.

Flesh separated from bone as red ribbons were flung into the air. The cartel pickup then spun past the assault truck's bumper and rolled over into an irrigation ditch on the side of the road.

Deckard brought his hand on the wheel back to the twelve o' clock position, straightening out the front tires to get them going down the straightaway again.

Sergeant Major Korgan rode on the back of his truck with the men. When the two convoys collided, those sitting on either side of him were shot instantly. One was dead, the other was applying self-aid with a tourniquet. The Sergeant Major ignored the blood pumping down his own arm and sighted in with his AK-103.

The barrel wavered back and forth as the vehicle moved. The M240B gunner in the cartel gun truck went cyclic but he was also unable to draw a bead on his target, the tracer and ball ammo combination flying high over their heads.

Cracking off several shots, one struck the windshield of the cartel truck as his own vehicle began to pull ahead. He had discovered the gun truck's weak point. They had welded metal plating all around the vehicle as armor but apparently they did not have access to bullet proof glass. Running a controlled burst across the windshield, Korgan watched as the gun truck jumped the median and flew into the opposite lane of traffic.

The cartel gun truck went head on with a city bus that was heading down the opposite lane. The truck disappeared in a cloud of dust as the bus slowed to a halt. Several bodies had been flung out of the bed of the truck and lay in the street. It had happened so fast, that Korgan didn't have time to process the event, or to think about his injured arm.

Instinctively, he held onto the truck with one hand with the AK in the other, the vehicle jerking to the side as the median to their flank exploded in a shower of concrete. The next gun truck was coming up behind them, a cartel shooter in the back firing an under barrel M203 grenade launcher attached to his M-4 carbine.

The PKM gunner rotated his turret to cover their six and opened up at the same time as the enemy M240B gunner. Several rounds from the M240B cracked dangerously close but the mercenary behind the PKM got a splash of sparks off the

M240B as he returned fire. The cartel machine gunner dropped down into the pickup, shot dead.

The injured mercenary sitting next to Korgan had gotten his tourniquet in place and stopped the bleeding. Shouldering his AK, the Samruk mercenary was back in the fight and launching rounds at the enemy gunmen with the grenade launcher. The PKM gunner in the turret tagged the enemy grenadier with a burst, causing the him to jerk the trigger as he fell out of the back of the pickup. With a pop, the 40mm grenade launched from the M203 and detonated in the street just behind the assault truck.

Walking his automatic fire down the front of the cartel pickup, the machine gunner then blasted through the windshield, causing the shards inside the cab to be sprayed with crimson. The pickup slowed to a crawl and the cartel vehicle behind it was unable to swerve out of the way fast enough. When they collided, the rear end of the second truck bucked up into the air, tossing more passengers out into the street.

Several bodies pinwheeled through the air with arms and legs splayed apart before gravity took hold and deposited them back to terra firma.

Jimenez watched the monitor as two of the mercenary assault trucks converged their fire on a strike force pickup truck. The driver evidently panicked because he yanked the wheel and took the truck off road. Overcompensating, the driver blasted through a chain link fence and went over a retaining wall where the truck landed on its side.

"What the fuck was that," Ignacio exclaimed. "How is this happening? These idiots don't know how to drive!"

"These idiots have escorted hundreds of shipments up north. They have traded fire with everyone from the Zetas to the Marines. This is happening because that gringo down there is motivated to win," Jimenez stated. He was not amused.

Scrolling through the numbers in the address book on his smart phone, Jimenez placed a call.

"This is why you create a layered defense."

CJ Reyes worked the chain on the pulley system hand over hand, bringing up the garage door. Inside was his baby. He had been working on it for several months. First sourcing the body and then the metal and welding equipment. Jimenez gave him as much money as he needed and it was every insane mechanic's dream come true.

Elsewhere, across town he could hear gunfire echoing throughout the city.

The phone in his oil stained jeans pocket began to vibrate.

"Yes, boss," he answered.

"Is it ready?"

"*Cebada* is ready to be deployed. I was just about to start him up."

"*Cebada*," Jimenez repeated. It was the name of the breed of bull with the most human kills of any of the breeds used for bullfighting. "I like that."

37

Nikita held his HK 417 under one arm as he staggered uphill. He was breathing hard and already covered in sweat. Aghassi followed just behind him. They had been running forward reconnaissance for the convoy in their indigenous vehicle when they heard of the enemy contact over the radio. Only a few minutes ahead of the main element, they had to act fast if they were going to respond.

Pulling off to the side of the road, they bolted uphill, grabbing onto small tree trunks and exposed roots to help make their way to a superior position.

"Here they come," Aghassi said.

Looking over his shoulder, Nikita saw the Samruk convoy, their comrades, involved in a pitched gun battle with a handful of cartel gun trucks. At first glance, it looked like the Samruk vehicles had already taken a beating. Sitting down on the incline was awkward. He ended up laying on his side. Curling up his knees, he let the rifle rest with the barrel oriented down into the street.

The convoy was moving fast and would blow by their position and be gone in just a few seconds.

Nikita focused in on one of the machine gunners in the armored turret of the nearest pickup. The area he had to fire through was the small gun port that the M240B's barrel was stuck through. The gap was maybe a little wider than his fist, and the target was moving.

Tracking his target, the 417's barrel gently moved as the battle got closer and closer. Stroking the trigger, his round went wide and harmlessly struck the armor plating. His follow up shot disappeared into the gap and the M240B went silent.

Next to him, Aghassi fired his AK-103 into the passengers riding in the back of one of the cartel pickups as it passed, spraying them with gunfire.

Then the convoy was gone, twisting around the cut in the hill.

"Shit."

"At least we thinned them out a little," Aghassi said. "Let's catch up."

Squinting to see through the blood splatter on the glass, Deckard turned the wheel as the convoy exited a long straightaway and began up the winding road that followed along the hill in the middle of the city. It was the same hill with the cellular phone towers on it that Nikita and Agassi had occupied the day before yesterday.

While reaching over the dead driver and steering the wheel, Deckard snatched the folder he kept secured on his Safariland holster. Flicking the switch, the spring-assisted blade locked into the open position. It was a small Benchmade folder that he carried for general purposes.

"Here," he said handing the knife to Kenny. "Cut yourself free and give me a hand."

Up above Kenny, the PKM gunner in the turret was rocking the gun sending hot brass raining down into the vehicle.

"Sh-sh-shit," Kenny said, stumbling with the knife.

"Hurry up," Deckard scolded him. I can barely see what I'm doing here."

Kenny cut through the plastic flexcuffs and looked up.

"Sh-shit!"

"What the-," Deckard's eyes went back to the road. "Shit!"

Jerking the wheel, the turret gunner lost his grip on the PKM and held on tight as the assault truck swung around a hairpin turn. If it wasn't for the vehicle being weighted down with guns, ammunition, and the mercenaries themselves, he probably would have dumped the Iveco truck on its side.

With the engine howling and spewing smoke from bullet holes in the hood, they rounded the turn with inches to spare as they left some of the truck's desert tan paint job behind on the concrete barrier at the edge of the road.

The cartel gun truck that had been close on their heels and gaining on them didn't see the turn soon enough with Deckard's vehicle blocking their view. Once he turned out of the way and the cartel driver saw the sharp bend in the road he didn't have enough time to make a correction.

The armored pickup truck jumped the curb and smashed right through the flimsy metal railing at the edge of the road before plummeting off the side of the cliff.

"Kenny, grab the driver," Deckard ordered while struggling to control the vehicle. The PKM gunner up top was firing again. As long as the convoy was still in contact, he didn't dare slow down or stop the vehicle.

Samruk's oracle grabbed the driver by his shirt and attempted to pull him out of his seat.

"What is that sticking out of him?" he asked.

Deckard frowned and stole a quick look away from the road and down at the corpse.

"That's an RPG rocket," he said looking back at the road in front of him.

Somehow the rocket had penetrated the vehicle and failed to detonate. More than likely, the shooter had gotten nervous during the fight and forgot to pull the nose cap off the rocket which protected it from accidental detonations in the event that it was dropped or fell out of the RPG launcher. Still, Deckard felt less than secure with a live RPG rocket lodged in the abdomen of the dead driver.

"Yeah, don't touch that."

They reached the hump where the road began to head into a decline as they shot downhill and back into the city as they circled around the edge of the hill. Picking up speed, Deckard slipped into the driver's seat as Kenny pulled the body out of the way. The PKM gunner was still firing wildly and they could hear bullets pinging off the armored cab. How that RPG had penetrated the armor, he didn't know but there was always that golden shot. Deckard could recall an American M1A1 Abrams Main Battle Tank that had been taken out by an RPG in Iraq.

"Reloading!" the PKM gunner yelled as he popped open the feed tray cover and reached for another belt of ammo.

The side view mirror on his side was now missing, but using the mirror on the passenger side, he could see his men riding in the back turn their Kalashnikov rifles on the tires of the cartel vehicle now lagging behind them. With two burst front tires, the enemy gun truck spun out, spiraling down the road. The Samruk vehicles following Deckard in the convoy sprayed the gun truck with more gunfire as they passed by.

The needle on the speedometer ticked up as they picked up velocity going downhill.

Rounding the final turn and blasting into the city, Deckard's jaw hung open as he saw the road blocked up ahead of him. Slamming on the brakes, Kenny shot forward into the dashboard as he hung onto the body of the former driver. The PKM gunner was thrown onto his gun as Deckard held his foot down, burning rubber in a trail of smoke behind them. The back tires threatened to spin out from under them, forcing Deckard to milk the wheel to compensate and keep the vehicle under control.

Leaving a streak of black skid marks, they finally jerked to a stop. Deckard looked up at the medieval contraption rolling towards them, the exhaust spewing a cloud of black smoke. He threw the assault truck in reverse and the engine died. Gray smoke was pouring out from under the hood. They had absorbed a few too many rounds.

The *clack-clack-clack* of tank treads filled their ears as the machine moved to take up Deckard's entire field of vision through the windshield. The PKM gunner let off a stunted burst that was nothing more than a token show of resistance. He might as well have been firing rainbows and sunshine instead of the 7.62x54R API rounds that bounced right off the steel beast.

"OUT!" Deckard yelled.

The assaulters launched themselves off of the outward facing seats in the back while the PKM gunner dismounted the machine gun from its pintle mount. Climbing out of the turret, he grabbed an extra belt of bullets, jumped down onto the hood, and then down onto the pavement. Meanwhile, Deckard grabbed the deceased driver. He was about to order Kenny out but then saw the passenger side door hanging open and the seat empty. Kenny didn't need to be told once, much less twice.

Aware that bumping the RPG round could detonate it, Deckard grabbed his AK and yanked the body out behind him. The tank treads were just a few meters away. The assaulters who had been on the back of the truck came over to help him handle the corpse.

From inside the metal beast, gunfire sprayed from several port holes, narrowing in on the rest of the Samruk convoy coming down the hill. One by one the assault trucks swerved to avoid oncoming machine gun fire. The heavy *ka-chunk ka-chunk* and massive muzzle blast alerted Deckard to the familiar sound of the M2HB machine gun inside the monstrosity. The twin streams of gunfire hosing down the street also told him that the crew inside was running a dual machine gun set up with two of the .50 caliber machine guns firing side by side from one trigger mechanism. Lucky for them, the guns were elevated inside the armed vehicle and the operators were unable to drop their gun barrels to target the mercenaries right in front of them. Instead, the driver would just run them over.

The mercenaries carried the driver away but Deckard found himself crawling up the side of the assault truck in a flash. Pushing a tow strap out of the way, he threw stray bottles of water aside looking for an ammo can kept in the back of the truck. The tank treads were coming straight down on the stalled vehicle, just feet away.

Deckard's teammates screamed at him in Russian as the machine threatened to grind him up underneath it. Sweeping empty shell casings out of the way, he found the green ammo can he was looking for. One of the boys had written on the lid with a paint marker.

It read: BLAMMO.

Deckard grabbed the ammo can by the handle and propelled himself off the back of the truck just as the treads made contact and pushed the vehicle slightly backwards before climbing up the hood. When his boots made contact with the street, he went into a roll and came up on one knee. The cartel-made tank rolled right over the top of the assault truck, completely destroying it.

Getting to his feet, Deckard could now see that the behemoth was a bulldozer that had been heavily modified by wielding hardened metal plates around the entire vehicle, fashioning a giant brown tower on top of the treads. Gun ports at the top of the tower allowed the dual .50 caliber machine guns to fire on anything that got in its way.

The Samruk assault trucks moved to cover, or shot off onto side streets to avoid the improvised tank and its large bore machine gun.

"Find a corner and hold it down," Deckard ordered the mercenaries who had escaped his truck.

Popping open the blammo can, he reached in and

grabbed two large black thermo-baric grenades. On his pistol belt he had a dump pouch for stashing spent magazines which now pulled double duty as a grenade carrier.

The tank continued to clank down the street, looking for his men and firing bursts whenever the gunner inside spotted them. Some of the mercenaries had dismounted their vehicles and were prepping their own RPG-7 launchers with anti-tank rockets. Letting a few fly, one grenade detonated harmlessly in the metal blade of the bulldozer. A second rocket bounced off the armor and exploded in the street next to Deckard's group, covering them in sulfur smelling white smoke. The third rocket exploded against the armored tower and the machine gunner inside began homing in on the RPG gunner squatting behind a car at the base of the hill.

It only took a nano-second for the twin barrels to spit enough lead to turn the car into a sieve as sparks flew around it like angry bumblebees. That was the last they heard from the RPG gunner.

"All stations on this net," Deckard said into his radio. "Cease fire and attempt to evade. Drive on to the objective."

Kazakhs called in to acknowledge the order as Deckard ran up behind the tank, passing his now demolished assault truck. Sticking out from the armor at the rear of the bulldozer was a three pronged ripper that would normally be used to loosen dirt prior to excavation on a work site. Slinging his rifle, Deckard reached out and grabbed the ripper while the bulldozer was still on the move.

Lifting his feet up, his boots scraped up against the sides of the ripper while he found a hand hold. Wiggling his way up, he stood on top of the metal claws. The sides of the armor plating were slick and getting up to the top of the tower was going to be a challenge to say the least.

They could stand around and shoot at the giant death machine all day and maybe that was the point. If Deckard let it, the tank would wear down Samruk's resources until they had nothing left to fight with.

The tank lurched, threatening to shake Deckard off. Finding a bump where one armor plate was welded to overlap on top of another revealed a very small handhold but it would have to do. Pushing off with one boot against the plate, Deckard flung himself up and got the tips of his fingers on the metal lip.

Grunting, he got his other hand onto the lip and walked his legs up until his knees were almost in his chest. He would have to make one more reach to the top of the metal tower and his strength was already giving way.

He was dangling by his fingertips and unlike a rock climber, he was outfitted in body armor, rifle, grenades, magazines, and other tools of the trade.

Suddenly the entire bulldozer quaked beneath him causing one hand to slip off the lip. The next thing Deckard knew, sheet metal was raining down around him. Rocks were dropping down and clanging off the roof of the tank's tower. Something hard struck his shoulder and he lost his grip.

Deckard kept his feet and knees together but still nearly blacked out when he impacted the street below. Groaning, he spat dust out of his mouth. Propping himself up with one arm, he saw the bulldozer smash the rest of the way through the entire corner of a warehouse. Bricks rained down around the dozer and the sheet metal roof collapsed in entire sections. The tank simply rumbled right over the debris and turned back out onto the street.

They must have had cameras somewhere on the outer skin of the tank and had seen him climbing up the back end of it. The mercenaries left the street corner they had taken shelter behind and moved up to help their commander out.

Deckard handed his rifle to one of them before unplugging his head set from his radio and undoing the Velcro on the cummerbund of his body armor. Ripping off the plate carrier he handed that off as well as his radio headset. All he kept with him was his pistol belt that had his 1911 pistol, extra pistol magazines, his knife, and his dump bag with the grenades on it. He needed to be light and agile if he was going to scramble up the side of the tank. It was a calculated risk.

Up ahead of them the tank driver threw one control level forward and the other backward to turn each of the two treads in opposite directions to spin the tank around to face the mercenaries.

"Hurry up," Deckard yelled as he took off towards the tank. Once again, running away would have been futile and they would have been cut down by the machine guns. In this case, they needed to get back under the gunner's arc of fire. Closer was safer, relatively speaking.

The mercenaries sprinted up and followed Deckard as he dodged to the side of the tank and ran around the back again. Out in the middle of the street, the driver must have realized that he didn't have any obstacles to run up against and knock of any sappers crawling up the side of his hull. Throwing the tank in reverse, Deckard was nearly impaled by the ripper but managed to climb up on top of it again.

Frantic screams beside him made it clear that one of the mercenaries had not gotten out of the way in time. Deckard reached out and grabbed the Kazakh's hand as his eyes went wild. He was trapped under the treads and was being crushed. His hand was violently ripped from Deckard's as he was crushed to death. As the tank tread rolled over the mercenary it had the effect of rolling a tube of toothpaste from the bottom up to the top. Deckard looked away as the mercenary burst in a tide of blood and gore. He braced himself against the armor plating, he was dizzy and about to vomit.

The tank was backing up into a brick wall and if he didn't move fast, Deckard knew he would be crushed as well. He hopped back up and found purchase on the lip of the armor plating, then reached up with his free hand and grabbed the ledge at the top of the tower. Executing a pull up, Deckard climbed up on top of the tank.

Reaching into his dump pouch, he palmed one of the thick cylindrical hand grenades. Pulling the pin, he lay down on his stomach and looked down over the front end of the tank where the port hole was. He could feel the heat through his uniform and gloves. Without hesitating a second longer, he plunged his hand through the port hole and dropped the grenade.

Panicked shouts came from within the metal beast.

Hanging off the edge of the tower, Deckard pushed off and was airborne for what seemed like forever before he hit the ground and stumbled down to his knees. Knowing there was probably only a second or so left on the grenade's time delay fuse, he threw himself to the ground and covered his head with his arms

The formal name of the thermo-baric grenade was the Anti-Structure Hand Grenade. Thermo-baric, meaning heat plus pressure made for a longer blast duration than conventional hand grenades as well as increased thermal output. The PBXN-109 inside the grenade created enough heat and pressure to collapse a building's walls, collapse an underground tunnel, or drop the top of a cave on top of pesky Taliban insurgents.

When the grenade went off it performed as advertised. Rather than some big fiery explosion, the thermo-baric grenade collapsed the tower built on top of the bulldozer by creating a short burst of over pressure. One of the side panels crashed to the ground causing the roof to cave in. Deckard got to his feet and dusted himself off as the tank came to a halt. Whoever was inside had been pulped and would have to be soaked up in a sponge if someone wanted to attempt a funeral.

The mercenary commander turned and walked away.

"Now we have two dead," Deckard said to the remaining mercenaries unemotionally. "One we can do nothing about and the other has live ordinance lodged inside him. Hide the body inside that warehouse that the tank drove through. We can't risk transporting him and having that RPG rocket go off."

"Yes sir," one of the Corporals confirmed.

"If I die," Deckard added. "Make sure you come back and recover the body."

38

"Backblast area clear," the Carl Gustav Assistant Gunner screamed above the sound of the firefight. When the Samruk ground convoy rolled up to the enemy stronghold they immediately began receiving effective fire. They would be pushed off the objective area entirely if the mercenaries didn't act fast.

The Goose gunner sighted in using the M10 scope attached to the recoilless rifle's v-slide lock mount. When he squeezed the trigger, the over pressure was so great it felt like he was underwater for a moment. The flechette round cleared off an entire section of the high walls of cartel gunmen. They had taken up positions on the walls to repel the mercenaries but the anti-personnel flechette round made mincemeat of them.

"Cock safe," the gunner yelled while cocking the weapon. The Assistant Gunner popped open the venturi at the end of the Goose, yanked out the expended shell casing and slammed home a fresh 84mm round.

"Backblast area clear," the AG yelled above the gunfire around them as he slammed the venturi shut.

The gunner aimed at a different section of the wall and let the flechette round go. A pink mist hung in the air as an entire row of gunmen went down under the metal shrapnel he had fired.

"Get the ladders up," Sergeant Major Korgan ordered his men.

With PKM machine guns from the assault trucks offering suppressive fire against any enemy left up on the walls, the assaulters surged forward from behind their vehicles and ran to the walls with their homemade wooden ladders.

The former convent had been converted into a cultural museum by the government of Oaxaca before Jimenez had taken it over. The walled compound and stone cloistered buildings inside provided fortification to the defenders. Whether or not it was impregnable remained to be seen.

The ladders went up and like medieval crusaders the mercenaries began scaling the walls.

Meanwhile, the Goose gunner lowered his recoilless rifle. They were out of the game for the time being with friendlies having moved into their field of fire. The Samruk mercenaries got to the top of their ladders and climbed up onto the roof where the firefight picked up intensity all over again.

The chatter of PKMs sounded alongside the *chunk-chunk-chunk* sound of the enemy's M240B machine guns. AK-103s popped off intermittently with sharper sounded M-4 carbines firing the smaller 5.56 round mixed in between. The sounds of death permeated across the entire city as civilians scurried indoors as fast as humanly possible.

"What's going on here," someone said from behind the Carl Gustav team. Turning, the two Kazakh mercenaries saw their commander arriving with seven other Samruk shooters. They were covered in sweat, some of them covered in blood as well.

"They just went up the walls," the Goose gunner yelled. "Sergeant Major Korgan is leading them."

Deckard nodded. He knew his man and he would be leading from the front.

His chest heaved under his plate carrier and his uniform was completely soaked through with sweat. They had run about ten blocks from where they had killed the improvised tank to the objective. With their truck demolished they had little choice. They also had to shoot their way through a check point in the middle of the street manned by cartel gunmen. Jimenez had planned his defense in depth with layers or concentric rings of obstacles and fighting positions arrayed around his compound.

"Six, are you out there yet," Pat's voice came over Deckard's radio headset.

"We just got here," Deckard answered, panting between the words.

"We've got wounded up here. They had fighting positions prepared for us and we are getting pinned down."

"Where is Shooter-One?"

"He is up here with us."

"Tell him to make his way back down and find a flanking position on an adjacent building. Maybe he can give you some breathing room to maneuver."

An RPG rocket whistled over the top of the convent and zoomed off into the city.

"I'm going to take my element in from another direction and probe their defenses. If you can fix the enemy in place and keep them from withdrawing we should make it out of this. I need you and Korgan to hold out."

"We will," Pat said over the sound of gunfire.

Deckard knew he may have just handed his men a death sentence. It was a chance they had to take.

"Goose gunner," he said. "What rounds do you have on you?"

"We have an HEDP round in our assault pack, the rest are on the truck."

"Perfect. I want you to blow the gate."

There was a small wrought iron gate that led into the compound. The mercenaries had wisely chosen the high road rather than the low one as they didn't want to get trapped in the cloistered courtyards with the enemy firing on them from the museum rooftops. Now, with the enemy distracted and fixated on Samruk's main force, Deckard would attempt a different method of entry and see if he could get behind the cartel gunmen. From there, they could launch a devastating assault against the soft underbelly of the cartel's defenses.

"Roger," the Kazakh affirmed.

The AG loaded up the High Explosive Dual Purpose round and shut the venturi. He waved several of Deckard's teammates out of the way before declaring the backblast area clear. The gunner fired and the wrought iron gate blasted open on impact, jolted right off its hinges.

"Nice job. Load up some HEAT rounds," he said referring to the Gustav's High Explosive Anti-Tank munition. "Just in case. I think you'd prefer that over a thermo-baric grenade if another tank shows up."

Taking the lead, Deckard's AK-103 led the way as he jogged across the street and stepped over the remains of the metal gate. Moving through the doorway, he quickly ran through the thick stone entrance and out into the vaulted ceilings of the overhang that lined the near side of the courtyard.

The firefight was raging above them. Tracer fire could be seen in the daylight, zipping overhead with occasional RPG rockets crisscrossing the sky. Down on the ground level, Deckard saw several corpses belonging to cartel gunmen. M-4 rifles lay next to them as a pool of blood leaked from under the bodies and between the cracks in the cobblestone floor.

After the mercenaries got up on the rooftops, those down

below quickly learned to stay out of the courtyard. Getting down on a knee behind the concrete banister, his eyes narrowed as he scanned the cloisters at the other side of the courtyard. It was almost too easy. Shouldering his AK, Deckard began firing into the shadows under the vaulted ceilings at the other end of the courtyard.

The amount of gunfire that replied back was nothing short of unreal. Deckard ducked down behind the banister followed by the other mercenaries. The cartel gunmen had been lying in wait. The decorative sculptures between the banister and the stone floor left a lot of openings, forcing Deckard to roll laterally to change his position as enemy gunfire focused on his position and collided with the space he had occupied a moment ago.

Sighting in, he burned through the thirty round magazine in his Kalashnikov in seconds as he fired a burst at every silhouette or muzzle flash that presented itself. Rocking the empty magazine forward, he tossed it aside and rolled again while reaching to the pouches on his plate carrier for a full mag. Flopping back on his belly, more gun fire attempted to catch up with him. Locking the new magazine in place he again pointed his AK barrel through the gaps between the ornamental sculpture foliage that decorated the cloisters.

The other mercenaries acted in a similar manner, firing and then ducking down behind cover and changing position, reloading on the move as best they could.

When Deckard acted on a hunch and fired on suspected targets, he drew a large volume of enemy fire but it simply was not as accurate as that of the mercenaries. Even though they were at a disadvantage and outnumbered two to one, the firefight was nearly over after several magazines worth of firing and maneuvering from each man. They had homed in on their targets and fired with both speed and accuracy, adding volume as appropriate.

"Cease fire, cease fire!" Deckard yelled.

There was plenty of gunfire raging on the roofs above them but there was no indication of enemy movement in the courtyard. Still, better safe than sorry.

"All stations on this net," Deckard transmitted. "I'm taking a friendly element through the northwestern courtyard. Check fire."

Deckard let his AK hang by the sling and opened a pouch on his plate carrier. Inside was a yellow smoke grenade canister.

"Who else has a smoke?" he asked in Russian.

One of the mercenaries produced a High Concentrate smoke grenade. Deckard's colored smoke was supposed to be used for creating visible signals for friendly helicopters and such while the Kazakh's was for concealing movement. Both would serve their purpose in this instance.

"You throw near and I'll throw far," Deckard told him. Pulling the pins, both men tossed their smoke grenades into the courtyard and waited for them to begin billowing smoke. In case of any cartel gunmen in windows or anywhere else, they wanted their movement concealed while they crossed the large open area to the other side of the courtyard.

"Go!"

Deckard shot off and disappeared into the smoke. The white smoke surrounded the mercenaries as they ran across the open ground. They had nowhere to go but forward. When he moved through the white smoke and into the yellow smoke he knew he was almost there. Emerging on the other side of the courtyard, Deckard found himself exposed out in the open but it was a short sprint back under the cover of the next exterior hallway.

Under the vaulted ceilings and somewhat behind the cover of the cloisters facing out into the courtyard, Deckard tried the large wooden door and found it locked. An explosion sounded up on the rooftop. Over the assault net, Deckard could hear dozens of voices. Some of them were high pitched, the firefight becoming an all out frantic battle for survival at close range. One by one, the Kazakhs emerged through the smoke and joined him at the door.

Deckard used his hand to motion laying a strip down the side of the door, a hand and arm signal to let his Kazakhs know that they needed to blow the door. One of the mercenaries came forward to unroll a flex linear charge. Peeling back the transparent film on the contact side of the charge, he stuck the triple strand detonation chord down the side of the door. With the task completed, he tied in the initiation system and the entire assault element backed off to a safe distance, the demo man trailing shock tube behind him that connected to the explosives.

The mercenaries stacked up, one behind the other. The first man pulled security on the door while the second initiated the charge. Wooden splinters went flying into the courtyard as the explosives ripped through the door. The Samruk International mercenaries pushed through the door and began clearing their sectors of fire.

As each assaulter high stepped over the destroyed door, they also had to step over the body of a cartel gunman who had been guarding it and had gotten a little too close to the blast. A wooden shard had penetrated his skull right between the eyes. They found themselves in an old archive with books and manuscripts overflowing from shelves that lined the walls.

At the end of the oblong shaped room was the next doorway. Deckard rolled his last fragmentation grenade through the door and held his men back as they waited for the blast. The rumble shook the ground beneath their feet. Flowing into the next room they were greeted by enemy gunfire. Another archive room had been prepared with a built up fighting position inside it, a sandbagged pill box that protected a M240B machine gunner. They had been waiting in ambush all along.

The sandbags had protected the gunner from Deckard's frag grenade, and now the first two assaulters were cut down by a wall of lead as they entered the room. On hearing the heavy rattle of the bolt hammering away at bullet after bullet, Deckard came in low. He was already halfway through the door as the number three man and was not able to turn around unless he wanted to get shot in the back.

It was a second archive room and scraps of shredded paper rained down on the former Special Operations soldier as he dived to the ground. The number four man also made it through the door and dropped down beside him. The remaining five Kazakhs halted at the door before the machine gun could slice them to ribbons. That didn't stop the gunner from wildly pouring fire through the door and raking it across the shelves of 15th Century manuscripts.

They had also thoughtfully removed the desks and other furniture from the room to give the gunner an open field of fire. Deckard clicked the selector switch on his AK-103 up from semi to fully automatic.

"Bound up," Deckard ordered the mercenary next to him. They only had a moment to act before the gunner realized

257

that they had dived to the ground rather than collapsed under his fire.

Coming to a knee, Deckard locked the AK into the pocket of his shoulder and held on tightly to the pistol grip and fore end, wrenching the rifle into his body. Holding down the trigger with a gloved finger, he sprayed the aperture where the machine gun barrel was blasting rounds from.

The gunner jerked a burst of fire that crept right up to Deckard's flank and sprayed just inches to his side and up the library shelf behind him. The mercenary on his opposite flank sprung to his feet and ran for the pillbox. The reciprocating charging handle on his Kalashnikov continued to cycle back and forth, the bolt spitting out hot brass as the M240B gunner pivoted his gun and homed in on the mercenary that was bounding forward.

Deckard's gun went dry but the other mercenaries were now coming through the door to support their comrades. Deckard dropped the mag and executed a combat reload in less than a second, but that second cost the mercenary running to the bunker his life.

Even with the other Kazakhs laying down their suppressive fire, their teammate was cut down before Deckard and the remaining four mercenaries converged their fire on the aperture and the M240B fell silent. Crossing the room, Deckard came into the pill box from behind and put a couple insurance rounds in the machine gunner. He examined the M240 but noted that the receiver had been damaged in several places, including the trigger assembly having been shot off.

So much for commandeering the weapon.

Coming up to the next door, they could hear men scrambling on the other side and the distinctive click and clack of weapons being made ready, magazines locked into place and bolts racked back to chamber the first round.

"It is clear," Deckard yelled in Spanish. "I machine gunned the gringos to pieces!"

When the door opened, Deckard held his AK out from behind the corner, only exposing the weapon and his hands while letting off a burst on full auto. The blind fire caused enough confusion to give one of the Kazakhs time to lob a frag grenade through the door.

The mercenaries chased the blast, stepping across the

258

threshold to opposite sides of the door. As Deckard moved behind them his vision suddenly whited out and he felt pressure in his ears. Stumbling backwards he tripped and fell. As his vision began to clear, two human forms in front of him abruptly merged into one, a man with long black hair and carrying an M-4 rifle in his hands. The shooter was reaching out to grab him by the collar of his camouflage uniform when Deckard got his AK back up and held down the trigger. He rattled through the rest of his final magazine but didn't hear a thing.

His would-be assailant spun and jerked as 7.62x39 bullets tugged at him, churning his insides into a mess before finally going down under the torrent of gunfire.

Before he could make it to his feet, he saw another cartel gunman turn towards him, having heard the shots from Deckard's Kalashnikov. He was still seeing stars floating across his field of vision as he acted on muscle memory, his dominant hand going down to the drop leg holster on his right side and thumbing down the retention hood as his palm came to rest on the grip of the pistol.

Yanking the 1911 out of the holster, Deckard held it out in front of him and squeezed off round after round until the gunman went down. Getting to his feet, he staggered forward, his empty Kalashnikov bouncing off his chest as it hung from its sling.

Through blurry vision, he saw the two remaining Samruk men being led off at gunpoint. The three of them had been stunned by a flash bang grenade giving the enemy enough time to pounce on them. They dragged the two Kazakhs off but were unable to capture Deckard alive before he gathered his wits.

Gaining target acquisition, Deckard took out one of the cartel gunmen who had been leading the Kazakhs outside. As he went down one of the other gunmen returned fire forcing Deckard to take cover behind an overturned desk. With his slide locked back on an empty chamber he reached for the magazine pouch on his pistol belt. The now empty AK was in the way so he shrugged out of the sling and sent it clattering to the ground before reloading the pistol.

Thumbing the slide release, Deckard rose from behind cover and fired a snap shot at the gunman standing in the door way. It was a rushed shot, but the .45 caliber bullet ricocheted off the stone wall and into the gunman's eyes, sending him bucking backwards.

The final gunman was pushing the Kazakhs forward. They had caught the brunt of the flash bang distraction device and were still suffering from its effects. Others reached through the doorway and pulled them forward as Deckard fired off a couple of rounds at the riflemen herding his comrades forward, just a moment too late.

Dashing forward, Deckard let his 1911 lead the way as he crossed through the door and into the bright light of another courtyard outside.

Something slammed behind him, causing the combat veteran to immediately go to ground. Behind him, he could see that a giant wood door had dropped down in the entrance way, trapping him in the courtyard.

With little option he continued into the courtyard.

Once outside he looked around and saw that he was surrounded by a giant wooden facade that completely encircled him. Directly to his front, standing up on a platform was Jimenez and his lieutenant, Ignacio. They had baited him into a trap.

They had lured him into their arena.

39

Deckard stood in the center of the arena.

Aiming down the iron sights along the top of his 1911, the mercenary squeezed off rounds into the center of the entourage surrounding Jimenez. Several cartel gunmen went down before the slide locked to the rear.

Jimenez tore a giant revolver from the holster on his hip and let loose a round that splashed in the dirt just inches from Deckard's booted foot. The gun in the drug lord's hand was massive, a Smith and Wesson Governor if he wasn't mistaken, chambered for .410 shotgun shells.

"Yeah!" Jimenez yelled at Deckard, glaring down at him from the elevated platform. "You just don't quit do you! Respect. But now we've got a gunslinger who has finally run out of bullets!"

Deckard let the slide slam forward and holstered his pistol. He stood in the middle of a circular wooden arena that Jimenez had constructed in the courtyard. Like a miniature Roman arena, there was stadium seating for spectators. This was where Jimenez and his boys stood laughing at him. Several who had absorbed Deckard's final barrage of gunfire were being dragged down below.

He could hear the firefight raging on the rooftops above and deeper in the converted convent but there was nothing coming over the radio headset he wore. Looking down, Deckard saw that one of his many near misses had resulted in a bullet pulverizing his radio with a neat round hole through the side of the metal casing. Unstrapping it from his kit, he dropped the radio along with the headset. It would only get in the way of what was about to happen next.

"Now we get to see what you are really made of," Jimenez lectured. "But I don't know."

Deckard stood with his arms hanging limply at his sides, his eyebrows pointed slightly upwards as his chest heaved. Sweat poured down his face and neck.

"You look pretty exhausted," Jimenez cautioned. "Are you sure you don't want to call off this little war of ours until tomorrow so you can get some rest?"

"I haven't got all fucking day Jimenez!" Deckard's voice

echoed off the high walls surrounding the arena.

"You're right of course," the drug lord laughed. "We have set loose the mad dogs of war. We couldn't stop them from fighting even if we wanted to! I know it has been grinding at you how I convinced all those soldiers of mine to assault your compound the other night. How I got them worked into a frenzy like that and all."

Deckard thought about the one they had taken prisoner, hugging his knees while rocking himself like a baby.

"We've been playing a game in this arena with the local townspeople, a game called Who Wants to Be an Assassin! I have people grabbed off the streets. Homeless bums, peasants, junkies, whoever and have them fight to the death. The survivors get to become *Sicarios*, my private army of crazed killers!"

"That's how you traumatize and brainwash these people into murdering priests and the disabled at a Christian mission? You sick fuck."

"Oh, fuck no. You got me all wrong. That wasn't me or my cartel. We don't know who that was. Santa Muerta did not grant her permission for anything like that. Maybe you've been pissing off the Zeta's up north? I don't know, do you have a secret admirer that you haven't told me about?"

What the hell, Deckard whispered.

"Indeed," Jimenez said having seen him mouth the words. "But that is just one of those unsolved mysteries in life. Some people say that aliens built those pyramids for the Mayans. Who the fuck knows?"

Through cross hatched metal bars sunk into the wooden frame of the arena on two sides, Deckard could see shadows shifting from side to side. A hand poked through the portcullis directly in front of him. The fist was holding a butcher knife, the sunlight from above reflecting off the blade. Several brown spots stained the ground around him, the remnants of spilled blood from past gladiator matches.

"So before we get interrupted by this little war of ours," the drug lord said with a smile, "let's see what you've got for me when there is no Army at your back, when you've run all out of guns. In this arena there is nowhere to hide. This is one place where we see people for who they really are."

"Fuck you."

Jimenez sighed and motioned to Ignacio. His lieutenant shouted and the two Kazakh mercenaries that the cartel captured after the flash bang went off were pushed forward. They had been restrained and one looked like he had been punched in the face with purple lumps around his eyes.

"You'll fight gringo," Jimenez said leveling the massive pistol to point it at the head of one of the Kazakhs. "Or I execute these men in front of you. Then I shoot you in both kneecaps and let our gladiators have at you anyway. Your choice."

"Let's get this over with Jimenez."

"I'm glad you think so."

The drug lord used his gun barrel to indicate to another cartel gunman to raise one of the portcullis doors. Pressing a button on a remote control, a pulley system somewhere inside the arena raised the metal gate. For a long moment nothing moved, only gunfire could be heard in the background as the war continued on all sides.

The man with the butcher knife emerged from the shadows, followed by a second knifeman, then a third. A fourth staggered out of the holding cell with a cleaver. God only knew how many of their fellow townspeople they had to stab to death in order to survive this long.

Deckard moved his non-firing hand towards the side of his pistol belt and undid a buckle.

The gladiators swarmed Deckard, snarling guttural screams as they descended upon him.

In one clean movement the mercenary's arm shot out, his hand a blur of motion as he chopped upwards and diagonally. The first gladiator's head snapped back as an arc of bright red blood that sprayed into the air before he fell down on his back. Deckard took a step forward and the second gladiator dropped his knife and brought his hands to his neck, making a futile effort to stop the flow of crimson that leaked from between his fingers.

The third knifeman also dropped his blade as the fingers holding it were sliced and completely dismembered from his hand. Then something hit him in the side of the head and he collapsed. The fourth gladiator tried to bring his meat cleaver down on Deckard but the mercenary pivoted out of the way and the gladiator suddenly found himself holding his own intestines. He fell to his knees, still looking at his insides when Deckard finished him.

The cartel men watching from the stadium seats stood in stunned silence, their mouths hanging agape. The American stood more or less in the center of the arena where he had been to begin with, surrounded by four dead gladiators. Pools of blood seeped into the dirt.

Deckard held his combat blade in a reverse grip in his left hand. The sinister profile of the double sided blade was soaked in blood as was the mercenary's glove and shirt sleeve. With ten inches of effective blade, the Grayman Sub-Saharan combat knife had more in common with a Roman short sword than with other military knives.

"Where the fuck did he get that thing from?" Ignacio blurted.

Jimenez looked frustrated.

"Let the second group out! What's wrong with you?"

The gunman with the remote control opened the second portcullis. Four more knifemen spilled out into the arena. Deckard tossed the knife into the air and caught it with his dominate hand before holding it with his thumb and pointer finger, allowing the massive knife to swing down back into a reverse grip.

The gladiators charged.

Deckard side stepped, putting the first gladiator between him and the second while the other two tried to circle around from the other side. Swatting the first attacker's knife hand away with the blade, Deckard then chopped it straight into the first gladiators face, dropping him. Gladiator number three had managed to come around on his flank. Deckard turned to meet him and dodged away from his first slash then grabbed him behind the head, yanking him down and plunging the ten inch Sub-Saharan into his enemy's clavicle.

As gladiator number two approached, Deckard repeated the same maneuver, putting number two between himself and number four, delaying the other man's attack and giving himself some stand off. When the second gladiator swung his butcher knife, Deckard brought his own knife up under the man's forearm, crossing the knife over his arm and snapping it down. Doing this he simultaneously wrenched and sliced the gladiator's knife out of his hand.

Deckard followed up with a stick between the ribs that deflated a lung and took all the fight out of his opponent instantly.

The fourth gladiator came right over the second to try to stab him in the chest. Deckard pivoted his body and swung the knife into a normal upturned grip. Bringing his arm right up over the top of the gladiator's attack, he stuck the knife in the would-be killer's throat.

Now Deckard stood surrounded by eight dead bodies.

Jimenez and Ignacio looked at each other.

Deckard looked on as they argued with each other in hushed tones. He watched the scene unfold as he struggled for more air, exhausted to the point that he had been moving and fighting based on pure muscle memory. Despite the physical training he put himself through, days in combat with little rest had taken their toll.

"Well gringo, all our other gladiators are out fighting your men so we are going to have to improvise here. I'm not going to lie. I'm impressed."

Deckard pointed the bloody knife at the drug lord, unable to talk.

"Listen," he shouted at his entourage. "Turn over your guns to Ignacio and select a weapon from one of the gladiator barrels."

The drug lord pointed to a wooden barrel full of hand weapons. Knives, axe handles, baseball bats, and other killing instruments.

"You want us to get in there with that fucking monster-" one of the drug lord's minions began to say when his words were cut off as Jimenez' Smith and Wesson erased his face from his skull. The .410 shotgun round exploded and the cartel lackey was dead before his body hit the ground.

"Rules are rules. He can't fight all of you off at the same time."

The eight remaining members of Jimenez' Personal Security Detachment turned their pistols and M-4 rifles over to Ignacio who disappeared into a back room somewhere. One by one they lined up and selected knives and clubs.

"Now get the fuck in the arena and finish this!"

Red in the face, Jimenez was infuriated.

The cartel PSD jumped off the stands, landing down in the arena.

"Hit him all at once," one of the security detail members

said. "Don't give him the chance to fight back."

Deckard bent down and retrieved a dead gladiators knife so that both of his hands were filled with a weapon. He kept his knees loose and settled into a shooter's stance as he prepared for the oncoming attack.

They came at once. Deckard rushed forward to meet them. He heard someone screaming but didn't realize that it was his own voice.

The butcher knife found its way into someone's eye socket, the Sub-Saharan chopped down on another cartel man's skull. An upward stroke sliced under another knifemen's ribcage before the inevitable happened. He was surrounded.

Beat down to the ground, a club glanced off the side of his head. A knife was plunged down into his back but stopped by the ballistic trauma plate he wore as body armor. Deckard fell down on all fours. Something hit his shoulder.

For a moment, he lost his grip on his weapon. Reaching for it as blows rained down, his gloved hand seized around the handle of the blade. He wasn't afraid to die but he was afraid to lose.

With the knife held in his fist, he brought it down on the nearest cartel man's foot. Yanking it free in a stream of blood he brought it back down on the next man's foot, stabbing downwards again and again in a hammering motion. Slashing horizontally, he cut through someone's Achilles tendon. As his support arm was swept out from under him, he lashed out and cut into another enemy's groin, separating him from his manhood.

Thrown on his back, Deckard rolled over on top of one of his disabled opponents. Stabbing him in the chest, his hand moved forward on the blade, choking up on it for better control. Someone reached for him and he swung, cutting right up the man's forearm.

Another enemy tackled him back down to the ground. As his opponent attempted to bring his knife down on him, Deckard slashed his bicep and then swung the blade around and stuck it into his mouth and though the soft pallet.

Someone else moved next to him so the mercenary put his boot in his neck.

Two more survivors stumbled forward with axe handles. Deckard kicked the first in the knee cap and the second tripped over his comrade's prostrate form. Throwing himself on top of the squirming bodies, the cutting continued.

Jimenez looked on as the American was straddled across one of his men's chest, plunging the evil looking black blade into his abdomen again and again. Like the other gladiators that the drug lord had sent into the arena, the modern day coliseum had the desired effect. The gladiator had been driven out of his mind.

Deckard looked up, his eyes red and bloodshot, just in time to see the drug lord flee the spectator stands and run into the corridor that led back into the old convent.

He blinked, everything was black for a moment. Then he was crawling up the side of the arena, straight up the wall and pulling himself over the top. Deckard felt his body red line but his mind did not acknowledge the command. His arms and legs felt like they were filled with acid, his heart threatening to rip right out of his chest. Deckard's mind, body, and heart told him, *no* but something else said, *yes*.

Deckard blinked.

He was inside the dark corridor.

He blinked again.

He was crouched down next to one of his mercenaries. One of the Kazakhs that Jimenez had captured. His face was a bloody pulp, done in by the drug lord's shotgun shell pistol. The drug lord had only needed one hostage. This one was expendable.

Deckard blinked.

Another cartel gunman came charging through the doorway at Deckard, the first shot from his pistol flying wide due to the Mexican's nervous aim. Deckard swung the massive blade downwards, splaying the gunman's skull open like a canoe.

Chasing after Jimenez, Deckard trailed him into the bottom floor of the museum. He could hear shuffling somewhere deeper inside the cold dark room. It was being used as a warehouse with wooden crates stacked nearly up the ceiling in some cases. Deckard recognized many of them as being military in origin, containing weapons and ammunition.

Holding his knife pointing outward at shoulder height, he carried it at the ready as he stalked aisle to aisle. Deckard homed in on feet scuffing across the concrete floor. Only a trickle of light was piercing in from the boarded up windows.

Jimenez' hostage was struggling with his captor.

Deckard tensed, his knife hand white knuckling around the handle.

Walking past row after row of weapons material, he strode out into the next aisle.

A sledgehammer strike knocked him flat on his back, the metal knife clacking across the floor as it fell from his hand.

Jimenez was shouting a steady stream of curses at him.

Finding that he was still alive, Deckard rolled back behind the row of wooden crates.

"What the fuck is this! Why can't you just die!"

Laying face first against the cool cement floor, sweat and blood dripped from the mercenary's face. That was when he realized that Jimenez had shot him with a shotgun round from his revolver. He felt like Satan himself had swatted him right off his feet.

Maybe the metal projectiles had penetrated his body armor, ripped right through the trauma plate and cut through his heart. Maybe deflated his lungs. Maybe this was how he died, face down in a pool of blood and sweat.

Maybe.

Maybe.

Maybe some other day.

Deckard reached out and grabbed the Grayman knife and pushed himself up, using one of the crates to brace himself and get to his feet.

"It looks like you are in the good favor of Santa Muerta, mercenary! You must know her well!"

He could barely hear what the drug lord was saying, not that it mattered.

"But I know you now, I saw how you fought to keep your men alive. It was too late for one but this one is still alive. If you want to keep it that way you let me pass and slip out of the museum before this war overtakes us both."

Deckard's stomach heaved. He was feeling light headed. Swallowing, he took a quick look down the aisle at Jimenez before quickly moving back behind cover. Jimenez was about twenty five feet from his position down at the end of the row of boxes. He held the flexcuffed Kazakh mercenary in a headlock with the barrel of the revolver pointed under his chin. The Kazakh tried to scream behind the gag that had been secured over his mouth.

He looked down at the knife. There was no way he could close the distance in time. Jimenez would have ample time to kill his hostage and more than likely would have time to turn the gun on Deckard and kill him in his already weakened state.

There was a warm burning in his chest from the impact. He still didn't know if any of the shrapnel had penetrated the body armor or not and suspected that he wouldn't be on his feet much longer.

Years ago he had picked something up from a couple Croatian soldiers, something he could hardly do on a good day much less today. As Deckard dug into his bag of tricks, he only had seconds to act and what he had in mind was the only tactical gambit he could come up with.

Readjusting his grip on the knife, he took a deep breath.

"Get out of the way gringo! We can both walk away from this, you and me-"

Deckard stepped out into the middle of the aisle with the Sub-Saharan held over his head.

"What-"

The drug lord's words were cut off as Deckard hurled the knife through the air in an overhand throw. The blade rocked across the distance between Deckard and Jimenez, the Kazakh's eyes went wide as the blade shot towards him.

Deckard had fucked up the throw, although it was on target, the blade spun in the air and the handle impacted the drug lord's face and glanced off. Jimenez bucked backwards in surprise as the blow struck him below the eye.

The Kazakh felt the arms around him go slightly limp as Jimenez was distracted and managed to tear himself away.

Jimenez tried to bring the Smith and Wesson back into play but Deckard was already on top of him. His fist hammered Jimenez in the nose, spraying blood down his shirt. A knee slammed the drug lord in the groin and then in the face as he doubled over. Once again he tried to align the pistol with his antagonist but it was torn from his hand.

Sprawled on the ground, Jimenez looked up at his attacker. What he saw was a nightmare of war. What he saw wasn't human.

Deckard reached down and picked up his weapon.

Reaching for the drug lord he clenched the hair on the top of Jimenez' head in his fist. Deckard held the black blade into the air.

"Wait, wait!"

As the blade swung down, Deckard began to chop.

40

"Order the offensive on the black side of the objective to fall back."

Pat triggered a burst of AK fire before finding cover behind a stone pillar. It was Deckard. His voice sounded like sandpaper. By now everyone thought that their commander was dead. He'd been radio silent for twenty minutes or so.

"Six, is that you?" Pat radioed back.

"Have our forces on the far end of the museum pull back. Give the cartel fighters a way out."

"Let them retreat?"

"Let them find their exit strategy. Set up a linear on Gurrion Street. I'm going to flush them all towards you."

"By yourself?"

"Make it happen."

The former Delta Operator did as he was told. Kurt Jager had arrived with Commadante Zero and his Zapatista rebels just as the Samruk mercenaries were going to be overrun. Kurt had taken the rebels through the botanical gardens on the back side of the museum turned cartel fortress and engaged the enemy. Talking to Jager on the assault net, he now explained Deckard's plan to him.

The German was unconvinced but acknowledged the instructors and began carrying them out.

"What was that?" Sergeant Major Korgan asked him as they waited for the next surge of fire from the cartel gunmen.

"Deckard," Pat answered. "He's alive!"

One by one, the black masked Zapatista rebels began falling back, abandoning their positions behind the walls and statues in the museum gardens where they had the cartel gunmen pinned down. Trapped between the Mexican revolutionaries on one side and the mercenaries on the other, the cartel men had found themselves in a double envelop. Before the rebels had shown up they were confident in a victory, now that reinforcements had arrived, they were certain to be cut down where they stood.

It was just a matter of time.

Now they had an opening, a way to walk away from the firefight but no one dared to defy The Beast. Many were survivors of the gladiator arena and had no desire to go back. Others were trusted cartel gunfighters and knew better than to betray Jimenez unless they wanted to be dangling under a bridge come nightfall.

A solitary figure came walking out of the first floor of the museum. He had what looked like a short sword in one hand and a clump of something in the other. The cartel men were still receiving some fire from the mercenaries but the two forces had basically reached a stalemate. From the windows, alcoves, and rooftops, the cartel gunmen craned their necks around to look at the newcomer.

His desert camouflage uniform was torn open at the knees and other places on the legs and arms, some of the holes exposing bloody wounds. His clothes were also stained red with blood. His equipment was torn and frayed, magazine and grenade pouches hung empty.

"Jimenez is dead!" he shouted at them in Spanish.

Thrusting his hands in the air, the cartel men could now see the bloody knife and the severed head of Jimenez, the one they knew as The Beast. The decapitated head was ragged around the neck from chopping blows that separated it from the body. The jaw hung down as flies were already beginning to accumulate inside his open mouth.

The knifeman threw the severed head in the dirt.

"This war is over!"

The cartel men didn't need to be told twice. If the mercenaries and the rebels had gotten what they came for and now they were giving them away out, they would gladly take it. Dropping their M-4 rifles, some held on to their pistols, some didn't, most just ran without giving it another thought. They dashed out of the museum, leaving their posts and fighting positions and ran past the guy with the giant knife without daring to look him in the eyes.

Close to fifty gunmen flooded out the back gate and out on the street.

Deckard waited until he heard Kurt Jager initiate the ambush as the cartel men ran right into the kill zone before moving on.

"You need to get right with god or whoever the fuck it is you talk to in times like this," Pat explained. "Because you're gonna die."

Ignacio looked up at him with tears forming in his eyes. His legs had been shot to hell, turned into ground meat as a mercenary caught him with a burst of PKM fire.

"Don't leave me to die alone," the cartel lieutenant begged.

"I won't but I need you to help me."

"You, you, you have-"

"All these M-4 rifles, the M240B machine guns, where did you guys suddenly get all these American military weapons from?"

Ignacio was breathing heavy. He was losing blood fast.

"We raided a Zeta warehouse up north. We knew you were coming and needed to stock up on more weapons. Jimenez found out from one of his sources that the Zeta cartel had a s-s-stockpile of American guns."

"Where did the Zetas get the weapons from."

"I-I-I was told that they are being funneled..." Ignacio's voice trailed off into a mumble as he grew weaker. Pat leaned forward, getting close and listening to the dying man's final words.

Sergeant Fedorchenko stepped forward, holding his AK-103 at the low ready and fearing the worst. His commander lay face first in the dirt behind the museum.

Deckard had gone dark on comms for twenty minutes and the men assumed him to be dead. Then he grabbed a radio from a fellow mercenary who had been taken hostage, ordered the rebels to fall back and prepare an ambush, then comes walking out holding Jimenez' decapitated head. The head lay near the Samruk Commander, the hair mottled and thick with blood.

Fedorchenko bent down and rolled Deckard over onto his back. Sand was stuck to the sweat and blood on the side of his face but as the Kazakh held his hand in front of Deckard's mouth, he could feel his hot breath.

"Medic!"

The Platoon Sergeant had checked his breathing and airway so he moved on, looking for wounds, bullet holes, or broken bones. There were several deep gashes, one in his shoulder, another on his leg. His face and head were covered in smaller cuts and scrapes.

The medic came bounding up and dumped his aid bag down next to the casualty.

"Get some Hextend into him to get his blood pressure up and start pushing more liquids. I think it's heat exhaustion."

He had also found several bullet holes in the uniform and a large strike on his front trauma plate. Near misses with death.

"He might go into shock so keep an eye on him."

It took the medic several tries to find a vein but finally got an IV drip in him. Fedorchenko squeezed the bag to push the fluids faster while the medic continued to work, attending the wounds with bandages. Several other assaulters came up and began prepping a litter to transport him.

Cursing in Russian, Fedorchenko got to his feet while the medic removed the Hextend bag and got a Saline drip going.

What the hell had happened to Deckard, he could only guess at.

41

Deckard leaned back with his eyes half open. He was on some light pain killers, 800 milligrams of Motrin and it couldn't kick in soon enough. They had reconsolidated and moved back to their compound to treat the injured and prepare to head down to the airfield. The entire compound needed to be packed up, sensitive material destroyed, and a quick hand over conducted with Commandante Zero and Samantha before the Mexican military rolled into Oaxaca.

By that time they needed to be wheels up and on their way back to Central Asia.

Twisting the cap off a small plastic bottle, he downed a five hour energy shot. The medic was sterilizing his wounds and getting them closed with medical grade Cyanoacrylate super glue. He was feeling better now that his body had soaked in three IV bags of fluids after suffering from heat exhaustion. His core temperature and resting heart rate had finally returned to somewhat normal levels. Once the medic finished with him he needed to be back up on his feet to oversee Samruk International's redeployment to Kazakhstan.

Pat, Frank, and Sergeant Major Korgan were supervising and working the moving parts with Sergeant Fedorchenko but he needed to be present as well.

"Drink this instead," Samantha said handing him a bottle of water. She stared at him with large brown eyes.

"Thanks," Deckard replied, setting the bottle down next to him. "I will."

"What's up big guy?" Pat said coming to sit down next to him. The medic was finishing up before moving on to other patients that were laid out in the OPCEN. Meanwhile, Cody was rolling up wires and packing away computers.

"I've been better."

"Well, you pulled another win out of your ass," Pat smirked. "No doubt about that. I won't even ask what the hell went down in there for now. I'm just glad that you are alive."

"Something I can't get out of my mind Pat," Deckard said, shaking his head.

"What's that?"

"Jimenez told me that it wasn't him that ordered the

massacre at that Christian mission."

"So fucking what?" Pat asked. "Who cares what he had to say. He's dead."

"Yeah, but the thing is, I believe him."

"Listen, take a few more minutes to get yourself together. When you are ready, before we blow out of here in an hour, come meet me and some of the boys over in the loadout room. We need to have a pow wow about some things."

"What's up?"

"I'll fill you in then, don't worry about it right now."

"Alright brother, I'll make my way down there."

Pat slapped him on the shoulder as he walked away, causing Deckard to wince.

"IT IS FOR YOU," Cody said thrusting a cell phone in his face.

Deckard looked up at him and took the phone. Pressing it to his ear he answered.

"Hello?"

"Deckard, it's Grant. Nice work down there but now you have to cut the shit and high tail it out of Mexico, understand?"

"We're moving out as fast as we can."

"I'm helping facilitate the process. I found out that your An-124 was sitting on an airfield in Panama waiting for you to recall the pilots and have them fly back to Oaxaca to collect you. We just made sure the airspace was cleared for you. They are already in the air."

"Appreciate it."

"We've upheld our end of the bargain, we have also received word that the Mexican military is inbound. They got a one hundred vehicle convoy heading south on Mexican National Highway 135D. We want you out of there ASAP."

"Are you going to have that helicopter meet us again at the airfield."

"Yes, you said it is a source and his family."

"Right, we had another but he decided to bail and try his luck on his own."

"Good luck with that. Get your ass on the tarmac and we'll have someone there to evac them."

"I'll be there."

Deckard terminated the call.

"That's all I can do for now, I have other patients I need

to double check," the medic said, tearing off his latex gloves.

"Do it, thanks for the help."

Every muscle in body ached as he stood up. He had a gash in his shoulder and another in his thigh. His pants were in tatters, his body armor and shirt were cast aside, cut off by the medic as he was cleaning him up. One of the pant legs had been cut up with medical shears so he could get to the cut in his thigh. Some butterfly bandages had been applied to the nicks and gouges in his face.

"Black," Samantha said as she walked into the OPCEN. "Or should I say Deckard."

"Guilty."

"I need you to do one last thing before you guys take off."

"I'm a little busy."

"Come with me."

Samantha led him into the adjoining room, it was Ortega's game room with billiards tables and flat screen television sets. One entire wall was a constantly flowing waterfall back lit with neon lights.

"What is it?"

"Shut up," Samantha said slamming the door.

Before Deckard could turn around, she had jumped into his arms, wrapping her legs around his waist. Pressing her lips to his, she put her tongue into his mouth.

"This was what you wanted to show me? I could have used this before I was shot to fucking pieces you know?"

Samantha dropped her legs to the ground and began undoing his rigger's belt. Freeing it, she grabbed the belt with one hand and yanked it free from the belt loops with a snap of nylon.

"Jesus."

Tearing open what was left of his pants, she reached inside.

"You've been drinking that water I gave you?"

"No, why?"

"Well I guess it's not an issue for you, huh? I thought you might be too exhausted so I ground up a blue pill and sprinkled it into your water."

"What the fuck? You tried to drug me?"

Samantha yanked down his pants and pushed him down

277

onto one of the couches lining the walls. Crossing her hands she grabbed the bottom of her shirt and pulled it over her head and tossed it aside. She wasn't wearing anything underneath.

"Just try not to tear open any of those war wounds and you should be fine."

The loadout room was simply an emptied garage on the compound where the two Samruk platoons kept all of their tactical gear and rifles while carrying just their issued Glock 19 pistols when not pulling guard duty. Body armor and rifles lined the walls along with RPG launchers, a Carl Gustav recoilless rifle, a couple Mk48 machine guns, a .50 caliber Barrett sniper rifle and other random weapons. In the center of the room were tables set up with ammo cans full of bullets for the mercenaries to jam into magazines between combat missions.

At the moment, the room was torn apart with empty ammo cans, wrappers, and other trash strewn about. Needless to say, the men had been constantly in and out of the loadout room for the last week. Now that things were winding down, the Samruk men were packing the deuce and half transport trucks with equipment, their personal gear would be hand carried on the aircraft.

Aghassi stood next to one of the ammunition tables with his notebook computer open. Nikita and Pat stood to either side of him. Kurt Jager, fresh off his assignment with the Zapatistas watched from a distance.

The men looked up as Deckard walked through the door with a bottle of water in his hand. His face was taped up but at least he was back on his feet. He had changed into a fresh uniform and cleaned himself up a little.

"How you feeling?" Aghassi asked him.

"I'm not dead."

Deckard unscrewed the cap from the bottle but stopped short. Looking at the bottled water hesitantly, he dropped it in the trash.

"Is there any Gatorade in the refrigerator?"

"I got you," Kurt said opening the fridge in the corner of the room and throwing him a bottle of the red colored liquid.

Deckard took a couple gulps and capped it.

"So what can I do for you gentlemen. It looks like you are in here planning a mutiny against me."

"Not until your Samruk International corporate checks hit our accounts," Pat joked.

"Here is the thing," Aghassi said, spinning his notebook around so that Deckard could see the screen. "We uncovered our entire target deck and fleshed it out with the personalities we wanted captured or killed."

The screen showed the link chart that they had been working on since their initial reconnaissance mission to Oaxaca. All of the blank spots on the chart had been filled in with names and pictures in recent days. Each picture had been crossed out with a black X indicating that they had gotten their man.

"We thought we were taking down the entire structure of the cartel, from operations, to logistics, to communications, along with the command node of Jimenez, Ignacio, and their most trusted men. But what if there is a secondary command node above Jimenez?"

"You know this whole deal smells like shit," Pat added. "The high end US mil weapons? How the fuck did they end up with those?"

"You told me that Ignacio's parting words were to the effect that they did a smash and grab on some Zeta warehouse. It sounds like a weapons stockpile or bunker on a US military base got looted and the brass on the base is trying to keep it quiet. Meanwhile, the weapons were smuggled into Mexico by the Zetas to help them maintain control over their plazas. This would end the careers of dozens of Colonels and Generals."

"He also mumbled something just before his expiration date passed. I asked him where the Zetas were getting the guns from and he said they were picking them up at AMIZ. I thought he was just babbling nonsense. He died a minute later so I figured he was delirious but when I was telling Aghassi about it he had heard of this place."

"AMIZ," Aghassi cut in. "*Academia Militarizada Ignacio Zaragoza*, no relation to our Ignacio, it is named after a famous Mexican General who kicked the shit out of the French in the 1860's. AMIZ is a training and operations center for Mexican police. It includes classrooms, a forensics lab, shooting range, helipad, everything needed to train modern counter-insurgency forces."

"That many US military guns in Zeta hands," Kurt said shaking his head. "No way was this just a simple theft from an American military base."

"But we are not telling you anything that you don't already know," Pat said as he sat down on one of the tables. "Right?"

Deckard took a deep breath and leaned back against the wall.

"Yeah," Deckard said. "Yeah, I know."

"What is problem?" Nikita asked.

"That massacre you guys found at the Christian mission is the problem. When I talked to Jimenez he told me that it wasn't him that ordered it, that it wasn't his crew that killed those people."

"You believed him?"

"I'm afraid I do. Look, when we got attacked on Grand Cayman..."

Deckard rubbed his face.

"When we got attacked by those suicide bombers, we had successfully evaded the Mexican military. The CIA was supporting our mission with men and material. Whoever led that attack knew exactly where we were going to be and when. They also had the capability to move Middle Eastern extremists onto the island with a large quantity of explosives."

"What are you saying?" Kurt asked.

"That whoever planned that attack had a sophisticated intelligence gathering network and previous experience running Islamic fundamentalist terrorist operations. It wasn't Jimenez, it wasn't the Mexican government, it wasn't the CIA up to some kind of hijinx. It was a fourth force, a new player that we were not aware of."

"What the hell..." Aghassi trailed off.

"The massacre at the Christian mission was deliberately made to be as sadistic as possible. The message written in blood," Deckard frowned. "I think was directed to me personally. It was a psychological operation."

280

"A PSYOP," Pat added, using the military terminology.

"Designed to draw me out Pat, just like you told me afterwards. They were trying to provoke a response, get me to do something reckless and effectively end our combat operations here in Oaxaca."

"But who and for what purpose?" Kurt asked the obvious question.

"That prisoner that Pat captured in Guatemala called him The Arab. I think that is our guy, but he is as much a myth as a reality. The CIA can't find shit on this dude and they want him bad after killing their pilots."

"You think The Arab and these US military weapons are related?" Pat asked.

"I have no way of knowing but I've got a bad feeling about it."

"Shit," Pat grunted.

"Tell me what else you know about AMIZ?" Deckard said looking to Aghassi.

"It is a police academy in Puebla that was built and stood up just a few years ago. While they train police officers it also serves as a staging ground where Mexican military forces can conduct training and rehearsals for major operations. Right now the Mexican Marines and select Infantry units are using it to launch their missions against the Zetas and other cartels. It's a major offensive across the whole of central and northern Mexico at this point with pitched battles on both sides."

"Let me guess, it is all a part of the Mérida Initiative?" Deckard asked, referencing the international security cooperation agreement between the Mexican and American governments.

"That's right. Our government and theirs share intelligence information and we also provide them with war material, helicopters and whatever else they need to battle the cartels."

"Including hundreds of rifles and machine guns?"

"Most of their guns are bought from overseas vendors, they are not using straight off the shelf US military weapons so it doesn't make sense for them to turn up in massive quantities like this."

"We've been down this road before. The Mérida Initiative must also be serving as a cover for a number of covert operations."

281

"Yeah, American military advisers. I've heard the rumors but I'm going to have to make some phone calls and see if I can get something specific."

"Make those calls right now."

"I will," Aghassi said, stepping out of the loadout room.

"What do you think Deckard?" Pat asked.

Pat, Kurt, and Nikita stood by, waiting.

"This isn't over."

"What's the plan."

"Whoever is behind this is running an off the books unsanctioned operation. That, or it is compartmentalized to the point that no one who could take action against it is placed in a manner to know the full picture. That said, there are going to be simple physical requirements, logistical issues involved in moving large quantities of war material. It sounds like this operation is piggybacked on a Mérida Initiative project. This would allow it to use official government transportation to move the weapons around."

"What are you thinking?"

"We chase the logistics tail and ride right up along it to its source. Find out who is behind it and skull stomp those fuckers."

"I like it," Nikita grinned.

"I've asked these men to sacrifice so much and too many of them are flying back to Kazakhstan in bodybags," Deckard added. "They are exhausted and we have fulfilled out contractual obligations in Mexico. Understand that it is just going to be the five of us. We stay light, mobile, and agile. That way we attack and move on to the next target before the enemy can figure out what we are up to, but we will be on our own. I'm having Frank and Korgan take these boys home."

"We understand," Pat said.

"Once Aghassi makes his calls task him to find and hot wire a vehicle for us. Pat, I want you to set up the vehicle, Nikita you load contingency supplies before everything else gets packed on pallets and sent back to Kazakhstan, Kurt I want you to start building some charges. If we find another cache or a trans-shipment point I want to blow it sky high."

"Roger that," the German answered.

"So we are really going to do this?" Pat said smiling.

"Fucking A we are."

282

42

The An-124 created a pall of white smoke as its wheels touched down.

The massive Russian cargo plane was a welcome sight. The remaining assault trucks that hadn't been shot to hell or blown up were standing by with the three deuce and a half cargo trucks in a single file. The entire compound had been packed up and turned over to Samantha as she was the only local police presence. Taxing down the runway, the An-124 spun around, as the rear cargo door opened.

One of the largest cargo carriers in the world, the Samruk-owned aircraft had to lower its hydraulics so that the rear end of the plane could get low enough to the ground to start loading vehicles and equipment. There was even a crane inside that ran down the length of the fuselage in the cargo area and could be loaded from both ends as the nose of the aircraft could rotate up and swallow everything from train engines to smaller aircraft hulls.

Sergeant Major Korgan ran up to talk to the flight crew since they were all native Russian speakers and could communicate easier. They would hash out a load plan as fast as possible to make sure all the vehicles were distributed correctly inside the An-124 to avoid weight and balance issues.

Deckard sat on the hood on one of the assault trucks, watching the flight crew drop two metal struts down to the tarmac for the vehicles to drive up. The shadows were growing long and everyone had a rough day. It wouldn't be until later that they would be able to process it all.

Several pickup trucks pulled onto the airfield nearby and disembarked several passengers. As they walked towards Deckard he only recognized one because of the pipe sticking from the corner of his mouth.

"No scary balaclavas?" Deckard asked as he got closer.

"Not anymore," Commandante Zero answered. "It is time for the people to see our faces and know that we stand with them."

The rebel leader was older than Deckard would have thought, maybe close to sixty years old with his hair having gone mostly gray. His face and nose were broad, displaying clear indigenous Mexican heritage going back to the Maya.

"This is where your fight really begins. The cartel served as the only functioning institution in Oaxaca for a long time now, completely replacing the systems of government. Now that the cartel is gone, it won't be easy for you."

"I know," the revolutionary said. "Democracy does not just happen, people have to be ready for it. We will have competition from the criminals as well. Not just other cartels but from the biggest crooks of all, the politicians in Mexico City."

Deckard slid off the truck down to the ground and shook the rebel's hand.

"Together we bled for nothing other than a narrow one in a million shot at giving these people something worth living for."

"That's something," Zero replied. "Something more than they had yesterday. Now it is time for the Zapatista movement to become something else, more than an armed rebel group or political movement."

"Good luck. You've only got one policewoman but it is a start."

"Thank you for what you've done here. I never thought that our arrangement would actually work, but to tell you the truth our backs were against the wall. We had ceased to be a relevant opposition force since the military came down on us years ago."

"Now is the time to take that one in a million shot."

"We will," he laughed. "Now get your imperialist gringo ass the hell off our land!"

"I will, believe me. The military has a convoy that is just a few hours out by now."

"We have a plan, we are going to go underground and let them think it is business as usual. With the war going on up north they will be recalled in a week or two. Then we hold elections while they are distracted."

Commadante Zero waved goodbye as he slipped inside the pickup truck and drove off.

Switching up the order of movement, one of the deuce and half transport trucks was the first to roll onto the back of the logistics aircraft, followed by an assault truck. The vehicles were literally swallowed one by one. Each would have to be secured to hard points on the metal floor with ratchet straps to keep the vehicles from rolling around during flight.

Over the whine of the Antonov's jet engines, Deckard didn't hear the helicopter until it was right on top of them. The CIA helicopter set down behind the row of Samruk vehicles, the pilot keeping the rotors going and ready to take off at a moment's notice.

Deckard hurried over to Frank who was safeguarding the source, his wife, and child. It was a golden helicopter flight that would eventually take him to the United States, a house, a job, and more importantly a new name and the safety that came along with it.

The source looked at Deckard with sad eyes and shook his hand.

"Thank you for looking after us," he said, tears forming in the corner of his eyes.

"Get your family the hell out of here," Deckard yelled over the rotor blast. "This is your freedom bird."

The same tattooed military contractor that they had seen during the previous prisoner drop off got out of the helicopter and held the door open with his other hand resting on the pistol grip of his HK 416.

"I saw some of your men working on a van," the source told him. "I thought you were leaving the country?"

"Of course we are."

"Well, just in case," the Mexican dug into his wallet. "Take this decal and stick it in the window. This is what we used to have on our trucks when we transported drugs up north."

Deckard looked at the decal, a yellow Ferrari sports car logo.

"It's a recognition signal between members of the Zeta cartel and their allies. It lets allies pass through the drug corridors without getting shot to pieces. You might still get stopped at some Zeta check points and have to pay a bribe, but at least they won't execute you."

"Thanks," Deckard said, putting the decal in his pocket. "I'll hold on to this, just in case."

The source nodded and turned to his family, ushering them towards the helicopter. His wife helped their son through the door before they climbed on board. The military contractor got in last, closing the door behind them just as the pilot pulled up on the collective and got them airborne. In seconds the helicopter had disappeared from view.

285

Deckard turned to see the last deuce and a half roll up the ramp and into the airplane. The assault trucks were now fully loaded. Frank limped up to him, having left his crutches behind.

"I can't believe you are sending me back to Astana while you guys go on some kind of suicide mission."

"I'll make sure you are on the next one once you've healed up."

"How about once you've healed up? You look like hammered shit!"

"I'm the leader, I just sit back and stick colored pins on maps and walk around with a clipboard so who cares?"

"Fuck you, dude. We'll talk back in Kazakhstan."

Frank limped his way to the aircraft. He was pissed about getting left out just as any of his men would be if they knew what he was planning.

"There is one more item of business to attend to before wrapping this up," a woman's voice said from behind him.

Turning, Samantha walked right up to him and threw her arms around his neck. Pulling Deckard down to her she kissed him deeply.

"Give me a call the next time you decide to shoot in and out of Mexico."

"Even if it is two in the morning?"

"Especially if it is two in the morning," she said. "Especially if you are already five tequila shots deep in the night."

"I will."

Sighing, she released Deckard.

"I have to go now and act as a liaison with the Mexican military as they arrive in a couple hours. I also have to act as if I have no idea what the fuck has been going on in my city for the last week."

"I guess it is a good thing you don't know anything about what has been happening here the last week."

"You know it," she said smiling.

Deckard couldn't help but stare at her ass as she walked back to the parking lot.

43

Deckard, Pat, Kurt, Aghassi, and Nikita looked out the windshield as the convoy of Mexican military vehicles passed on the opposite lane of traffic down federal highway 135. There were approximately one hundred vehicles in the fighting column including HMMWVs, tracked infantry fighting vehicles, Silverado pickup trucks, and cargo trucks transporting several hundred Mexican Infantry soldiers.

With Aghassi behind the wheel, Deckard was grateful that Samruk International was in the air and already somewhere over the Atlantic Ocean, heading back to Astana, the capital of Kazakhstan. Once there, Frank and Korgan would make sure each man was paid from the bundles of cash they had confiscated from Ortega as well as what was found hidden away by Jimenez. They would have their work cut out for them attending to burials, hospital visitations, and making sure that life insurance payments were made in a timely manner to the families.

Meanwhile, the stay-behind element drove their van north while the military headed south, into their previous Area of Operations. They were just a few hours too late. Samantha would have her work cut out as well, playing dumb and doing damage control until the military withdrew from the area.

Thirty minutes later, the van pulled through a checkpoint manned by civilians with AK-47 rifles and bandannas covering their faces. In the night, they had not seen the checkpoint until they were right on top of it. The guards saw the Ferrari logo stuck in the upper left hand portion of the windshield and waved them through. The Zeta secret handshake.

The Zeta cartel was now the largest and most powerful drug cartel in Mexico. They controlled most of the northern portion of the country but were in competition with the Sinaloa cartel, the oldest cartel in Mexico. The Zetas had been elite Mexican airborne soldiers who defected to the cartels and eventually splintered off to form their own faction, bringing military training and experience with them. Efficient and ruthless, they came to dominate the drug trade and were soon moving into other lucrative ventures such as vehicle thefts, human trafficking, extortion rackets, real estate, and more.

With American monetary and intelligence assistance, the Mexican military had been engaged in combating the Zetas for years but had only recently pushed towards an endgame as their operations came to mimic American Counter-Terrorism tactics developed during the War on Terror in Afghanistan, Iraq, and beyond. Now the military and the Zetas were engaged in a full blown war for survival.

The five Samruk mercenaries had absolutely no interest in fighting it out with the Zetas. That was way over their head and best left to the military. Their goal was simple, identify where the large volumes of US military weapons were originating from and shut it off at the source. Anything they could dig up on The Arab would be an added bonus.

Nikita was fast asleep in the passenger seat. Aghassi was nodding in and out while driving. Kurt and Pat were both passed out on the floor of the van amid the tactical gear and weapons they were hauling. Deckard felt like he'd been hit by a train and was about to go down at any moment.

"Aghassi, pull over in this parking lot on the right," Deckard said.

Pulling into the lot Deckard nudged the other mercenaries to wake them up.

"We're halfway to Puebla, we can take six hours but might not be able to once everything starts moving again. Keep one guard up front at a time, everyone else needs to hit the rack."

"Sounds good," Aghassi yawned.

"Nikita, you've been racked out for a while now. You take first watch."

Deckard unbuttoned his shirt and balled it up to use as a pillow. Later, he wouldn't even remember laying down.

His sleep was deep and dreamless.

Aghassi drove through the outskirts of Puebla, making a lazy circle around the AMIZ compound as not to arouse suspicion. Located at the edge of the city, the compound was off site from the main AMIZ headquarters. The facility was surrounded by twenty five foot reinforced concrete walls with guard towers spaced at even intervals. It looked like many of the Forward Operating Bases that US forces operated out of in the Middle East.

Deckard knew that this was no accident. Mexico had been more violent and even bloodier than Iraq and Afghanistan for a number of years. These days the only other splatter fest that could compete with Mexico was Syria. The FOB had been built with American money and assistance so it was no wonder that it looked like a stronghold to wage a counter-insurgency from.

The area reconnaissance made clear to the mercenaries that the direct approach was out of the question. Going over the walls would be difficult and they would almost certainly he sprayed with machine gun fire. Nikita could easily take out a few guards in the towers with his suppressed sniper rifle but at this point they were not sure who was involved with the weapons trafficking and who wasn't. Who was corrupt and who was just a soldier serving their country was one of the questions they would attempt to answer.

"Check this out," Aghassi said, pointing towards a Mexican police convoy on the street up ahead. A half dozen pickup trucks were loaded with Federal Police carrying rifles and wearing assault vests packed with spare magazines. The convoy was heading towards the AMIZ compound.

Aghassi reached up and snatched the Zeta-Ferrari decal off the windshield and handed it to Deckard.

"Get up here and change seats with Nikita. It will do the talking but it will be good for them to see a white face."

"Shit," Deckard said, realizing what the former ISA operator was planning. "That is a hell of a risk."

"It's just crazy enough to work."

Accelerating, Aghassi brought the van up behind the convoy, getting close, but not so close that the Mexican police felt threatened.

"Wave this at them," Pat said handing him his ball cap. It had an American flag Velcro'ed to the front.

As the convoy snaked towards the front gate of the AMIZ compound, the mercenaries trailed close behind in their commandeered panel van. The gate guards slung their weapons and pushed the road blocks out of the way, another signaling the tower guard to press a button a retract the heavy metal gate. A giant bicycle chain began to rotate and drag the gate across the entrance on one wheel.

The convoy of Federal Police was then allowed to pass into the compound. The five mercenaries held their breath as they approached the gate. Rolling down the window, Aghassi waved Pat's American flag baseball cap at the gate guards and began speaking in rapid fire Spanish. It was hard for Deckard to pick out the words but he was telling the gate guards that they were American Special Forces advisers detailed out to the Mexican Federal Police and were coming back from an operation with them.

The gate guard nodded his head and waved them through.

Gassing the van through the entrance, the gate began to swing back into place behind them.

"I can't believe that worked," Kurt said.

"I've been on enough military bases overseas to not be surprised by this anymore," Pat replied. "I couldn't tell you how many times I rolled up to an American FOB in Iraq driving a civilian vehicle, dressed up like a local, and told the gate guards that I was an American and to let me in."

"And they just let you in."

"Just about every time," Pat answered. "The Delta Force special."

"The gift that keeps on giving," Deckard laughed. "Sort of like the clap."

Aghassi pulled off from the convoy and slipped down a side street. The complex even looked like a FOB from the inside with small trailers or Compartmentalized Housing Units that had been shipped in and in some cases joined together to form larger work areas. There were also trailers converted into offices and classrooms with a few larger permanent structures here and there. The van pulled into a parking space in front of a loading bay and stopped.

"So what's the plan?" Aghassi asked.

"Hold what you got. We're US military advisers here to conduct Foreign Internal Defense operations. If you run into the Federal Police tell them you are working with the military. If you run into the military tell them you work with the police, whatever you have to say to get out of a jamb. We'll split up, one Spanish speaker per group. Pat you come with me since you are worthless."

"I speak Thai."

"Like I said, worthless. Kurt, you go with Aghassi and take Nikita with you."

"Da," the Kazakh answered.

Switching to Russian, Deckard quickly explained the situation and added that he should probably just keep his mouth shut during this operation. Explaining Nikita would be a little more difficult if people heard his native language.

"Kurt, you look for the headquarters building and see if you can locate where the base commander and his staff are working out of. It's late but they just had men back from an operation so someone will be in there. This loading dock looks like the logistics hub so my group will go look for the logistics office and break in. Remember, we want to know about any other gun shipments, where they are, and who is behind them. Got it?"

"Yeah," Aghassi said. "Should be a cake walk."

"Hey, remember you recruited me for this mission, not the other way around. Let's go."

The men wore their camouflage uniforms and retained their weapons and plate carriers to complete the picture of being American military advisers. Aghassi's group broke off and Deckard went in another direction with Pat, walking around the loading bay.

Avoiding the golden glow of the overhead lights, the two mercenaries stayed in the shadows as they walked around the building, trying each door until they found one that was unlocked. Looking inside, the lights were on but nobody was home. Large I-beams held up the ceiling and the concrete floor looked like it had been swept recently. There was a forklift and a few empty wooden pallets on the floor but not much else.

"I hope this isn't a wild goose chase," Deckard said.

"All those American military weapons, the ones you turned over to Zapatista rebels in good faith I might add, were not a figment of our imagination," Pat answered back. "They came from somewhere."

"But did they come from here?"

291

Walking between the Compartmentalized Housing Units, everything was quiet. Bugs buzzed around the yellow bulbs hanging from bare fixtures outside each door. The two former soldiers crunched across the gravel, looking at the placards on the wall of each unit and deciphering the Spanish language words. So far they were coming up empty.

Hearing the crunch of footsteps approaching, both men looked on hesitantly. They could be in a world of shit depending on who they ran into. They might be able to fool some guards but if the base's operations or intelligence officer found them, their cover story would not hold up for long.

Out of the shadows appeared four figures, two women and two men. The men wore desert digital camouflage uniforms with built in knee pads, high end stuff made by Crye Precision. The women were in Mexican Army uniforms.

"You have got to be fucking kidding me," Deckard groaned.

"Isn't that Dusty and Flakjacket Fred," Pat said while squinting in the darkness.

"I'm afraid it is."

Dusty cracked a joke in Spanish and all four of the partiers broke out laughing. Flakjacket was holding a bottle of tequila in one hand with his arm around one of the girls. The Special Operations community was a relatively small one and if you worked in it long enough, you would run into the same people over and over again. Still, the two mercenaries didn't expect this. While they were running around pretending to be Special Forces advisers they had just run into two genuine military advisers from SEAL Team Six.

"Dusty!" Deckard yelled down the gravel walkway as they were about to disappear into their bunk room. "Did the commandante of the base forget to lock the liquor cabinet again?"

Dusty jerked his head around.

"Motherfu-" he paused. "Deckard? Are you kidding me man? What are you doing here?"

Deckard smiled as he walked up and shook the SEAL's hand.

"I'm on a contract with Wexler," Deckard said, making up a new modified cover story on the fly. He was in the dark and needed to feel the situation out. "Asymmetrical Warfare Group

292

sent us down here to study cartel tactics and make recommendations to guys like you."

"Study cartel tactics? Then what's with those fire sticks and blammo you guys are carrying?"

"New kit they have us testing out for the Force Modification office. If we recommend it, they will push this stuff over to Dev and Delta for further evaluation."

"I like it," Dusty said curling his upper lip. "That is one gangster looking AK you've got there."

"What's up?" Pat said stepping forward to shake hands with Dusty.

"Holy shit, you too!"

Flakjacket still had his girl hanging off his arm but reached out to shake hands with them both.

"Haven't seen you two since that job in the PI a few years back," the SEAL Team Six operator recalled. "They always pick brown skinned guys like us for that type of shit but who knows why they keep sending crackers like you."

"Because I'm the color of the boss man?" Deckard countered.

"Oh, shit." Dusty laughed. "Not for long, we're breeding you fuckers out of the gene pool!"

"How are things going for you guys down here?" Pat said, steering the conversation.

"Not bad, not bad, but we still wish we were back with our Squadron in The Horn. They get to shoot pirates all day and we're here doing a FID mission that they should have given to Green Berets."

Flakjacket popped open the bottle of tequila and passed it around. The two female Mexican military officers each took a long swig before handing it off to Deckard who downed a gulp. Painkillers, he told himself. Pat took a slug and handed the bottle off to Dusty.

"I was going to say," Deckard said. "You guys are SEALs and I don't see a lot of water in Central Mexico."

"Nope, me neither," Flakjacket said rolling his eyes. "But the SOCOM commander is one of ours and our own commander doesn't know how to say no to him so we get pimped out for every jive ass mission. I mean, the Mexican police and military are making some progress down here but it's an uphill battle."

293

"Corruption?"

"That's a big part of it. The Agency and the DEA have been compartmentalizing and hiding operations to the point that our missions are not getting compromised as much as they used to. As I'm sure you know, they've been rotating Spanish speakers in Dev down here for years now but it is still mostly advise and assist."

"Even if we get to slip the leash every now and then," Dusty said, looking as his lady friend. She didn't appear to speak English but giggled none the less. "So we have rolled up some High Value Targets here and there, mostly Zetas while we ride along with FES, the Mexican version of the SEALs, but also with the Marines and Federal Police like we did tonight."

"We have really just been jumping from base to base the last week and interviewing soldiers and cops about what tactics that the cartels have been employing," Deckard lied. "I've been hearing some things about large shipments of military grade weapons ending up in the hands of the cartels."

"Oh, yeah." Dusty confirmed. "No doubt. The cartels buy military grade shit from corrupt Central American military officers. Sometimes it is even stuff that the United States government is shipping to the Mexican military to help them fight this war. It is counter-productive of course because the cartels rip it off or buy it off from corrupt officials."

"What kinds of quantities are we talking about here?" Deckard asked.

"You know, a dozen AT4 rockets here, a dozen M203 grenade launchers there."

"What about really large shipments, as in hundreds of rifles and machine guns, tens of thousands of rounds of ammunition?"

"You've been hearing those rumors too?" Flakjacket said.

"Yeah, enough times that it is starting to concern us," Pat added.

"Sounds like you guys haven't been read in either," Dusty spat. "They are keeping all of us in the dark."

"What do you mean?"

"What do I mean?" Dusty repeated. "I mean there is some major league hero stuff going on down here. Some real Serpico shit."

"OBI has their hands in just about everything going on in Mexico," Flakjacket said. "The Agency's Case Officer working out of there had a hit put out on him by one of the cartels but was ordered to stay. They must be keeping him in place for a reason."

"Yeah, his PSD is shitting bricks over there in Mexico City. They are convinced they are going to get rolled up any day now."

"You think the CIA is up to something?"

"Maybe, maybe not," Dusty interjected. "I'm just saying that the orders coming out of OBI are pretty strange. They are deliberately interfering with and stalling military and police operations down here."

Deckard wasn't about to let on that he wasn't sure what OBI was at first but it hit him with the reference to Mexico City. The Office of Bi-national Intelligence was in a building next to the US Embassy in the Mexican capitol city. It housed liaisons from the CISEN, the Mexican intelligence agency, along with the FBI, CIA, DEA, and Homeland Security.

"What kind of orders?"

"Like arbitrarily freezing our operational areas so that we can't conduct raids. Just shutting down large swaths of certain cities for specific times and letting the cartels run amuck. Then we have to go in and clean up the mess afterwards."

"So you think OBI is intentionally sowing chaos and making the drug war worse than it has to be?"

"Well that is why I say, maybe not. I know some of the contractors working the CIA Case Officer's Personal Security Detail, some of them are former teammates. You guys probably know some of the former Army dudes working the detail. Anyway, when I give them a call they tell me that this Case Officer is as confused by these orders as we are. He doesn't get it but is being told to toe the line. He did, and that is probably why they are not yanking him out of country even though he has a bounty on his head. He is someone's lapdog now and they like him right where he is."

"Where is he getting his orders from?"

"Not sure, but OBI answers to NORTHCOM."

"What the hell is going on down here?" Pat asked.

"You got me brother," Flakjacket said. "We just got another month working this joke of a mission and then we pop back over to Somalia to do some real work."

"I hear you," Deckard said. "I don't have a phone with me but why don't you hit me up with your number and I will let you know if I hear anything."

"Right on," Flakjacket went inside and came out a moment later with a piece of paper that he handed to Deckard.

"Thanks, I'll let you guys get back to business."

"Take care Casper," Dusty joked. "You two better get under overhead cover because I think the sun is coming out. You could burst into flames if caught in direct sunlight."

Turning, Dusty slapped one of the girls on the ass on her way into the room and slammed the door behind him.

Dusty was right, it was almost dawn and none of them wanted to get caught skulking around AMIZ during the day when the base would be much more active.

Opening the sliding door on the van, Deckard and Pat climbed inside.

"Can you believe that shit?" Pat asked.

"Not really. It sounds like OBI is freezing down certain corridors at certain times."

"Long enough for the drugs to head north and for the guns to head south?"

"Yeah, that and maybe something more."

The door swung back open, causing them to start as Kurt Jager pushed someone into the van before getting inside. Nikita came in behind him and shut the door while Aghassi got in on the driver's side and took the wheel.

"Who is this?" Deckard demanded.

"Assistant S2 Officer," Kurt replied, keeping his AK pointed at the prisoner. They had captured the assistant to the AMIZ intelligence officer. "He confirmed that the guns are coming through AMIZ and being handed over to the cartels. Not just the Zetas, but to all of them."

"Were you compromised?"

"No, we convinced some of the police we ran into that we were American military advisers like you said but after we found this guy and interrogated him we figured we had to bring him with us."

"We're running out of darkness," Aghassi reminded them.

"Get us out of here."

Aghassi fired up the engine and headed back towards the gate. When he got there, Kurt held his hand over the prisoner's mouth and held his Glock 19 to his temple to inspire him to keep quiet. Aghassi explained to the guards that he had a couple prostitutes in the back that he had to drive back home. After bullshitting for a minute about prices and services rendered, the gate guards laughed and let them pass.

Hitting the main road, Aghassi took a right.

"Which way are we going?" he asked.

"Our prisoner knows," Kurt insisted.

"Where are the guns coming from," Deckard asked him in Spanish.

"Militar No. 3," the intelligence Officer said sheepishly. "Torreon."

Deckard leaned back against the side of the van.

"North," Deckard told Aghassi. "We're heading north."

297

44

The ceiling fan slowly spun round and round, cooling nothing and no one in the sweltering heat. Flies buzzed around the corners of his eyes until he swatted them away. Outside, someone was honking their car's horn. Further away, someone else was popping off some shots, the sharp cracks distinct over the other background noise.

He began to fidget in his seat, rubbing his hands together. He never felt comfortable during long periods alone without a task or a distraction. Alone with his thoughts was alone with his nightmares. Times like this brought him back to another time and place.

A knock sounded at the hotel room door before his assistant entered.

"East Torreon has been shut down," the assistant informed him. "The Marines are throwing up roadblocks to the south but we have a clear shot into the sector for the next few hours. Our contact says he will have OBI keep it open as long as we need."

"This will be over before then," The Arab replied. "Did you get what I asked you for."

The assistant handed him a few packs of cigarettes from the local market. The Arab lit one up and took a drag.

"Thank you Abdullah," The Arab said, patting the back of his assistant's head. "Let us go and do what we do."

Grabbing his backpack for him, the assistant followed The Arab and locked the door behind them. The sun was just starting to peak and whores were beginning to stagger back to the hotel after working the streets all night. The Arab pushed several out of the way as they made their way down the stairs to the street.

Geographically, Torreon was right smack in the middle of the war between the drug cartels as a major way station between northern and southern Mexico. The war had been raging for months now as evident by the rotting corpses in the streets that The Arab's assistant had to avoid as he negotiated his way to their target.

The Arab lit another cigarette, took a puff and rubbed his eyes.

He had seen these streets before, grown up on streets just like them in Iraq. He was barely old enough to walk when his father came home from work and kicked his mother out of the house. He wanted to take another wife so she had to leave and the child with her. Rejected by her family they slept in filthy streets flooded with stagnant black water. He hadn't understood it at the time, but she had sold her body to men passing by just to keep them both fed with one meal a day.

Finally, with both of them starving, his mother rejected him as well and left him to die on the streets, hungry and alone. He had not yet reached maturity when he too was forced to turn to prostitution. In southern Iraq, it is easier to have a boyfriend than a girlfriend and there was never any shortage of clients.

As a teenager he had grown big enough to find additional ways of surviving. He learned how to fight and fought anyone and everyone he could find, taking what he pleased. For a time he ran with a gang of youths who would steal and run scams but most of the time he worked alone. After Saddam was captured by the Americans things only got worse as Iraq slid into chaos.

The next gang he worked with was mostly into kidnapping. There were no rules, they would drive into Baghdad and grab girls right out of the University campus. They would be raped for days on end until their family paid the ransom. If the family didn't pay up they would be killed or sold off to locals as sex slaves. There was no one to stop them and the Americans were busy going after foreign fighters and bomb makers.

If they needed a place to stay or a new hide out they would simply knock on the door of some rich person in the nice part of town and tell them that if they were not allowed in that they would rape his wife. If they refused, the gang would force their way in, if they complied they raped the wife and cut the heads off babies they found inside anyway simply because that was what they did.

Wandering the back alleys one night, stumbling over holes in the street big enough to swallow a tank, he finished a bottle of whiskey and decided he had had enough. Drunk and disoriented he flipped open the straight razor he always carried. The rusty knives were only used for the home invasions. Tearing off his shirt, he snarled, externalizing every moment of self hatred he had ever experienced.

299

The car came to a halt alongside a black sedan that was idling alongside the road.

The Arab was shaken back to reality, dropping his cigarette out of the window as he was about to burn his fingers. The driver's side window was lowered, revealing his Arab-to-Spanish translator.

"The local we hired has the house under surveillance. They are home."

"The area will be clear of soldiers for several hours," The Arab stated. "Plenty of time for us to get in there and do this."

Motioning to Abdullah, the assistant took the lead, driving into the target neighborhood. The men in both vehicles pulled ski masks over their heads. Arriving on the correct street in the area that had been operationally frozen for the Mexican military, they met with a local who had been keeping tabs on the family living in the house they told him to watch.

A few words were exchanged before the money was handed over from the translator in the second sedan. The local informant walked off and both cars parked in front of the house they were interested in. The translator opened the trunk of his car and the other occupants of the vehicles retrieved their sledgehammers.

The Arab thumbed the scars running down his forearms as the death squad went to work on the door. The residents were just waking up as the door gave way. The killers drew pistols, moved inside, and quickly secured everyone they found, flexcuffing their hands behind their backs. Grabbing his bag, The Arab followed them in, lighting up another cancer stick as he walked inside.

It was a family of four, kicked down to their knees in the living room while Abdullah set up the digital video camera on its tripod. The biggest and baddest of the Sinaloa cartel assassination teams called themselves TT and their leader went by the name of Ghost Killer.

The death squad now had Ghost Killer's family hostage. His mother, his sister, his niece, and his cousin. Tears were streaming down their cheeks but no one said a word to them. None of the killers were interested in gathering information or holding them for ransom. When one of the prisoners began to whine or speak out, one of the death squad members would take a plastic bag and hold it over their head. Letting them squirm for a moment, it would give them reason to keep their mouths shut the next time.

The Arab reached into his bag and grabbed his rusty knife, sticking it down his front between his belt and his pants.

The cameraman signaled that they were rolling. The Arab stood behind the prisoners with his arms crossed in front of him, the knife clearly visible. The Spanish speaker came forward and began reading a prepared speech from a piece of paper, declaring themselves to be Los Zetas assassins who were retaliating against the Sinaloa cartel. Another member of the kill team hung cardboard signs around the necks of each captive, declaring them to be whores, traitors, and patsies.

Once the speech had concluded, The Arab went back to his bag for the second piece of equipment he needed, a three foot length of 2x4 wooden plank. He had a lot of experience in his line of work and decapitating adults was much different that slicing the heads of children and infants. He had tried other measures like drugging the victims but it never seemed to work in a timely manner. It would take too long for them to go under, or worse, they would collapse while filming and not wake up.

Walking up behind the Ghost Killer's cousin, he wound up and slammed the 2x4 into the back of his head, knocking him face first on the floor, unconscious. The niece received the same treatment, then the teenage sister, and finally the overweight mother. Knocking them out first was suitably violent on camera and kept them from kicking too much during the cutting.

The camera man adjusted the angle to point down at the prostrate forms. The Arab drew his knife and went to the mother first. Exposing her soft neck by pulling back on her hair, he started the cutting.

He kept his work fast and efficient. After all, they had a second job today. The death squad would have to call their control to have another zone frozen to keep the military out while they went and paid a visit to the family of a Zeta assassin in different neighborhood.

45

Flinging open the sliding door, Aghassi slowed down just enough for them to toss the Mexican military officer out of the van alongside the dusty highway before speeding off again. The mercenaries couldn't bring themselves to execute the guy in cold blood. He hadn't been part of the gun running ring but since he was an intelligence officer stationed at AMIZ, he had seen the comings and goings, listened to the encrypted radio traffic, and had eventually put two and two together. In short, he was a good intelligence officer.

Aghassi looked in the rear view mirror and saw the young man standing on the shoulder of the road looking dejected as the mercenaries continued driving north. They had made it very clear to him that it would behoove all parties involved if he never mentioned his kidnapping and instead concocted a story to explain his absence to his superiors involving tequila and hookers.

According to the S2 Officer, the guns were being flown to Military Base Number Three which was adjacent to the civilian airfield in Torreon. From there, the guns were being distributed to cartels across Mexico. It wasn't just one cartel being armed, but nearly all of them. To Deckard's ears, it had shades of the Iran-Iraq was in the 1980's where the United States had armed both sides of the conflict to weaken both parties.

From Torreon, truckers would be contracted to haul the guns south to AMIZ under armed escort from Private Military Contractors, the military, or guns for hire. The north/south running corridor would be frozen during this time on orders coming by encrypted radio signals from the OBI office in Mexico City to allow the convoy free passage. Once the guns arrived in AMIZ, select military officers and intelligence agents would divide the weapons up and use the loading bay as a distribution point. One day the Zetas would pull their trucks in and load up the largess. The day after, the Sinaloa cartel would send their own trucks to pick up an equal number of weapons.

Who was flying the weapons into Military Base Number Three and where were they coming from? The S2 Officer didn't know and was only familiar with the stages of the operation that passed through the hub at AMIZ where he worked. He did know that everyone at the military base in Torreon was corrupt. The base served as the major way station for the flow of weapons to the cartels and the soldiers and civilians working there facilitated the violence that had plagued Mexico.

Aghassi watched again in the rear view mirror as Deckard downed two more Motrin pills along with a bottle of water before passing out on the floor of the van. They had a long seven hundred mile drive ahead of them, right up the spine of central Mexico.

The mercenaries rotated drivers all day, only stopping for a couple piss breaks and to pick up some food along the way. When not driving, they took advantage of the free time to catch up on some sleep and perform weapons maintenance.

Deckard opened Aghassi's notebook computer and checked his encrypted Samruk International e-mail account. He had one e-mail from Samantha to tell him that the military was already getting bored as they had not found any mercenaries, cartels, or communist rebels to fight. So far, so good. Frank shot him a quick note to inform him that they had arrived in Kazakhstan with minimal fanfare. Sergeant Major Korgan was getting the injured situated in the hospital in Astana.

Then an e-mail from an address he didn't recognize appeared in his inbox. Clicking on it, he read its contents:

-Begin PGP Encryption-

Deckard, one of my sources tells me you were not on that airplane out of Mexico. You blatantly violated our agreement. There will be repercussions for that. In the meantime, I will not be reporting this indiscretion to my superiors. I have a good idea of what you are up to and I want you to know that the Clandestine Services support you in spirit but not in any tangible manner for reasons I'm sure you can understand. We know

something stinks to high hell with this man called The Arab.
Understandably, you don't have a high opinion of my employers
but this isn't one of our operations. Good luck.

- G

-End PGP Encryption-

Deckard snorted. Agent Grant of the CIA had just given them an underhanded endorsement. Who would have thought? Additionally, Grant had added a web link at the bottom of the e-mail. Clicking on it, Deckard was taken to a publicly available youtube.com video. As he watched three women and one man kneeling on the ground, he knew what was coming next.

Someone was reading some kind of diatribe off camera about how they were Zeta hit men striking back against the Sinaloa cartel. The executioner whacked each victim on the back of the head with a board before he began slicing their heads off. Deckard noted long horizontal scars running up the executioner's forearms as he worked the rusty blade through the older woman's throat. He closed the laptop and put it away.

The website indicated that the video had been uploaded just an hour ago. The narration given in the video indicated that the quadruple murder had taken place in Torreon.

It was nine o' clock at night when the mercenaries rolled into town.

"This is about as far as we are getting," Pat said as he coasted the van off to the side of the road.

"Grab your kit and we'll move out on foot," Deckard ordered.

They had been driving around the edges of Torreon for nearly an hour, running into one roadblock after the next. Some were cordons set up by Mexican Marines but most were being run by cartel members. According to the map, Militar No. 3 was in the center of the city along with the airport. Kitting up, the mercenaries locked up the van with their go-bags full of emergency supplies and proceeded deeper into the city.

Deckard carried explosive charges, Nikita a small aid bag filled with medical supplies, Pat a pair of large bolt cutters, and Kurt a Hooligan tool. Aghassi has his usual breaking and entering kit.

The Zetas and the Sinaloa cartels were engaged in an all out battle for control of the city. Automatic gunfire thudded throughout different sectors of Torreon with red and green tracer fire streaking through the night sky. The occasional grenade or RPG explosion lit up the night and the *crump-crump-crump* of mortar fire walked across one of the derelict neighborhoods.

The cartels were going bone to bone to see who was bigger and whoever had the largest body count would win the day. Whoever uploaded the most violent videos onto the internet would achieve victory in the propaganda war.

And it was all on someone else's dime.

Squeezing through a filthy alleyway filled with trash, the mercenaries circumvented a Sinaloa cartel roadblock. One at a time, they sprinted across a four lane highway and passed a hollowed out gas station with shattered windows. Just as Nikita cleared the road, he hit the dirt as headlights flashed above him and a five vehicle convoy of blacked out Suburban Sport Utility Vehicles blasted down the street.

Paralleling the road, the five men shook out into a single file, maintaining a separation between each man. Lowering their night vision goggles, they were able to see their surroundings and stay well away from any other human presence as they were in an approach into the city that was not built up, consisting of knee high brush. Under the green tint of the night vision goggles, light sources were amplified and the gunfire shooting into the sky looked like lasers from some kind of science fiction movie.

Deckard led the patrol through an empty construction site where they passed between stacks of cinder blocks and rebar before climbing a dusty hill and dropping down into what had been some kind of resort with a golf course and artificial ponds. Moving through the abandoned resort, the mercenaries stuck to the low ground where they would not be silhouetted and pushed

305

deeper into the city.

With years of experience conducting Direct Action raids and Unconventional Warfare, in and out of the military, Deckard made a careful route selection based on his map reconnaissance. The haphazard and confusing nature of urban war zones and the danger they posed was worth avoiding as much as possible so to that end, he kept them away from the built up areas where the gunfire was coming from. This wasn't their war and their goal was to cut the conflict off at the source, not get embroiled in every bushfire gun battle.

On the other side of the resort, Deckard found a high wall and a gate that would take too long to go around. A smaller gate for foot traffic was secured with a chain and padlock. Motioning Pat forward, the former Delta operator used a pair of wide grip bolt cutters to shear through the lock. With a snap, the metal gave way and the padlock fell to the ground.

Both men quickly ducked back into the alcove as another convoy passed on the street outside. This time it was pickup trucks full of Marines. One thing was clear, this area had not been operationally frozen by OBI in Mexico City. This was a free for all and everybody was invited.

Waiting to make sure the coast was clear, the mercenaries dashed across the road, avoiding a corpse sprawled in the street as they reached the opposite side. Hopping a small fence, Deckard looked down at the small Garmin GPS Foretrex strapped to his wrist. The industrial park in Torreon was warehouse after warehouse with a barren strip running down the middle where a set of railroad tracks had been laid. Following the tracks, the patrol continued heading north.

From the single shots ringing out across the industrial area, it sounded like someone had posted snipers up on the overpass on the other side of the warehouses. More mortar fire was raining down on a position somewhere on their left flank. Ignoring the distractions, they moved through the war zone until Deckard took a tactical pause at an intersection.

Two burnt out car hulks sat in the middle of the road, one of them with flames still flickering inside. Charred corpses were twisted around inside until they became unidentifiable from the rest of the wreckage, but the mercenaries did recognize the smell of burning flesh from previous battles. With no signs of immediate enemy presence, they made another road crossing, one man at a time while the others faced out and pulled security.

Along the main commercial ribbon, there was a residential area that Deckard guided the patrol through towards an open lot. The houses were small, single story affairs with windows barred up, hardly a single light shining through the windows. Many of the locals had fled the area long ago as the cartels heated up the plaza.

Taking a gulp of water from his Camelbak, Deckard took them through the open lot, skirted around a condominium complex, and across another open lot. It was slow going, but worth the effort. Five men, no matter how good, wouldn't last long against the kind of fire power rolling around Torreon on this night. The mercenaries crawled through a dump and dashed across another road, nearing the airfield.

Now they only had to cross three blocks to the airstrip beyond. Moving with his AK-103 at the ready, Deckard motioned for the mercenaries to push up alongside the houses on his right side where they disappeared into the shadows. As their leader took a knee, the other four men followed suit. In a few moments, they saw why Deckard had halted them. A half dozen cartel gunmen carrying American-made M-4 rifles were also out on patrol. They were well trained, maintaining noise and light discipline as they stalked through the neighborhood. The mercenaries waited several minutes after the enemy patrol passed before picking back up.

The airport was surrounded by a double barrier, a concrete wall and barbwire chain link fence. The bolt cutters would be awkward on the fence so Kurt Jager found some thick pieces of cardboard in the trash outside one of the homes. The concrete wall was easy to scale, but then they had to lay the cardboard over the barbwire and shim their way over one at a time. Pat took a knee next to the fence to allow the others to step off his upper leg and pull themselves over.

Inside the airport perimeter, the mercenary unit headed to the military base as several helicopters lifted off from the other side of the runway. Deckard looked at the twin lines of blue lights alongside the runway, the landing lights wavered and twinkled through the heat mirage coming off the tarmac.

This was how they fought, warfare on the margins. They were slipping through a conflict, a fight to get to the fight.

Finding an irrigation ditch, Deckard led the mercenaries

down into it as he spotted guard towers looming in the distance, silhouetted against the dull glow of burning fires somewhere in the city. Getting down to the prone, the five infiltrators high crawled through the stinking mud and garbage. When they got within a couple hundred meters, he called Nikita forward.

The sniper extended the bipod legs on his HK 417 rifle and turned on the Universal Night Sight attached to the rail system in front of his ten power scope. They were not close enough for Nikita to use sub-sonic bullets, they would bleed velocity to the point of ineffectiveness by the time the rounds reached their targets. With the suppressor in place, the bullets would dump some velocity as it was, going from super-sonic to a trans-sonic snap as they left the barrel. With a full-fledged war raging in the city, no one would notice a couple suppressed shots.

An eight foot tall concrete wall with a couple rusty strands of barbwire ringed Militar No. 3 with large pre-fabricated circular guard towers facing outwards and spaced around the perimeter. They were the type used by American forces abroad. The concrete sections were poured and cured in country, then shipped out to Forward Operating Bases where each section would be stacked on top of one another with a crane. The modular tower system could then have a ladder placed inside that led to a platform at the top that included overhead cover.

Nikita settled into a slow, rhythmic breathing pattern. At the bottom of his breath, he squeezed the trigger. The 417 snapped and he quickly transitioned to the next target. The gun let out another snap and both of the tower guards facing in their direction had been eliminated.

Moving while crouched over, the mercenaries jogged towards the wall. This time it was Deckard that took a knee and helped each man hurtle over the wall. With the barbs on the barbwire only occurring every few feet, it was easy for them to use the wire as a handhold and avoid the sharp parts. With Pat sliding down the opposite side of the wall, Deckard kicked off the side of it, reached up to grab the wire, and then pulled himself over the top.

His joints were sore and stiff, the wound in his thigh burning with the strain, even if the pain was dulled by the pills he had been taking. He could use something stronger from the aid bag he carried, morphine for instance, but the opiates would affect his situational awareness. They were cutting corners as it was, with his senses at half capacity or worse he was sure to get them all killed.

Inside the military compound, they saw a few hangars, what looked like barracks, and some other outbuildings, but it was the warehouse that drew their attention. The mercenaries stayed behind a half empty water tank while they waited for a two man roving patrol to pass. Nikita made a hand signal to Deckard, asking if he should take them out.

Deckard shook his head.

Once the patrol has passed he looked over at the four mercenaries.

"Let's hit the warehouse. If they are really moving war material through this base that is where it is going to be stockpiled until they can have it driven down to AMIZ."

Finding a row of palm trees, they used the shadows to disappear into and stay well away from any light sources until they came to the warehouse. Taking a knee, Deckard watched and listened, trying to figure out the best way inside. Across the airfield they could hear the thumping of another helicopter readying for takeoff.

The military base was adjacent to the civilian airport and it shared the same runway. A taxiway led from the runway and right into the military base where there was a hangar prepared to receive aircraft. The warehouse itself looked locked up but Deckard noticed that high up on the side of the brick wall were a series of windows that had been canted open for ventilation. An old two and a half ton truck collecting rust alongside the warehouse would help them gain access.

Hurrying across the open area, Deckard climbed up onto the hood, leveraging himself off one of the front tires. Once on the roof of the truck, he could reach up and grab the windowsill. Conducting a pullup, he took a quick look inside. The hot air blasted him in the face, but he instantly knew that he had found what they were looking for.

"This is it," he hissed as the other mercenaries looked up at him.

With his AK slung over his shoulder, he pulled himself through the window and hung inside the warehouse. The heat accumulating inside was nearly enough to kill him on its own, the effect only exaggerated by the fact that he was wearing body armor and a helmet. An I-beam stuck out of the brick wall where it helped hold up the roof. Grasping the edges, Deckard straddled it with his feet and slid down to the ground. Pain shot up his leg when he hit the floor as he had aggravated his wound.

The warehouse was absolutely packed. Down the center were two rows of armored vehicles. Along the sides were crates stacked nearly to the ceiling in some cases. There was pallet after pallet packed with boxes of ammunition, each box containing at least two ammo cans of 7.62 or 5.56 bullets. Others looked to be eastern bloc ammunition, 7.62x39 AK-47 bullets and RPG rockets.

As his teammates slid down behind him, Deckard walked closer, examining crates with stenciled markings indicating that they contained AT-4 Anti-Tank missile launchers.

"Damn," Aghassi said. "I can't believe I'm seeing this."

"I'm afraid I can," Deckard said.

"These armored vehicles are straight out of Libya."

"Are you sure?" Deckard said, turning to face him.

"Yeah, that is a Konkur," he said pointing to a wheeled Armored Personnel Carrier.

"It looks like a BRDM-2," Deckard added.

"It's a variant that was sold to Libya by the Russians. Look at the BMP-1 vehicles," he indicated the tracked vehicles. "They still have the Libyan military color scheme on them."

"Are you positive?"

"Yeah, dude. I was on the receiving end of that 73 millimeter cannon more than once during the Libyan Civil War."

Pat walked over to a metal tub and cut off the lock with his bolt cutters. Opening the lid, he pulled out a dusty AK-47.

"Look at this," he said, holding the rifle out to them. "Check out the Arabic markings. This is an Iraqi Tabuk."

Deckard slipped off his assault pack and handed the explosive charges to Pat.

"Wire this place to blow. There is enough live ammunition and explosives in this place to sympathetically detonate and render everything in the warehouse destroyed. Kurt, give him a hand and I will take the other two to find the base commander."

"Sounds like a plan," Kurt said with a smile.

"A combination of brand new American hardware and military hardware captured in the Middle East," Deckard thought aloud. "What the hell is the point behind all of this?"

"They are just flooding the country with all the guns they can get their hands on," Aghassi said.

"But who is *they*?" Kurt asked the six million dollar question.

46

Once outside, Deckard had an easy time locating the building that housed Militar No. 3's Commanding Officer. It was the only building with air conditioners sticking out of the windows. A single guard stood outside the door. Loading his magazine of sub-sonic ammunition, Nikita gifted the guard with a third eye. The only sound from the sniper rifle was the hammer striking the firing pin inside the gun.

The guard dropped to the ground like an empty jacket. Deckard moved to the door and used Kurt's Hooligan tool to pry between the door and the frame, creating a decent working space. Working the pry bar deeper and deeper, he managed to pop the lock right out of the frame and the door swung open. Setting the tool down, he shouldered his AK and stepped inside.

The first room was an office with a desk and computer sitting in the corner. The Mexican flag hung on the wall. The name card on the desk read that it belonged to General Gonzalez. Easing open the door to the second room, he found the General asleep in his boxer shorts, snoring while the air conditioner cycled cool air into the room.

Slapping the General in the face, Deckard rolled him out of bed and onto the floor. His pot belly broke his fall.

Nikita delivered a few kicks before Deckard and Aghassi grabbed him under the arms and helped him stumble through the door and into his office. Gonzalez hadn't even gotten a word out before they shoved him down into his swivel chair and put him in flexcuffs.

"W-what is the meaning of this?" The general stammered. The commanding officer of the only military base in town had been working on his beauty sleep while the city fell apart around him. To Deckard, it was a clear signal that the escalating war raging just outside the base's walls was all part of the plan.

"What's the meaning of enough American and Arab weapons to outfit an Army in that warehouse right next door?" Deckard answered his question with a question.

"Are you mad?" The General spoke reasonably good English. "You're American, we got all that shit from you guys. You told us to store it for you."

"What are you talking about?"

"Who are you?" the General demanded. "Military advisers that the Yankees sent down to work with the military? Listen, we both get our orders from the same people. Call down to OBI, they will fill you in. You are making a huge mistake here."

"We are not military advisers," Nikita said with his heavy Russian accent.

The General's eyes widened as he looked at the mercenaries. An American, a Russian, and a Mexican looking guy working together didn't fit.

"Mercenaries," he said under his breath. "Who hired you? Los Zetas? The Templarios? I know Jimenez and Ortega are out of the game. Did the Sinaloa cartel send you? This doesn't make any sense."

"Exactly what I was thinking," Aghassi agreed.

"Where are the guns going?" Deckard demanded. Using the Hooligan tool, he pinned the General's chin between the pry bar and the steel spike at the end of it to help get his point across.

General Gonzalez gulped.

"The Arab shit is getting shipped out across the country to the cartels, the AK-47s, old PKM and RPD machine guns, RPG-7s, that sort of thing is all getting shipped to the Zetas and the Sinaloa cartel. It goes out from here and from AMIZ."

"Only those two cartels? Why not any of the others?"

"Because that is not part of the plan. The Zetas and the Sinaloa are the two biggest players in the drug trade. The guns go to them, they wipe out the smaller cartels and consolidate their power. Then we let the Zetas and Sinaloa cartels fight each other for a while until they are both weak, that's when OBI will order us to cut off the supply of weapons and equipment to the Zetas."

"So the drug trade gets consolidated under one single cartel," Aghassi stated the obvious.

"Yeah, that's right," the General confirmed. "The plan has never been to end the drug trade but rather to manage it. The cartels have split into too many factions and have gotten too violent. OBI has been calling the shots and deciding who lives and who dies."

"Why is the Sinaloa cartel being singled out to rule the drug trade?" Deckard asked.

313

"They are the oldest cartel in the country with the deepest institutional ties. They also launder their money through Wall Street which ingratiates them to our neighbors up north."

"And you are just following orders," Deckard asked, still holding the Hoolie tool under the Mexican Officer's chin.

"I've worked for the Sinaloa cartel since I was a Captain so I was practically a shoe in. I've been promised a top spot in the cartel once this is all over in another year or two. Most of the players out there slinging bullets will be dead by that time and OBI is going to want some kept men running the show for them."

"And the dead piling up in the streets? The civilians caught in the cross fire? The families having their heads sawed off are just collateral damage?"

"War is an ugly thing," the General replied. "You should know that with all the wars the gringos start all over the world."

"What about the US Military hardware," Aghassi cut in, seeing that Deckard was about to take the General's head off. "Is that going to the Zetas?"

"No, that is for safekeeping. The heavy shit is being stockpiled around the country, under the control of trusted Generals. People like me."

"Then how did the Jimenez cartel arm themselves with American rifles and machine guns by breaking into a Zeta stockpile?"

"I heard about that. That was no Zeta stockpile, it was a cache that belonged to the Mexican Marines. They were supposed to be safeguarding those weapons as a part of contingency planning."

"What contingency?"

"In case one of the cartels became too powerful and completely overthrew the Mexican government, or the violence leaked into the United States to the point that a real crackdown was needed. Mostly though, those armored vehicles and missile launchers are for the coup."

"What the fuck are you talking about?"

"God damn, just let me go!"

"What coup?"

"In case CISEN, the CIA, OBI, whoever the hell," Gonzales said nervously. "In case they can't keep the Mexican government under their control they will arm the cartels with

314

heavy weaponry. You saw some of it in our warehouse. Armored vehicles, Anti-Tank weapons, Surface to Air missiles, and more. Then we have a re-enactment of the Iraqi insurgency. Same as Libya. Same as Egypt. Colonels will replace Generals, the government will be killed or forced into exile."

Deckard dropped the Hooligan tool. Even he was shocked by the balls on these people.

"Who?" Deckard asked. "Who is behind the weapons trafficking and these contingency plans?"

"I told you, I take my orders from OBI. I'm a made man and it isn't my place to ask questions."

"Where are you getting the guns from Gonzales?" Deckard yelled. "They are not just materializing via fucking magic!"

"The planes come in during the middle of the night. Civilian chartered aircraft. I never even see the pilots. Our forklifts pull up and start unloading pallets until the plane is empty. Then it takes off back where it came from. Sometimes they pick people up-"

"What?"

The General coughed, realizing he'd been so scared that he started running his mouth and had volunteered information.

"Sometimes the same flights drop people off and then pick them up later."

"What kind of people?"

"I don't know, I don't know!"

Aghassi pulled his notebook computer out of the Kifaru Koala pouch he wore on his kit. Starting it up he played the beheading video uploaded earlier in the day from Torreon.

"Yeah," the General confirmed. "The guy with the scars on his forearms. He's been through here a couple times. Sometimes he has a team with him. Sometimes it is just him and one other guy. They come in at night, do their work, and fly out the next day."

"You knew that this was the kind of work they did?"

"I suspected. OBI freezes the area to deny my soldiers from entering the area. These massacres occur, and the area is opened back up as this guy is getting back on the plane and flying out. We never speak to them, just provide vehicles for them as instructed from OBI. I don't think they speak Spanish or English. They look Arab."

The Arab.

Deckard raised the Hooligan tool high over his head. The General closed his eyes, accepting what was coming. With a thud, the mercenary slammed the metal spike into the General's desk. Papers and office litter flew across the office as Deckard growled, upturning the desk and spilling everything on the floor. Walking away, Deckard flung the door open and walked outside.

"Where is this Arab?" Aghassi asked.

"Flew out this afternoon. They didn't say where they were going," the General said around the sweat running down his face.

"The next arms shipment. When is the next airplane due in?"

Gonzalez didn't even hesitate in answering as his eyes shot to the clock hanging on the wall.

"Look out the window."

Deckard watched as an airplane touched down on the Torreon airport runway. It was flying blacked out with all of the flight and interior lights switched off. The only way you flew into a war zone without getting shot down.

Slowing, the cargo carrier plane turned off onto the taxiway the led into Militar No. 3.

"This is Six," Deckard said as he clicked the transmit button on his radio. "How are those charges coming?"

"Almost done," Pat reported in. "How long you want on the time fuse?"

"Ten minutes."

"That's it? I can cut an hour's worth," Pat explained. "That would give us enough time to make it back to the van and be out of the city before the blast."

"We're not taking the van," Deckard told him. "Change of plans."

Outside, the aircraft was lit up by the lights above the

hangar doors. He could now identify the airplane as a Lockheed L-100 cargo plane, the civilian equivalent of the military's C-130 Hercules. As the rear ramp began to lower, a forklift was driven up to the back end to begin removing the pallets of weapons and ammunition.

"Save one of those charges to bring with you and start the count down on the time fuse as soon as possible. Let me know when it is burning."

"Roger," Pat acknowledged. "I can't wait to see this plan of yours because this is going to be a big bang. Big enough to shatter half the windows in the city."

By now, Aghassi and Nikita had finished using a roll of duct tape to secure General Gonzalez to his chair.

"Leave him," Deckard said. "We're leaving."

Locking the door behind them, they left the General secured inside his office. He was going nowhere fast. Taking a knee, the three mercenaries watched as a crew of Mexican soldiers climbed onto the L-100 aircraft and began pushing pallets across the rollers set into the floor of the plane and onto the forklift where they were set down next to the hangar.

"Six," Pat's voice crackled over the radio. "Ready to initiate?"

"Do it. Then meet us in front of the General's office across the way from your position."

"Roger, we're burning. Ten minutes."

Thirty seconds later, Kurt and Pat ran up to meet them.

"We need to get the fuck out of here," Pat urged. "We'll be lucky to escape the blast as it is."

"That's our freedom bird right there," Deckard said, pointing towards the airplane with the barrel of his gun. "Nikita, you're on overwatch. The rest of us will assault from where they are downloading those pallets next to the hangar. We don't stop until we go right up the fuselage of the aircraft and into the cockpit."

"Now that's a plan," Kurt Jager said with a grin.

"The General knew a lot but didn't know the source of the weapons he was receiving. Time to find out."

Nikita's uniform shifted colors as he stalked off into the night to find an acceptable overwatch position while the remaining four men cut across a road and crept up behind the pallets that were now sitting beside the hangar.

Taking cover behind them, Deckard took one final look as the forklift was re-positioning itself to carry off the next pallet.

"There are three pallet pushers and one forklift operator. The pallet pushers look to have side arms. I don't know about the driver behind the forklift."

"Let's move," Pat urged. "We're talking about less than eight minutes here."

"Nikita, do it," Deckard said over their radio net.

The crack of the gunshot couldn't be heard above the jet engines but the forklift operator suddenly slumped over in his seat. As the mercenaries sprung out from behind the pallets, Deckard let off a single shot that caught one of the pallet pushers in the chest. He bobbed forward and took a swan dive off the back of the ramp.

Climbing up the back of the forklift, Aghassi and Pat stood on top of it and took careful shots at the remaining two men. They had to be careful not to damage the aircraft in the process or they would all be shit out of luck if they couldn't get off the ground. Luckily, the human body was an acceptable bullet trap. One of the Mexican soldiers was caught completely by surprise, the other reached for the pistol on his hip but was just a second too late as Pat cut him down.

Shimmying across the blades of the forklift, the two mercenaries ran down the fuselage of the aircraft, dodging between several pallets that had yet to be unloaded and the exposed metal guts in the sides of the plane. Deckard clamored up behind them.

"Nikita, get your ass up here," he ordered the sniper before he got left behind.

By the time Deckard got to the front of the cargo plane, Pat had already kicked in the cockpit door and taken the pilot hostage. The former Delta operator had plenty of experience with aircraft take downs and other tubular assaults.

"What the fuck are you idiots doing in my airplane," the pilot complained. There was so much noise that he didn't hear the gunshots. "Are you guys with Task Force 7?"

Deckard looked the pilot right in the eye.

"In five minutes this entire military base is going to explode. Every bit of ordnance you've been ferrying into Torreon over the last month is rigged with C4 plastic explosives with a time fuse burning down to detonation."

Looking over his shoulder, he saw Nikita set his rifle down inside the back ramp and then pull himself inside.

"We are leaving right," Deckard wasn't asking. He was telling. "*Now.*"

The pilot looked like he was about to have a heart attack. Closing the hydraulic operated ramp, he turned off the air brakes and started back down the taxiway. Gaining speed, the black tarmac was rushing underneath them as they watched through the cockpit windows. Making an abrupt turn, the pilot brought them onto the runway.

"Four minutes," Pat said, looking up from his watch.

The pilot accelerated down the runway as fast as he possibly could, pulling on the yoke and getting them airborne. The L-100 felt like it was almost going vertical, forcing the mercenaries to find something to hold onto as tracer fire flashed across their vision from someone in the city shooting at the airplane.

"Once you get some altitude," Deckard ordered. "Bring us around at a safe distance. I want to see this for myself. I also want you to see that I mean fucking business with you tonight."

For a moment, the pilot looked as nervous as General Gonzalez had. The same General Gonzalez cooling his heels while ducked taped to a chair in his office, Deckard enjoyed recalling as he peered out of the cockpit window. They flew blacked out, the same as when the L-100 had come in to avoid ground fire and were now several thousand feet in the air above Torreon. Below, Military No. 3 was clearly lit up by the base's ground lighting. The hangar, the warehouse, guard towers, and even the General's office were clearly visible in the night.

"Thirty seconds," Pat announced.

"We'll give you plus or minus five seconds with the time fuse Pat," Deckard said sarcastically. "If your det is too far over or short of your estimate then you've failed the demolitions course."

"I was a Master Breacher in Delta," Pat snorted. "I've got this."

"I hope so or you owe me a case of beer."

"Well, we will see in another ten seconds."

The Lockheed cargo plane slowly orbited the Mexican military base while the pilot looked on nervously.

"That is more than five seconds," Deckard criticized. "I'm going to make this fucking pilot land and send you down there to inspect-"

The Samruk International commander choked on his words as the warehouse blew outwards in all directions. General Gonzalez's office looked like a shanty caught in the shock wave of a nuclear explosion like in some black and white test footage from the 1950's. The cement guard towers shook and tipped over as the blast rolled over the entire compound. Secondary explosions tore through the fuel depot and vehicles were tossed aside like matchbox cars caught in a tornado.

Several seconds later the airplane suddenly dropped a dozen feet as if it had hit some serious turbulence. In a way, it had. It took a moment for the explosion to propagate outwards before the heat and pressure wave bounced them through the sky. The pilot maintained control of the aircraft as the mercenaries looked down on the burning military base. Nothing was left.

General Gonzalez was with the dust.

47

Nikita and Aghassi went into the back of the airplane to take a look inside the pallets that had not been downloaded by the ground crew while Pat and Kurt loomed over the pilot. Deckard took the seat where the co-pilot would normally sit. The weapons trafficker had been flying solo.

"Who are you guys?" the pilot asked nervously. His knuckles were white on the controls.

Internally, Deckard had to concede that it was a valid question. They were not even mercenaries, not really, not any more. They had traveled deep into the night and found a third layer of war, a third layer occupied by players with no names, where conspiracy theory was soon revealed as conspiracy fact. Beyond Special Forces, beyond the CIA, was a rogue network of criminal entrepreneurs. This network was not a governmental organization but rather one that appeared to be overlaid across numerous commercial interests, one that had hijacked systems of government, using spies and soldiers alike as pawns in their grand scheme of things.

Where did that leave the five Samruk International mercenaries?

There wasn't a name for them, the closest label that fit was vigilantes.

"What is your flight plan?" Deckard asked, ignoring the question.

"Flights like this don't have a plan," the pilot answered.

"Where did you fly out of before arriving in Torreon?"

The pilot hesitated.

"You saw what we did to an entire military base. We probably are not the type of people you want to fuck with."

"Fort Bliss."

"Fort Bliss," Deckard repeated, looking up at Pat and Kurt. "And where did you plan on flying back to?"

"Back to Bliss."

"And on to your next destination?"

"No," the pilot shook his head. "I would then be turning the plane over to another pilot and I'd take commercial air back home. It's a compartmentalized program. Everyone only knows their one little leg of the journey, their one little piece of the operation."

Compartmentalization was normal during military and intelligence operations, Deckard knew from his own experience. Working in this manner, one compromised cell could not divulge information on the other components of the operation. The technique worked as the five mercenaries had been struggling to unravel the gun trafficking ring and met with serious resistance in unmasking who the players were behind the scenes. Some CIA case officer working out of OBI wasn't the senior man in charge.

"Let me guess," Deckard said. "You work for a commercial venture that has leased a hangar on Bliss?"

"Yeah, that about sums it up."

"Then take us to Bliss."

"Are you nuts? Are you guys going to try to blow up an active US military base like that last one?"

"Our fight isn't with the US military, or even the Mexican military for that matter, only those who are actively participating in turning Mexico into a blood bath. Now tell me, which firm do you work for?"

"Kepper Airlines."

"A CIA front company?"

"They front for the CIA on occasion."

"On this occasion?"

"You gotta believe me, man. I just don't know."

The pilot was sweating it out as he checked his instruments and got them on a heading towards Ft. Bliss.

"Who leased the hangar on Bliss?"

"G3 Communications."

"They have provided non-official cover for Delta operations in the past," Pat added.

"What's your name?" Deckard asked the pilot.

"Ed."

"Well Ed, as you can see, I want to know who the puppet masters are behind sowing death and destruction in Mexico."

"I'll tell you what I know."

"How are you making these illegal border crossings with an aircraft loaded down with guns?"

"We fly in a safe corridor, whoever is flying that corridor doesn't get harassed or searched by customs. They know to stay hands off."

"In other words, someone freezes the operational area during your overflights so you can pass through unmolested?"

"No, not really. It's a permanent corridor that is run by the Defense Intelligence Agency. It's been in place since the mid-1970's."

Deckard rolled with the punches. He knew it was going to get a lot worse before it got better.

"For running covert operations in Central America?"

"Among other things. There used to be a series of radio beacons stretching from Colombia all the way into the United States that pilots could home in on. Nobody flying the corridor would be intercepted as long as they transmitted the correct response transmission signal. Today, everyone uses GPS so the radio towers were dismantled."

"What is the correct transmission signal?"

"Hotel Tango Romeo 585."

"That's the pass phrase you will have to give when we cross over the border?"

"Only if they radio and ask for the *bonafides*. The radar operators are so used to these black flights that they don't even bother asking as long as you are in the right corridor."

"So how does Ft. Bliss figure into this?"

"Briggs Army Airfield on Ft. Bliss is considered a power projection platform by the Department of Defense."

"Basically, it's like an aircraft carrier but instead of in the ocean, it is on land at a strategic location," Deckard said.

"Yeah, like that. Ft. Bliss also hosts the El Paso intelligence center which deals with analyzing narco-terrorism coming out of Mexico. I drive onto the base when Kipper Airlines calls me in, get on a plane that has already been loaded with cargo and fly it to Torreon. Then I fly back and go home until the next call."

"And cash the paycheck," Deckard added. "Did you ever question where all these weapons were heading?"

"I thought they were being used to fight against the drug cartels. We sell guns to the Iraqis, Afghanis, and dozens of other less than democratic countries. So we sell guns to Mexico? This is hardly the biggest skeleton in Uncle Sam's closet."

"Yeah, it does kind of pale in comparison to the Arabs you've been flying in and out."

Ed jerked at the controls.

"You know about that?"

"Who are they?"

"I've never spoken to them and they've never spoke to me. Spooky guys. They get on the aircraft, I fly them in, and they get off. When OBI makes the call, my dispatcher at Bliss has me fly back in to pick them up."

"They are being housed at Ft. Bliss?"

"I don't know. I doubt it. There are other flights as a part of this operation. They don't tell me what their destination is, but I never got the sense that they were staying at Bliss. A bunch of shady looking Arabs hanging around a military installation would certainly raise some eyebrows."

Just then, Aghassi opened the door and walked into the cockpit.

"He's packing some heavy shit back there. 90mm recoilless rifles and armor penetrating rounds. AK-47 ammunition, and get a load of this," Aghassi held out a drab green colored tube.

"LAWs," Deckard said, recognizing the Light Anti-Tank weapon. "Make sure you grab a few. I have a feeling we are going to need them."

"I never really knew what I was flying in and out, I just picked up the pallets and-"

"Shut up and fly Ed," Deckard cut him off. "By the way," he said turning back to Aghassi. "Can I borrow your notebook for a second? I think Ed needs to see something."

Aghassi went into his kit and withdrew his notebook computer, handing it to Deckard. Opening the computer, he pressed the power button to get it fired up.

"Let me ask you Ed, have you ever seen one of the Arabs you ferried around with some really gnarly scars on his arms?"

"Like some deep cut marks on his arms?"

"Yeah, exactly like that."

"There was one guy who had these crazy scars that walked all the way up his arms. One time I saw them when he was wearing a short sleeved shirt in the summer. He is the one I see most frequently, I think he is the leader of the group."

"Take a look at this," Deckard said turning the computer screen towards Ed. The Torreon beheading video played, The Arab's scars clearly visible on his arms as he sliced the head off a living teenage girl.

"Jesus Christ."

"Hardly. The first time I encountered this guy was on Grand Cayman when he killed a couple CIA pilots by sending suicide bombers after us. The next time I saw his handy work was at a Christian mission. Listen Ed, it was a massacre. They lined up mentally disabled people and recovering drug addicts. Even the padre and the nurse who I found with her panties around her ankles. This Arab put them against a wall and executed them."

"I have to ask you again man, who the hell are you guys? You obviously are not SEAL Team Six or Delta Force."

"We are mercenaries. Freelancers. We fight and we get paid for it. This is what we do. This is what we are good at. When someone kills my men, when some coward takes the fight to civilians, when they cut the heads off teenage girls and execute the sick, then they have taken the fight to me. This isn't about money Ed, not anymore. This is about justice. We blew up that Mexican military base because those bastards were supporting this shit, just like you."

"I had no way of knowing."

"Now you do. Decision time. Make the call. You just ran out of gray areas to hide in."

The pilot looked away, wiped his hand across his face, and then set it back on the controls.

"What do you need?"

"Who from Kepper or G3 Communications works at the hangar? You said something about a dispatcher."

"There is a dispatcher and an operations officer who monitors black flights shooting up and down the flight corridor."

"They will be there when we hit the ground?"

"Oh, yeah."

"Okay, are there any phase line code words you need to pass to them as we approach?"

"Just regular communications with the flight control tower."

"Then play it off like any other day."

"What are you going to do?"

"We are going to do what we do."

"I can't believe this is happening. This means I've been helping that Arab group murder civilians, but why would G3 have someone doing that?"

325

"Because someone contracted them to transport these people. We still don't know who is behind all of this. But the murders are about pitting the Zeta and the Sinaloa cartels against each other. They murder members and family members from both of the two largest cartels in Mexico, then they stage it to look like the opposing cartel committed the crime. This gets them to fight and wipe each other out."

"That is the anti-drug policy?"

"Maybe it is part of it anyway. The real objectives may be laying in wait, in a holding position somewhere in the background until the time is right for capitalizing on these massacres and making a strategic gambit, maybe for all of Mexico considering the amount of hardware you've been transporting into the country. Then we will see what this is really about. Someone is inducing a crisis in order to create political capital for them to advance their own agenda. You never want a good crisis to go to waste Ed."

"That's sick."

"You know what the funny thing about war atrocities is? Once you start killing, it is hard to stop. I mean, what do you do for an encore? All you can do is continue to escalate the level of violence in order to scare, intimidate, or outright kill your opposition. You cut off some girls head off, so your enemy disembowels someone and shows them their insides, then what do you do? Raise the stakes, film some torture porn that is even worse. It goes on and on."

"But you said, once you start killing. You just blew up a base full of corrupt Mexican soldiers. Killing is what you do too."

"I never said that we were not a part of this shit Ed."

48

Briggs Army Airfield was dead quiet in the hot summer night. As a part of Ft. Bliss, the air base was located on the far western tip of Texas, was the home of a number of US Air Force strategic airlift capabilities that moved American soldiers and war material in and out of the Middle East and Asia. As a logistics hub, it was well situated for a covert logistical airlift company to hide behind the regular legitimate activities of the military base.

The Lockheed L-100 flying in from its milk run down to Mexico received a radio transmission from the G3 Communications hangar when it was fifteen minutes out. The flight dispatcher had received reports about a massive explosion at Militar No. 3 in Torreon and thought that he must have lost a pilot and an airplane. The concern was quickly alleviated as the pilot confirmed that he had escaped the blast and was soon calling in to the Air Traffic Control tower for permission to land at Ft. Bliss.

Cleared for landing, the L-100 touched down at Briggs Army Airfield in the early morning hours and taxied towards the leased G3 Communications hangar. The massive hangar doors retracted open and swallowed the aircraft whole before shutting behind it. The airplane had a tail number but no official markings of any kind.

The flight dispatcher left his office to meet with the pilot. He had been scrambling to assemble what information he could about the explosion in Torreon. His employers would be demanding answers. With the engines powering down, he walked to the rear of the aircraft as the ramp lowered. Five commandos with non-standard weapons and equipment walked off the ramp and into the hangar. They were clearly para-military troops.

The dispatcher was outraged, marching over to meet them. He knew damn well from the flight manifests that they were not scheduled to pick up or drop off any contractors. They were running a compartmentalized program and this was a serious security breach. He opened his mouth to say something but only wind escaped his lips as one of the commandos slammed the butt of his rifle into the dispatcher's stomach.

Deckard flung open the office door and walked right in as if he owned the place, which at that moment, he did.

"Are you the operations manager?"

The man behind the desk stood straight to his feet, "Who the hell are you?"

Three other mercenaries flowed in behind Deckard, pointing their rifles at the man.

"House cleaning," Deckard answered. "Now sit your ass back down and keep your hands where I can see them."

Nikita pushed the flight dispatcher into the office and flung him into a chair next to the operations manager. He was still clutching his stomach where he had been butt stroked.

"What are your names and duty positions?" Deckard demanded.

The two middle aged men looked away. The flight dispatcher was overweight, bald, and wore eye glasses while the operations officer looked trim despite his age. A former military or intelligence man no doubt.

"Kurt?"

Kurt Jager handed over his Hooligan breaching tool. With a pry bar on one side and a spike and another pry bar sticking out of the other end, it looked like some kind of war hammer straight off a 14th Century battlefield.

"Now hold out the bald one's hand."

Nikita and Pat grabbed his arm and held it out in front of him.

"Wait, wait, wait!" he pleaded.

Deckard didn't believe in torture, but in this case he might make an exception.

"I'm Danny," the fat one said.

Deckard looked over at the second prisoner.

"Chris."

"Your job here?"

"I'm a dispatcher," Danny said.

"Ops manager," Chris answered.

"I'm going to keep this simple then. Where are the guns coming from?"

Both men clammed up.

"I'm not going to ask a second time."

A single bead of sweat dripped down Chris' face.

Deckard slammed the spike coming off the side of the Hooligan tool down on Danny's hand, impaling it on the desk. He let out a scream that was more terror then pain. His body was already going into shock, the pain would come later.

"We're just logistics people for G3 Communications," Chris pleaded for his friend.

"Start talking or you're next," Deckard said as he pried the Hoolie tool free from Danny's hand.

"They don't usually tell us where the guns are coming from," Chris explained. "We've seen them flown in on US military aircraft but also on CIA chartered aircraft. We think the foreign weapons are coming out of Libya, maybe Iraq as well."

"Enemy weapons captured by the US military?"

"That or weapons captured by rebel fighters in the Middle East and then bought from them by the CIA. There were also a number of Private Military Companies in Libya during and after the civil war to secure Gaddafi's stockpiles. He had warehouse after warehouse of small arms, that's probably where most of it is coming from."

"So they're flown here to Ft. Bliss. Then what?"

"The guns are loaded on chartered aircraft and flown to Mexico. The Office of Bi-National Intelligence in Mexico City coordinates with the El Paso Intelligence Center here on Bliss to instruct our pilots as to what airfield to drop the weapons off at."

"Who is giving the orders?"

"We get our orders from the El Paso Intelligence Center, on the receiving end, the Mexicans get their orders from OBI but these are just coordination centers, not decision makers."

"So G3 Communications is the shot caller? They get to decide who gets what?"

"Maybe," the operations manager said. "But I hear it goes up to NORTHCOM and the National Security Council. G3 doesn't do shit on their own. I've worked for this company for almost ten years now and they always have paper to protect themselves. Paper that goes straight to the top."

Deckard hesitated. He knew he was now deep into a nebulous area where privatized military, intelligence, and logistical companies merged with the US military and the civilian government. Five men were not about to wage war against NORTHCOM or the NSC, the White House's national security team. The President of G3 Communications was probably somewhere inside the beltway as well. They needed priority targets before their opposition figured out that a rogue group of mercenaries was back tracing their gun running operation and took counter-measures, the type that would quickly leave them dead.

"What about moving people around the battle space? What about the Arabs moving in and out."

"What Arabs?"

"They know all about it Chris," Ed said, peering through the door. "They know about The Arab."

"Jesus, Ed! You are working with these people?"

"I am now," the pilot said stepping inside. "Those people are butchers. I saw what they did."

"You can't be serious," Chris snorted. Danny held his injured hand and whimpered to himself.

"Did you know we were ferrying death squads in and out of Mexico?"

"I didn't know and didn't ask Ed. I knew better and thought you did too. We both knew we were not playing paddy cake down there so don't pretend you are innocent in all this."

"Where?" Deckard interrupted. "Where are they being flown back too? Where the hell are these guys working out of?"

Chris took a deep breath.

"Area 14," he said with a sigh. "The Nevada test site."

"No fucking way," Pat snarled. "You are trying to tell us that some group of Arab terrorists is being housed on a US government facility?"

"You know where that is?" Deckard asked.

"Yeah, it's a Department of Energy Facility where they used to do test detonations of nuclear bombs back in the old days. It is separated into different areas but there is nothing much out there today. There is an aircraft bone yard where we used to train up on aircraft take downs when I was with Delta. There are a few other facilities out that way but like I said, it's

330

pretty empty."

"We are not told where the flights are coming from," Chris said. "But between me and Danny, we've put two and two together over the years. They are being flown out of the airfield at Area 14 and then flown back after their missions are completed."

"The Department of Energy is putting them up?"

"Who knows?"

It wouldn't be the first time that a covert operation was buried behind official cover. It was actually a common practice for CIA agents to operate under official cover as State Department employees. By some estimates, more than half of State Department employees were actually working under the auspices of the CIA. DOE was nondescript enough to offer plausible top cover for a foreign fighter terrorist cell operating in Mexico, no one would look for a covert operation of that nature hidden inside the DOE.

"Are they there now?"

"The Arabs? Yeah. We had another pilot fly them back to Area 14 about seven or eight hours ago," Chris said.

"You thinking what I'm thinking?" Pat said from behind Deckard.

"I sure am," Deckard replied.

Chris saw the expression on their faces.

"They must have an entire compound over there full of those guys. With the amount of different faces we've seen over the last couple years coming through from Area 14 there must be a platoon if not a company strength element. You'll be shot to pieces."

"I'll fly," Ed offered.

"I appreciate that Ed, I really do," Deckard said sincerely. "But I lost an airplane full of my men the last time I tried to air land on a hostile airfield that hadn't been cleared. I won't ask my men to do that again."

"Before I took off today I saw that the Golden Knights are here. I got to talking to one of them and they are here at Bliss to train up for a parachute jump into a Texas Rangers game next week."

"Sky trash," Aghassi snorted. "I was doing solo HALO infils into Pakistan while those sky divers were telling the girls war stories in the bar."

331

Pat laughed. He had been on a few similar infils with his Delta team. Some went better than others.

"Yeah," Ed said. "But you guys are like some kind of black ops team that takes out the trash so why don't you just borrow their parachutes and jump into Area 14? They left everything in the hangar next door."

"Aghassi, go make that happen," Deckard began assigning tasks. "Four parachutes, one tandem rig since Nikita has never done a free fall jump. Ed, get your plane refueled and warmed up. Pat, start preparing weapons and equipment for the jump."

"What about me?" Nikita asked.

"You can hog tie these two knuckleheads," Deckard said pointing to Danny and Chris. "And dump them both in a mop closet where they won't be found until our business has been concluded."

49

Hot air rippled up from the surface of the Nevada desert. Even in the darkness of night, the mirage could be seen with the naked eye, obscuring the hills far off in the distance. The desert nights could be brutal but not as brutal as the one The Arab had lived in.

He couldn't sleep. Tossing and turning, he was always restless, always had to keep moving. Whenever he stopped, the world came crashing in on him. As he looked out across the desert, The Arab ran a hand under his shirt and across the uneven grooves lined over his belly. The deep scars continued all the way up his chest, the horizontal slash marks matching those on his arms. More scars ran down his thighs and some on his back, as far back as he had been able to reach with his blade.

Sometimes the scar tissue tightened and pulled at his skin, becoming extremely painful. Once a year or so his masters would have him visit a plastic surgeon to help relieve the tension.

Lighting a cigarette, he thought about that night seven years ago. Finishing a bottle of whiskey he wandered the back streets of Baghdad, stumbling and falling every few steps. He was ready to check out. A life of poverty, petty crime, murder, and prostitution had left him with nothing. The Arab knew that he was spiraling out of control, consuming everything in his path.

He had killed people for no reason at all, stalking them down the dark streets and sinking a knife into them. Men and children alike were his targets, whoever was vulnerable and alone. With his gang of thieves they had tracked down a man who had owed them money in a neighborhood. The Arab held him down while they took turns gang raping him.

The Arab couldn't feel anything anymore, the alcohol didn't numb him, it but made him disoriented. Reaching for the razor blade he carried he decided to end it. The sharp blade parted skin and flesh up and down his arms, legs, and torso. Bleeding and alone he screamed, laying in the street in a drunken mess.

Closing his eyes, he let go and the darkness took him in. His next memory was hazy. He woke up in a hospital bed with attendants looking over him. He came to find out later that he was in Camp Ashraf north of Baghdad. As it had turned out, the followers of a radical Sheik named Massoud had found him and taken him in. He would come to learn that they had use for a man like him.

The following months were painful in more ways than one. As his wounds healed, he was also compelled to confess his sins to Massoud. Massoud had been a quiet and patient man, the only father figure that The Arab had ever really had. The Sheik was the leader of the group housed at Camp Ashraf, a type of refugee camp established after the 2003 American invasion. There lived the People's Mujaheddin of Iran, or MEK as they were known to the occupation forces.

Once Massoud was convinced of The Arab's loyalty, his skills were then put to use. With additional training and access to weaponry, he spent much of his time in Iran conducting midnight border runs. MEK had been a Marxist terrorist organization that had fought inside Iran since the 1960's. Saddam had given them refuge, and now the Americans. He did well in Iran, launching kidnappings, assassinations, and bombings against government officials.

Later, he was sent elsewhere in the Middle East. He even did a six month job in Chechnya. Massoud gave him orders and The Arab did not question. For the first time in his life, he had a purpose. The criminal skills he had acquired, the brutal ways of the Baghdad streets were actually seen as an asset. What once made him an outcast now made him a trusted fighter that other MEK members looked up to.

From Libya, to Saudi Arabia, to Bahrain, The Arab did what was asked of him. Today it was Mexico, but his communications with Massoud indicated that they were just closing the net, preparing the battlefield to finally finish off Iran. The Arab looked forward to that day, the day when a piece of Iran would be handed over for him to rule over as a warlord.

The dead gave him no cause for concern. The motivations behind the kill orders were immaterial. There were no humans involved.

Looking up at the moon, The Arab turned and walked back to his dormitory.

Deckard ate shit when he hit the ground.

First his feet collided with the desert floor and then he belly flopped right into it. Spitting the grime out of his mouth, he groaned, his entire body feeling like it needed a tune up. Night landings were always rough when you couldn't see the ground and had to judge it by looking at the horizon. He should have pulled his toggles halfway down to slow his forward momentum a lot sooner.

From the sound of things, his comrades were not fairing much better. Pat slammed down somewhere to his front. He came down heavy as he had to tandem jump with Nikita strapped to his parachute harness. Aghassi touched down beside him, apparently lighter than a feather as he pulled down on his toggles to slow the parachute's forward drive and executed a stand up landing. The black and gold colored parachute collapsed behind him.

Grimacing, Deckard shrugged out of his parachute harness and balled it up with the parachute. They would have to hide them somewhere before moving on to their objective. Ed had lowered the ramp and put them out right over Area 14. Apparently, there was another black flight corridor established from Bliss to the Nevada test site so they did not have to worry about being picked up on radar.

Jumping at 12,000 feet, they froze at the high altitude before they pulled their rip chords at 4,000 feet. With parachutes stolen from the Army's Golden Knights demonstration team, it was a little awkward when it came to rigging equipment. They wore the parachutes over their plate carriers and secured weapons under the chest and leg straps. Additional equipment had to be jerry-rigged as carefully as possible.

They were right in the center of the airplane bone yard that Pat had told them about. The rusting hulks of 747 jumbo jets all the way down to private Lear jets littered the desert all around them.

"You okay?" Aghassi asked as he carried his own chute

over to him.

"It is never enough to kill me, just enough to hurt really, really bad," Deckard complained.

"I hear you."

Up ahead, Nikita got to his feet and dusted himself off while Pat unclipped him from the parachute. They looked none the worse for wear.

"How was your first jump?" Deckard asked Nikita.

"Cold."

"Have you seen Kurt?" Pat said.

"Shit," Aghassi said. "No, we haven't."

Just then they heard someone shuffling up behind them. The four mercenaries struggled to free their rifles and chamber a round from the magazine. Putting their weapon into operation should have been the first order of business once they hit the ground, but this wasn't exactly a traditional jump.

"*Ich bin lebendig,*" Kurt said in his native German.

"What?" Aghassi asked, relaxing now that they knew it was their missing team mate.

Under the moon light, Deckard could see Kurt's hands twitching slightly.

"You okay? You're shaking like a French soldier."

"Fuck you. I came down on my reserve chute. I didn't have silk over my head until I was five hundred feet off the ground."

"What happened?"

"The main canopy had a total malfunction so I had to cut it away at 3,000 feet. Then the reserve had cells on it that started to collapse on me. I had to tug the toggles and mess with the suspension lines the entire way down."

"Next time we pack our own parachutes," Deckard said.

"Agreed."

Stashing their parachutes in one of the empty airplanes, the mercenaries moved out. The airfield in the distance was partially lit, guiding them in towards the objective area. If The Arab and his gang were on Area 14, they had to locate them and maneuver to contact as soon as possible. Not only was dawn hours away, but it was only a matter of time before the command and control node for the entire gun running and death squad operation figured out what was going on after Militar No. 3 was destroyed and the Ft. Bliss G3 Communications facility had gone dark.

Sticking to the shadows created by a massive passenger aircraft, the mercenaries weaved their way towards the airfield, keeping landing gear or loose aircraft debris between them and their target to help conceal their movement. Nearing the edge of the airfield, they crawled forward to get eyes on.

There were two large aircraft hangars next to the runway, no control tower, and a series of trailers that looked to be used as housing units. What really caught all of their eyes was the compound next door to the far hangar. Surrounded by a high barbwire fence was a box shaped building with an antenna farm on the roof. A tall communications mast rose from the roof alongside various High Frequency antennas, and satellite dishes.

Nikita passed Deckard his HK 417 sniper rifle so he could take a closer look. Using the ten power scope, he scanned the security features for a moment before passing the rifle on to Aghassi.

"What do you think? Those look like active alarm systems inside the perimeter."

"Yeah, it's an overlapping system of bi-static microwave sensors," Aghassi replied. "The transmitters are those dishes you see in the gravel. They send out the microwave frequency to the receivers. If they detect a minute difference between the sender and the receiver it will trip the alarm."

"And bring down God only knows what."

"That has to be our priority target," Kurt added. "That's the nerve center for this logistics system we have been back tracing."

"Tracking down The Arab will have to wait," Deckard agreed. As bad as he wanted him, killing a General was always going to be more important than killing a foot soldier. This was a war and targets had to be prioritized.

"If we manage to bypass the sensors, what kind of security is on the door?"

Aghassi moved the sniper rifle to take a closer look.

"Bio-metric lock. Looks to be both thumb print and face scan."

"Can we get passed it?"

"With time and proper planning."

"Neither of which we have," Pat muttered.

"We will have to improvise something," Aghassi said as

he handed the rifle back to Nikita. "It might work."

"I see a two man roving patrol moving around the far hangar right now," Deckard said, squinting as he looked across the runway.

"And a third having a smoke break over by the housing units," Nikita said as he looked through the scope.

"What does he look like?"

"All three of the guards look like Arabs as near as I can tell."

"Alright, here is the new plan," Deckard said. "We are going to have to improvise some kit if we are going to get into that command and control center undetected. Kurt, go back to the parachutes and cut lengths from the suspension line that we can use as tethers. I'm going to find the rope. Pat, you find something we can use as a grappling hook and a way to muffle the sound when we throw it. Aghassi, you get together whatever you need to get through the biometrics system. Nikita, find a firing position somewhere in one of these airplanes where you can give us cover fire if need be."

"Roger that," Pat said, picking up on what Deckard was planning.

"And try not to get killed."

Nikita slipped into the fuselage of an old Boeing MD-80, finding a port for his sniper rifle through a rectangular window that was missing the clear plexiglass. Settling in, he scanned Area 14 for targets and waited.

Kurt Jager jogged back to where they had dropped off the parachutes. His Samruk issued Ka-Bar fighting knife made quick work of the 550 chord suspension lines that secured the parachute to the harness. He cut enough safety lines for each of the mercenaries before moving back to the rendezvous point.

Deckard and Pat evaded the two man guard patrol with Nikita informing them about enemy movements over their radio.

The padlock on the door to the hangar was easy to pick and they were soon inside the dark interior. Using red lens pen lights, they each rummaged through the boxes of discarded airline equipment and garbage.

Pat had the shock of his life when he ran into a drab colored military van with Cyrillic lettering across the side. Area 14 was apparently being used as a staging ground for covert operations all over the world.

Eventually the former Delta operator found a large metal hook that would normally be used to attach to a tow strap. Locating some rubber matting, probably torn up from the floor of an airplane, he sliced it into pieces and wrapped it around the hook before securing it in place with some string.

Meanwhile, Deckard found a couple of ropes in the corner of the hangar. Some were dry rotted, but when he tied the others together with square knots he ended up with a long enough length for what he had in mind. Looping the rope back on itself, he flung it over his shoulder. Linking back up with Pat, he headed out to meet the others.

Outside, Aghassi crept closer to the command and control center. He had to admit to himself that he was stumped. The fingerprint reader could be bypassed, but without knowing who had access to the building he was at a loss to figure out how to get by the face scanner.

As luck would have it, he was crouching in a ditch nearby the facility at exactly four in the morning which turned out to be a shift change. A white Ford Escort pulled up to the gate. A slight man emerged from the vehicle and was buzzed in on foot. He scanned through the biometric locks and went inside. Knowing what was happening, Aghassi scrambled through his Kifaru Koala pouch for his digital camera.

When the relieved night guard opened the door and headed to the Escort, Aghassi was ready. Zooming in on the man's face as closely as he could he began snapping pictures. He was a young guy, probably in his thirties with slightly graying hair and a doughy face. A Rear Echelon Mother Fucker if ever there was one, Aghassi knew.

The Escort took off down the runway and disappeared into the night, heading back home or back to a security hub elsewhere on Area 14 or one of the many other areas established on the former nuclear test site. The former ISA operator scrolled through the pictures on his digital camera and breathed a sigh of relief.

He nailed it.

"You are clear," Nikita's voice came over the radio. "The guards are moving over to the housing area."

From his firing and observation position, Nikita instructed the four mercenaries on where the enemy was going and where they were coming from.

"Roger," Deckard replied.

The mercenaries climbed out of the ditch and skirted around the runway, heading for the far hangar. There was a metal ladder attached to one side that would allow them to climb up to the roof. One by one, they slung their weapons and began the climb. Hand over hand, their boots vibrated off the metal rungs as they tried to be as silent as possible. Deckard brought up the rear and was halfway up when he heard Nikita's warning over his radio.

"The roving patrol is on its way back. They are on my side of the runway now but will see you if you don't get to the top in another minute."

Deckard and Kurt were the two still on the ladder and both now stopped trying to be quiet and rushed up the side of the hangar. Their legs and arms were burning by the time they got the top. He was glad that he had Kurt cut safety lines because after all he had been through, he felt like he was losing dexterity.

The four mercenaries stayed low to avoid being spotted by the patrol and crept across the top of the hangar to the side that faced the Command and Control facility. From the edge of the hangar, the communications mast on the target building was a good thirty feet away. It was a long distance, but it was still a security design flaw in putting the mast so close to the hangar. It was a flaw that the mercenaries would be more than happy to exploit.

There was one exterior flood light that needed to be taken care of before they began to infiltrate.

While Pat was tying their half-assed grappling hook into their half-assed climbing rope, Deckard got on the radio with Nikita.

"Has the patrol passed you yet?"

"Yes, they have moved on into the aircraft graveyard."

"Can you do something about the flood light in front of the building?"

"Roger," Nikita replied. "Wait one."

A few seconds later the flood light popped and blinked out as a silent sub-sonic bullet shattered the bulb inside.

"That works, thanks."

"No problem."

Deckard turned to Pat.

"Who is going to give it a go with this contraption?"

"I played baseball in college," Pat informed him. "That's why I got a good grenade arm."

"You went to college?"

"For six months."

"Well, take a shot at it. If you miss and the hook crosses through the path of those microwave transmitters below we are fucked but no pressure or anything."

"Some of us like the pressure," Pat said as he rotated his arm, warming up his shoulder.

Grabbing the hook, Pat wound up, feeling the weight in his hand for a few mock practice throws. Kurt tied off the free running end of the rope around a fixture for a lightning rod at the edge of the hangar roof. Bolted firmly in place, it would be able to support their weight.

Thirty feet away was the three sided communications tower with antenna and satellite dishes hanging off the side. Pat took a deep breath. Stepping forward with one foot, he overhanded the metal hook through the night sky. The mercenaries winced as the hook passed through one of the metal cross bars and thudded off the side of the mast. It made noise even with the rubber padding.

Kurt slowly retracted the rope and as if by magic the hook snagged on the metal cross member.

There was the ghost of a smile on Deckard's face.

"Who owes who a case of beer now?" Pat boasted. "I

gots some skills."

Kurt carefully untied the knot around the lighting rod fixture and retied it using some mountaineer knots to make the rope as taut as possible. The former GSG-9 commando then handed out the 550 chord lengths he had cut. Aghassi was going across first. He used the chord to tie a loop through his belt and then across the rope bridge which would act as a safety line if he slipped and fell.

The mercenaries had constructed the rope bridge across thirty feet of empty space, crossing over the microwave sensors and barbwire fence below. The drop was about forty feet, enough to kill you in and of itself. Aghassi looked somewhat less than confident as he felt the rope creak and strain under his weight. Laying on top of the rope, he attempted to commando crawl across but with his AK-103 and other combat equipment making him top heavy, it was not long before he slipped and was dangling under the rope, holding on with his hands and feet crisscrossed over the top.

Grunting his way across the rope, Aghassi crossed the chasm and pulled himself onto the communications tower. Wiping his face with the sleeve of his uniform, he was visibly tired. Kurt went next, tying himself into the rope and them shimmying across. Aghassi was already climbing down the tower to the roof of the command and control building.

The other mercenaries pulled security, watching for signs of enemy activity. If one of their own was spotted on the rope, the climber would be helpless while he was taken apart by gunfire.

Kurt managed to commando crawl across the top of the rope the entire way, with one bent knee and ankle locked into the rope while the other leg hung underneath to help him keep his balance. Not bad for a guy who was medically discharged from the German military after a rappelling accident.

Once on the other side, Pat tied his tether in and started across the rope.

"Shooter-One?" Deckard said over the radio.

"All quiet here."

"Let's hope it stays that way."

When Pat was almost to the other side, Deckard tied in and waited until Pat came off the rope and scooted down the tower to join the other two mercenaries. As he began his commando crawl, Deckard got that sinking feeling. It wasn't just a fear created by vertigo, the rope really was stretching to its limits as he was now the last man across. With the loss of dexterity, he had a hard time maintaining his grip. His forearms were also about torqued out. As he reached out with his hands, he pulled himself forward with his ankle resting over the top of the rope.

Every movement was a struggle. The Oaxaca campaign had taken him well over his threshold. How much longer he could hold out, he had no idea. There was little experience in the world in pushing this hard or coming this far. They had traveled into the unknown.

"Six, freeze right there!" Nikita's warning came over his headset. "Two guards just came from behind the far side of the hangar. They are walking towards you between the chain link fence and the hangar.

Without forward movement to help stabilize him, Deckard's body slowly rotated off the top of the rope where he hung upside down underneath. With his plate carrier and rifle hanging off his body, it was simply too difficult to maintain his balance.

In the darkness, he could hear voices in Arabic advancing below him.

He tried to lock his fingers around the rope, securing them in place like a vise but knew that he was slowly losing purchase as his grip gave way. His gloved hands slipped so he tried to regain a better grip but was unable to clench his hands around the rope.

The improvised tether tied around his belt and the rope saved him from falling. It pulled tight as he hung upside down with his arms out. His feet were crossed and locked into the rope.

Gravel crunched under approaching footsteps. As blood ran to his head, Deckard heard their voices as one lit up a cigarette. The words were in Arabic.

"No one knows what happened in Mexico?" one of the guards asked the other.

Deckard was struggling to stay alive but picked up the gist of the conversation.

"It just exploded. It might have been an accident but no one knows. Maybe someone was smoking in the ammo dump again," the other guard said, grabbing the lit cigarette out of his partner's mouth. The smoker laughed as he grabbed it back and took a puff.

"I just can't wait to get out of this place."

"No kidding. They are talking about sending the entire group to Syria in a few weeks."

"I've heard the rumor."

The guards were passing right under Deckard as he hung helplessly. Nikita might be able to get off a shot if he were compromised but not before the guards filled him with lead. Feeling movement across his neck, Deckard panicked. The sling on his AK-103 rifle was sliding right over his head.

Swatting out his hand, he managed to hook it through the sling just as it was about to fall through the night and land beside the guards. Deckard closed his eyes as he hung on to the sling, the rifle swinging below him.

"I think they have another group working Syria already and just want to send us for the final push. Once Syria falls to the Brothers then we will be going into Iran."

"If Allah wills it."

The guards moved on, turning around the corner of the hangar and out onto the runway.

"You are clear," Nikita said, letting out the breath that he had been holding.

Deckard managed to get the sling back over his head and shoulders. He had to use his forearms as hooks, bending at the elbows and throwing them over the rope. His hands were next to useless at the worst possible moment. Inch by inch, he moved like a caterpillar across the rope to the communications tower.

When he finally got there, his face red and dripping with sweat, he held onto the metal structure, standing on it with his boots and resting for a moment. Testing his grip on the handle of his Sub-Saharan knife, he pulled it free and cut through the tether chord. Placing the knife back in its sheath, he slowly made his way down the tower.

"Are you okay?" Pat asked him once he got down on the roof. "I thought we had lost you for a second there."

"Me too," Deckard said. "Me too."

50

One by one, the mercenaries dropped off the roof of the windowless building. After a careful examination for an easier way in, there was no other entrance aside from the single doorway on the ground level. Hanging off the side of the building, each man let go and fell a few feet down to the gravel. Once on the ground they were at the outer wall and outside the range of the microwave detectors that were arrayed between the building and the fence.

Deckard, Pat, and Kurt took up positions around the front entrance where the biometric sensors were located while Aghassi started pulling out his tools.

"Let's watch MacGyver get us out of this one," Pat said breaking his balls.

"You fuckers are going to eat your words," Aghassi promised.

Retrieving a small tube of finger print powder, he blew a small amount over the glass fingerprint scanner installed next to the door. Next, he booted up his notebook computer and set it down while the operating system loaded. Waiting on the computer, he pulled a small sandwich bag from his kit and shook his beef jerky out of it, dumping the Slim Jims in his cargo pocket. Taking a few hits off his Camelbak water bladder, he spit some of the water into the plastic bag.

"Hold this," he said, handing the bag to Kurt while he went back to his computer. Clicking through the ToughBook computer he brought up the picture he had taken of the relieved command center staff member who he had photographed during the guard shift change. Transferring the image from the camera onto his notebook, he cropped the image of the man's face and put it against a flat black background.

"Give me that bag," Aghassi said, grabbing it from Kurt.

Holding the computer screen up in front of the camera that conducted the bio-metric face scan, he placed the bag of water on top of the powder that had stuck to the oils left behind by previous user's finger on the scanner.

The face scanner measured the distances between distinct physical features on the face in front of it, thirty seven different measurements in all from ear to ear to nose to lip, to

345

eye to eye, and so on. The water bag pressed down on the powder residue sticking to the fingerprint, simulating the flat pad of the finger itself. Both scanners hummed as they operated.

After a few seconds there was a click within the door as a deadbolt lock retracted back inside the heavy metal door.

Deckard reached out and grabbed the handle. The door easily swung open on its hinges without so much as a squeak.

"Eat your words," Aghassi reminded him, just to say he told them so.

The mercenaries stepped inside, moving to the walls of the corridor as automatic overhead lighting kicked on. The walls were painted flat off-white with linoleum tiles on the floor, completely nondescript with nothing on the walls, not even a fire plan with directions. The door clicked shut behind them as Aghassi slipped inside while stuffing his computer back into his kit.

At the end of the hall, a door opened. The mercenaries held their weapons at the high ready as a figure appeared looking around, surprised that the overhead lights had flipped on. He was going business casual in khakis and a polo shirt.

"Oh," his mouth hung open as he spotted the four shooters zeroing in on him. The Samruk International men walked forward, their muzzles not wavering from center mass of their target.

"Well," the man conceded. "This is a surprise. You are coming in from Mexico?"

"Open the door," Deckard ordered.

The black site employee scanned his access card and the glass door clicked open. As he opened it, Deckard pushed him inside. They were in some kind of war room. There were work stations lined up on desks, the screens blacked out as they were all in sleep mode. Six flat screen television sets were hung on the far wall. Five were turned off, the other was running a 24 hour news network but was on mute.

"Who are you?"

"Greg Soloman. I'm a special activities manager for G3 Communications," he volunteered.

"Greg Soloman, special activities manager," Deckard repeated. "Where is the safe?"

"What-"

Greg's words were interrupted as Kurt slammed a fist

346

into the manager's stomach.

"Where is the safe?"

The G3 manager was struggling to catch his breath.

"Stand up straight," Deckard said as he pulled him up. "Take us to the safe."

Greg led them into the adjoining room where there was a shoulder high safe sitting in the corner of an office. Turning the dial, he opened the heavy composite metal door.

"Clean it out," he said looking at Kurt and Aghassi. "Pack up whatever we can carry with us."

Inside the safe were three ring binders filled with documents, compact discs, thumb drives, security access cards, portable hard drives, removable classified hard drives, manila folders packed with documents, and plenty more.

"Let's go Greg," Deckard led him back out into the war room and pushed him into one of the swivel chairs. The chair rolled backwards and slammed into a work station. Deckard leaned over and got right in his face. Greg looked at the beard stubble, the sweat stains around the collar of his uniform, and every bruise and cut on his face that it had taken the mercenary commander to get to this point. "We are going to have a talk."

"I get it, I get it, I get it," Greg started talking a mile a minute. Apparently a G3 special activities manager wasn't a field operative who knew how to keep his cool. "I'm under duress. The insurance companies will cover for G3. I'll tell you what you want to know."

"That's a good thing because you've got one of your boys cooling his heels in a mop closet with his battle buddy. Needless to say, he is going to be pitch hitting if he wants to jack off anytime soon."

"What do you want?"

"What is the code name for this operation?"

"Which one?"

"How many are there?"

"Maybe fifty that are active and a hundred that are passive."

"Holy shit," Pat cursed. "This place is a murder factory."

"Who are the Arabs patrolling around outside?"

"Those are MEK imports from Iraq."

"The terrorist group?"

347

"We just got them removed from the State Department's list of terrorist organizations."

"These are the guys you have been sending down to Mexico?"

"Yes."

"What is the point of sending death squads down to Mexico? The cartels seem to do a pretty good job at killing each other on their own."

"Not a good enough job," Greg said nervously. "We used to have a couple big cartels, big drug lords that ran their operations but didn't wage open war. Then came the Pablo Escobars that tried to challenge the state. Guys like you went down to Colombia and took care of them but then the cartels split into factions and started warring with each other."

"G3 was hired to help them with that task?"

"Basically. We sent operatives in to escalate the level of violence, get the smaller cartels to shoot it out with each other and the larger cartels until only the big ones are left."

"Fuck," Pat said shaking his head.

"Yeah," Deckard agreed. "We played right into your hands."

"You are the guys from Oaxaca? The ones who took down Ortega and Jimenez?"

"The same."

"We would have gotten around to them, but yeah, we could have been on the same side."

Deckard grabbed him by the throat.

"We would never be on the same side as scum like you. Scum like MEK." Deckard released him. "G3 has also been running guns to the cartels. Was that operation to run in tandem with the death squads?"

"Yes," Greg said gasping for air. "The massacres provided the motivation, the guns provided the means. It is a layered operation that relied on allowing straw buyers at American gun shops to smuggle guns into Mexico but that is a drop in the bucket compared to the shipments of military weapons we are sending to the Mexican military. We send them to the military for distribution to the cartels directly after acquiring the weapons from the Middle East. Other times we send the weapons along official US military logistics channels as part of the Mérida Initiative and tip off the cartels so they can run transit heists. Other military grade weapons are put into the hands of select Mexican military commanders."

"For the coup?"

Greg's eyebrows shot up in surprise, "that is just a contingency plan in case everything falls apart in Mexico and we cannot control the government. There are other contingencies. SOCOM has one drafted to send the entire Special Operations Task Force into Mexico and clean the place out. It would take the lessons learned from Iraq and Afghanistan, combine them with our studies of cartel tactics and apply them on the ground. Delta and Rangers would finish the cartels in five or six months. Total war. It is a backup plan if all else fails."

"What is the primary objective?"

"Once we reduce the cartels to just the most powerful we help them go to war with each other."

"The Sinaloa and the Zetas."

"Yes, this is the stage we are at now. We help them weaken each other, then we help one destroy the other."

"The cartel that walks home with all the marbles is pre-determined?"

"Yes, the Sinaloa is the favored cartel. They have the deepest institutional ties."

"You mean they launder their money through all the right banks on Wall Street?"

"I can understand why you would make the inference, but I have no way of knowing the motivations of those who have employed G3 Communications for this job."

"Log into your work station. I want to see what you have."

Greg took a deep breath and logged into his computer.

"Once you've weakened the two largest cartels, then what happens?" Pat asked.

"Then we help the Sinaloa destroy the Zetas. The war between these two organizations would be so violent that the leaders of both groups will more than likely be killed, replacing them with younger, more pliable leadership. If not, such leadership will be supplied by inserting select officers from the Mexican military into the Sinaloa cartel."

"The same officers that you have handed all these weapons over to?" Deckard interjected.

"They will be the new ruling class of Mexico."

349

"What fucking think-tank lackey clown came up with this dumb fuck idea?" Deckard spat.

"Mexico has turned into an ugly place," Greg tried to explain. "We have been fighting the war on drugs for years without any real results. This is a way to lower the violence to levels that everyone is comfortable with. We can't end the war but at least we can manage it. This is the best option for everyone on both sides of the border."

"And a fat fucking paycheck for the managers!" Pat screamed.

A map popped up on the computer screen as Greg's login information was accepted. There were blips all over the world where G3 was running operations.

"What is that on your desktop," Deckard said pointing to an icon. "North American Community?"

Greg opened the folder by double clicking with his mouse.

"The operations you have asked me about are a periphery to the overall national security agenda that we have been, in part, tasked with carrying out," Greg said as he opened up a file showing a map of North America where there were no borders between the United States with Mexico and Canada.

"What the hell is that?" Deckard said.

"The North American Union," Greg explained. "It is an amalgamation of the North American continent, joining Canada, America, and Mexico together as one for mutual security, economic cooperation, and a shared system of taxation."

"What?" Deckard rubbed his forehead, trying to wrap his mind around the bizarreness of it all.

"When things really collapse in Mexico, whether it is at the height of our planned war between the Sinaloa and the Zetas, or because one of our contingency plans has to be enacted via a coup or direct US military action, there will be a push by all three governments for a mutual security agreement. At that time, the citizens of all three countries will be sensitized to the situation with feelings of uncertainty and insecurity. This will provide the political capital for all three countries to ratify an international treaty calling for the North American Union."

"No," Deckard answered. "No."

"We are shutting this down tonight," Pat agreed. "Fuck this."

"Who else is in on this," Deckard demanded. "Who is pushing for this shit?"

"What do you mean?" Greg exclaimed. "Like I said, the elites of all three countries are and will be pushing for it. This is the plan, this is what is going to happen. If governments oppose the plan they will be moved and compelled to support it. I don't know who all the players are, I just manage a small handful of operations from behind a desk. You would have to ask the CEO of G3 Communications."

"I will-"

Deckard's words were cut off as something hissed inside the war room.

"They have initiated the destruction sequence," Greg informed them. The room was already filling with smoke. "You managed not to trip it when you broke in here but they are watching," he said pointing to the black ball mounted on the side of the wall. It was a security camera.

"Someone off-site?"

"Yes."

Suddenly, flames were crawling up the walls. Black smoke was rising to the ceiling as the war room heated up. The place had been rigged with thermite and an initiation system that could be remotely triggered by whoever was watching on the security camera. Jogging over to the glass door leading to the hallway, Deckard saw that it was filled with flames. With their exit cut off, they were stuck in a death trap.

Aghassi and Kurt walked into the war room, coughing and choking on the smoke. Each held a clear plastic garbage bag filled with documents and other materials taken from the safe.

"We definitely got what we came here for," Aghassi said. "But I'm not sure if we are going to survive long enough to do anything about it. We need to get out of here."

"It won't be easy," Deckard said with tears running down his face as the smoke stung his eyes. "Our exit is an inferno. Push into the office where there is less smoke."

The mercenaries had to crouch down to keep their faces out of the smoke, the heat was intense, almost overwhelming as the walls were quickly being consumed by fire.

"If we don't have an exit out then we will just have to make one."

351

The Arab bolted upright in his bed.

The trailer was pitch black and silent other than the steady hum of the air conditioner and the sudden vibration of his cellular phone as it slid across the night stand.

"*Nam?*" he said, answering the call.

He listened intently to the voice on the phone. Their security had been breached. Someone had not only penetrated Area 14 but also the Command and Control center. The destruction sequence had begun. The mercenaries would be liquidated along with the on-duty special activities manager, the one they knew as Greg. It was a necessary sacrifice in order to eliminate the threat and maintain operational security.

The quick reaction element that had been training at Area 17 several miles away was being called in but in the meantime he was to wake his MEK squad members and move directly to the command center to provide containment if it became needed.

The Arab indicated his understanding before hanging up the phone. Reaching for the AK-47 propped up next to his bed, he flung open the trailer door and began screaming for his men to grab their weapons and follow him.

Slipping on his boots, he rallied the death squad.

Someone had followed him back from Mexico.

He had a feeling he knew exactly who that someone was.

51

The explosive charge blasted a hole through the roof, the sheet metal tearing and peeling outwards with the blast giving the appearance of a giant bullet hole. Through the smoke that poured out from the gap in the building's roof, a heavily armed mercenary appeared. Climbing out of the hole, he turned to help his team mates up.

Deckard pushed Greg up where Kurt Jager firmly grabbed him by both shoulders and hauled him up before dropping him on his side at his feet. The G3 communications manager hit the roof with a thud, his body bouncing off the surface with a gasp of escaping air from his lungs. Deckard emerged from the column of black smoke, coughing and gagging.

"Shooter-One," Pat said, taking charge while Deckard was trying to regain his voice. "What's going on?"

"We have lots of movement," Nikita reported. "About a dozen men waking up and kitting up from their sleeping quarters. They are starting to move to your position."

"Slow them down."

Nikita had transitioned back to regular long range sniper rounds, ditching the sub-sonic ammo. Still, the hollow crack of the suppressed rifle could hardly be heard. Pat failed to identify a muzzle flash from the aircraft graveyard which spoke well for the sniper's hide site selection.

"I got two of them," Nikita radioed in. "But then they realized the general direction I was shooting from and took another route, behind the hangars. They should be on top of you guys in seconds. I will do what I can when they get out in the open."

"Okay," Deckard said as he regained his voice. "Let's get off of this roof before it collapses, fall back to a defendable position, and-"

His words were cut short as a RPG rocket barreled into the communications tower on the roof and exploded into a ball of fire. Releasing a high pitched creak of metal on metal, the tower fell sideways across the roof. Deckard and Kurt dived out of the way as the twisted metal hulk slammed into the roof, the end of the tower snapping off as it hit the edge of the roof.

"Kurt, you're with me. The rest of you get out of here while we lay down suppressive fire."

Deckard and the German mercenary ran to the contact side of the building and began returning fire at the ten Arab shooters who were trying to surround them. Both triggered rapid bursts of fire at the death squad that was attacking them. Deckard's AK ran out of rounds first.

"I'm black," he shouted to Kurt who picked up his rate of fire to compensate.

Deckard ducked down behind the lip of the roof and reloaded. He moved laterally to change his position before popping back up and rejoining the fight. By now Kurt was empty and had to reload. Meanwhile, Pat and Aghassi threw their prisoner off the roof before jumping down beside him.

"Let's go, let's go," Deckard said as he slapped Kurt on the shoulder and fell back, running across the roof. He stumbled as the roof gave way beneath him. Sliding backwards and down into the inferno that had opened up below, he reached for the wreckage of the communications tower to stop his descent. He was still slipping when Kurt circled around the opening and gave him a hand. Yanking him up, the two turned to the edge of the roof and dropped down.

"Get down!" Pat warned as he threw a frag grenade at the chain link fence. Hitting the deck the mercenaries braced themselves as the grenade exploded and tore a small hole in the barrier. One by one, they slipped through the ragged opening.

Out on the flight line, they saw a convoy of headlights heading towards them.

"Shooter-One?"

"I see them," Nikita informed them. "I count eight vehicles."

"That's funny," Pat said dryly. "I count ten."

In seconds the convoy would blast right down the runway, cutting between them and their sniper in the aircraft graveyard. They would then be trapped between the convoy and the death squad on their opposite flank. Deckard didn't think they had killed any of them as they had been behind a pile of gravel which meant his team was outnumbered two to one on one flank and maybe thirty to one on their other flank.

The only terrain feature that even offered the illusion of cover and concealment from which to fight from was the

354

drainage ditch that Aghassi had made his photographs from earlier. Bounding forward, the mercenaries descended into the waist deep channel and got down in the prone. Pat and Aghassi sat Greg down and dumped their bags of intel taken from the safe down next to him.

If they had continued forward, even at a sprint, they would never make it to the far side of the airfield before they would be overtaken by the convoy and caught out in the open where they would be run down and shot to pieces.

Greg was trembling uncontrollably.

The four combat veterans had seen more than their share of firefights. They had all had their nose bloodied a few times in the past. They knew what was coming. It would be the fight of their lives. It wasn't that they were not afraid as much as their calmness was really a resignation that fear would be not a productive emotion at this point. Their training took over. The terrain and the enemy had made the decision for them and now they had to ride it out, hoping that their asses came along for the ride.

Each man made sure they had a full magazine loaded and a round in the chamber. Several laid an extra magazine or hand grenade next to them for easy access. Pat had the LAW rocker launcher that he had liberated from the weapons shipment that they had intercepted. He pulled the retaining pins out and extended the tube. The former Delta operator readied the LAW, aiming down its sights.

Fingers tightened around triggers.

Behind them, the ruins of a conspiracy burned.

The Arab held his hand out, halting his men.

An injured animal would go to ground and wait in ambush. This what the mercenaries had done. They would not walk into their kill zone. He would wait for the quick reaction team to arrive. The mercenaries would be cut down or forced to retreat, right into his death squad. Then, they would feast on the American's bones. The Iraqis would act as a stopper force and block off their escape.

The convoy was rapidly approaching. Their role as a quick reaction security force was only while in garrison at their training areas in Nevada. They were actually a strike force made up of several platoons of MEK gunmen. While The Arab and his men specialized in sabotage, assassinations, and black propaganda, the strike force's role was one of direct combat.

They were being trained to go into Iran with CIA paramilitary forces ahead of the planned invasion where they would soften up Iranian military and even civilian targets before coalition forces pushed across the border. Heavily armed, they would make quick work of the feeble mercenary force. They were fools to even attempt to infiltrate Area 14 with such small numbers.

Going from position to position, The Arab set his men down on their bellies in the dirt at even intervals where they would be able to cut off any avenue of escape that the mercenaries might attempt. Finally, he got down on the desert floor himself and shouldered his AK-47 just as the MEK strike force screamed down the runway.

Pat pulled out the safety, aimed, and fired the LAW rocket launcher. The warhead shot down the runway and scored a direct hit on the lead vehicle. Both front doors on the HMMWV blasted open as smoke and fire billowed out. The turret gunner did a Peter Pan impersonation as he launched out into the night. Discarding the empty rocket tube, Pat scooped up his AK and joined his comrades as they fired bursts into each vehicle they could draw a bead on.

On the other side of the airfield, Nikita thinned out their ranks, transitioning from target to target as fast as he could. Hitting moving targets in low light conditions was no easy task, even with night vision but he managed to take out four of the turret gunners before they could even open fire.

One HMMWV driver panicked and drove straight toward their position, not knowing where the gunfire was coming from. Aghassi came up to one knee and fired on fully automatic, walking his gunfire through the windshield. He rolled out of the way a nano-second before the military vehicle crashed into the ditch, bottomed out, and then lost control as it climbed the opposite side and rolled over in a cloud of dirt.

Another HMMWV stopped short, identifying several muzzle flashes. The turret gunner swung his M2HB .50 caliber machine gun on the mercenaries and opened up with a heavy staccato burst that chewed up the ground less than a foot away from Kurt Jager. The machine gunner suddenly pitched forward, a sniper's bullet slapping him in the back of the skull.

The vehicle's doors were flung open as more MEK gunmen spilled out onto the runway. At less than forty feet away, Deckard threw a hand grenade that bounced off the tarmac and rolled right into the middle of their ranks before exploding.

Kurt fired into the next nearest HMMWV. Killing the driver, the truck crashed into the first HMMWV that was now disabled, jolting its passengers.

The firefight was lightning fast and frantic as the enemy had no idea how close they were to the intruders. The Iraqis had been taken by surprise and now they were trying to draw down on their targets but found that each of them already seemed to have giant bulls-eyes painted on their heads.

The Samruk International team had gotten their licks in, but the writing was on the wall. It was a matter of tactical calculus. They were outnumbered and outgunned. Looking over his shoulder, Deckard saw that Greg had already gotten zapped. He lay in a puddle of his own blood, staring up at the purple, black, and blue early morning sky.

"Fuck it," Deckard said. "I'm dead already."

Sprinting out from behind cover, he ran straight for the crashed HMMWV. The passengers who had been rattled by the crash were now emerging from the vehicle. Deckard fired on the run, blasting ragged holes into all three of them with stunted bursts of fire that blasted through the unarmored doors.

Gripping the dead driver around the throat, he callously pried him out of the HMMWV and dumped his corpse on the runway. Slipping into the truck he keyed his radio.

"Don't shoot, I'm getting on the gun," he warned Nikita.

Clawing his way into the gun turret, Deckard saw that there was not a machine gun mounted but rather an MK-19 grenade launcher. The MK-19 was jumbo sized machine gun that fired linked 40mm grenades. With the chain of High Explosive rounds already fed into the feed tray, Deckard reached forward and grabbed the charging handles on either side of the weapon. Muscling the massive bolt inside the receiver to the rear, he made the weapon ready to fire and flicked off the safety switch on the sear mechanism.

Ignoring the rear sight and front sight blade, Deckard held down the butterfly trigger and walked the exploding grenade rounds towards an approaching HMMWV. Inside the MK-19 the bolt slammed home, delivering a 40mm grenade down range as the expended shell casing fell out of the bottom of the receiver.

A line of grenades launched from the barrel in a steady but hollow sounding *thwunk-thwunk-thwunk* until the MEK vehicle was stitched from side to side. Each grenade exploded with a brilliant flash of yellow light, a shower of sparks accompanying each mini-detonation. A cyclic rate of 350 rounds per minute equaled a lot of ordnance going down range.

With the HMMWV reduced to a rolling fireball, Deckard transitioned to the next vehicle. His grenade fire shredded the HMMWV's tires, causing it to skid across the runway before stopping. Deckard's next burst of fire easily punched right through the flimsy metal doors and got inside the vehicle, reducing its occupants to a red vapor mist.

Behind him, Kurt Jager jumped onto the hood of another disabled HMMWV and dropped down into the gun turret, taking control of the .50 caliber machine gun, adding it to the fray. Each bullet was about the size of a finger and was absolutely devastating on the unprotected enemy vehicles.

Another group saw the carnage and attempted to dismount from their vehicle before being torn to shreds. Deckard turned the MK-19 on them as they attempted to run to the cover of the hangars. The grenade launcher spat 40mm rounds into their path, ripping them into red ribbons of flesh. Disembodied arms and legs spun through the air as the MEK terrorists were caught in the open.

For the first time in a long time, The Arab was shocked. Somehow the mercenaries had quickly turned the odds in their favor, to the point that they had captured two of the strike force's crew-served weapons and put them into operation against the other MEK vehicles.

The Americans were not retreating back into their position but were instead charging right into the strike force, killing them, and tearing them limb from limb. As The Arab watched one of the men take command of the MK-19 grenade launcher and rip through a half dozen MEK men, he knew the battle had reached a tipping point.

"Come Abdullah," he said to his nearby assistant. "Now is our last chance. While they are distracted, we can hit them from behind where they are exposed."

Motioning to the remaining nine men in his squad, The Arab, along with Abdullah, led them toward the firefight. Moving abreast of each other, they formed a hasty assault line. Two of the mercenaries were in the MEK trucks using the heavy weapons while the other two were using them as cover to fire at what was left of the strike force.

The Arab moved down into the drainage ditch where the infiltrators had taken cover from the initial assault. He found the body of a white devil, but not a soldier. It was the facility manager. Next to him were two bags filled with documents. They were of no concern to The Arab, so he continued to lead his men, closing on the enemy positions.

Once they had the mercenaries in sight, The Arab raised his AK-47 and fired.

Deckard felt something slap his back as he was pushed on top of the MK-19, forcing him to release the trigger. Bullets smacked into the HMMWV like heavy raindrops, each round landing with a *thwack*. Pulling down on the handle, Deckard rotated the gun ring around as he realized that they were taking fire from behind them. Another bullet punched through the green ammo can holding the linked 40mm grenades, while another shot grazed across the roof of the truck.

In the vehicle beside him, Kurt collapsed and fell from the turret, disappearing from view inside his HMMWV. Aghassi began climbing up and into the gun as Deckard sighted in with the MK-19. The death squad they had encountered earlier had finally decided to engage, probably waiting for them to be weakened by the second MEK element.

Thumbing down the trigger, he let off a single round before another hammer blow struck him in the chest, ripping him off the grenade launcher as he staggered backwards into the edge of the turret. First he had taken a round in the rear trauma plate in his plate carrier and now another round in the front plate.

Aghassi opened up with the .50 cal just as Deckard thumbed down the MK-19's trigger a second time. At close range, the effects were absolutely devastating. The 40mm rounds were tearing off legs below the knees as the grenades bounced off the tarmac before they had a chance to reach minimum safe distance and arm themselves. In one case, a MK-19 grenade struck an advancing MEK terrorist in the face, dropping him.

The .50 cal machine gun was chewing through the enemy as they walked right into Aghassi's stream of Armor Piercing Incendiary rounds. Pat had dropped to the ground and was returning fire with his AK-103 while Deckard and Aghassi shot right over his head. Looking over his shoulder, Pat shouted up to Deckard.

"That guy is getting away!"

Deckard looked to see someone dart behind the first disabled HMMWV, the one Pat had shot with the LAW. He was somewhat more clever than his late comrades, using the vehicle as cover he then ran down the runway making sure to place Aghassi's HMMWV between himself and Deckard so that only one of them could fire at a time. At that moment, Aghassi was still shooting and couldn't hear Pat or Deckard above the chaos.

"Take the gun," Deckard yelled down to Pat. Deckard suspected he knew who was making a run for it.

"You're going after him?" Pat said as he stepped up onto the hood to take over on the MK-19. They were still taking some more gunfire from what was left of the strike force. "I want to come with you."

"I saw Kurt go down, Aghassi needs to treat him while you keep up the rate of fire."

Deckard jumped out of the truck and ran down the runway. Halting, he adjusted the focus ring on his PVS-15 night vision goggles until he spotted the black form of a human being running off in the direction of the aircraft graveyard.

Maybe he could arrange an interception.

"Shooter-One," he radioed. "Give me a sitrep."

"I fired through all five magazines for my sniper rifle. Down to just a pistol."

"Move forward and pick up an enemy's weapon, then coordinate a link up with Pat."

"Roger."

Holding his rifle at port arms, Deckard ran across the landing strip, keeping the fleeing terrorist in sight until he disappeared into the shadows of one of the jumbo jets off in the distance. After that, all he could do was vector in on the 747 where he last saw the runner and try to pick up the trail again as he got closer.

The Arab swung around, snarling as he spotted one of the Americans. Somehow, he knew that his pursuer had to be the mercenary commander that he and his squad had been targeting south of the border. It was the only answer that made sense. Amazingly, he had escaped the suicide attack on the island. Later, the executions at the Christian mission had failed to draw him out. Psychological studies drawn up by his employers said that it was almost certain that he would throw his forces into a fray immediately after a massacre of that magnitude.

Finally, there was the IED. The Arab had triggered the explosives with a cell phone detonator, striking the lead vehicle in the Samruk International convoy as they departed Oaxaca. The mercenary commander appeared to like leading from the front. Only later was it discovered that he had been in another vehicle. Since cutting a deal with the United States after the invasion of Iraq, MEK had never been on the defensive like this before. Now their terror cells had been annihilated in the blink of an eye.

Running under the belly of an old jumbo jet, The Arab continued to a mid-sized aircraft and settled down behind the forward landing gear. This was his last chance.

The loss of Abdullah and his men did not concern him. He could not feel for them even if he wanted to. His only concern was escape and if he didn't finish off the American mercenary he would be looking over his shoulder for the rest of what would probably be a short life.

Lining up the rear u-shaped notch sight with the front sight post on his AK-47, The Arab didn't have to wait long.

Then the mercenary appeared, looking from side to side as he stood underneath the jumbo jet.

The Kalashnikov bucked up into his shoulder and his target dropped.

Deckard jolted backwards, his body having a sympathetic reaction that dumped him onto his backside as the PVS-15 night vision goggles were torn from his helmet in an explosion of glass and plastic. Thankfully, his clear lens Oakley glasses saved his eyesight.

Rolling away, he found cover behind an old air conditioning unit.

"*Shloonkum il-yoom?*" a voice called out to him. "*Intu laazim ta baaniin.*"

Deckard blinked, ignoring the superficial cuts caused by his night vision goggles getting shot off. Using the EO Tech holographic sight mounted on his AK-103, he squeezed off several shots in the direction of the voice.

"*La-tutluq in-naar!*" The voice said with a laugh.

It took Deckard's mind a few seconds to catch up. He was speaking in Iraqi dialect Arabic, another language that he had a passing familiarity with. The Arab let off a couple shots of his own which rattled into the air conditioning unit he was behind.

Getting of fix on the death squad leader's position, Deckard returned fire before quickly bounding behind the rear landing gear of the 747 he was under.

"Listen to me you white devil," The Arab continued to taunt Deckard in his native language. "You wanted me and now you have found me but what is it that you are really looking for out here in the desert tonight? Are you sure you want to find what you are looking for?"

Deckard understood the words but was barely listening. His adversary's strength was not as a fighter but rather as a cunning manipulator. He was the battlefield's landscaper, making both sides of conflicts believe what he wanted them to believe.

"We have never met, I am sure of it, but I know your work and you know mine. I've seen the way you move. You move like those commandos in Iraq. I bet you never considered that it was me doing the cutting in so many of those beheading videos did you?"

Sticking to the shadows, Deckard kept low and attempted to circle around by taking cover under another aircraft. The Arab fired a few probing shots, a recon by fire to elicit a response so he could pin point Deckard's position. He didn't take the bait.

"Listen, you need me as much as I need you. I create the nightmares you need American! You could not exist without someone providing these horrors. Men like you are only switched on when your nightmares are clear, like now, like tonight you see?"

Deckard moved silently around The Arab's flank. If he

could take him alive, there was no end to what they could get him to confess to on camera. They could blow the entire conspiracy wide open.

"America needs these nightmares," The Arab lectured. "Your country needs these monsters even as it denies that they exist. Without these fears they would have to look in the mirror and confront who they really are. Without me, you would have to confront what you really are. Then you would see that you are just like me. Blood for blood. I take a head and you set out to take a dozen. I play my games and you play yours."

Looking down, The Arab saw a subtle shift in the shadows.

Pivoting on one foot, The Arab spun to confront Deckard. He attempted to bring his rifle into play but Deckard was a blur of motion as he parried the weapon aside with his own. A low kick connected with The Arab's inner knee causing an explosion of pain inside the joint. A butt stroke from the American rode right down his forearm and stripped the AK-47 out of his hand.

"Not as easy as cutting the head off unconscious women is it?" Deckard asked him.

Against a professional soldier, a butcher like The Arab was simply out classed.

With a guttural scream, The Arab moved with surprising speed. Reaching out, he grabbed the barrel of Deckard's AK-103 and attempted to muscle it away so that it was no longer pointed at him. Deckard simply took a knee, using his leverage to his advantage as his opponent attempted to push the gun barrel up and away. By dropping to a knee, the gun barrel was now realigned with The Arab's torso.

Three shots cracked out in the night.

The Arab stood there for a moment, his hands exploring his stomach and finding his palms suddenly slick with blood. Calmly, he sat down in the desert sand before laying down on his back. As blood poured from his wounds, he accepted that he was going to die.

Deckard stood over him, his face expressionless.

"Who are you?" The Arab asked with blood splatter around his lips.

"Nightmare's end."

Now Deckard could recognize the scars that ran down

364

the arms and legs of the bleeding man as he only wore a t-shirt and shorts. Lifting his shirt he saw that they extended in deep lines across his stomach and chest as well.

"Who did this to you?"

"I did," he said, his voice growing faint.

Deckard let his rifle hang by its sling and rotated it to his side. Drawing the Sub-Saharan combat knife, he knelt down beside The Arab.

"Do it," the dying man gasped. "I would do the same and worse to you."

Amid the killing and the violence, Deckard could feel himself spinning out of control. The drug cartels had escalated the level of bloodshed to levels that even the Iraqi insurgents had difficultly matching. Once they starting killing, they then started creating massacre after massacre to try to one up each other. Once you started down that path, it seemed that there was no end to it. The only future in that cycle was mass graves filled with bloated, rotting corpses. Now he was a part of that as he had cut off Jimenez' head just to get his point across.

The Arab was not a soldier, a mercenary, or really even a terrorist in the conventional sense. He was an artist. He manipulated and destroyed biological life wherever he went, all to advance someone else's political agenda. Someone else. Some player with no name.

"Who do you work for?" Deckard asked.

"None of us really know the names behind these wars we fight," The Arab answered. "I am no more enlightened then you are."

Reaching into a pouch on his plate carrier, Deckard pulled out a black marker and began writing across the top of The Arab's shirt collar.

"What...what are you doing?" His eyes were slowly closing.

"Making sure that whoever you work for gets my message."

Finished writing, he put away the marker and balanced his knife in one hand. Flipping it over into a reverse grip, Deckard plunged the blade into his fallen enemy's chest cavity, slicing through his heart. With a final heave of his chest, The Arab settled to the ground and died.

Deckard left the knife sticking out of the dead man's

chest and began walking back towards the runway.

Behind him, he left a river of corpses, demons, and ghosts in his wake.

Four men walked across the airfield.

Deckard unclipped his helmet and held it under one arm, watching and waiting as the mercenaries approached him. Behind them, the hints of dawn were peeking from behind the distant hills. As his men grew near, he could see that Kurt wore a tourniquet around one arm where he had been shot while manning the machine gun. Pat had the lower portion of one pant leg cut away where a bloody bandage had been secured in place. Nikita had his sniper rifle slung and carried the weapon of a fallen terrorist. Aghassi limped forward.

They stopped short, looking at him expectantly.

"It's over," Deckard confirmed.

Kurt nodded. Pat smiled. Aghassi frowned and surveyed the carnage all around them. Nikita's expression was neutral. They were tired, but ready for whatever came next. It was just then that Deckard noticed that Kurt and Aghassi were carrying plastic bags that had been thrown over their shoulders. The documents from inside the command center.

"You guys thinking what I'm thinking?" Pat asked.

"Is the beer light on?" Aghassi wondered aloud.

"What is beer light?" Nikita questioned.

"Not a bad idea," Kurt said, looking toward Deckard for approval.

"Find a vehicle that is still running so we can get the hell out of here."

"Then?" Pat asked again.

Deckard shrugged his shoulders.

"Vegas is only an hour away."

Epilogue:

Bodyguards led the way through the secret back entrance into the exclusive Others Club in the upper east side of Manhattan. Behind them, their principal ambled up the steps and into the elevator. With a 60,000 dollar initiation fee, membership in the Others Club was one of the most coveted, and expensive, in New York City. The principal, flanked by two former Secret Service agents as he rode the elevator, would know as he was one of the founding members.

When the doors pinged open the old man went to his favorite room in the clubhouse, walking past servers and staff preparing for the coming day. Nearly ninety years old, his humble beginnings in Europe continued to hold him back among the city's elite circles. He was denied entry into several of the older, stuffier clubs for New York socialites, one of the reasons why he started his own.

A server greeted him at the door and had him seated at a table that had been arranged specially for him and his guests in the library. While the Yale Club and the Century Club were filled with blue bloods sitting on overstuffed antique leather chairs underneath hundred year old glass chandeliers that would have sunk with the Titanic, the Others Club was modern and vibrant. The morning light shined through the windows and glowed amongst the white book cases and modern art work hanging on the walls.

He established the club for a new kind of wealth, and a new kind of man. The Others Club boasted a membership consisting of not just Ivy League alumni, diplomats, and politicians but also of actors, film producers, media personalities, artists, and writers. Those who could pass the thresholds for entry anyway.

It wasn't long before another set of bodyguards showed up and his guests entered the room. The old man rose to shake their hands. The twin brothers were movers in shakers in business as well as domestic politics. The Biermann brothers jetted all over the country during the year, held their own conferences, and chaired political organizations not to mention running candidates for elected office. They were major players in the game. They were also one of the old man's primary antagonists which made them perfect for membership into his club.

The closer they were, the easier it would be to develop a consensus when the time came. A time like today. Like it or not, Manhattan was where finance met and influenced power brokers in government.

"You mentioned something about," one of the brothers began with some hesitation. He was the younger of the two by eight minutes. "Complications?"

"Don't worry. My people swept this room for bugs before we got here," the old man said dismissively. "Yes, I've gotten word about the destruction of a Mexican military base early last night. I've delayed them, but the media will be picking it up eventually. I've been assured that we have some time to prepare our mitigation strategy. Meanwhile, my people are looking into this situation in a discreet fashion which ensures that we are all protected."

"We have a plan in place in case something does come out in the press," the older Biermann brother stated.

"I can mobilize the Occupy movement through various media watch dog organizations," the old man agreed. "If the public hears about the government smuggling guns into Mexico we will make it look like a Republican conspiracy theory against a Democrat President."

"And we can mobilize thousands of Tea Party supporters through our own media outlets," the brothers said almost in unison, an annoying habit that the twins had. Looking at each other, the older brother continued. "We can get them outraged by the scandal and channel their anger towards the President which will fit nicely with what you have planned."

"That way," the younger brother said, picking up the conversation, "the entire scandal turns into nothing more than left wing versus right wing demagoguery and the subsequent investigation will go nowhere with both political parties pitted against each other."

"During an election season," the older brother laughed. "Its' a slam dunk. Silence a few whistle blowers, threaten to sue any journalists that get out of line, and the entire affair will peter out on its own."

The old man pursed his lips.

"Maybe. Let's see what the damage is first before we

worry about containment."

The waitress brought them their breakfast, including three glasses of bourbon, a tradition the three men had started several years prior.

"The military base in Torreon could have been an accident of some kind but on the way here I found out about the Ft. Bliss facility going dark. Now we are getting nothing but radio silence from Area 14. It can't be a coincidence."

The old man's assistant came in and sat down at another table. Propping a black case in front of him he opened it to reveal a computer screen and keyboard. The twin brothers had a similar system as did many others in their network, up to and including various commanding generals and select members of the President's National Security Council.

Nicknamed, the "Pirate's Net" it was a communications platform developed as a part of Cold War continuity of government planning. In the event of a nuclear war, military planners had decided that the mechanism and functions of government needed parallel systems to allow them to survive. This included a means for the civilian government to talk to the military even after key facilities and satellites had been destroyed by intercontinental ballistic missiles.

Normally run by the Office of Naval Intelligence, the Pirate's Net transmitted signals by bouncing them off the ionosphere rather than by satellite, and this gave it the added advantage of making it impossible to tap into and eavesdrop like normal communications. The National Security Agency was recording nearly everything these days, ostensibly for purposes of counter-intelligence but since the 9/11 attacks they recorded civilian communications traffic as well.

Communications nodes in their network had to use a system that could not be recorded or cracked by any agency, anywhere. The stakes were too high.

"Sir," the assistant said. "Military Police on Ft. Bliss have found the crew at the G3 facility retrained and locked in a closet. Other than a non-life threatening wound, they appear to be fine."

"What the hell is going on here?" the younger brother asked. Nothing like this had ever happened before. No one had the gall to challenge their power.

"Get Ted on the phone for me," the old man said,

demanding to talk to the CEO of G3 Communications.

"He locked himself in his panic room when he heard about what was happening. His body guards are trying to talk him out," the assistant said, looking away from the computer screen.

"When was this?"

"About half an hour ago."

"What about Area 14?"

"Updates show that a security detachment from Creech Air Force base is just arriving. I see a new message being forwarded to us from our contact in the National Security Council."

The three oligarchs nervously ate their breakfast while the assistant read them the message traffic. They never touched the Pirate's Net but rather let surrogates handle it for legal reasons. Technically the system never should have been outside the hands of ONI as it was piece of classified government technology.

"The reports are coming in through NORTHCOM," the assistant updated them. "The G3 command and control center burnt to the ground."

"Now we know why Ted is hiding out in his panic room," the old man said. "He must have ordered the destruction sequence."

"The Iraqi contingent appears to have been completely destroyed."

Forks rang off porcelain as the brothers dropped their utensils on their plates.

"They are counting the dead now, but there are dozens of bodies and destroyed vehicles. It appears to be the entire MEK strike force."

"What about the provocateur element?" The old man specialized in propaganda and manipulation. When needed, his provocateurs acted all around the globe to help advance his schemes in tandem with various non-governmental organizations.

"They appear to be among the dead, sir. Wait, there is something else coming in."

The assistant's hands danced across the keyboard and a picture loaded on the screen.

"Uh, you might want to take a look at this," he said

sheepishly.

The old man lumbered from the table, followed by the twins. As they stood behind the operator of the Pirate's Net, their faces went white. The Air Force security detachment had uploaded a picture from the scene of the disaster to the Pentagon, who in turn forwarded it to the White House, and finally to them.

The old man had never met him of course, but the corpse in the photo was the provocateur operative that he knew only as The Arab. A giant black knife was sticking out of his chest. The twins looked faint. Across the top of The Arab's shirt were hastily written words, hashed out with a black marker. The old man's eyes followed across them as he read aloud.

"His boss is next on my target deck."

Read about the adventures of Deckard's father, a Vietnam veteran turned professional mercenary during the 1980's in the PROMIS series. Here is a sample from issue #3, PROMIS: South Africa...

12SEP83
0032hrs
South Africa

Streetlamps cast golden light down on the long empty roads that twisted throughout the Eastern Cape, insects creating a steady buzz that filled the darkness of night with their presence. The occasional window was still illuminated, only to be dashed as the locals tossed a curtain into place and prepared to bed down for the night. Although not still, the night was calm until the blast rocked through several neighborhoods, shaking people from their beds and setting off alarm systems on several warehouses located in the area.

South Africa was having another one of those nights.

0030hrs

An aluminum ladder thudded silently against the side of the prison wall, the strips of rubber tire treads tied to the top of the ladder damping the sound as it made contact. The ladder had been specially cut for one specific task, to help two black-clad men scale that specific wall. After scrambling up the rungs, the first man tossed a carpet over the barbed wire before uncoiling a rope ladder down the opposite side of the wall.

Crawling over the lip, the two operators did their best to keep a low profile as not to silhouette themselves against the moonlit skyline. Sliding down the rope ladder in a kind of controlled fall, they then slung their AK-47 rifles off their backs. The safeties slid off without the normal distinctive click, the levers wrapped in black electrical tape during mission rehearsals that had been conducted over the past week.

Finding themselves in the courtyard of Middledrift Prison, they sprinted to the heavy steel door that led into the prison itself, their rifle muzzles leading the way and scanning for threats. Black ski masks concealed their features from the ever watching CCTV camera on a pivot mount above the doorway.

372

Reaching into a satchel, the larger of the two operators produced a specialized door charge made of P4 explosives. Developed years prior during the Rhodesian Bush War, the charge was often called by its nickname, the *Gate Crasher.*

If there was anyone on the other side of the door they were in for a world of hurt from the steel bending and giving way under the explosive force of the detonation. The charge lived up to its name. The two assaulters stood on either side of the door as the plastic explosives blasted a shower of debris out between them, rattling windows for blocks in every direction.

Inside, the cell blocks consisted of cinder block walls that were covered in peeling paint, the walls themselves seeming to stretch on forever. The black-clad interlopers cut right and sprinted down a side corridor, knowing exactly where they were headed. A scale mock up had been constructed with wooden planks and Hessian cloth where they familiarized themselves with the floor plan. Together they had run rehearsals through the improvised prison again and again until they knew the layout like the palm of their hands.

Approaching the wing of the prison where the target was being held, they saw two guards as they rounded a juncture in the hallway. With AK-47 muzzles bearing down on them, one of the guards threw his hands in the air. The other reached for the revolver holstered on his hip just a second too late as one of the intruders butt stroked him across the cheek, drawing blood and knocking him to the concrete floor.

"You," the attacker said to the remaining guard who had prudently surrendered. "On the fucking ground!"

The prison guard could see the edges of the man's lips and eyes under the balaclava he wore. He was the smaller of the two, also white, but his accent was not that of an Afrikaner. It was a strange voice like he had never heard before except maybe on television. American?

In seconds the gunmen had handcuffed the prison guards to a pipe sticking out from one of the nearby walls and were hurrying down the hall to complete their mission.

Turning another corner, their boots thudded down the corridor towards the entrance to the wing that housed solitary confinement, usually reserved for those deemed to be too dangerous to be left in general population. However, there was also another type of prisoner consigned to solitary confinement.

Political prisoners.

At the sliding barred metal gate that served as an entrance to solitary, a lone guard sat behind a desk half asleep. When he saw two men storming up to him with Kalashnikovs held at the ready he jolted fully awake, his heart rate suddenly skipping up well over a hundred beats a minute. Reaching for the pump-action shotgun lying across the desk, a spray of 7.62 bullets shredded the wooden desktop, sending the shotgun spinning to the floor. The guard retracted his hand as it was now bleeding from several shrapnel wounds.

The larger assailant strode up to the guard and punched him in the face, toppling him over. No demands, just another obstacle to crush on the way to their objective.

Reaching for a key ring in his pocket, the shooter with the American accent produced a key, jammed it into the lock on the gate and turned it open. The key, and others, had been given to the operators several days prior by a guard who was currently off duty. The American had used some key impressioning techniques to make copies before rushing the originals back to the prison before anyone noticed them missing. The door slid on its rollers until it came to a stop with a loud *clang* that resonated throughout the solitary confinement block.

The jail breakers took off, jogging down the hall as prisoners reached through the bars of their cells attempting to catch hold of them. They screamed and shouted in a half dozen languages and dialects. Aside from the actual prisoners, the cells themselves were empty cement cubes with a lone slop bucket, the only amenity provided. It was no wonder that they begged to be released. Most of them looked malnourished; some looked positively sickly with boils across their skin and covered in feces.

In cell Twelve-Alpha they found their target, Josef Menzi.

Although it could be debated whether or not Josef was a psychopath, he was kept in solitary for purely political reasons. The ruling government, particularly the current president of the breakaway state of Ciskei, didn't want Josef spreading his political ideas among the other prisoners, afraid that it would lead to another coup attempt. It didn't help that the current President of Ciskei was also Josef's brother.

One by one, the various black ethnic groups were

granted strategically located black homelands, Ciskei being one of them. The idea was purely Machiavellian on the part of the South African government. With black homelands granted, the rest of South Africa was reserved as a white *Volkstaat* by a matter of deduction. Besides, with the various black tribes split up into separate provinces it was even easier for the Apartheid-state to play them all off against each other.

With the fall of Rhodesia and the expansion of the communist menace, the South Africans weren't taking any chances. That was where Josef came in.

Frail and underweight from years of captivity, Josef looked up at the two white men as he sat with his back against the wall. Were they liberators or murderers? Hard to tell.

"Tell us your mother's name," one of them demanded, slinging his rifle over his shoulder. This one's accent was Australian, he was sure of it.

"Your mother's name dickhead!" The other sounded American.

"Phelisa," Josef croaked.

"Where were you born?" the American asked.

"Bisho."

The American pulled out a key ring and quickly located the appropriate key while the larger Australian kept an eye out for armed guards. Swinging the barred door open, the paramilitary soldier reached in and helped Josef to his feet.

"He sounds like a fair dinkum," the Aussie said.

"You stay with me, you do what I do," the American told Josef. "If you so much as shit your pants without me giving you permission first and I will put a bullet in the back of your fucking head. Understand?"

Josef nodded.

What else could he do?

The next few minutes were a blur as the two black-clad gunmen half dragged, half carried Josef through the prison, shooting their way out as several guards gave a half-hearted attempt to prevent them from escaping. After the quick exchange of gunfire, both guards threw down their weapons and made a run for it. Dying was simply outside their paygrade.

Walking right out the front door of Middledrift Prison, the three of them stood silently as police sirens sounded in the distance. Headlights flashed and a white van ground to a halt in front of them. Flinging open the side door, the two commandos pushed Josef inside and piled in behind him. Before they had the door closed the driver stomped on the gas and accelerated down the street.

Their driver made the first right hand turn they came to. A half dozen police cars missed them by a margin of several seconds as the police vehicles skidded to a halt in front of the prison.

Josef was handcuffed, gagged, and blindfolded before being laid down on the floor of the van. The prisoner needed to safeguarded at all costs. A lot of people had a lot riding on him tonight.

"Don't move," Sean Deckard ordered the political dissident as he yanked off his balaclava.

"Are we clear?" Robin asked from the driver's seat.

"I think so," James responded, tugging off his own mask to reveal a massive caterpillar of a mustache on his upper lip. "Looks like we lost them."

Sean dropped a half empty magazine from his AK, topping it off with a fresh one from his chest rig. Golden light flashed through the van as Robin gunned it down a labyrinth of side streets. They had a long drive to their destination, and he knew it was going to be an even longer night.

For years he'd been fighting one war after another. From Vietnam, to Laos, to Cambodia, Rhodesia, Zambia, Mozambique, Angola, and now in South Africa he plied the ancient trade of soldiering whenever and wherever he could, but tonight would be different.

Tonight he was fighting to prevent a war.

If he failed, the resulting genocide would make Mugabe's reign over Zimbabwe look like a walk in the park.

Holding on tight, Robin nearly balanced the van on two wheels as he rounded a corner and sped off into the darkness.

Acknowledgements:

Where to even begin...

You start off writing a novel thinking that it will be a solitary process, you sitting by yourself in a corner somewhere smoking cigarettes and drinking whiskey while you pound out your manifesto on a laptop. The reality is that writing a book like this is much more collaborative than I ever would have thought.

If I were to judge Target Deck by its cover I would give it an A+ and that is thanks to my awesome cover artist Marc Lee. He knocked it out of the park once again. Now if you didn't find the content of the book as inspiring as the cover, well, please don't blame Marc for the errors of my ways.

I also want to thank Ted and Laura K. for putting eyeballs on the text of the book and slogging through my butchering of the English language. Thanks so much for your patience with me! I'd like to thank Uri for consulting on some of the technical aspects of the book. Brandon Webb gets a huge shout out for giving me a job at SOFREP.com and providing me with lots of great advice about publishing. I also want to thank Dan Tharp, Chris Martin, Iassen Donov, Federico, Rob, Peter Nealen, Hank Brown, Laura W., John Meyer, Jack Badelaire, Jack Silkstone, and many others who cannot be mentioned here for your friendship and support.

As always, I need to thank and apologize to my wife, Caterina. Sorry that this whole writing deal turns me into an anti-social hermit for long periods of time honey.

Glossary

.300 WinMag: Sniper rifle chambered for the .300 Winchester Magnum cartridge.

.410 shotgun shell: Smallest size shotgun cartridge which is about the same width as a .45 caliber bullet

160th Special Operations Aviation: Helicopter aviation unit composed of the world's most highly trained pilots and flight crews who fly Special Operations troops where they need to go on combat operations

1911: .45 Caliber pistol

40mm grenade: A grenade fired from a grenade launcher rather than thrown by hand. One type is fired from the M203 under-barrel grenade launcher and another type is fired by the MK-19.

550 chord: Parachute line, also used by soldiers to tie down equipment and just about everything else you can think of

AC-130: Aerial gunship

AG: Assistant Gunner, carries ammunition, spare barrels, and tripod for a machine gunner or extra ammunition for a recoiless rifle gunner. Also preforms reloading duties.

AK: See AK-47

AK-103: An updated form of the AK-47 rifle that can be fitted with a variety of different optics.

AK-47: Avtomat Kalashnikova-1947, following the standard Soviet weapons naming convention. Avtomat meaning the type of rifle: automatic. Kalashnikov comes from the last name of the inventor, Mikhail Kalashnikov and the year 1947 is when the rifle went into production. The AK-47 is the world's most ubiquitous battle rifle, having been used in virtually every conflict since the Cold War.

AMIZ: Academia Militarizada Ignacio Zaragoza, Mexican police academy

An-124: Large Russian-made cargo airplane

API: Armor Piercing Incendiary ammunition

Arystan: Kazakh Anti-Terror unit

AT4: US military single shot anti-tank rocket

Barret: .50 caliber anti-material rifle

BMP: Russian tracked armored vehicle

BRDM: Russian made four or eight wheeled armored vehicle

C4: Composition Four, military grade plastic explosives

Camelbak: Plastic bladder used to carry water in, commonly carried on a soldiers back and drank through a long tube that acts as a straw

Carl Gustav: 84mm Recoiless rifle that can fire HE, HEDP, and HEAT among other types of rounds.

CDMA: Code Division Multiple Access, a way to access channels utilized by various radios

Celox: A hemostatic agent which quickly clots bleeding injuries

CHU: Compartmentalized Housing Unit

CIA: Central Intelligence Agency

CISEN: Mexican intelligence service

Comms: Communications

COMSEC: Communications Security

CP: Control Point

Crypto: Cryptography

DEA: Drug Enforcement Agency

Delta Force: US Army counter-terrorist unit

Det-Chord: Detonation Chord, used to sympathetically detonate larger explosive charges

Dev: (see SEAL Team Six)

Direct Action: A mission tasked to kill enemy soldiers or terrorists

DLI: Defense Language Institute

DOE: Department of Energy

F-5: Fighter Jet

FARC: Fuerzas Armadas Revolucionarias de Colombia, Colombian guerrilla group

FBI: Federal Bureau of Investigation

FES: Mexican maritime commandos

FID: Foreign Internal Defense

Flashbang: A distraction device which can be thrown into a room and creates a flash and a bang

Flexcuff: Disposable plastic handcuffs

FOB: Forward Operating Base

GAFE: Mexican Counter-Terrorist unit

Glock: Austrian made brand of pistols

GPS: Global Positioning System

GSG-9: German Counter-Terrorist unit

GUARD: Global Unconventional Aid, Rescue, and Defense, a US-based Private Military Company

HE: High Explosive

HEAT: High Explosive Anti-Tank

HEDP: High Explosive Dual Purpose

Hextend: A blood plasma extender

HF: High Frequency

HK 416: German made carbine rifle with a gas-piston upper receiver chambered in 5.56

HK 417: German made big brother to the 416 but chambered for the 7.62 bullet

HMMWV: High Mobility Multipurpose Wheeled Vehicle

Hoolie tool: Also known as a Hooligan tool, this metal pry bar is used for mechanically breaching doors

HUMINT: Human Intelligence

HVT: High Value Target

IED: Improvised Explosive Device

IR: Infrared

Iridium phone: Mobile satellite telephone

ISA: Intelligence Support Activity.   Unit   that   conducts intelligence gathering operations for Special Operations.

ISR: Intelligence, Surveillance, and Reconnaissance

Iveco: Truck manufacturer

JDAM: Joint Direct Attack Munition

Ka-bar: Military fighting knife.

Kaibiles: Guatemalan Special Forces

Kalashnikov: See AK-47

KIA: Killed In Action

LAW: Light Anti-Tank rocket launcher

LOA: Limit Of Advance

M-10: Scope used to sight in a Carl Gustav recoiless rifle

M-1950: Green canvas bag used to hold and protect a para-trooper's rifle during a parachute jump

M16: Standard issue American combat rifle

M203: Under barrel, breach loaded, 40mm grenade launcher

M240B: 7.62 belt fed General Purpose Machine Gun

M249 SAW: Squad Automatic Weapon, belt fed and chambered for 5.56

M2HB: .50 caliber machine gun

M4: Shortened M16 carbine, commonly carried by US forces

MAC-10: American made Sub-Machine Gun

MBITR: Multiband Inter/Intra Team Radio

MEK: Iranian terrorist organization sponsored by the United States

Mérida Initiative: American aide package given to the Mexican government to help them fight drug cartels

MK-19: Automatic belt-fed 40mm grenade launcher

Mk48: A 7.62 machine gun that is smaller and lighter than the M240B

MP5: Heckler and Koch 9mm sub-machine gun

MSR: Main Supply Route

MSS: Mission Support Site

NAFTA: North American Free Trade Agreement

NORTHCOM: Northern Command

NSA: National Security Agency, handles signal intercepts

NSC: National Security Council

NVA: North Vietnamese Army

OBI: Office of Bi-National Intelligence

OGA: Other Governmental Agencies, euphemism for CIA para-militaries

ONI: Office of Naval Intelligence

OP: Observation Post

OPCEN: Operations Center

Overwatch: A stationary element that provides security, and cover fire if need be, for a maneuver element

PCI's: Pre-Combat Inspections

PIT maneuver: Pursuit Intervention Technique, a technique to ram and stall out a car

PKM: Belt-fed Russian machine gun

PL: Platoon Leader

PMC: Private Military Company

PND: Mexican political party that came to challenge the PRI

PRI: Mexican political party that dominated the country for 71 years

PSD: Personal Security Detachment

PSYOP: Psychological Operations

PVS-14: Single tube night vision goggles

PVS-15: Dual tube night vision goggles

QRF: Quick Reaction Force

Rangers: US Airborne Light Infantry unit

RPG: Rocket Propelled Grenade

RRD: Regimental Reconnaissance Detachment, now known as RRC

RTB: Return To Base

S2: Intelligence staff section in a military unit

Samruk International: A Private Military Company based out of Astana, Kazakhstan. See Reflexive Fire for the origins of this company.

SATCOM: Satellite Communications

SBF: See Support by Fire

SCUBA: Self Contained Underwater Breathing Apparatus

SEAL: SEa Air and Land, US Navy commandos

SEAL Team Six: US Navy Counter-Terrorism unit. Also known as Naval Special Warfare Development Group or just Dev for short.

Sicario: Spanish word for assassin.

SIG Blaser: State of the art sniper rifle with interchangeable barrels to allow more than one caliber of bullet to be used by the same platform

SIGINT: Signals Intelligence

Sinaloa cartel: Mexico's oldest drug cartel

SITREP: Situation Report

SOCOM: Special Operations Command

Special Forces: Also known as Green Berets, specialize in training indigenous forces. A separate unit from SEALs, Rangers, and Delta Force

Support By Fire: Can be an overwatch element, usually a line of machine gunners which fire on the enemy to support advancing riflemen who assault the objective

Sunkar: Elite Kazakh police force

SUV: Sport Utility Vehicle

Swedish K: Sub-machine gun

385

Technical: Improvised combat vehicle. Usually a pickup truck with a machine gun mounted in the back

Thermite: Burns at high temperatures and is used to destroy enemy equipment

Thermo-baric: Heat+Pressure, a type of explosive designed to collapse structures from the inside

TNT: Trinitrotoluene explosives

TOC: Tactical Operations Center

UAV: Unmanned Aerial Vehicle

UHF: Ultra-High Frequency

UW: Unconventional Warfare

Uzi: Isreali made Sub-Machune Gun

VDO: Vehicle Drop Off

VHF: Very High Frequency

Weapon's Squad: One of four Squads in an Infantry Platoon. Weapons Squad employs machine guns while the other three Squads are composed of riflemen.

WIA: Wounded In Action

Zapatistas: Mexican populist rebel group

Zetas: Drug cartel founded by Special Forces soldiers who defected from the Mexican military.

Growing up in New York, Jack Murphy enlisted in the US Army at age nineteen. Completing Infantry Basic Training, Airborne School, and the Ranger Indoctrination Program, he was assigned to 3rd Ranger Battalion. As a Ranger, he served as an Anti-Tank gunner, Sniper, and Team Leader, and also graduated from Ranger School and Sniper School.

After several deployments to Afghanistan and Iraq, he attended the Special Forces Assessment and Selection Course and was selected as a Special Forces Weapons Sergeant. Over a year was spent training in the Special Forces Qualification Course, including further weapons training, SERE School, language training, and more.

Assigned as the Senior Weapons Sergeant on a Military Free Fall team in 5th Special Forces Group, Murphy was again sent to numerous schools and training courses before being deployed to Iraq. Acting as the senior trainer and adviser to an Iraqi SWAT team, his Special Forces team conducted Direct Action and other missions across Northern Iraq.

Having left the military in 2010, he is now working towards a degree in Political Science at Columbia University. Murphy is the author of Reflexive Fire, Target Deck, the PROMIS series, and numerous non-fiction articles. He has appeared in documentaries, on national television, and syndicated radio.

Jack's work appears frequently on SOFREP.com, the #1 source for news and information about US and Allied Special Operations. He also has a blog at Reflexivefire.com.

Written by a former Reconnaissance Marine and veteran of Iraq and Afghanistan, Task Force Desperate is the gritty, fast-paced beginning of a new series of military thrillers. Jeff Stone and his team of Praetorian Security contractors are marking time on counter-piracy duty aboard a freighter in the Gulf of Aden when the boredom ends abruptly. A major US base on the Horn of Africa is overrun in a well-coordinated terrorist attack, and those base personnel who survive are taken hostage. With the world economy tanked, and most of the Western militaries dangerously thinned, the Praetorian operators find themselves to be the hostages' only hope of rescue. The mission wasn't going to be simple, or easy. But as events in East Africa accelerate, and outside players start to show their hand, the Praetorian shooters start to realize just what a desperate gamble they are embarked upon, and what this particular job is going to cost...

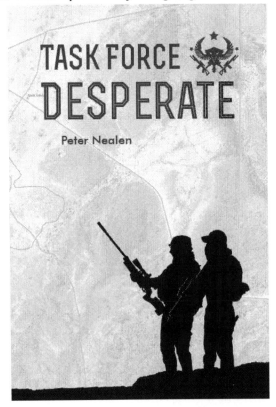

Dragged Back to Battle

Tommy Scarred Wolf thought his commando days were all behind him, until somebody messed with his family. Jennifer Scarred Wolf and her college girlfriends were in the wrong place at the wrong time, and now face death and worse. The kidnappers probably assumed nobody would be crazy enough to come after them.

The Shawnee Green Beret is going to show them the danger of assumptions.

Tommy needs friends, funding, and firepower to accomplish what no government is willing to try. Hardly a stranger at pulling off the improbable, he soon assembles all three, and steams for a vice-ridden hellhole halfway around the globe.

His hand-picked team includes Dwight "Rocco" Cavarra, a former SEAL team commander; Jake McCallum, a Delta Force veteran; and Leon Campbell—an unflappable sniper whose conscience has been declared M.I.A. These are the survivors of Tommy's last suicide mission, from an outfit unofficially known as Rocco's Retreads. Together they are bound for two deadly jungles—one of trees and undergrowth; one of brick and iron. Waiting for them are modernday pirates, gunhappy sex traffickers, and an ultra-secret black ops team so dangerous even the CIA can't touch them.

Soon it's obvious there's something more sinister than "white slavery" going on. What starts as a rescue mission rapidly degenerates into a small-scale war, with no quarter asked or given. Death is dealt with everything from bare hands to automatic weapons, but it's going to take a lot more than brute force for the Retreads to fight their way out of this deathtrap.

***Tier Zero* is sequel to Henry Brown's *Hell and Gone*, both available wherever books are sold online.**

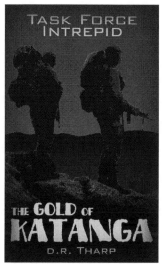

TASK FORCE
INTREPID

THE GOLD OF
KATANGA
D.R. THARP

Kruger and his team are indicative of the evolution of warfare, they are former elite soldiers working for a Private Military Company that exists in the gray area between government and business. As security contractors they sometimes, but not always, work on behalf of the US Government essentially as a proxy force that can be denied when things go wrong.

The action clips along as Kruger's men are called into the Congo to retake a gold mine that has been captured by rebel fighters. Again, the scenario is anything but fiction and reminded me of the Port Soyo mission that Executive Outcomes executed in the 1990's. DR does his homework in regards to the geo-political perspective as well as the tactical aspects of this book. Although DR is a Navy veteran, he doesn't have any background in Infantry operations, something that is surprising as the action scenes are so spot on. Even the verbage and terminology is accurate to the point that I'm starting to think DR might be some kind of military contractor himself! Got anything you want to tell me DR?

Things get ugly for our protagonists as they move on to a secondary objective that they hadn't anticipated, a hostage rescue of some missionaries that have been captured by the same group of rebels. Teaming up with a Special Forces trained indigenous unit, Kruger's team has the odds stacked against them. They might be able to pull off the impossible, but it won't be pretty.

-Reviewed by Jack Murphy

Made in the USA
Columbia, SC
25 July 2020